Ruth and Boaz

Also by Terri L. Fivash:
Joseph

To order, **call 1-800-765-6955.**
Visit us at **www.reviewandherald.com** for information on other Review and Herald® products.

Ruth and Boaz

Strangers in the Land

TERRI L. FIVASH

REVIEW AND HERALD® PUBLISHING ASSOCIATION
Since 1861 | www.reviewandherald.com

This book was
Edited by Gerald Wheeler
Copyedited by Delma Miller
Cover design by GenesisDesign
Cover illustration by Robert Hunt
Typeset: 11.5/13.5 Bembo

PRINTED IN U.S.A.

12 11 10 09 08 7 6 5 4 3 2

R&H Cataloging Service
Fivash, Terri L.
Ruth and Boaz: strangers in the land.

1. Boaz (biblical figure). 2. Ruth (biblical figure). I. Title.

222.35092

ISBN 978-0-8280-1818-0

~ Dedication ~

This book is dedicated to
my mother and father
for the wonderful home
I grew up in.

– Acknowledgments –

Many people have helped me prepare the background for the story of Ruth and Boaz. I would especially like to thank Oystein LaBianca and Randall Younker for their time reviewing this manuscript and for the information on culture and society that they provided. Jim Christianson and Josef Greig gave me much information about sheep. Leona Running was an invaluable guide to the intricacies of Hebrew words and grammar and gave of her expertise time and again. John C. Banks came to my rescue with information on genetics and hereditary traits. As always, thanks to my advance readers and my family for their time, patience, editing skills, ideas, support, and interest in this project.

To Parents of Younger Readers

Because the range of what is considered appropriate for children of various ages is so varied, and because my target audience is for adults, I have decided to include this notice to parents who might wish to read this book to their children, or let their children read it. One of my goals in presenting this biblical narrative is to stay within the cultural thinking of biblical times as much as possible. This includes, of course, thoughts and ideas on human sexuality. Ancient peoples had differing views on what was acceptable and unacceptable in regard to sexual behavior and the appropriate times and manners for it.

In the original Hebrew the biblical author has heavily laced the interactions of Ruth and Boaz with marital allusions and double meanings. At the threshing floor Ruth was very explicit about what she wanted from Boaz. In writing this story I have tried to give the full meaning of the narrative, which is normally lost in translation to English. At the same time, the biblical narrative does not go into intimate details, and neither have I. However, because thinking on this subject today does have such a wide range of reactions, I recommend that parents review the relevant sections on the story and judge for themselves whether or not they wish their children to read them.

To the Reader

I do hope you will read this before you start the book, because I think you'll enjoy the book more, knowing the following information.

A Word About Chronology

Historians tie all ancient dates to Egyptian chronology because the Egyptian king lists give us the longest measuring line. However, the king lists are incomplete and fragmentary, and the only B.C. date agreed upon by scholars is 664 B.C., when the third intermediate period of Egyptian history ended. All dates previous to this are guesses. They can be based on various hints from ancient sources, archaeology, astronomical phenomena, etc., but they are still guesses. For every historian who accepts a certain date for an event, another will have a good argument for a different date. To be blunt, we just don't know for certain. Therefore, the dates that I give for the lives of Ruth and Boaz are also guesses.

I have placed Ruth and Boaz at the end of the period of the judges, but some historians place them at the beginning. Why? Because Boaz is the "son" of Rahab, and Rahab lived in Jericho when Joshua came to town. Now, if Boaz had Obed, and Obed had Jesse, and Jesse had David, that means three generations span the period of the judges, which is generally accepted to be about 300 years long. Three generations probably did not cover 300 years. Who's lying? Nobody. The key lies in the use of the Hebrew words for relationships, such as *son, father,* and *begat.* These words can mean an immediate relationship, as we use them, or they can indicate *descendant, ancestor,* and *descended from.* This is how Christ can be called "the son of David, the son of Abraham" (Matt. 1:1) and how the scribes and Pharisees can claim Abraham as "our father" (John 8:39). Compare Matthew 1:8 with 1 Chronicles 3:11, 12 for an instance of skipped generations using the Hebrew word for begat.

Since there may not be any clue in the text as to which meaning the author intended, dating genealogies presents a problem. Matthew 1:5, 6 can thus mean that Salmon and Rahab had a direct descendant named Boaz, who married Ruth, or that the descendant born to

Salmon and Rahab (as opposed to another wife Salmon had?) was the ancestor of Boaz, who married Ruth.

In the case of Boaz and Ruth, Scripture tells us that they had a son and named him Obed. Therefore the terms there probably refer to immediate descendants. We also learn that David's immediate sire was Jesse. What we do not know is whether any generations intervene between Rahab and Boaz, or between Obed and Jesse. For the sake of convenience, I chose to put the intervening generations between Rahab and Boaz. Be aware, however, that they could just as easily come between Obed and Jesse, or, given the fact that all dates are guesses, maybe they don't come anywhere at all, and historians have simply overestimated the length of time in the period of the judges. We just don't know. And while we're on the subject of people, here's . . .

A Word About Names

Names in biblical times were extremely important, since people equated them with the individuals themselves. Names all had meanings, and changing a name meant a significant transformation in the person. That is why God changing the names of Abram, Sarai, and Jacob is significant enough for the Bible to mention. (Please notice, also, that everyone gets new names in the New Jerusalem [Rev. 2:17].)

We know for certain the meaning of only one name in the story of Ruth, and that's Naomi. Her name meant "pleasant." *Boaz* may have meant "strength." Chilion and Mahlon probably had names that indicated some kind of sickness or weakness, and I couldn't find any satisfactory meaning for Ruth or Orpah. Naturally, biblical interpreters have offered lots of theories and guesses, but we just don't know. I did not make significant points of the meanings of names in the story except for Naomi, and the wordplays on her name are inherent in the Hebrew text. Which brings me to . . .

A Word About Dialogue

As I did the research for this story, I discovered that half of the story gets lost in the translation. The Hebrews *loved* wordplay. Since most Hebrew words had multiple meanings and connotations, the manner in which the writer of Ruth put words together becomes a vital part of the total story. This applies especially to the dialogue between characters.

For instance, in Ruth 2:12, Boaz asks God to grant Ruth His fullest blessing because she has come to trust under His wings. The word translated "wings" is *kanap,* which also means the edge or hem of a garment. To trust under Yahweh's wings is to seek refuge under the hem of His garment. Ezekiel 16:8 uses that phrase with the word *kanap* in a strongly sexual context and as a euphemism for marriage. Ruth and Boaz spoke the same language, and both would have understood the double meaning conveyed by the words, as well as the fact that Yahweh's fullest blessing involved granting Ruth many sons. That she caught the double meaning is clear in her reply in Ruth 2:13. Her phrases "comforted me" and "spoken kindly" to me are words that describe the activity of lovers.

None of this is evident in the English translation. The biggest challenge in writing this book was to convey the whole meaning of the Hebrew words and the dialogue in much the same way we would need to unpack a word for a non-English speaker. If you leave a friend with a wave and say "Later," your friend interprets this as "I've got to go now, but I'll meet with you in the near future, and we will continue our conversation at that time."

The words and dialogue in Ruth are the same, only more so, since they can also carry social connotations along with everything else. In Ruth's first conversation with Boaz she describes herself with a word indicating the lowest possible position for a female on the social ladder. At the threshing floor she refers to herself as a social equal, eligible for marriage. Words in the dialogue, then, can reveal not only hidden information, but much about the character speaking and spoken to. Again, the English translation misses this entirely. I tried to return this type of information to the story, and as I did, the story came alive for me. Finally, I'd like to give you . . .

A Word About Society

Please keep in mind the word *small.* Most towns had 50 to 100 people. I made Bethlehem a bit larger, but in reality it probably didn't have more than 100 people in it when Ruth lived there. A very large city might have had almost 1,000 people in it, but only a few such places existed in the ancient Near East at that time.

To help scale down the picture, think of the old American West. Ruth's society was analogous to frontier society, with the same concerns, dangers, and challenges. Life could be just as uncertain, and the number of people in a town and associated ranches around it was about the same as that of biblical towns and farmsteads. The Indian wars of the 1800s compare well with those of Saul and David against the Philistines, and both were conducted in much the same manner.

As portrayed in the story, the land of Palestine looked much different during the time of the judges. Some experts have estimated that as much as six feet of topsoil has eroded away since the time of the Romans, nearly 1,000 years after the judges lived. During Ruth and David's time the land was heavily forested. Valleys between hills had fewer trees and could be used for farming. Animals, both wild and domestic, were everywhere. Rainfall was more abundant as well. The land little resembled what it looks like today.

I hope the above helps you understand the story of Ruth and Boaz. Please turn the page and read on.

— Cast of Characters —

Characters listed with an ★ are biblical. I have supplied names for some.

Pronunciations:

A pronounced as "ah," spelled "ah"; occasionally as short "a," spelled "a"
E pronounced as long "a," spelled "ay"; occasionally as short "e," spelled "eh"
I pronounced as long "e," spelled "ee"
O pronounced as long "o," spelled "oh"
U pronounced as "oo," spelled "oo"
AI pronounced as long "i," spelled "aye"

Italics indicate the stressed syllable.

Abiaz—principal troublemaker in Heshbon of Moab
★ **Abigail**—Naomi's maternal half aunt whose death started a war
★ **Abimelech**—son of the judge Gideon who wished to be a king
Ahinadab—Ammonite pottery merchant from Jebus looking for sweet figs
Alya—singer to Kemosh who got a sore throat
Amarel—citizen of Dibon in Moab who dreamed of being king
Amos—a youth of the Habiru
Anamot—wife of Ahinadab who insisted on having sweet figs
Banael (Bah-nah-*ayl*)—man of Bethlehem looking for the trash pile
★ **Besai** (Beh-*saye*)—father of Tobeh
Bilgai (Bil-*gaye*)—elder in the gate who supported Tobeh
★ **Boaz**—the one man in town who didn't care what Tobeh thought
★ **Chilion**—(Kilion), son of Elimelech and Naomi who didn't know quite enough
Deborah—granddaughter to Eprah and wife of Tobeh, in that order of importance
Domla—merchant of Tekoa who did not like to pay his debts
★ **Eglon**—former overlord of Moab who oppressed the people of Benjamin
★ **Ehud** (Ay-*hood*)—leader of Benjamin who put Eglon in the past tense

★ **El-Shaddai** (Ayl Shah-*daye*)—God of Jacob

★ **Elimelech**—husband of Naomi, who tried to become a wine merchant

Eliram—dispossessed landowner who had sweet figs for sale

Elsa—Heshbon midwife who never knew what others did

Eprah—second most honored elder in Bethlehem, who doted on his granddaughter

Ezer (*Ay*-zehr)—Naomi's father, with a low opinion of "tainted" blood

Gaali (Gah-*ah*-lee)—elder of Bethlehem who supported Boaz

Gaddi—youth who wanted to be a Habiru and learned the hard way

Gershed—Phoenician servant in Boaz's house

★ **Gideon**—former judge of Israel who saved his people from the Midianites

Hamioh—gleaner in Boaz's field

Hamir—midwife in Heshbon who, unfortunately, drew Abiaz's attention

Hanan—head elder in Bethlehem, tired of sitting on that cold, hard stone at the gate

Hannah—wife of Tahat and determined to collect her just recompense

Hasi (Hah-*see*)—weaver in Bethlehem who needed more help

Hattush—servant of Tobeh, with an interest in women from Moab

Hissil (Hee-*seel*)—local king of Heshbon who knew the value of his shepherd

Ithmah—scribe to King Hissil with two daughters, or was it only one?

Kalkol—farmer near Bethlehem determined to collect money not owed to him

Karmet—apprentice to Hamir

★ **Kemosh**—Moab's god who was never at home

Kemosh-dan—current overlord of northern Moab

Kemosh-natan (Keh-*mohsh*-nah-*tahn*)—son of Eglon and father of Kemosh-dan

Ladel—half Edomite who fell into Boaz's hesed

Lilith—demon of the desert night that haunted Boaz's dreams

Maash (Mah-*ahsh*)—heir to King Hissil who annoyed Abiaz

Madana—Ezer's wife who taught her daughter Naomi to remember Aunt Abigail

Madiya (Mah-dee-*yah*)—Ruth's friend in Bethlehem who liked to talk

⋆ **Mahlon**—son of Elimelech and Naomi who first understood Ruth's value

Mattan (Ma-*tahn*)—son of Meshullam who took over as dahveed of the Habiru

Menahemet (May-nah-*heh*-meht)—Boaz's first wife who fell when her brother Ladel fell, only in a different way

Mesha (*May*-shah)—prince of Moab who never quite made it to the throne

Meshullam (May-*shool*-ahm)—war leader, or dahveed, of the Habiru who saw the future in Boaz's eyes

⋆ **Naomi**—wife of Elimelech, who believed as her father taught and never could change

Negbi—elder of Bethlehem who supported Boaz

Nehebet (Neh-*heh*-beht)—gleaner for Boaz with a curious mind

⋆ **Orpah**—Ruth's sister, provided that both were daughters of Ithmah

Pash—Yidla's name for Pashur

Pashur (Pah-*shoor*)—Habiru wool merchant who kept Boaz up-to-date, militarily and mentally

Patah—Mattan's son who played the fly on the wall

Qausa (Kah-*oo*-sah)—elder of Bethlehem who supported Boaz

⋆ **Rahab**—ancester of Boaz

Raham—supporter of Tobeh in a hurry to have an heir

Rapa (*Rah*-pah)—farmer near Bethlehem not wishing to pay what he did not owe

⋆ **Ruth**—Moabite raised in Heshbon and firmly convinced that Yah could do anything

Sakar (Sah-*kahr*)—son of Hissil

Sarnahal—large Habiru good at reaping and rescues

Shahar—elder in Bethlehem who supported Boaz

Shimrith—wife of Ithmah and mother of Orpah, who gave birth to another daughter (or son?)

Tahat (Tah-*haht*)—dispossessed farmer of Bethlehem and Tobeh's first mistake

⋆ **Tamar**—Judah's daughter-in-law and wife who long after she died gave Naomi ideas

Tashima (Tah-*sheem*-ah)—woman of Bethlehem, Ladel's wife, and always in the thick of things

Tawy (*Tah*-wee)—Egyptian master singer in Heshbon who paid Ruth more than she expected

⋆ **Tobeh** (*Toh*-beh)—Naomi's half cousin with dreams of conquest and riches

⋆ **Ushna** (*Oosh*-nah)—Levite who gave all his kind a bad name

⋆ **Yah**—hill spirit who was always at home and who was much more than he seemed

⋆ **Yahweh**—the God who brings His fields to harvest

Yatom (Yah-*tohm*)—son of Boaz and Menahemet, who asked to see his immi

Yattir (Yah-*teer*)—Ammonite resident of Bethlehem and elder who helped Tobeh

Yidla—Moabite shepherd with a simple mind and direct connection to his God

Zakkur—best friend and chief adviser to Tobeh

Zippor—musical instrument maker in Heshbon who unknowingly made a very famous harp

– Vocabulary –

Pronunciations:

A pronounced as "ah," spelled "ah"; occasionally as short "a," spelled "a"

E pronounced as long "a," spelled "ay"; occasionally as short "e," spelled "eh"

I pronounced as long "e," spelled "ee"

O pronounced as long "o," spelled "oh"

U pronounced as "oo," spelled "oo"

AI pronounced as long "i," spelled "aye"

Italics indicate the stressed syllable.

Abbi (*ah*-bee)— "my father," term of endearment, i.e., "daddy"

Adon (ah-*dohn*)—masculine title of respect: "lord," "sir"

Cypriot White Slip Ware—type of pottery from Cyprus, white with minimal straight-line decoration in brown

Dahveed (dah-*veed*)—probably "beloved one." May have designated an important or "beloved" leader in war. It is used in this context in this book, although much argument rages over the word's ancient usage and meaning

Dodi (doh-*dee*)—"my uncle"

Elohim (eh-loh-*heem*)—generic Canaanite name for supernatural beings and/or the gods

Ephrathite—descendant of Ephrath, one of the founders of Bethlehem

Geber (*geh*-ber)—masculine title of respect: "master" or "sir"

Geberet (geh-*behr*-eht)—feminine title of respect: "mistress" or "ma'am"

Gerah (geh-*rah*)—unit of monetary value applied to both silver and gold, 50 silver gerahs equaling one gold gerah

Girdle—wide, long cloth or supple piece of leather that was wrapped around the waist more than once to form a belt. It could also be used to hold small items that the wearer would tuck into the folds.

Goel (goh-*ayl*)—closest male relative financially able to purchase land and return it to someone who had sold it to support his family;

also responsible for purchasing back land rights that have been sold for the same purpose

Habiru (hah-*bee*-roo)—name for bands of nomads, usually small, that roamed Israel during the time of Ruth. Consisting of landless family units or displaced persons from the 12 tribes or any of the surrounding nations, their main occupation was as mercenaries, but many bands simply supported themselves by robbery and murder. Habiru can refer to the entire band or a single member of it.

Hamsin (hahm-*seen*)—harsh, sere east wind from the desert; it could wither and dry out a crop overnight

Hesed (*hehs*-ehd)—voluntary kindness on the life-saving level done by the sole person able to do it. God's grace to us is hesed.

Henna—a plant-derived reddish dye used to color skin and nails

Immi (*ee*-mee)—"my mother," term of endearment, i.e., "mommy"

Krater—large shallow bowl useful for serving fruit, etc.

Leben (*leh*-behn)—curdled milk used for food

Levirate marriage—duty to impregnate the widow of a brother or nephew who died without leaving an heir to continue the family name. The responsibility applied only to brothers and uncles of the deceased.

Nahsi (nah-*see*)—also Nasi, masculine title of respect: high/governing lord; carries the connotation of political/judicial authority

Papyri—plural of papyrus

Papyrus—writing material made from the papyrus reed and forerunner of paper

Pithoi—plural of pithos

Pithos—singular noun for large round storage jar, three to six feet tall, used for food items such as grains. Once set in place, they were rarely moved.

Qedeshah (keh-day-*shah*)—feminine singular noun of the name for the women who served as prostitutes in the high places in which religious virility/fertility rites were celebrated. The masculine form of the word, qadesh (kah-daysh), referred to the male prostitutes who provided the same service.

Qedeshim (keh-day-*sheem*)—masculine plural noun for the above

Qedeshot (keh-day-*shoht*)—feminine plural of the above.

Salt Sea—ancient name for the Dead Sea

Sar (sahr)—masculine title of respect: "prince"

Shabbat (*shab*-baht)—seventh day of the Israelite week, their day of rest; Sabbath

Tate (*Tah*-tay)—Egyptian office of vizier, second only to the pharaoh

Travail—childbirth labor

Usufruct rights—legal right of a widow to derive her living from her dead husband's estate until she herself died

– Cultural Notes –

Thank you—Saying "Thank you" to someone did much more than express gratitude. In the culture of the times people spoke the words only when recipients of a favor either considered themselves below the giver in status or knew they would not be returning the favor either because they could not or they didn't wish to. In the never-ending game of taking and receiving honor, saying "Thank you" brought an end to the transactions with the acknowledgment that the giver was more honorable than the receiver.

Fringe—fringes on a robe indicated status. The longer the fringe, the higher the status. A person could quite accurately place another in the correct status level simply by noting the color, ornamentation, and material of their clothes.

Tassels—Yahweh Himself ordered the Israelites to wear tassels on the corners of their robes to remind them of the covenant He made with them at Sinai. (See Numbers 15:38, 39.)

Honor—Honor was the grease that made ancient society work, much as money does in Western societies. Honor can be thought of as the respect and approval of one's community. To understand honor, think of it as a credit rating. Without honor, the avenues open to a man to support himself and his family were severely limited, much as a bad credit rating limits a person today. Anything that would make people think less of a person or their family reduced the family honor. Keeping and maintaining honor, therefore, was of primary importance, and one had to measure every action against what people would think of it.

Open your ear—The actual Hebrew idiom is to "uncover your ear." The phrase meant that the speaker had vitally important information for the listener, and the listener could only learn the information from the speaker. The idiom appears twice in the Bible, once when Boaz speaks to the other kinsman at the gate, and once when Jonathan swears to warn David if Saul is still angry with him. (See Ruth 4:1 and 1 Samuel 20:13.) In both texts the idiom and its connotations completely vanish in the English translation.

Hesed—Most modern English versions of the Bible translate the word as "loving-kindness." Sometimes they render it as "mercy," but both translations again leave out some of the important connotations of the Hebrew idea. Hesed can only come from the one person who must act in order for another's life to be preserved. This makes it the perfect word to describe what God does for us. If He didn't act, we'd all die, and He is the only one whose action will give us life. Therefore, He gives hesed.

Elohim—The elohim were supernatural beings, from spirits and demons up to the gods. Spirits were everywhere and were capable of action for or against humans. It was wise to remain on their good side with sacrifices and gifts. Fortunately, all spirits and gods were tied to a geographical location, and their power weakened quickly when outside the geographic area. Crossing a border meant leaving the power of one god and coming under that of another. House gods, teraphim, could only guard a single house, a hill spirit could only operate on that single elevation, etc. Thus when Ruth crossed the Jordan, people understood that Kemosh, the god of Moab, would be severely handicapped if he wanted to help her, leaving her at the mercy of the Israelite God. A god's power was directly tied to the amount of territory he could operate in. Therefore, when Ruth heard that the Israelite God could work anywhere from Egypt to Ur, she could assume that He must be higher in status and thus more powerful than all the national gods in those areas, just as a national god would be higher in status and more powerful than a hill spirit, which would in turn be higher in status and more powerful than teraphim.

Creation beliefs—Yahweh taught a much different concept of creation than the surrounding myths and legends in ancient times. Most creation myths stated that the world and everything in it came from either sexual activity by the gods or by a violent struggle of some kind involving a war between a good and an evil deity. Yahweh does neither to create. He simply speaks, demonstrating His complete supremacy over the world and everything in it. He was also different in that He commanded humanity to remember His creative acts rather than having humanity constantly remind Him to continue the process of creating and thus keep the universe from collapsing back into chaos. The Sabbath was to remind humans of what Yahweh had made. The sexual practices involved in the worship of other gods were designed to show the deities exactly what needed to be done to ensure that the land would continue to produce food. Thus, for an Israelite to participate in these practices was a denial of Yahweh's claim to be Creator.

Names—A person's name was much more than just a label in the ancient Near East. In some mystical way the name was the person. Thus people considered disparaging someone's name the same as a physical attack. (Think of the third commandment.) Being able to give someone a name meant having the power to control that person (remember God changing the names of Abram and Jacob, and Nebuchadnezzar giving Daniel and his friends different names), and knowing someone's name represented a measure of power and control over that individual. You gave your name only to people you trusted, and one of the simplest defenses against the elohim was to deny them knowledge of your name, since if they didn't know it, they couldn't touch you.

Preserving a name—The most important thing in the culture of the ancient Near East was to preserve a name and/or an inheritance. Although the Egyptians believed in a full afterlife and the Mesopotamians in a rather shadowy one at best, the ancient Israelites believed that when you died, you ceased to exist. Their earliest understanding of eternal life was actually the concept of eternal remembrance. If a person's descendants remembered their name, that's how the person survived death. They lived on in memory, for a person's name was the person. It made having offspring of utmost importance, since who else would preserve your name? To die childless was the ultimate death. The chances of having descendants to remember you greatly increased if they had land to live on, thus making the preservation of the family land of paramount importance also.

Units of measure—I decided to use modern units of measure for units of length so the flow of the story would not be interrupted while the reader tried to equate ancient units with modern ones. Units of volume, however, presented more of a problem, since we are not certain how big they were. I used the ancient names and tried to give some indication in the text for the amount of the unit. If the indications are vague, it's because we don't know precisely what the ancient terms represent. I chose to use later ancient units of money, since we have somewhat of an idea about them. In this book I have arbitrarily set a day's wage at 1 silver gerah. Its value as a metal would be at the time of this writing about 36 cents, but the buying power would be about $18. I also arbitrarily set 20 coppers as equal to a silver gerah, making the buying power of each copper about 90 cents and the value as a metal about 1.8 cents.

The Time of Planting and Early Rains

This is a harvest story. Not about grain, but about Yahweh's harvest of life, for He works with people. Our fields produce food—His fields life, happiness, and security for those He has chosen for His own.

Zadok, the high priest, asked for the story, but he wanted a truncated tale that represented but a small portion of the whole. How can you truly celebrate the harvest unless you have first planted and worked the fields, prayed for the rain, and spilled your sweat in the labor of reaping? Surely a whole story must include what went before, so that you can appreciate what the harvest meant. But no, Zadok desired only the end of the story. He has it now, for whatever good it will do him.

You, I am sure, will not be satisfied with such a partial telling, so make yourself comfortable and pull the lamp closer. There are figs, dates, and apricots on the table with the fresh-pressed new wine. Do you have enough? Good. Now we can begin.

We must go back to the beginning of things—things Yahweh planted almost 170 years ago, when Israel had no king and the judges lived; when the Philistines from the coast raided eastward; when Midianites, Ammonites, and Aramaeans harassed the tribes; and when Israel forsook Yahweh, to our shame. Back then, even in peace, bands of Habiru roamed the country, and life could be full or empty, depending on Yahweh's will.

We must begin with a child, a seed that Yahweh carefully planted and cultivated, for he would be the beginning of many things, most of which came to harvest long after his death. He was a typical 7-year-old boy playing outside of Bethlehem with his friends, unaware that there was anything unusual about him or that Yahweh had chosen him. His name was Boaz.

Summer
Ab, fifth month, Boaz's seventh year
(1136 B.C.)

Boaz, what are you doing?"

"Getting something to use for a staff so I can play Barak, Elimelech," the boy replied, rummaging just inside the courtyard gate while his skinny step-cousin shifted impatiently from foot to foot. It was Shabbat morning and hot already.

"But I'm playing Barak.* Come on!" Elimelech urged.

"You can't be. Naomi said I could play Barak." Boaz pushed his thick, dark chestnut hair over his shoulder and grabbed for the stick he had found.

"You're playing Sisera and get killed. Tashima is bringing some spoiled wine so she can make you look all bloody. She's going to be Jael."

Frowning his annoyance, Boaz stepped into the street with the stick. "But I don't want to play Sisera. I'll get my new robe all spoiled." He looked down in satisfaction at the tassels on the robe. He was old enough now to wear those important reminders of the commandments Yahweh had given His people. "Besides, it's your turn to be Sisera, Elimelech."

"I can't play Sisera, 'cause I don't have any Canaanite blood, and you do. Now come on. Naomi gets snooty if she has to wait too long."

His stepcousin's smug tones angered Boaz, and he clenched his fists. "Well, Naomi promised I could play Barak this time. She likes me better than you, so we'll let her decide."

"She does not! She likes me!" Elimelech answered, glaring at his younger relative.

---

* See Judges 4 and 5 for this story.

"Tashima likes you," Boaz retorted. "Now who's making us late? Come on." He ran down the narrow street toward Bethlehem's west gate, his long legs easily outdistancing his rival, the blue thread in the tassels showing as they swayed. Naomi had said he could play Barak, and, after all, he was tallest of all the boys.

She sat primly just outside the gate, the sun bringing out the highlights of her honey-colored hair, already pretending to be Deborah, the woman judge who had saved Israel. Boaz stopped beside her.

"What took so long?" she asked, eyeing the stick he had in his hand. "That's not long enough for a spear. You're playing Sisera, and he needs a spear."

"But you said—"

"I'm here, Naomi," Elimelech interrupted, panting from his run.

"You said I could play Barak," Boaz insisted.

"That was before." Naomi stood up as the other children looked uncertainly from Boaz to her.

"Before what?"

"Before she found out that you have Canaanite blood!" Tobeh, Naomi's older cousin, said triumphantly. "That means you can play only Sisera from now on!"

"That's not fair!"

"Well, that's the way we'll play," the older boy replied. "Abbi says the only thing Canaanites are good for is to be killed, so you'll have to be killed."

Naomi walked away. "Come on, Tashima; let's get ready. Did you get the spoiled wine?"

Boaz looked around, gripping his stick tightly, anger choking him as the others turned and followed her.

"Canaanite!" Tobeh taunted in a whisper.

"I am not a Canaanite! I'm Ephrath clan just like Elimelech! It's not fair," Boaz shouted, chest heaving as he fought to keep from slamming his stick into the older boy's smirking face.

No one paid any attention. Elimelech edged closer to Naomi, and Tobeh laughed.

As they crossed the road to the little hollow by the wall, Boaz whirled and ran. Dashing the tears of rage from his brown eyes, he fled down the valley beside the town and up the opposite slope, his feet swishing through the dry, brown grass. Once under the cool pines topping the hill, he threw himself down under a huge tree, sobbing.

It was bad enough that Tobeh's goading could make him cry, but why couldn't he play Barak? His ancestor Rahab was honored for saving the Israelite spies when they came to Jericho, and for forsaking Baal to worship only Yahweh. What was wrong with being her descendant?

"Boy?"

Boaz flipped over, gaping at the thick-muscled legs beside him. Wearing a soldier's kilt and helmet and carrying a naked sword, a Habiru warrior stared down at him. His bow was slung over his shoulder, and arrows showed thick in the quiver. The man's dark-gray eyes bored into his brown ones. Too angry and startled to be afraid, Boaz stared back.

For an instant the man's gaze wavered. Then he pointed with his chin toward Bethlehem. "Run to the town, lad. There are raiders coming up the south road. They'll ask to trade in the market. Once there, they'll attack. Tell the watch."

"Yes, geber," Boaz gasped, scrambling up. As he ran he threw a glance over his shoulder, but the man had vanished.

Suddenly frightened, Boaz flew back down the hill, thankful that his long legs enabled him to cover the distance quickly. He burst through the last of the trees near the valley floor and jumped the dry streambed at the bottom. Once he was across the small plain, the land rose to the walls of Bethlehem.

It was too far. He'd never get there in time, for hard as he ran, he seemed to be standing still. He pressed his hand into his aching side, then stumbled and rolled several feet before he recovered and sprang up again, his legs pumping harder than before. Unexpectedly the wall loomed above him, and he whirled around the corner not far from the west gate, dust spurting under his sandals. "Raiders, raiders," he screamed. "Coming on the south road. Raiders!"

The man on watch darted toward him. "What did you say, boy?"

"Raiders! Coming from the south to attack the town," he gasped out, almost falling. The sentry grabbed his arm and pulled him through the gate.

"What's this about raiders?" Adon Hanan, one of the elders sitting on a stone bench by the gate, demanded.

"I looked up, and there was a Habiru," Boaz panted. "He said the raiders would ask to trade, then attack when they were in the market. He said I should warn everyone."

The sentry glanced around. "That doesn't make sense. It's Shabbat. The market is closed."

"He could still be right," another man spoke. "I heard just this morning that two homesteads east of here have been burned out. Those Habiru don't care about Shabbat, or Yahweh, either."

"Rouse the town," Adon Hanan decided. "Bring the men to the market. We all know what Habiru can do."

"Is something wrong?" Naomi's mother asked, hurrying over. "Boaz, have you seen Naomi?"

"She's playing outside the wall in the hollow, Geberet Madana."

"Bring the young ones in—we have word that raiders are coming to the town," the sentry commanded.

Her face pale, Madana rushed out of the gate, calling for her daughter.

Boaz dashed home, bursting into the house with his story. "Abbi, Abbi, there are raiders headed for town. You're to go to the west market."

Without a word, his father grabbed his sword and rushed out the door.

Hearing his voice, Immi came in, gripping his shoulder while he told the news. Her fingers squeezed until it hurt as the servants gathered their weapons and stationed themselves to guard the house or went to help with the battle. She stared into the corner where Rahab's teraphim stood. The family's ancestor had brought them from Jericho when she married Salmon, one of the spies she saved. They were four postlike pieces of wood of various sizes with curious whorls and knots on them. The largest was as tall as Boaz and had a rounded top like a head.

When he was younger, he'd been afraid to go past them in the dark, since they were supposed to be the abodes of the spirits that guarded the house. Now he avoided them and kept his head down when he walked by them. Immi bit her lip, then went to the baked-clay, box-like shrine to Yahweh, taking out a bit of incense.

"Get a coal from the fire, Boaz," she said.

He went to the courtyard and scooped up a coal with a piece of wood. His mother added the incense and put it in front of the teraphim. Then she took him upstairs. Silently, her face white, she stood beside him on the flat roof of the house next to her loom, the dagger in her hand nearly hidden in the folds of her robe.

Boaz never forgot the tense waiting, the sudden confused shouts and screams of the battle in the market, his mother's grip tightening still more as the noise moved closer.

"It'll be all right, Boaz," she said again and again.

"I know, Immi," he answered each time.

Then new voices reached their ears, an authoritative bellow rising above the clashing of metal and the twang of bowstrings and the whistle of arrows. Silence fell. Gradually the servants relaxed their taut watchfulness, lowering their weapons.

Finally his mother's hand fell from his shoulder, but the ache from her grip remained.

"We can go down to the courtyard now," she said. "Your father will be back soon."

Her voice shook, and he glanced at her, catching the worried look on her face. What if Abbi didn't return? Down in the courtyard Immi told him to get a drink from the cistern and lie down if he wanted to. But she didn't let go of the dagger, and she didn't sit under the grape arbor as she usually did when she waited for Abbi.

When the gate finally opened, Immi whirled to face it. The dagger fell from her hand, and she threw herself at her husband as Boaz ran forward. Abbi held her for a long time, murmuring into her ear as her shoulders shook. Then he scooped his son into his arms, hugging him.

"It's a good thing we had warning," he said. "Adon Hanan had our men hidden around the market and as many stalls open as we could in the short time we had to prepare. I kept thinking the Habiru would notice something wrong, but they spread out around the square and simply attacked.

"If we hadn't been ready, or it hadn't been Shabbat with all the men here, they would have taken the whole town. Instead, four of them were killed immediately. They're trained fighters, though, and recovered from our surprise. They had pushed us from the market into the streets when Meshullam and his band attacked them from behind."

Immi raised her head from Abbi's shoulder. "Meshullam?"

"He's a dahveed, a war leader, from a different Habiru band, and the one who spoke to Boaz."

"Dahveed? Why do they call a war leader 'the beloved'?"

"Because the survival of the band depends on him," Abbi replied, smoothing Immi's hair and setting Boaz back on his feet. "He decides whom they fight, plans the attack, collects the payment, and all the rest. Without a good dahveed, they die. Thank Yahweh that Meshullam threw his men in on our side. Otherwise, things would have turned out very differently." He pulled Immi to him and hugged her again, one arm around Boaz, who clung to his leg.

"How many died?" his wife asked.

"Twelve of the attackers, including the enemy dahveed."

"How many of us?"

He grimaced. "There are about 10 wounded, two severely, but only four died, including Besai." Abbi shook his head. "It was the strangest thing. Besai fought right beside Meshullam and knew the Habiru was defending us. But after the attack he turned on the man, who reacted predictably. None of us can figure out why Besai did such a crazy thing."

His legs suddenly feeling weak, Boaz sat down soberly. Besai was Tobeh's father and half brother to Naomi's mother.

Later he and his mother went into the house, and Abbi looked into the corner when he smelled the incense. "Yahweh is more powerful than Rahab's household gods," he said gently to his wife.

"I know," she replied. "But I didn't want to take any chances."

Boaz looked from Yahweh's shrine to the teraphim and decided he should avoid both from now on.

The rest of Shabbat blurred into the hurried burials for the dead. Tobeh stood stiffly at the entrance to his father's tomb, his lips pressed together, his eyes glittering and bitter. Worried about Naomi's tears and bewildered by the sudden changes since the morning, Boaz watched from where he clung to Immi's hand. But strangely, the clearest detail he remembered afterward was that no one said a word about spoiling his new clothes.

With the permission of the grateful town elders, Meshullam's band built a stronghold in the hills east of the town. They came to trade in twos and threes to avoid the latent prejudice of some of the townsmen, who looked on the nomadic Habiru as a necessary evil, tolerated for their fighting skills, but paid off and wished away as soon as danger ceased. Habiru life was hard, and many bands did turn to pillage and robbery to support themselves.

Meshullam's group consisted of mostly displaced members of the tribe of Dan, but a family of Edomites traveled with him, as well as a Hittite and a Philistine. The dahveed kept his people firmly in check, and if a stray sheep or goat never returned once in a while, most farmers ignored it. The protection that Meshullam provided against the more rapacious bands of Habiru, as well as the occasional forays of the Midianites or Ammonites, was more than worth such a small price.

Time passed, and Boaz became fast friends with Pashur, one of Meshullam's sons. As he grew he spent many hours with the Habiru practicing with bow and arrow, sling, sword, and, when he became tall enough, the long infantry spear. In Bethlehem no one ever again mentioned his Canaanite blood, but Tobeh always looked down on him with contemptuous gray eyes.

Spring
Abib, first month, Boaz's sixteenth year
(1127 B.C.)

Glancing down nervously to be certain his girdle* was in place and the tassels on his robe hadn't come off, Boaz hoped his best garments looked all right for his appointment with Naomi's father, Ezer. His robe was dark red, embroidered with black to match the fine black sash and the black trim on his light-gray cloak. He wished Abbi could go in his stead, as was proper, but his father had been ill for several weeks. As he walked down the narrow street to Naomi's family compound, Boaz reviewed his father's instructions, wondering again about Abbi's reluctance to let him ask for Naomi's hand.

---

* See Vocabulary.

"Go if you must," his father had said. "Be respectful and call him 'geber.'"

"Should I say adon?" Boaz had asked anxiously.

His father sighed. "He is not your lord, and I pray he never will be. Geber is enough. You are his social equal."

"I'll remember, Abbi."

Pausing before the correct gate, he made himself knock, then fidgeted, fingering the fringe on his girdle. Immi had combed his thick, dark chestnut hair, smoothing out the parts that tended to curl, so he knew his hair looked all right. He had loved Naomi for so long, and before Abbi fell ill, he had helped build a one-story house in the compound so his future wife would have a house of her own, even if it was small.

As footsteps approached the gate he straightened and lifted his chin. He must not be intimidated, for he came from one of the best households in town, and he would be geber of it all one day. Maybe someday he would even be adon.

A servant opened the gate. "Yes?"

"I would like to speak to Geber Ezer."

"Wait here, please."

Boaz followed the servant into the dimly lit private court of Ezer's house on one side of the family compound. Laughter and the aroma of lentils seasoned with garlic and dill drifted over the wall to him. *Ezer's household must be holding a feast here tonight,* he thought. He tried to remember if he'd heard any news of visitors to the family, but he'd been too preoccupied building the small house and planning for Naomi's arrival. He rubbed his sweaty hands on his cloak as the minutes crawled by. It seemed odd that Ezer would keep him waiting like this. Well, if Naomi's father was having a good time, maybe he'd be in a good mood and say yes to his request immediately.

Ezer caught him adjusting his clothes when he appeared, still chewing a bite of food and looking him up and down. Feeling small under that critical stare in spite of his still-growing height, Boaz flushed.

"So what business do you have that is so important?" the older man asked abruptly.

The slightly sarcastic tone threw Boaz off balance. "T-There was something I wanted to discuss with you," he stammered.

"You told me that in your message. Out with it, boy. I've guests, and I can't leave them all night."

Gulping, Boaz tried to still his shaking legs, realizing that Ezer wasn't even going to invite him to sit down. "I wished to speak with you about—about Naomi, your daughter."

"I know she's my daughter—I've raised her. What about her?"

His face a fiery red, Boaz stared at the ground. "I-I wish to marry her."

"Marry?" The man's eyebrows shot upward. "You?"

"Yes, geber," Boaz said, cursing himself for forgetting to be polite. "She—well, she has been very kind to me, and—"

"And you take her kindness as permission to press for her hand?"

Boaz looked up. "It's been more than just kindness, geber. She has been very pleasant to me, and I believe she feels as I do. A-About marrying, that is."

"Of course my daughter is pleasant; that's why we gave her that name. And you think I would look favorably on a match?"

The acerbic play on Naomi's name made Boaz flush more. "I-I hope so, geber. It will be good to join our houses, and I love Naomi very much, and you know I will inherit all my father's land. I can take care of her very well with my inheritance, and our houses—" His voice trailed off under Ezer's hard stare, and his face reddened even more.

Suddenly the man laughed. "You and my daughter? You, of all people! And what does your father think of this?"

Boaz swallowed, wishing he could sink out of sight. "He was willing for me to ask, geber."

"I'll bet he was, but he wasn't terribly taken with the idea either."

Clenching his hands to stop their shaking, Boaz stared down again. How could Ezer know that?

"You should pay more attention to your father, boy." The man's voice was suddenly angry. "If you were the last man in Bethlehem, I would never give Naomi to you! Do you think I would ally my house with yours? stain her pure blood with your tainted blood?"

"Tainted?" Boaz echoed, raising puzzled eyes to him.

"Polluted, I should say," the geber continued. "You're nothing but a dirty Canaanite, son of a Jericho whore. How dare you even consider my daughter? Get out of this house!" he shouted, jabbing his finger toward the gate. "Don't ever come here again, and if I find you anywhere near my daughter, I'll have you beaten, understand? Get out!"

"But—" Boaz started to say, then felt himself whirled around and rushed to the courtyard gate, a rough shove sending him sprawling as it slammed.

Stunned, he lay in the street, trying to clear his head.

"I'd say Ezer doesn't like you," an amused voice commented above him. "What happened?"

"I asked for Naomi's hand, and he called me a Canaanite," Boaz replied, trying to gather his wits and stand at the same time.

"Did you honestly expect Ezer to give his daughter to Rahab's blood? How could you be so stupid?"

Boaz stared blankly at the other man. "Tobeh?" His voice cracked.

"Tobeh?" the older youth mimicked, peering down his long, thin nose. "Yes, it's Tobeh. Landing in the street is the least of what you deserve. I'll see you in the dust yet!"

"What have I done to you?" Boaz stammered in a daze.

"Have you forgotten so soon? My father died because of you!"

The sheer rage in the words overwhelmed Boaz. "Besai was killed in the attack by the Habiru years ago!" *What could that have to do with Ezer's refusal?* Boaz wondered as he climbed to his feet.

"Do you think *I've* forgotten?" Tobeh hissed. "You brought word about an attack, remember? Why didn't you mention that the second band of Habiru would be on our side? If you had, my father wouldn't have attacked the Habiru dahveed and gotten himself killed!"

"No one knew the second band was coming, least of all me! Meshullum saved our lives!" Boaz protested, trying to make sense of what reached his ears. "Your father fought beside him. He knew the dahveed was on our side."

Tobeh laughed venomously. "My father was the only one who could see that Meshullam wanted to be king, and that's why he killed him. Those treacherous Habiru will turn on us one day. They should all die—just like Canaanites!"

"What are you talking about? They're Danites and haven't bothered anyone!"

"No? What about all the livestock that vanishes every year? And what about the supplies that went out the gates three weeks ago and disappeared into the hills? When I'm king—uh, old enough—I'll make sure people see things in their true light." Turning on his heel, the older youth started to the gate.

"Tobeh, Meshullam's band just drove off the Habiru that had raided west of town and killed three farmsteaders! They've spent so much time defending us this year they couldn't plant their own fields. We have an obligation to help them," Boaz said, straightening his robe.

"Paying them off is closer to the truth. You're as blind as the rest. Go home, Canaanite. Just because your grandmother married into the oldest clan in Bethlehem doesn't make you an Ephrathite. You're a polluted son of Rahab!"

Mouth open, Boaz watched him pound on the courtyard gate. The same servant opened it.

"Be off with you, Canaanite," Tobeh threw over his shoulder as he entered.

Mocking laughter rang in Boaz's ears as he fled, swinging over a low place in the town wall and racing across the meadow grass grown long between two vineyards. He took the terraces of the grain fields as if they were stairs, desperate to find the solitude of the hilltop forest, driven by the humiliation that burned in his heart. Was he the only one too stupid to realize Ezer's attitude? And then to have Tobeh see him thrown into the street like a slave!

Shame lent wings to his steps, and he twisted and turned down the winding forest paths until he could run no farther. Throwing himself to the ground, he pounded his fists in futile rage as sobs drained what strength he had left. All his hopes having turned to shame, he cringed at the disgrace he'd brought on himself and his father's house. Ezer's contemptuous refusal burned in his heart. It had never occurred to him that he might be unacceptable as a husband. Had he also misjudged Naomi's attitude toward him? What if no one else would marry him? His mind in turmoil, he finally drifted off into sleep.

And dreamed. He walked alone through the lands across Jordan that bordered the great eastern desert, watching the grasses fade to clumps of withered brown and then sparse patches of thorny vegetation that merged into the sand and rocks beyond. The sun set behind him, casting his shadow before, bringing his first hint of terror as the shadow moved and shifted on its own. He dared not stop, but kept walking on and on into the wasteland of gods and demons, far from the comfort of human companionship and aid. The farther he went, the more his shadow came to life, shape-shifting into vague hints of fearsome or beautiful creatures no matter how he tried to control it.

Sleepiness began to overwhelm him, and as it did, fear seized him. Somehow he knew that if he slept, his shadow, feeding off the power in the wildness around him, would transform completely out of his control, and he would be helpless before it. But sleep he must, and with growing trepidation, he chose a spot in the sand and pulled his cloak closely around his shoulders.

As he lay there he sensed the malevolent force drawing closer. Desperately he tried to awaken himself, to warn himself of the danger. But no, he must watch himself sleep while his treacherous shadow crept into the silver light of the rising moon, separating itself from him. The hamsin sprang up, whistling eerily. The dry, withering east wind ruffled his hair and plucked at his cloak. It swept his shadow into itself, whirling it around and around, transforming it into the shape of a beautiful woman.

She stepped out of the hamsin as it died, tall and lithesome in Canaanite wedding garments woven from the night's darkness and gleaming with silver stolen from the moon. When she turned she noticed him, waking him with her look.

But instead of a bride he saw Lilith, the night demon of the desert wastes, who, everyone knew, preyed on lonely travelers. Somehow he must resist her if he wished to live, but he couldn't drag his eyes from her. She smiled, her cruel eyes mocking him as he lay there paralyzed. He could not resist as she leaned over to grant the yearned-for kiss that would draw the life from his bones.

His body shuddering, faint derisive laughter on the wind of the nightmare echoing in his mind, Boaz jerked awake. He drew his cloak closer, heart still pounding, and huddled against the damp chill of the night, terrified the dream would return. Clouds obscured the stars overhead, and the west wind brought the faint smell of the sea. Shivering, he drew his knees tighter and dug his back into the dead leaves caught by the brush. They smelled musty and slightly rotten. His cloak would never be the same, but he was too frightened to move. The next thing he knew was the warmth of the sun on his face.

Pashur lounged on the meadow grass not far in front of him. His black hair was bound back in a knot, and his eyes looked more blue than gray this morning. "You ran as if Lilith herself was after you. What happened?"

Boaz paled, shivering at the memory of his nightmare. "I asked for Naomi's hand," he finally answered.

The Habiru's eyes widened. "I can't imagine Ezer was flattered."

Brushing his disheveled hair away from his face, Boaz said, "He threw me out. Did everyone know he hated my Canaanite blood except me?"

"That made you run?" his friend asked, ignoring his question.

"No. Tobeh saw what happened."

"That overbearing flea-host saw you land in the street?"

"Yes." Boaz rubbed his face, anger rising in him again. "I ran from him, Pashur. He laughed at me, and I ran. What will Abbi say? I lost family honor last night."

The Habiru studied the clouds rising in the west. "Your father will tell you that someday you'll have the chance to redeem your reputation, and Tobeh will be the one slinking away with people laughing at him."

"He sounded as though he really hates me. Did you know he blames me for his father's death?"

"I've suspected it, even though my father killed him." Pashur sighed, rubbing the back of his head. "According to Mattan, Tobeh says Besai was justified in attacking Abbi, and he means to change the town's opinion of his father."

"Does your brother know that Tobeh thinks your father is plotting to be king of Bethlehem?"

His friend looked sober. "No. That's a new one. I'll tell Abbi, but there's not much we can do except leave it in Yahweh's hands." At Boaz's startled look he added, "We do worship him, you know. We're Danites."

"I know. It's just that I've never seen you at the altar here in Bethlehem or at the tabernacle in Shiloh." Boaz flushed uncomfortably.

"We tried it once, both places, but our reception was chilly, so father set up an altar by our stronghold. We can't offer a lamb very often, but we try to sacrifice a turtledove whenever we can or sometimes burn some grain if that's all we have." Pashur's voice trailed off, and his face reddened slightly.

Tactfully Boaz stared at the trees, wondering if his family would be that faithful if they had as little as the Habiru did. He went with his father every fall at Yom Kippur to Shiloh with the sacrificial animals for the atonement, and if Abbi didn't go to the other major feasts, he at least sent something by Gershed, their Phoenician servant. "I'm sure Yahweh understands," he blurted.

"He does."

Boaz chewed the inside of his lip a moment, studying the young man next to him. "Why do you stay here?" he asked suddenly. "I know it's hard for your band in a lot of ways, and surely there would be more profit around Beth-shean or the cities in the Shephelah or even up north by Dan."

The Habiru was silent so long that Boaz thought he wasn't going to answer.

"I don't know if I'm the one who should open your ear about this or not," he finally replied.

Boaz stared. Open his ear? He could understand that the answer to his question could come only from Pashur or another Habiru, but why would the information be considered vitally important to him? "If you'll get into trouble, don't tell me," he said, trying to smooth things over.

"It's something you should know," his friend said, picking up a stick and tossing it back into the trees. "We will never leave," he went on, his voice low. "A couple of years before my birth our band was nearly wiped out, most of the warriors killed by betrayal in a disastrous battle. Meshullam was one of the few left—and became dahveed. That winter the band almost starved. Mattan remembers some of it. He said they ate a lot of bitter vetch and sycamore figs along with whatever game they could hunt down. Once, they found some wheat in an abandoned silo. They took it all, only to find it filled with scabious seeds, making the flour and bread bitter. But they ate it anyway. He remembers one day when the only food they had was bramble berries, and he got a stomachache from it."

Boaz stared at the grass he twisted in his fingers, unable to imagine that sort of life. "What happened?"

Pashur pulled his knees up against his chest and stared into the distance. "Abbi was desperate. There were only three warriors left who could fight or work, and almost 20 women and children who had survived the winter. Mattan says Abbi went out alone one night willing to offer himself as a sacrifice—anything to gain Yahweh's hesed for the rest of them."

Boaz looked away. Pashur had never been this serious before.

"Abbi never did say what happened that night. When he got back, he slept for the whole day and had a long scar across his chest. That's what made the others believe his dream."

"Why?" Boaz couldn't resist asking.

Pashur met his eyes challengingly. "It was a scar, not a wound. And it hadn't been there when he left. So when Meshullam said he'd been given a dream of a place and a man that would bring us peace, everyone believed him. Things went a little better after that, but Mattan says they wandered for three years, looking for the place in the dream. I was too young to remember much of that, but when we found the spot in the hills east of Bethlehem, Abbi recognized it."

Intrigued, Boaz sat up. "Did Meshullam also see the man from his dream?"

The Habiru hesitated, then threw a twig he had found in the grass back toward the trees towering over them. "No, not the man. That was too strange. The man stood on a sheep's fleece with a scepter lying behind him on it and wore the robes of an adon over the kilt of a warrior. He had a brilliant gold ornament shaped like a harp around his neck, and he held out a sheaf of wheat to my father. The only thing my father understood was that the man was offering him food. He knelt and took the sheaf. Anyway, Abbi vowed that if Yahweh would give us food and rest from our wandering, we would stay at that place until all of the dream was fulfilled, whatever that was."

"But how will you know when that is?" Boaz leaned back on his hands.

Again Pashur rubbed the back of his head. "I don't know. Maybe the dream is about something yet to happen, or something that may happen or not. But whatever it is, we'll be here."

"I'm honored that you would tell me this, Pashur," he said, meeting his friend's gaze.

"I'm honored that you would listen to such foolish stories as we have," the young Habiru replied. "Are you ready to go back? We ought to get started," he added, casting another glance at the sky.

Boaz looked up. "Why?"

"Because we're going to be lucky to get home by noon as it is, and I think your abbi will worry."

"Noon! Where am I?" He jerked upright.

"About a stone's throw from Tekoa. And you took the roundabout route. Keeping up with you last night was a challenge, let me assure you," the young warrior chuckled.

"That far? And I have only my belt knife. What if that lion around here had found me?"

"To say nothing of us dangerous, unpredictable Habiru," Pashur added wryly, standing and picking up his bow and quiver.

Boaz stood also, shaking the dead leaves from his cloak. "You've been a good friend, Pashur. I won't forget that."

A shrug. "You've done much for me. Let's go. Maybe the rain won't start until we get back."

Tired and wet from the rain, Boaz pushed open the gate to his home, worried that he'd ruined his clothes.

"Geber Boaz! Thank Yahweh you have arrived!" Gershed gasped, running up to him. "You must come at once! Your mother has been out of her mind."

"What is it?" The servant's agitation alarmed him. "Immi didn't worry, did she? Pashur was with me."

"Geber Boaz, your father died last night."

The ground lurched, and the world crumbled around him.

Early summer
Tammuz, fourth month, Boaz's seventeenth year
(1126 B.C.)

Trying to keep his voice under control, Boaz watched the wine buyer closely. "You know the worth of our vineyards, geber," he repeated. "We have an exceptional pressing this year. A gold gerah per jar is only 10 silver gerahs more than last year, and the wine is well worth it."

A shadow flitted across the corner of his eye, and Boaz's stomach knotted. Tobeh. Desperately he tried to ignore his rival's unnerving stare and concentrate on the wine buyer. He needed the better price badly. Tobeh's interference had cost him much recently. His inheritance included six entire grain fields, two olive orchards, a large vineyard, and two garden plots, but he was barely making ends meet. He found it impossible to concentrate on business with Tobeh's disconcerting gray eyes watching him at every turn.

The wine buyer stroked his beard thoughtfully. "An exceptional pressing, you say?"

"I thought Boaz was disappointed with the wine this year, didn't you, Zakkur?" Tobeh said to his companion just loudly enough for the merchant to hear.

Flushed with anger, Boaz refused to look at the two men.

"I wouldn't want to say, exactly," Tobeh's best friend murmured, giving the merchant a significant glance.

The wine buyer's eyes narrowed.

"The wine is perfectly good, geber, and worth one gold gerah," Boaz assured him.

"Canaanite!" Tobeh jeered softly as he walked on by.

"I'll pay only last year's price, 40 silver gerahs a jar," the buyer said with a suspicious stare. "That's my final offer."

Defeated, Boaz accepted the price, grinding his teeth in impotent rage at Tobeh's tactics. He'd counted on a higher price for the wine to provide funds to purchase extra grain so he could send his share to the communal granaries without shorting his private ones. Despite all he could do, Tobeh's slurs were having an effect, and the only reason many men in town continued to do business with him was that he had fulfilled his grain obligations last year after rust swept the town's wheat fields and ruined more than half the crops. Failure to do so this year would be a deathblow to his reputation and thus his livelihood.

When he returned home, he was in no mood to attend Elimelech and Naomi's wedding feast. Entering the gate into his family's compound, Boaz glanced across the central court, the empty one-story house he had built for his bride-to-be mocking him. The storerooms and shed on his right were empty, and worry creased his forehead. If he didn't learn to handle his inheritance better, they might have to rent the house and rooms or even leave the compound. He stared at the cistern in the center of the court. Didn't his mother's maid normally get water about this time? Was something wrong? Had the cistern gone dry already?

For a moment, Boaz stopped breathing, his chest feeling crushed. Had he forgotten to check the cistern? Was it leaking? Then he remembered it was connected to the town system and had been inspected late last summer with all the others.

As he walked into the private courtyard of the two-story house he noted that the cover was off the opening to the cistern. Replacing it, he made a mental note to speak to Immi's maid about her leaving it off. Where was she? Straightening, he stared at the shed for the milking goats and small storeroom. They were empty also, since the last old nanny goat died just two weeks ago. They would have to buy milk or do without until next spring when two female kids would freshen for the first time. A wave of fatigue washing over him, he leaned against the wall. *I'll lose it,* he thought. *I'll lose it, because I can't stop Tobeh.*

"It will come out all right, Boaz."

Immi stood in the doorway of the house. He was taller than she now, and gray streaked her hair. Losing Abbi had been hard on her. "I'm not so certain," he confessed. "I barely got last year's price for the wine after Tobeh and Zakkur commented on its value in front of the buyer. I can't stop him, Immi. I'm losing everything Abbi built up for us."

"You're still learning, son. We have enough this year, which is more than can be said for other years. It will come out all right."

Boaz walked over and hugged her.

"And even if we lost everything, I'd still have my greatest treasure," she assured him. "But I don't think you should worry. Someday you'll sit in Adon Hanan's place as chief elder. Now, are you ready to go to the wedding?"

Boaz looked down into his mother's face with a smile, noting the exhaustion in her brown eyes.

"Yes, after I change. You, however, are going back up on the roof and rest."

"No, I'm already dressed."

"But you're too tired to enjoy this, as I can easily see. I'll be fine by myself, Immi. Besides, how can I court the other available women if my mother is hovering around?" The flash of relief that crossed her face confirmed his suspicions.

"You're certain you'll be all right?"

"I'll be fine, Immi. The sun will stay warm for a long while yet, so go on up again. I'll come for inspection after I'm dressed. Where's your maid?"

"She's gone right now."

He looked at her still face and then at the cistern. "I'll help you upstairs," he said, offering her his arm.

Slowly they climbed the interior stairs he and Gershed had built to make it easier for her to reach the second story. She went to the balcony and climbed the stairs there to the roof. Someday he needed to put some outside stairs to the balcony. From habit, he glanced in the corner where Rahab's teraphim stood. The faint scent of incense reached his nose, and he looked closer. Nothing. Checking the shrine to Yahweh, he found a small charred piece of incense. Somehow it heartened him to know that Immi wasn't desperate enough to invoke Rahab's household gods as she had the day Meshullam's band had first arrived.

"Please, Yahweh, show me what to do. Preserve our inheritance before You," he whispered, bowing to the shrine, and then opened the clothes chest to get dressed.

When Gershed appeared beside him, he asked the servant, "Did Immi dismiss her maid?"

"Yes, geber."

"Bring her back. Immi needs someone, and I haven't lost everything yet."

"Yes, geber."

Although he put on a cheerful face for his mother, despondency welled back up in him on the way to Elimelech's house. This should have been his wedding. Then he sighed, knowing he hadn't had the courage to approach Naomi after Ezer threw him out. She hadn't seemed to care whether or not he attempted to court her, and she had certainly returned Elimelech's advances quickly enough.

Had his attraction for Naomi been all one-sided? Had he mistaken things that much? Not that he'd had time to do much about it, for learning to manage his inheritance kept him well occupied. Then his mother had sickened.

The aroma of spices and cooking beans drifted out of the open compound gate, and a vaguely familiar young servant conducted him inside. Without asking his name, the youth led him to a place of honor close to the married couple's table in the private courtyard of Elimelech's house. Guests spilled into the common courtyard where more tables groaned under the food. Servants hurried among them, carrying pitchers of wine, baskets of bread, and large shallow kraters of figs, early melons, pomegranates, and dates.

"Wine, geber?" someone asked, and Boaz nodded.

The servant poured the last of his wine from the pitcher and hurried away to refill it from the storage jar in the corner. Barley bread and raised wheat bread sat in a basket nearby, and half a roasted lamb was fast disappearing as another servant sliced pieces for the guests. Side dishes of broad beans and lentils sat in bowls for anyone to dip into, and everyone tried to keep the flies to a minimum. As he helped himself to the food, the thought crossed Boaz's mind that Ezer had appreciated the advantages of a connection with the Ephrath clan after all. But he'd managed it without tainting his descendants with polluted blood.

"I'm surprised you dared show your face, Canaanite," Tobeh hissed, pausing by him and smiling benignly, his gray eyes contemptuous over his thin nose.

"Tobeh, you're wanted," Tashima said shortly, stopping beside Boaz with a plate of sweet breads in her hand.

Giving the shorter young woman a nasty look, Tobeh stalked away.

"Don't pay attention to him, Boaz," she said. "He's Besai's son, which is explanation enough."

"I know. But Besai might have put a rein on Tobeh if he hadn't died."

Tashima's greenish eyes narrowed. "Good riddance, I say. My immi has never forgotten what that man did to his own sister, Abigail. And Tobeh's growing more like him every day."

"This is a celebration, Tashima. Don't rake up the past."

She smiled. "Then don't you let that arrogant donkey upset you." Setting the full bowl down, she snatched up an empty one and hurried away to the cooking fires for more.

Boaz watched Elimelech sitting with a smug smile by Naomi. She turned to speak to someone, and that honey-colored hair brushed her new husband's arm. Abruptly Boaz shifted his gaze elsewhere.

"It's good to see you here, Boaz," Elimelech said a moment later. "I know your mother has been ill. How is she?"

"Not well enough to attend this feast, I'm afraid. She wanted me to be certain to wish you Yahweh's blessings from her."

"Send her our wishes for Yahweh's healing," Naomi put in, smiling kindly.

"I will. And I'll tell her that she missed seeing the most beautiful bride in Bethlehem." He raised his cup in salute to the couple.

Naomi blushed. "Thank you, Boaz." She turned to her husband with an expression of complete satisfaction on her face.

Boaz swallowed the lump in his throat. Naomi had never looked at him like that. Maybe it wasn't just Ezer. Perhaps she could never have forgotten his "tainted" blood either.

"No, we'll make a place for him." Tobeh's voice rose just enough for Boaz to catch the words. He glanced up. Naomi's cousin escorted a richly dressed guest his way, and Boaz wondered where the man would sit, for all the spots around him were filled.

Then Tobeh's malicious smile when their glances met told him that the guest would receive his place. He'd been maneuvered into the public humiliation of being sent away from a place of honor at the most important wedding of the year. And he could do nothing about it.

"Geber Boaz, a message for you." The youth who had escorted him in stood at his side. "Your mother requires your presence."

"Surely you don't mean to go, Boaz?" Naomi asked, seeing him stand. "You just arrived."

"Immi has sent for me. She must have taken a turn for the worse. Please, forgive my leaving so soon." With a slight bow, he hurriedly followed the servant outside the compound.

"Geber Boaz, I must confess that my message was false," the young man said as soon as they could not be overheard.

"It was perfectly timed, however," Boaz replied, finally remembering where he had seen the youth before. "And may I ask what Pashur's oldest nephew is doing serving at Elimelech's wedding?"

"I'm helping out. Normally I serve in Geber Tobeh's household."

Hastily suppressing his laughter, Boaz stared at him. It would be just like Meshallum to set a spy in the enemy camp. "I should have guessed. You have done me a great service, Patah, saving my honor."

The lad's face clouded. "Your honor is worth saving. Which is more than I can say for my geber."

"Be careful how you speak, Patah. You must not be heard criticizing your geber. I'll remember your help today. Again I owe the Habiru a debt."

The youth bowed. "I am happy to serve you."

Winter
Shevat, eleventh month, Boaz's nineteenth year
(1124 B.C.)

I should be used to the numbness, Boaz thought, standing bareheaded in the cold drizzly rain, but it hit just as hard now as it had when his father died. He hardly heard the weeping of the women around him as his mother was laid to rest in the tomb. At that moment he didn't know if his hands and feet were numb from the near-freezing chill or from the harsh realization that he was now alone. Did it matter?

"Poor woman. No doubt living with a man of Canaanite blood drove her to an early grave. Well, perhaps it's for the best."

Boaz stiffened, outraged that Tobeh had chosen this moment for another slur on his house and blood.

"How true," Zakkur, Tobeh's best friend, agreed. "It must have been a hard life."

Deliberately Boaz closed his eyes. He had learned to ignore his antagonist for the most part, but he sensed the crowd shifting behind him, and his mouth twisted ironically. By the time he left, most of the younger men in the town would have clustered around Tobeh, and only a few of the older men would remain with him. He couldn't blame anyone. Tobeh was doing much better with his inheritance and family honor than he was with his.

Tobeh's continued comments penetrated his thoughts no matter how he tried to block them out, and once the tomb was sealed, Boaz walked swiftly away, knowing in his heart that he was running from Tobeh once again. As his rage intensified, his pace increased. Lately his temper had become harder to control, and he knew he must get away before it got the better of him.

That night, when he fell exhausted onto his sleeping mat, the memories of Tobeh's taunts ushered him into the throes of his dreaded nightmare of Lilith, the night demon. Desperately he fought to awaken himself, to keep himself from wandering farther and farther into the wilderness across Jordan—but to no avail.

As usual, he woke at the same place in the dream, shaking and terrified. Wrapping himself in his cloak, he huddled against the wall, trying to block out the thoughts of Tobeh, and Lilith, and of what he would do now that he was completely alone.

Just before dawn he pulled on a short robe and knotted the girdle. He wrapped his feet against the chill before strapping on his sandals, and took his thickest cloak, a dull green that blended well in the forest. Dropping over the wall at his usual place on the east side of the town, he strode swiftly along the muddy path through the garden plots and vineyards, headed for the trees.

"God of my fathers, what has happened to my life?" he spoke aloud. "I don't know which way to turn. Everywhere I go, Tobeh is there before me. He even drove me from my mother's grave!"

Silent tears ran from his eyes as he walked along, shivering from the cold. "Am I to lose the inheritance You gave to my fathers? Will our name vanish from before You among Israel? Have I offended You in some way? I know I have not been to Shiloh since Abbi died, but I have sent offerings and sacrifices every year. I have kept Your covenant as best I know how. Take pity on me, Yahweh, for I have nowhere else to turn."

As the sun rose, sending shafts of light between the trees, deer faded into the dimness at his approach. Down in the valley by the streambed a coney vanished into its hole as an eagle soared overhead. Boaz stopped and watched a fox on the other side of the stream creep forward and pounce, tossing a mouse into the air and swallowing it.

Would he be the mouse and Tobeh the fox? "Hear my prayer, Yahweh, or my family shall disappear from memory," he muttered.

He strode onward, empty of all but grief, ignoring the slap of wet branches against his cloak. His breath hovered white in the chill air that numbed his feet and hands. Then the sounds of swordplay reached his ear, stopping him and sending his hand instinctively to the belt knife in his girdle. Glancing around, he realized he was close to a clearing in which the Habiru drilled. Slipping through the trees, he crested the hill. His mother's failing health had kept him close to home for almost a year, and he had not seen Pashur in that time. Below him, two lines of men practiced with swords and shields. He started forward, passing the sentry who had already recognized him.

"Shalom, friend," Pashur called up to him.

"Shalom, Pashur."

"What happened? You look terrible. I've been away establishing myself as a wool buyer and looking for a way to transport it."

"We buried my mother yesterday."

His friend stepped instantly from the line of men. "I grieve with your loss, Boaz. Had I known, I would have come."

"You would have been welcome. Tobeh drove me from the grave with his tongue."

Pashur regarded him oddly. "Did he?" he asked softly, rubbing his black hair. "I think you've had quite enough of Tobeh. Come, get a sword, and I'll make you forget him for a while. We will spar, and then you can tell me about your mother."

Boaz wasn't interested, but he put on the arm guards anyway, appreciating his friend's concern for him. Gripping the handle of the old shield, he chose a stout wooden practice sword and stepped to the sparring line. Now that all his father's house had died, maybe he should sell his inheritance and try to start over somewhere else. The thought of leaving the land bequeathed him by his ancestors made him shudder. But how else would he ever be rid of Tobeh? If he had a son to follow him, to carry his name, it would be different—he'd fight to the last copper to keep his land. But with Naomi married to another there was little chance of—

The sting of the flat of a wooden blade on his cold, bare leg yanked his mind back.

"I need the practice, even if you don't, Boaz," his friend said.

Once through the drills, the warriors paired off to spar. Pashur circled and struck. Boaz turned the other wooden sword easily with his own, thrusting in his turn. The exercise warmed his body, but the thought of his mother soon intruded, bringing with it Tobeh's mocking laugh.

"You're not paying attention," Pashur said in disgust, whacking the other leg this time. "Are we going to spar, or are you going to brood about Tobeh?"

Flushing, Boaz backed away, his leg stinging. He raised the shield again.

"Why don't you forget the little coney?" Pashur asked, advancing. "Has he grown so big that he's the only thing you can see?"

"It's the way he maneuvers me into impossible situations that galls," Boaz replied, grunting as he landed a solid blow on the bronze center of Pashur's hardened leather shield.

"And you can't stop him, can you, Canaanite?"

The hated name exploded in Boaz's mind, shattering the walls restraining his anger. Silently he flew at Pashur, raining blows as fast as he could lift his arm. The Habiru parried, turned, and blocked, dancing out of his reach. Just as Tobeh always did.

Grimly Boaz lunged forward, only to turn his foot on a stone and fall, barely avoiding a strike from his opponent as he rolled to his feet. The impact reined his temper back to a controlled heat. Obviously a frontal assault couldn't overwhelm his opponent.

Something more flashed over him, intensifying the light and colors around him and blocking out everything except his immediate vicinity and his desire to win. Remembering the steep rise of the hill by the boulder on one side of the clearing, Boaz circled toward it, subtly encouraging Pashur to follow him through the maze of sparring men.

Acutely focused, he didn't notice those he effortlessly drove out of his way in his attempts to corner his opponent, nor did he notice them stop to watch the intense conflict between Pashur's quick agility and his own relentless strength.

He retreated before a rain of blows, drawing the Habiru warrior after him, the wooden sword clacking as he parried with it. Occasionally he drove forward as they turned and twisted, gradually drawing nearer to the bank. Although panting, the sweat streaming from him in the cool air, Boaz felt strong and quick, and he burned to beat down Tobeh's memory just as he planned to do to the fighter before him. Wood against wood, he blocked and twisted, nearly ripping the practice sword from his adversary's hand. He circled a final time, putting the man's back to the steep hillside.

Instantly the man saw the trap, but Boaz drove inexorably forward, using his strength to keep his opponent from breaking into the open where his agility gave him the advantage. At last he had him pinned against the boulder, unable to move. Grimly Boaz hammered against the shield, beating the man holding it to his knees.

"Boaz, I'm not Tobeh."

Of course he was Tobeh—who else would he be fighting?

"Boaz!"

Dropping his weapons, Boaz wrenched aside his opponent's shield and, grasping the man's sword wrist, yanked him to his feet, spread-eagling him against the bank.

"Believe me now?" Pashur asked wryly.

Breathing hard, Boaz stared at the face inches from his own, his mind gradually becoming aware of his surroundings.

"If you could call on that skill at will instead of only when you're angry, you would be the best Habiru in the land," his friend said softly. "You going to let me go?"

"Before you drop your sword? Your father taught me much better than that!"

"Will you loosen your grip so I can?"

"Not until you yield."

"I'm beaten."

When Boaz relaxed his arms a trifle, Pashur dropped his sword. Hearing the murmured comments of the other men, Boaz stepped back, reddening with the usual embarrassment that flooded him whenever he lost control of himself.

"Anytime you want to join us, tell me. You could lead our band as dahveed."

Boaz shook his head. "I don't wish to live my life angry all the time, not even as a dahveed of the Habiru. Are you all right?"

"I'll be sore in the morning." Pashur grimaced. "I seldom get this kind of punishment!"

Leaning against the high bank as the other warriors drifted back to resume their practice, Boaz watched his friend slip the guards from his arms. "You deliberately provoked me, didn't you?"

Pashur shrugged. "You needed a taste of victory over Tobeh. So far, my friend, you have fought that man as clumsily as you fight with a spear." Stretching, he rubbed the backs of his arms. "Make Tobeh fight on your terms, Boaz. I don't know when you began your advance. You seemed to do nothing but retreat until I suddenly found myself cornered with surrender my only option."

The Habiru squatted down, resting against the bank. "Handle Tobeh the same way," he continued. "You won't conquer him in a day, or a week. Maybe it will take years. But if you fight him as you just did me, you'll be able to destroy him if you wish."

Boaz kicked the sword on the ground in frustration. "But I don't want to destroy him—I just want him to leave me alone!"

"That's beside the point," Pashur retorted in exasperation. *"He* wants to destroy *you.* The point is whether or not you let him. And if you play your strength against his weakness, he won't be able to withstand you any more than I could."

Afterward the two friends went hunting as they had used to do, saying little. As dusk approached, they returned to the clearing. "It's been good to spend the day with you, Pashur," Boaz said quietly.

"Then come again," the Habiru replied as he disappeared into the trees.

~ ~ ~

During the next couple days while the cold rain kept everyone from the fields, Boaz sat for several hours listening at the town gate, learning that Tobeh had enlarged his father's inheritance by two fields and had secured a lucrative contract with a merchant in Jebus for fine olive oil. From comments and conversation he learned which merchants and landowners Tobeh usually did business with about town.

That night Boaz watched the flame of the oil lamp slowly grow dimmer as he paced in the room on the compound that he used for his business activities. "Pashur is right," he muttered to himself. "It's time to fight on my terms."

Using an old sheet of papyrus, he recorded every name mentioned in connection with Tobeh, then wrote down every business contact he had inherited from his father. Interesting. Tobeh had only one or two tentative associates outside of Bethlehem's vicinity. But he himself had more than a half dozen in Jebus and two in Jericho. An intriguing possibility rose in his mind, but it would require him to operate on two fronts, and he would need to know Tobeh's goals in order to avoid him for the first few years.

Straightening up from the small table, he threw the reed brush down and paced again. How could he discover what his rival really wanted? A faint memory tugged at his mind, and he paused, staring at the flickering lamp as he dredged his memory, absently stroking the soft dark hair of his growing beard. Something about Tobeh and the whole town. Yes, that quickly corrected comment, "When I'm king—uh, old enough." Just a slip of the tongue? Or did it reveal what was really on his mind?

Thoughtfully, Boaz sat down on a three-legged stool by the table, reaching for some dried fruit in the bowl. Just suppose Tobeh was planning to become king of Bethlehem. How would that influence his thinking and actions? He might concentrate totally on Bethlehem and its environs, ignoring what might be happening over the horizon. The man had a tendency to hold one idea in his mind and disbelieve anything contrary to that view, as evidenced by his opinions about Besai's death.

Boaz frowned, turning that thought over in his mind. How could he use it to his advantage? Another memory intruded. Tobeh had begun wearing new, showy clothes, claiming his increased wealth was a result of Yahweh's pleasure in the extra offerings he'd sent to the tabernacle in Shiloh. Now, why would he risk his family's good name by opening himself to an accusation of greed, that he was taking more than his due? Or was he preparing the ground for future advancement in status? Kings could accumulate all the wealth they wanted, since it brought honor to the entire community.

Stroking his beard again, Boaz stared blankly at the door. He'd have to pay special attention to which people in town accepted Tobeh's display without comment. That might reveal who supported him. And, since the man appeared eager to flaunt his success, would he assume that appearance automatically correlated with actual wealth? Would he cling to that idea even to his own detriment? Boaz leaned back against the wall and folded his arms. Suddenly lots of intriguing possibilities flooded his thoughts.

For his own part, he must maintain his own inheritance first, perhaps enlarge it a little if the chance came, but nothing obvious. That would provide a solid base from which to operate. At the same time, he must establish himself outside of town beyond Tobeh's influence. It would work only if his rival concentrated his energies on Bethlehem for the next several years and waited until he was at least 30 before attempting anything.

Uneasy, Boaz resumed pacing. It was a chance he must take. Then he smiled grimly. Maybe Yahweh was thinking ahead of him. With the poor grain crops the past two years, he'd been wondering what to do with the unexpected increase of his donkeys. Rather than selling those extra five animals, perhaps he should use them to transport goods. Hadn't Pashur said he needed some way to ship wool?

Ideas spinning through his mind, Boaz paced faster. What about that neglected fig tree he and Pashur had found near Tekoa, the one that always had the sweetest figs he'd ever tasted? Was it the tree or the soil? If he could help someone settle on a farmstead near there something might come of it.

It wouldn't be easy at first. He must handle most of the business outside of Bethlehem on his own and still oversee his lands here. The townspeople would comment on his long absences, since people rarely traveled out of town unless they were merchants who sold goods they did not produce and lived on the fringes of honorable society. Also, he must make every move with the thought of how Tobeh would see it and interpret it.

"Geber Boaz?"

Irritated at the interruption, he swung around. "Yes, Gershed?"

"There is a man, Tahat, at the door looking for work. He owns a farmstead west of town, and his father recently died."

Why is anyone looking for work at this hour of the night? Boaz wondered. "Show him in, Gershed."

Moments later he inclined his head to the slightly older man wearing a faded brown-striped robe. His visitor looked both tired and defeated.

"Shalom, Geber Tahat. Please come in. There is wine on the table and some fruit. Refresh yourself, then tell me the reason you have come to see me."

"Shalom, Geber Boaz. Your hospitality is most generous."

Tahat eased down on the stool near the low table and reached for a dried apricot. Gershed silently returned, poured wine into a cup, and added some raised wheat bread to the food.

After eating a small amount, Tahat slid back on the stool.

"Now, tell me what has happened," Boaz invited. "Gershed said your father recently died?"

"Yes. It was only then that I realized we were indebted to Geber Tobeh. We lost one barley harvest to smut, and the next year thieves cleaned out our granaries. They broke all the farm implements they could find and ran off with our oxen. Yattir, the Ammonite, expressed great concern about Father's misfortunes and very generously offered to lend a hand, making a deal that my father would pay a certain amount of wheat, barley, and olive oil every year to work off the debt. He said that if we couldn't pay everything required one year, we could just add it on to the next."

"That was three years ago?"

Tahat nodded.

"I remember the raids. The thieves hit almost every farmstead in your area. A small band of Habiru, wasn't it?"

"Yes. Meshullam's band drove them off. Anyway, Yattir helped several of us on the same terms. Only one or two were able to pay him off completely. The amounts he asked for sounded reasonable, but most of us had to postpone payment until another year, and then another, and the debt kept getting bigger. At Father's funeral Tobeh informed me that he had bought the loan from Yattir, so now I owed it to him."

"And he demanded you pay immediately."

The visitor sighed. "I asked him to wait until harvest—the crop coming on now is the best I've ever had. But he insisted that I pay now. I told him I couldn't, so he suggested a way to settle the debt. Everything I harvested would go to him."

"Leaving you with nothing for next year to plant or eat, which meant that you'd have to go into debt again to start over. Undoubtedly, Tobeh would arrange things so you would have to borrow from him."

Grimly the man nodded. "That's how he got his first new field. It wouldn't surprise me if Yattir had been fronting for Tobeh from the first. I told that scrawny hyena that if he wanted my land worked under those terms, he could send someone from his own house to do it. He did."

Again Boaz began to pace the room. "Why did you come to me?"

"You are one of the few in town who might have enough to lend me the amount I owe," Tahat replied, studying the floor.

"Particularly since my inexperience or my rivalry with Tobeh might work in your favor? I'm young, Tahat, but not stupid. My harvests haven't been any better than anyone else's the past two years."

His visitor looked ashamed. "I've been to three other men in town before I came here," he confessed. "Even Adon Hanan turned me down. But he suggested that you might have some way of helping."

Boaz paused, studying the man. "What bothers you most, Tahat? Losing the land, or being under Tobeh's thumb?"

Surprised, the farmer jerked his head up. "How can you ask? It's my family's inheritance!"

"You walked away from it readily enough."

Tahat flushed. "What gives you the right to ask such a question?"

"You came to me for money."

Struggling to decide what to do, Tahat glared at him. At last he looked down, his shoulders slumping. "What does it matter?"

"I'm considering two options, and your answer will determine my offer."

With a sigh, his visitor rubbed his face with one hand. "Father was the farmer, geber. I never could settle into it, and I hate being under Tobeh's thumb. He's lording it over me as if he were a king."

Boaz chuckled. "Good. I think you and I can deal, Tahat, if you're willing to take a risk with me."

"I'll do anything to get out from under that leech!"

"All right, go along with him. Go to the gate tomorrow and make the contract to give him your entire harvest this year to fully clear any indebtedness. But stipulate that he must provide the labor. Since you will be destitute at the end of the year, that seems fair."

"I certainly will be. He'll take everything."

"I have five donkeys," Boaz continued, "and with those donkeys you will transport wool for a friend of mine just starting as a buyer. When he gets paid for his services, he'll settle up with you and probably introduce you to others who need something taken back to Jebus, or Jericho, or any number of other places. Charge a price a little on the high side, then be absolutely certain that the goods arrive on time and in perfect condition.

"I'll give you one year to establish a reputation as the best donkey caravan between Jericho and the coast. At the end of the year you can decide whether you'd like to continue what you're doing, or take your payment and return to your land."

"Who is this friend of yours?" Tahat asked, his eyes intent and interested.

"Pashur, of Meshullam's band. It's a gamble, for if we fail, I will lose half my donkey herd."

"But I will be no worse off than I am now. Why would you give me such hesed?"

Flushing, Boaz ceased his pacing. "Hardly hesed, for this may not be a kindness, let alone lifesaving. At the end of the year you may be dead, or left with the bare land and nothing to work it with."

"I'm there already. This looks like hesed to me. I have nowhere else to turn and have no reason to expect anything from you." Tahat shrugged. "I'll do whatever you ask."

"You're too kind," Boaz said uncomfortably, turning away. "If you can be at the gate tomorrow, I'll try to have the donkeys ready."

"As you wish, adon."

"I'm not your lord, Tahat."

"Maybe," the man replied. "I am curious, however. What was the other option?"

"That would only suit someone who likes to farm," Boaz replied, deciding to ignore his visitor's enigmatic reply.

"Oh? My neighbor lost his land to Tobeh with the same kind of deal he's pulling on me. Losing his inheritance has devastated him."

"Who is he?"

"Eliram. He would give anything to be back on a farmstead."

"Tell me, Tahat, does Eliram like figs?"

Late fall
Kislev, ninth month, Boaz's twentieth year
(1123 B.C.)

Boaz looked over the last of the three fields he had cleared. He had worked alone, day after day, felling the trees, clearing the brush, cleaning out the stones and using them to build terrace walls. He would be ready to sow the field tomorrow. Smiling, he yanked out another small bush by its roots.

All his recent business ventures had prospered. Tahat had not 10 but twice 10 donkeys working in two caravans. Pashur had suggested that his Habiru train all the caravanners to fight, and it wasn't long before the bandits on the routes learned to leave Tahat's caravans alone. The man had decided to continue as caravanner, splitting the profits with Boaz and Pashur.

Eliram had done well also. The new farmstead near Tekoa now had a house along with a garden for kitchen crops to one side. The farmer had cleared and terraced two fields and put in a small walled vineyard. The watchtower would be positioned between the fields and vineyard, and the walls around the fields were partially complete.

Farther up the hill, in a depression that seemed to wind around the entire hillside, Eliram had planted five fig trees in various places near the one Boaz had shown him. Many of the trees nearby were taller than those in the surrounding forest. Eliram's family loved their new home, and his wife had already gained a reputation in Tekoa for her fig pasties, which she sold daily during fig harvest.

Stretching to his full height, Boaz studied the new terracing he'd just completed here on his second farmstead investment. He had chosen the site carefully, studying the lay of the land for months, watching where water flowed from the hillside and observing frost patterns and other indications of the land's usefulness. It was farther from town than most farmsteaders liked, although Meshullam's Habiru made living away from Bethlehem safer than it used to be. And even though Bethlehem was relatively free from the Philistine harassment beginning farther west, most farmsteaders wanted to be nearer town just in case.

With this in mind, the Habiru had helped Boaz build a house designed to hold off attack and allow escape through the stable into a shallow ravine overgrown with shrubbery. The watchtower was taller than normal, with a low wall around the platform at the top and built to be an offensive position as well as a lookout for enemies or predators in the fields and gardens.

With a grunt, Boaz picked up another stone and added it to the terrace wall, remembering Tobeh's barely disguised scorn at the gate two days ago when the man had sold grain to him at an outrageous price. But Boaz had nothing left of his own crop to sow here, and he estimated his three new fields would yield nearly as much as his other fields combined because the slope of the land channeled an unusual amount of water down into the fields. He had made the bottom layer of gravel in the new terraces extra thick to accommodate the runoff and allow it to percolate to the next terrace down. A layer of dirt, another of gravel, and the final one of topsoil should ensure an abundant crop yield.

Working steadily, he added more stones to the wall and dug some stubborn shrubs from the far corner. Noticing a particularly mushy spot under his foot, he dug down, uncovering what appeared to be a small spring! He spent the rest of the morning lengthening the terrace wall to capture the water flow. As he did so he planned how he would have Tahat transport the grain from these fields west before selling it, thus allowing him to preserve a low profile around Tobeh and Bethlehem.

Another rock slipped into place, and Boaz rested briefly, pondering the biggest problem on his mind. He desperately needed an overseer. Keeping his activities outside of Bethlehem as quiet as possible meant he often worked alone and had to use hired help to tend his inheritance, which looked noticeably neglected. Last year he had not been able to prune his vineyards properly, and the resulting harvest was not as abundant as it could have been. He had little time or energy to oversee the laborers after keeping up his business contacts in Jebus and Jericho coupled with hard physical labor like his work today. But his exhaustion left him sleeping so deeply that it suppressed his nightmares of Lilith.

He knew the townspeople wondered at his frequent absences, but his open replies, which told nothing, to any queries had so far averted suspicion of wrongdoing.

At noon Boaz walked to the house and sat at the table, removing the plug in the wineskin for a long drink. He had almost completed that third field and should have it entirely sowed by— The small scuffing sound from the stable made the hair on his neck rise, and he jerked, spilling a little wine on his foot. Instinctively he knew that an animal had not caused the noise. Rising stealthily, he crept toward the stable door. Whoever was in there probably wasn't friendly. He grasped his staff tightly, a long oak rod polished from much handling and so hard he'd broken more than one sword blade with it.

The stable door shifted under his touch, and he was certain he'd latched it yesterday. Standing to one side, he used the rod to push it open. Nothing moved inside the stable. He checked the area. The front and side wall across from him were only half built yet. Staff ready, he stepped forward and stood in the center of the space, eyes watchful, ears searching for any sound.

Nothing. Puzzled, Boaz slowly turned, surveying the entire room. All was as it should be. The chill on his foot gradually reached his mind, and Boaz looked down. Why would he feel that low a draft? The hidden door to the ravine was open just a crack! The small flow of air had cooled his wet skin.

Studying the ground, he noticed a moist spot or two. Bending cautiously, keeping his eye on the door, he touched the spots and rubbed his fingers together, smelling them. Blood.

"Come on out," he spoke quietly. "I'm not in the mood for a fight today, but I do take exception to guests that hide themselves."

Although he thought he heard a small intake of breath, he received no reply.

"I know you're hurt," he went on. "You bled on the floor. If I have to drag you out of there, I'll probably do more damage than it's worth."

Almost imperceptibly the door shifted. Boaz stepped to the side, putting himself just in the line of sight of whoever was there. He waited tensely, ready to leap aside should the door open enough to admit a knife or arrow.

"I'll come out, but I have a sword."

"And I'm out of your reach," Boaz replied.

Slowly the door opened, and a man about his own age stepped into the room, left arm pressed tightly into his side. He was slender, with an intelligent face and long fingers that gripped the old sword in his hand, its blade corroded and chipped in several places. Dried blood stained his tattered robe, one brown eye was nearly swollen shut, and he was covered with bruises and cuts.

Boaz relaxed. One strike of his staff would snap that blade. "My name is Boaz, of the Ephrath clan in Bethlehem. What did you run away from day before yesterday?"

His visitor blinked. "How did you know—" He stopped. "Never mind."

"As you wish," Boaz said mildly. "You going to let me do anything about your wound?"

The man looked down at his injury. "Just give me some food, and I'll be on my way."

He's no warrior, Boaz thought. *Trained fighters never take their eyes off their opponents.* "You won't get far, and out in the open you're in real danger. I can smell the blood on you, which means everything else out there can too. You feel up to fighting off wild dogs? Or the lion that favors this area? I'm afraid it's me or them."

"We'll stay," another voice said, and through the doorway came a woman with the most gorgeous head of hair Boaz had ever laid eyes on. He gasped, mouth hanging open.

The dark chestnut color matched his own, but her hair blazed with subtle red highlights that glittered and shifted in the light. She had pale skin that would be silky smooth when it was clean, and her nose tilted up just a bit.

The man tightened his grip on his sword, dark-brown eyes boring into Boaz.

"Welcome to both of you," Boaz finally managed to say, collecting his wits. "Come with me into the house. There's no one here but me."

While the two strangers followed him, Boaz reached outside for the water skin he'd hung there on the wall.

"Have a drink," he invited, holding the skin out to the man, ignoring his companion.

The other hesitated, then grimaced in defeat and dropped the sword, reaching for the water with the hand he could still move.

"Have you decided to trust me enough to let me look at your woman without trying to gut me?"

"I'm not his woman," she said. "I'm his sister. Habiru raiders overran our settlement a week ago. They seized Ladel as a slave. I'd managed to hide, and I followed them for two days before one of them spotted me. It took another day to figure out why I was around, and then they beat Ladel trying to make him tell them where I was.

"Night before last someone passed out strong wine, and most of them got drunk on it. We took the opportunity to leave."

"How did you find that back door?" Boaz asked.

She made a face. "My brother fell into the ravine."

"And what's your name?"

"Menahemet. Most people call me Mena. Father was an Edomite. My mother was from this area, near Tekoa. We hoped we could locate her family."

"Tekoa is a couple miles south and higher in the hills. You can go there after we take care of your brother. Clean him up with that water, and here's some food. Then get him back into the ravine. I'm returning to Bethlehem. Later this afternoon my servant Gershed will bring food and other supplies to this house. Keep out of sight. You and Ladel can stay until he's better."

"May Yahweh reward your hesed to us, Boaz."

"It's not hes—" he started to say, then shut his mouth. If she wanted to think he was being kind, let her. It might be easier that way to convince her and her brother to remain here and take care of the farmstead. He would need someone here and—

"And you want any excuse you can find to keep her near you, you fool," he muttered, striding down the road to Bethlehem.

Early fall
Heshvan, eighth month, Boaz's twenty-first year
(1122 B.C.)

"You wished to see me, Boaz?"

"Yes, Ladel. There was something I wanted to discuss with you."

"Oh?" The man looked at him with knowing brown eyes.

Flushing faintly, Boaz glanced down. Now that Ladel was here, he didn't know how to broach the subject. His stomach felt sick from the memory of what happened the last time he asked for a woman's hand. But he had to do this sometime. By now he was older than most unmarried men, and he needed a family so that he could fill his place in society adequately. Besides, he was lonely. Up to now, he'd been too busy, or not attracted to any of the eligible women, to think of marriage until he'd seen Mena standing in her torn robe covered with dirt and leaves, that magnificent hair tumbling down her back. His pulse pounded just thinking about it.

"Boaz?"

"Uh, yes. I was distracted there for a minute."

"Yes, Mena has that effect."

Although Boaz looked up quickly, his friend had a perfectly sober face. "She does?"

"Yes. I've already had three requests for her hand in the past month. One was from a very wealthy merchant in Jericho."

His heart froze. Of course someone like her would attract a lot of attention. He was well off, but most of his enterprises were still more promise than profit. In another few years it would be different, barring disasters and given Yahweh's blessings, but now? He certainly didn't want to stand in the way of an advantageous match for Mena. Maybe he should keep quiet.

"Boaz? What did you want to discuss?"

"Uh, I wanted to ask you about something."

"You said that."

"It's about the farmstead," Boaz blurted, shifting the papyri on the rough table in front of him.

"Is something wrong? I've tried to do everything you wanted there," Ladel said anxiously. "The walls around the fields are done. We haven't started plowing yet, but we haven't had a hard enough rain to loosen the ground."

"No, no; you've done just what I asked. It's just that I wonder if you're a bit cramped there." He put the papyri back where they had been and picked up the brush pen.

"Not at all. There's plenty of room for both of us."

"Not cramped for space," Boaz corrected. "Cramped by being held to something not really suited to your talents."

Ladel dropped his gaze. "You saved our lives, gave us a place to live, helped us locate our mother's clan. I don't want to leave you without someone to take care of the place."

Boaz put the pen back down. "Don't worry about that. Meshullam has a couple families who would rather farm than fight and who are willing to stay that far from town."

"Then what do you want?"

"I've noticed that when I talk a problem over with you, you usually come up with some very shrewd advice. As you've seen, I need an overseer." He knew that he was really just avoiding the subject of Mena, but then her brother would be perfect as an overseer. Maybe something would come of this interview after all.

His tenant frowned. "It's a tempting offer, but to be truthful, I'm not excited about working as a hireling."

"I see." Expecting him to leave, Boaz looked puzzled as the man continued to sit comfortably, watching him. "Would there be other circumstances in which you'd consider the position?" he asked cautiously. The more he thought about the idea of Ladel as overseer, the better he liked it.

"Yes. If I had a share of the profits, and could perhaps purchase the farmstead I've been working as an inheritance for my descendants."

"Oh," Boaz said, relieved. "Yes, I think that can be arranged. I've helped out one or two other men that way."

"I know; I've talked to them."

"Checked me out, did you? I thought I'd been honest with you."

Ladel had a crooked grin on his face. "Yes, but there are circumstances in which a man wants all the information he can get. And you must admit that you do have some rather strange habits, Boaz. You just disappear periodically. I know that sometimes you go to Tekoa, other times to Jebus or Jericho. But at still other times, fairly regular ones, you simply vanish."

"I hardly think that's any of your concern," Boaz said stiffly.

"Normally, I couldn't agree more," Ladel replied calmly. "But as I said, there are circumstances when a man wants to know everything he can. For instance, starting a business partnership—or becoming family."

Boaz chewed the inside of his lip. Becoming family, he had said. Had Ladel noticed his feelings toward his sister? What did he think of them? More to the point, what did Mena think? He didn't want to be mistaken again about a woman's attitude toward him.

"Something else on your mind, Boaz?"

"Well, I—sort of."

"Yes?"

"It's about Mena. She's very beautiful." Boaz flushed, wishing this were just a straight business deal. He could keep his wits during them. But when it came to marriage and women, he never knew what to say or how to say it.

"Been thinking of Mena?" Ladel asked matter-of-factly.

"Well, she is very nice to think about. For me, anyway. Not that I have dishonorable intentions," he hastened to add. "She's just so beautiful with that hair."

"So you've said."

Boaz glanced away in desperation. This was going as badly as the first time. Why couldn't he just ask for her hand? Better drop the whole subject. "Anyway, I wanted to ask you about the overseer's job. If we arrange for you to receive part of the profits and to purchase the farmstead, would you accept?"

"I'd give it serious consideration, provided some other circumstances are cleared up. But I thought Mena was under discussion."

"Could we put that off until another time? I do have much to do."

Ladel shook his head. "I don't think that would be a good idea. My sister would probably take my head from my shoulders if I left now."

"Oh." Boaz shifted on the seat, sweat forming on his forehead. Thinking of her made him uncomfortable. That hair. It had brushed against his hand once, and he could still feel the softness. He shifted in his seat. Why was it so hot in here? Pushing the papyrus in front of him around on the table, he asked, "What about Mena?"

"I believe you were telling me how beautiful she was."

"Well, yes, and—and she's been very kind to me, too."

"Kind?" Ladel's eyebrows climbed again. "I would have thought she was more than kind."

Avoiding his friend's gaze, Boaz cursed himself. He was babbling exactly the same inanities he had to Ezer years ago!

A twinkle showed in Ladel's eyes. That little crooked smile didn't help either. "Just ask, Boaz," his friend said, taking pity on him.

"How do I know she wants me to?" he burst out, standing and turning his back. "It's not as if I'm the best catch she can make. Yes, I guess I'm well off, but for a few more years any setback could wipe out all of what I've done. With the Philistines getting bolder, that's a real possibility. What if the Ammonites or Midianites take it into their heads to raid? Droughts, locusts, any number of things could—"

"And lightning could strike you dead tomorrow, Boaz. I don't think she would accept that as an excuse."

"What has she thought about the other offers you've had?" he asked, pacing the floor.

"She told me that she'd sell me back to the Habiru if I tried to marry her to anyone but her choice."

Startled, Boaz stopped. "She has someone in mind?"

"I'd say so, yes."

"Oh." Boaz sat down, putting his head in his hands, his heart sinking. He'd been mistaken again. At least Ladel wouldn't throw him into the street.

His friend shook his head in wonder. "My sister told me she would only marry the man who fell in love with her the day she looked her worst and then had the temerity to completely ignore her minutes later by offering her brother a drink as if she weren't even there. Mena was quite emphatic about it. She seemed to feel that marrying this man would give her sufficient opportunity to make him curse the day he dared to ignore her in such an outrageous manner, because she was going to make certain that he never in his life looked at another woman and—"

"Ladel, will you give me Mena's hand in marriage?" Boaz interrupted before he had time to think about what he was saying.

"I think that can be arranged if you will tell me where you go when you disappear."

For a moment Boaz hesitated, wondering how Ladel would feel about connections with the Habiru after his experiences. "I visit friends up in the hills."

"Let me see your sword hand."

Without thinking, Boaz started to hold out his right hand.

Ladel's crooked smile stopped him. "I take it these friends are Habiru?"

"Yes," he admitted. "They provide protection for Bethlehem and are nothing like the band that destroyed your home. You've already had business dealings with one of them and are living in a house that they helped build. The wool merchant, Pashur, is a son of the dahveed—and my friend."

With a sigh Ladel shook his head. "The more I know of you, Boaz, the deeper I find you," he chuckled. "Maybe Mena has finally met her match! Keep her in hand, would you? And ask her soon, before she drives me to Lilith with her impatience."

"I'll do what I can," Boaz promised, flushing.

Fall
Heshvan, eighth month, Boaz's twenty-sixth year (1117 B.C.)

Geber Boaz, I'm sorry to interrupt, but I have an urgent message."

Boaz looked up at the panting messenger who had just entered the room where he sat with Ahinadab before a Jebus magistrate finalizing a business deal. The Ammonite merchant had the best pottery in the city, and he had offered to acquire a set of large pithoi of the white ware from Cyprus for Boaz.

"What is it?"

"If you would step outside, geber?"

"Excuse me," Boaz said, rising, his stomach suddenly in knots. What could be wrong? Mena? She was carrying their second child.

"What is it?" he repeated as soon as they were out of the room.

"Geber Ladel sent me. Your wife is not well."

Boaz grabbed the messenger's shoulder. "What do you mean, 'not well'?"

"Geber, she went into labor yesterday. The midwife came, and, well, after several hours she called for Geber Ladel. After he talked to her, he sent me for you. He says you are to come immediately."

"What is wrong with Mena?" Boaz demanded. But he could read in the messenger's eyes what the man could not bring himself to say. "Yahweh preserve her!" he groaned, rushing out the door without bothering to get his cloak from the other room. Once away from Jebus's gates, he headed for the Habiru trail between Jebus and Bethlehem. In the trees he stopped long enough to pull his robe up between his legs and tuck it firmly into his girdle. Then he ran, keeping a good pace that he could maintain for miles. The wind quickened, bringing with it a pouring rain that pounded his skin and made it hard to breathe. His head ducked low, he slowed as the trails turned to mud. Slipping and breaking a leg would help nothing.

Streaming water and panting hard, he saw Bethlehem's wall at last. His hair had come unbound and stuck to his soaked robe. He darted through the gate and across the empty market without pausing. Bursting into his family compound, he rushed to the private courtyard.

Ladel spotted him immediately and ran toward him. "Thank Yahweh you're here."

"What happened? How is Mena?" Boaz gasped, leaning against the wall.

"It's bad. Something went wrong with the birth. The baby was born dead; and from what I can understand from the midwife, Mena is bleeding, and they can't get it stopped."

"Oh, Yahweh, no." Boaz slid down the rough wall to the ground. "Surely the midwife can do something! Mena didn't have any trouble when Yatom was born. Why now? Where is she?"

"In the small house. The midwife won't let me in. Here, wash the mud off yourself and get a dry robe. I'll go check on her again."

In a daze Boaz shed his robe, splashed some water over himself from a jar, and pulled on clean clothes that Gershed brought, tying back his hair hurriedly without bothering to do more than wring most of the rainwater from it.

Ladel waited at the door. "The midwife won't answer my questions," he said simply.

Feeling as if he had walked into a shower of hail, Boaz went to the door.

"Geber Boaz, you must not go in," the maidservant outside protested, trying to restrain him.

Silently he moved her aside and entered, followed by Ladel. How pale Mena looked! Glancing around, he bit his lips. Blood soaked the bedclothes.

Unable to speak, he sank down beside the bed mat, reaching for his wife's hand.

When he touched her, she opened her eyes and turned to him. "You're back," she whispered.

"Yes."

Her hand tightened on his. "I'm sorry."

"For what? You're going to be fine," he said between clenched teeth.

She smiled faintly. "I'm going to die, Boaz. I can feel it, and I've been at enough births to know what this much blood means."

He glanced at the white-faced maidservant. "Get a clean covering," he snapped. She reappeared moments later.

"Spread it over her." Boaz pulled it up himself, covering the soaked cloth all around his wife.

"Make sure there is someone there for Yatom," she said when he took her hand again.

"There is," Boaz said firmly. "Right here."

She smiled again. "Not for long. Something is pulling at me. Is everything covered up?"

"Yes."

"Bring Yatom, would you? I want to see him."

When Boaz glanced at his brother-in-law, he nodded and left the room. "Ladel is going to get him," he told his wife. "He'll be here soon."

"Hurry," she replied, a catch in her voice. "The room is getting so dark."

Clenching his jaw to keep his chin from trembling, Boaz patted her hand, then kissed it. The smell of incense reached his nose, and he glanced around. Someone had brought the shrine to Yahweh and Rahab's teraphim from the big house and set them in a corner, charred incense lying in front of both. A shiver of his old remembered fear ran up his spine, and he looked away. Maybe they brought comfort to Mena. Although he'd never seen her make offerings to either Yahweh or the teraphim, she'd kept both the household gods and the shrine dusted and maintained a supply of incense.

Moments later Ladel entered with 4-year-old Yatom, who looked very afraid.

"Where's my little man?" Mena asked almost as she usually did.

"I'm here with you," the child replied, his voice unsteady.

Boaz put his son's hand in hers.

"You be a good boy for Abbi now. He'll take care of you, and so will Dodi Ladel."

"Where will you be, Immi?"

"Immi has to go with your sister and take care of her."

"But I don't want you to go away. Why can't sister be here with us?"

"She needs me as you needed me when you were younger, so I have to go with her. But don't you worry. Whenever you want me, just call my name, and I'll be there in your mind, and you can remember how much I love you. Give me a kiss now, and go get some supper."

Somewhat reassured, Yatom leaned over and kissed his mother, then went out with his uncle.

Head bowed, Boaz held Mena's hand. Its trembling told him the effort it had taken for her to appear natural for Yatom. In his heart he cried for Yahweh to have compassion and give life back to his beloved.

"Are you here, Boaz?" she asked after several minutes.

He gripped her hand harder. "Yes, I'm still here. I haven't gone, not for a moment."

"I can't see—the room is all dark. Talk to me, love. I want to hear your voice."

Tears streamed down his face, but he swallowed the lump in his throat. "Remember when I first saw you? Standing there in the stable looking like a wild thing? And Ladel so injured, he could hardly stand. But he wouldn't let go of that absurd sword."

She struggled to smile. "I remember."

"I fell in love with you right then, you know. I couldn't resist. And how your eyes flashed when I ignored you! But I think it was sending Ladel to propose to me that really took my heart—"

"What?" she interrupted weakly. "I did no such thing!"

Boaz stroked her hair. "Well, you told him not to leave until I'd offered for your hand, anyway. I'd never have dared to ask for you otherwise."

"Silly you," she murmured with another weak smile.

"The past five years have been the best of my life, Mena. Since I've had you, I've never looked at another woman, and you gave me little Yatom, the best son a father ever had, and we are very happy, aren't we?"

Her hand was limp in his, and the only thing he could think of was how beautiful her hair looked, its red highlights gleaming in the light of the lamp.

Early summer
Sivan, third month, Boaz's twenty-seventh year
(1116 B.C.)

Are we almost there?"

"Yes, Yatom. Just over the next hill," Boaz answered, leading the donkey up the trail toward its crest.

"And that's the place where you met Immi?"

"Yes."

"And Dodi Ladel will be there?"

"He should be. Your uncle owns it now—he set his sandal on it not long ago."

"But didn't he need his sandal, Abbi?"

His father smiled. Yatom could be so literal about words. "That means he took ownership of it. You've seen people pace off a piece of land to buy or sell?" The boy nodded, looking around with wide brown eyes just like his mother's. At the sight of them Boaz looked away, a pang striking his heart, and continued his explanation. "If it's a large piece, the buyer will pace the land off with the seller in order to show where the boundaries are. With smaller pieces of land, the buyer will just step on the land before witnesses to finalize the sale. That's what Dodi Ladel did.

"Now, sometimes, if it's a piece of land that both parties know, the whole sale is handled at the gate. In that case, the seller takes off his sandal as a symbol of ownership or rights to the land, and gives it to the buyer, who accepts it, meaning he has purchased ownership or rights to the land."

"But what does he do with the sandal after that?" Yatom asked, brushing a fly away from his dark auburn hair.

"He gives it back," Boaz smiled, tousling Yatom's hair affectionately. The promise of red in Mena's hair had been fulfilled in her son's. "Now sit still, or you'll fall off the donkey."

Yatom settled down, but one hand clutched his father's robe. For weeks after his mother had died the child had refused to let him or Ladel out of his sight. At first Boaz had been helpless to know what to do for his son. Having the boy with him every minute was a great hindrance to the work he needed to do.

But somehow he and Ladel had managed with the help of the women servants, and now Boaz was giving serious consideration to another wife. Yatom needed a mother, someone who would love him, not just pay halfhearted attention because they were supposed to.

The thought made him sigh. Finding the right woman was harder than he had anticipated. All the marriageable girls seemed so young and giddy. Bethlehem had its share of widows, but he did not feel comfortable with any of them.

As for himself, if the woman was reasonable to look at and willing to accept him, he would be content. He'd never find anyone to match his first wife. Her loss still made him ache unbearably whenever he thought of her, which was often. More than once he'd found himself reaching for her when he half-wakened in the night. Then her absence felt like a sword thrust. Although Yatom no longer cried for Mena, Boaz wished he could say the same for himself.

They breasted the hill, and there across the small valley now carpeted with red and yellow spring flowers was the house, snuggled up against the trees, looking as if it had grown there with them.

"It's pretty," Yatom said. "Who's that woman?"

"Why, I don't know," his father replied, squinting to see better. "Let's go ask."

The woman waited for them to enter the courtyard.

"Shalom, Boaz."

"Shalom. This is my son, Yatom."

"Ladel mentioned you might come by. Come in and refresh yourselves."

Thoroughly puzzled, he followed the familiar-looking woman into the house. Her manner was not that of a servant. "I apologize, but I don't remember your name," he said as she ushered him in and indicated a small table with fruit on it.

"I'm Tashima."

"Shalom," he said again, not much further enlightened. What was she doing here?

"Ladel should be here any minute," she added. "I'm sorry to leave you, but I must check the fire, or your food will be inedible."

At his nod, she hurried back into the courtyard and the cooking fire.

"Where is the stable, Abbi? The one where you first saw Immi?"

"It's through that door in the side wall," Boaz pointed. "Back then it was almost a lean-to with half walls on the front and far side and a roof made of pine branches. Dodi Ladel has built the walls up with mud brick now and put on a proper roof. We must wait for Dodi before we go there. Here, try this fig."

"Oh, this is the sweetest fig I've ever had!" the child exclaimed.

Boaz smiled. If all went well, he would soon market those figs.

"You got here earlier than I expected," Ladel said as he entered. "Shalom to you."

"Shalom. Ladel, who is the woman who met us?"

"Tashima. Don't you recognize her?"

Puzzled, Boaz shook his head. "Who is she?"

"She's my wife."

Boaz's jaw dropped. "When were you married? Wait a minute! Wasn't she betrothed to someone a while ago?"

"That was more than 10 years ago, Boaz! Her betrothed died in the same raids that wiped out Tahat's father. Her family had a series of setbacks during the next four years that left them heavily indebted. Tobeh hinted that he could help the family recover if Tashima was his wife, but her father had already seen the way Tobeh 'helped,' and he prudently refused. Tobeh retaliated by heading off any suitors for Tashima's hand."

With a wince Boaz well remembered how Tobeh's comments at appropriate—or inappropriate—times could ruin a deal.

"If you recall, I got acquainted with Tashima at your wedding," Ladel went on, "but I wasn't ready to remarry yet."

"Mena mentioned a sister-in-law, but I didn't realize it was your wife. Did the Habiru that captured you also kill her?"

"Yes," Ladel said tightly. "When I did think of marriage again, I asked for Tashima. She warned me about Tobeh, but I knew we'd be living out here and not in town. You left on your business trip before I could tell you about her, and then Mena died. We were married two months afterward in Tekoa, where her mother is from. I mentioned it to you once, but you were still too grief-stricken for it to register, I guess. And you've kept yourself very busy since then," he finished, his eyes full of sympathy.

Boaz studied the wall, searching his memory. "I do remember your mentioning marriage to me, but that's all. May Yahweh bless you both and fill your house."

"Your good wishes are welcome. What is it, Yatom? You're sitting there bursting to ask something."

"May we see it now? The stable where you and Immi first met Abbi? May we see it?"

With a chuckle the boy's uncle stood, holding out his hand. "Yes, we may go see it now, and I'll take you through the hidden door and show you just where I fell into the ravine."

Boaz watched the two disappear into the stable, then looked around, suddenly realizing how deeply he'd buried himself in his work since his wife died. When was the last time he'd discussed anything but the next shipment with Tahat, or asked Pashur how his family was doing? In the stable he could hear Yatom crowing with delight as his uncle opened the hidden door. Shaking himself out of his reverie, he joined them.

The next day the two men went to the pasture where Ladel kept a small flock of sheep. Yatom ran everywhere and got into everything, his inquisitive bent reminding Boaz again of Mena.

"I would guess Yatom is both a comfort and a hardship," Ladel commented softly as the boy headed for the trees on the slope a short distance away. "He's so much like his mother. You still miss her, don't you?"

"Yes," Boaz admitted, barely able to keep his voice steady. "Maybe I always will. The only thing that helps is keeping my mind occupied with something else."

"I guessed as much. What do you think of the improvements I've made here?"

"You've done very well, Ladel," Boaz said, glad to change the subject. "I had an idea this piece of land would be very productive, and you've certainly—"

"AAABBBIIII!" his son's panicked scream jerked both men's heads around.

The boy ran from the trees, heedless of where he was headed.

"Yatom!" Boaz shouted, racing toward him. "Watch out for the ravine! Don't—"

His son screamed again as the ground disappeared in front of him, and he tumbled into the gully.

Horrified, Boaz ran to the spot, sliding down the steep sides to the bottom of the rocky defile that channeled runoff from the hill.

"Abbi, Abbi, it was a bear! I saw it, and it tried to get me! I saw it! And I ran. Then the ground went away. Abbi, it hurts."

Grimly Boaz looked down at his son. Yatom had plunged onto the rocks propelled by his own momentum, and from the way the boy lay, his father knew that the fall had broken several bones. "Just stay still, son."

"But Abbi, the bear will get us!"

"No, it won't. Dodi will drive it away."

"How is he?" Ladel asked from the top of the bank.

"Not good," Boaz replied tersely. "He says a bear frightened him. It is possible?"

"Very. There've been reports of a crippled beast that has taken to hunting even during the day. The inhabitants of Tekoa have organized two hunts, both unsuccessful. I'll go have a look around."

"Be careful. If it's crippled and desperate from hunger, it won't hesitate to attack."

"I'm not going far, but I do need to see if it's hanging around." His brother-in-law disappeared.

Boaz turned back to his sobbing son.

"Abbi, I hurt so much!"

"Yes, you took quite a fall. Dodi will be back soon, and we'll carry you out of here."

"Don't, Abbi. It'll hurt; I know it will."

"I know, Yatom, but we can't leave you here."

"We could wait. I've always stopped hurting before. Then we can go back to the house."

"This kind of hurt isn't going away very soon," his father said gently. "You'll have to be as brave as you can when Dodi and I lift you."

"All right, Abbi."

"It is that bear," Ladel said from the top of the embankment. "The tracks are plain. We've got to get Yatom into the house." He slid down the steep slope, quickly taking in the situation. "How shall we carry him?"

"Get my staff," Boaz said, untying his girdle. "I think it's on the ground above us." He stripped off his robe. "Run our staves through the arms and twist the bottom around them. It'll make a stretcher that way, and we'll tie Yatom on it with our girdles."

Once they were ready, Boaz looked at his son. "We're going to lift you now and put you on Abbi's robe. Then we'll carry you out of here and back to the house. Are you ready?"

"Yes," he sniffed.

As gently as they could, the two men picked up the boy, easing him onto the robe and binding him to the stretcher. But as they lifted the stretcher, Yatom started to scream.

~ ~ ~

Boaz glanced up as the healer entered the room.

"I must speak to you," the man said.

Putting down Yatom's hand, Boaz stepped outside, finding his brother-in-law there too. "Well?"

"I can do no more. The child is too injured inside. It's a wonder he's lived these past two days."

"I can't lose Yatom!" Boaz exclaimed savagely. "Surely there is something you can do!"

"I'm sorry, but—"

"Get out!" Boaz said quietly, a cold, deadly numbness rushing over him. "Get out of this house! Never let me see you again. Go!"

"I'm sorry," the man repeated. "I wish—"

"Get out!" Boaz shouted, lunging forward. His brother-in-law struggled to hold him back as the healer scrambled away, still murmuring that he was sorry.

"Boaz, stop it," his brother-in-law shouted into his ear. "It's not his fault."

"Yatom can't die! He's all I have left!"

Ladel didn't answer.

That night Boaz sat outside in a torn robe, ashes smeared on his skin. "Yahweh," he whispered, "what have I done that my family must die? Let Your wrath fall on me and not my son. Yatom has done nothing."

Bitterness filled his heart. Mena had been the flame lighting his life, the warmth that surrounded him. What was wrong that his God would punish him so? Because of Rahab's blood? Boaz shivered. Had Yahweh turned against him because he was descended from a Jericho prostitute? The hours passed, leaving him in the gall of his unanswered questions.

As dawn flushed on the horizon Ladel touched his shoulder. "Yatom is asking for you."

Taking the cloth his brother-in-law held out to him, he wiped the ashes from his face and hands. Then he went back to sit and bathe his son's hot face while his heart bled at the moans of pain he could not stop.

Hour after hour it was the same. Night came again, and once more he sat under the stars, challenging Yahweh to answer him, to reveal his sin that had caused such a thing. He cursed Yahweh, daring the deity to slay him; he challenged Him to answer the charges he hurled to the stars. Although he pleaded, bargained, wept, and insulted his divine adversary, no answer came.

"What is he doing?" Tashima asked her husband as they stood in the courtyard looking at the figure huddled under a huge pine on the slope. "How can he say such things to Yahweh? Does he want to die?"

Ladel put his arm around his wife and rubbed her shoulder. "I think he is wrestling with his God somehow—or trying to."

"Like Jacob at the Jabbok?" Tashima whispered. "Ladel, what will happen if Yahweh doesn't answer?"

His grip tightened. "He *must* answer! He has to! If He doesn't, I'll—I'll bring Him down from the skies myself!" Then he spun on his heel and strode to the house, unable to bear the sight of his friend's suffering.

Another endless day passed, and when darkness fell, Boaz took his place under the pine, too tired to think, simply enduring the agony in his soul. What more did Yahweh want of him? Sacrifices at the tabernacle in Shiloh? Would it do any good to offer his own blood for his son? Or was his blood the problem?

"Why will You not answer me?" Boaz cried, slumping down, filled with a sudden loathing for himself. Perhaps Tobeh was right. Maybe the only thing Canaanites were good for was to die. Beside him sat the cooked leeks, bread, olive oil, wine, and figs Tashima had brought out hours ago. There was also a bowl of water in which to wash his hands. The knife she had sent along with the food gleamed in the moonlight.

Picking it up, he drew the edge across the back of his forearm, watching the blood well out. It looked black on his arm and dripped into the water, staining the moon's reflection on its surface.

"How much of it do You want, Yahweh?" he asked bitterly. "Or shall I take it across Jordan to the desert of my nightmare and give it to Lilith? Are Tobeh and Ezer right? Am I worthy only of Your rejection because my blood is not pure? Is that why everyone I love is destroyed? How do I atone for who I am?"

Head in his hands, Boaz sat in despair, ignoring the blood flowing from his wound. Gradually the bleeding slowed. He knew his life was not enough to save his son. Only the greatest hesed could save Yatom, and there was no one to give it. His name and his family line would die before Yahweh, and no one on earth would ever remember them.

"Is there no way to save my son?" Boaz groaned.

*"The Lord your God, He is God, the faithful God who keeps covenant and mercy for a thousand generations with those who love Him and keep His commandments."** *"The Lord . . . set His love on you . . . because the Lord loves*

---

* Deut. 7:9, NKJV.

you, and because He would keep the oath which He swore to your fathers."★

The words sprang from his memory, from his visits to Shiloh with his abbi when he had listened to the reading of the ancient law. But they didn't make sense. Yahweh loves you because He loves you? How could that be? Surely gods favored only those who brought sacrifices and worshipped in the temples regularly.

"I will have mercy on whom I will have mercy, and I will have compassion on whom I will have compassion."†

The blood had stopped flowing from the cut on his forearm. The red reflection of the moon in the bowl of water caught his eye again. If all the sacrifices at the tabernacle in Shiloh were not a bribe to induce Yahweh to favor His people, what were they for? Could they really be a substitute, so that human beings would not die when they sinned? Was it possible that Yahweh would honor His promises and keep mercy for a thousand generations just because He chose to?

"Yahweh . . . set his affection on you . . . because Yahweh loved you and kept the oath He swore to your forefathers."

A splinter of hope burst into Boaz's mind, and he clung to it desperately. "But I am not wholly of Israel," he whispered. "Is there something for one such as I?"

"In you all the families of the earth shall be blessed."‡

He remembered his father reciting the words, telling him the story of Yahweh's promises to Abraham, how the patriarch's descendants would provide the promised Seed who would bring an end to the evil one and his works and would bless all the families of the earth.

"Even Canaanites?" he whispered.

All.

Boaz trembled. All. He bent forward, digging his fingers into the dried pine needles that carpeted the ground. "Then grant me Your hesed, Yahweh. Please, I beg of You. *Give life to my son!*"

Unable to breathe, he waited. A strange stillness settled in the trees. The sounds of the insects faded from the night, and absolute calm stilled the small rustlings of the woods.

★ Deut. 7:7, 8, NKJV.
† Ex. 33:19, NIV.
‡ Gen. 12:3, NKJV.

"He and his descendants will have a covenant of [peace] . . . because he was zealous for the honor of his God."★

The words flashed the story in his mind—how Aaron's grandson, Phinehas, had killed the Simeonite, Zimri, for blatantly and publically defying Yahweh while the Israelites were mourning their sin with the Moabite women at Peor.† Yahweh had granted Phinehas a covenant of peace and one of a lasting priesthood. And the descendants of Phinehas served even now as priests of the tabernacle in Shiloh.

Boaz bent forward until his head almost touched the ground, sweat dripping from his face, seizing the possibility of peace for his tortured mind. But could he put Yahweh's honor before his own? Yatom was all he had, the only chance that his blood and name would continue beyond his death, carrying his own life beyond the grave. Dared he trust that to Yahweh?

He clenched his hands, his stomach twisted with tension, the muscles in his arms as rigid as wood. What about Abraham? He had trusted the same thing—even more, since Isaac had borne the promised blessing. Pounding his fist into the ground, he upset the bowl of water and splashed himself, the resulting sharp sting making him gasp. The wound had reopened, and once more, blood spilled over his arm.

His chest aching for relief from the pain that seemed to bear down on him from all sides, Boaz stared at the blood. *A covenant of peace.* The thought gleamed like a tiny sliver of light in the darkness of his thoughts, and he strained toward it with every fiber of his being.

The dead needles imprinted his forehead as he ground his skin against them, fingers digging into the earth still soft from the winter's rains. The price of that covenant was yielding himself—and his son—to Yahweh's honor. As Abraham had had to do. And Jacob, and Joseph.

"Yahweh, I cannot!" he cried, tears flooding his eyes. "Yatom is my life, my hope for remembrance before You after I return to the dust I was made from. He is all I have left! What good is my life if he is gone?"

The stillness continued, the only sound that of his breath, the only movement the shudders of his own body.

★Num. 25:13, NIV.
† See Num. 25.

"You are Yahweh! You know I cannot fight You for long! How am I to live without my son?"

Eyes closed, Boaz knew his hope for peace, for any kind of understanding, was slipping away.

"I will have mercy upon whom I will have mercy."

Finally he could struggle no longer. Like Jacob, he had strength left only to cling to the one gleam of light that promised peace. "I am only a man, Adonai," he choked out, "and You are the God who created all. You give and take life when and where You will. I don't understand why this evil has come to Yatom and me. All I beg is that somehow, in whatever way, You will bring an end to the suffering of my son and remember my family before You when we are gone."

*"I will do the very thing you have asked, because I am pleased with you and I know you by name."**

Boaz froze, the blood in his veins seeming to stop from amazement. Very slowly he lifted himself from the ground and turned his face to the stars. "You know me by name?" he gasped. The tiny sliver of hope grew in his heart, until the light blazing from it drove out the darkness. His tension drained away, leaving him exhausted and limp. For several minutes he rested, then the sting from his arm intruded into his thoughts.

Taking the wine, he doused his arm liberally, gritting his teeth as it flowed into the raw flesh, then poured the olive oil over the wound and bound it with the cloth Tashima had wrapped the bread in.

Sitting back once more, he looked up at the sky. "Forgive me, Yahweh," he whispered. "With my fathers, I will wait until Your promised Seed comes to make things right again. Then justice and mercy and recompense will be granted to all. Even to me and my son."

Utterly spent, he slumped to the ground, fading into sleep.

"Boaz? Boaz! Are you all right?"

Jerking awake, he opened his eyes, staring around in the darkness. "Ladel? What's wrong?"

"It's Yatom. Please come quickly."

Rising stiffly, he went to his son, kneeling on the floor by the sleeping mat. "Abbi's here," he said, taking the small hand in his. His child looked so pale in the dim light of the lamp.

Yatom opened his eyes. "Abbi, I feel so strange. I can't stop it any-

---

*Ex. 33:17

more, and I know you don't want me to go there." Tears spilled down the boy's face.

Boaz tightened his grip, suddenly wondering how much pain his little boy had endured because his abbi didn't want him to "go there." The thought broke his heart.

"Don't you worry about that now, Yatom," he said, steadying his hand to stroke the boy's face. "That doesn't matter now. That strange feeling is just sleep so you won't feel the hurt anymore. It's all right to go there."

Yatom nodded, a little smile crossing his face. "It's stopping the hurt already, Abbi."

"It won't be long then," his father assured him. "Close your eyes. This will be a good sleep. When you wake up again, everything will be all right. I promise."

"Will Immi be here too?"

Boaz hesitated, closing his eyes and clenching his teeth to steady his voice. "Yes, Yatom. Immi too," he answered firmly.

With a nod the child slid peacefully into death.

His father stayed by the bedside until Ladel led him away. Blindly he returned to the place of his mourning under the pine, stretched out on the ground, and let the earth drink his tears. As he wept, he seemed to feel arms around him, larger, stronger, and more comforting than any he had ever known.

After the burial he turned again to hard labor to forget, working himself to exhaustion each day while he struggled to master his grief and stave off the dreams of Lilith that plunged him into dark moods. As he cleared the fields and planted them in the fall, time eased the sharpness of his pain, and the nightmares came less often, fading in intensity until he could sometimes forget the mocking laughter that always accompanied them.

Fall
Tishri, seventh month, Boaz's twenty-eighth year
(1115 B.C.)

Boaz idly stared out the tiny window at the patch of blue sky, contemplating the newest information he'd gleaned about Tobeh. The man no longer maintained his fields. None of them now lay fallow, therefore his cattle did not graze there, depriving the field of manure fertilizer. Ladel reported that this year Tobeh had stopped burning the stubble for ash fertilizer, and apparently had no plans to spread any ash on them at all.

Chewing on his lip, Boaz considered the information. Besai had been an opinionated, stubborn man, but he had been canny about farming and had built his fields up until they were the best-producing ones in the area. His son still rotated crops, but that was all. It didn't make sense. At this rate the land would be all but useless in 10 years. Why would Tobeh deliberately ignore his livelihood?

"He's a fool, unless he's planning on supporting his household by other means by then," he muttered aloud. What else could he be counting on?

"When I'm king—" His mind replayed that hastily corrected comment. For the most part, so far Tobeh had acted as expected if he was working toward kingship, although Boaz still had difficulty crediting the thought. Could Tobeh seriously be planning such a thing? Within the next 10 years?

"Well, if he is, I've got only 10 years to be ready for him," he said to the ceiling.

"Geber Boaz, you are wanted at the south gate," Gershed said, entering the room.

"What for?"

"Adon Hanan has requested that you come to witness a dispute."

Surprise held Boaz still for a moment. "You are certain Hanan asked for me?"

"Yes, geber. You specifically."

This was an unusual honor for someone not yet 30, the age at which society considered a man to have attained mature judgment and thus able to help uphold the social and legal fabric of the community.

"Bring my brown robe, Gershed, the one with the green trim."

By the time he had untied his girdle and slipped out of his old robe, the servant had returned. "I brought your second-best cloak, geber," he said. It was a lighter shade of brown, trimmed with a fine dark-brown wool that matched the girdle the servant had also brought.

"Very good, Gershed."

Taking his staff, he hurried to the south gate, where a group of men waited.

"Shalom, Boaz," Hanan greeted him. "Thank you for lending us the benefit of your judgment. Please sit down, and we can get started."

"Shalom to you all," Boaz said, taking a place in the back. He did not expect to say anything, for he was clearly the youngest one here. As he settled himself, a local beggar hurried into a side street. Boaz smiled grimly to himself. Tobeh had an efficient information system, and he would be raging that Boaz, though younger, had been summoned as an elder before him.

"Kalkol, we are ready to listen to your complaint," Adon Hanan announced.

"Yes, adon, gebers. I bring complaint against Rapa. He has stolen one of my sheep, a valuable ram."

"What makes this ram so valuable?" Hanan asked.

"I purchased it from Moab two years ago, from the Yidla line."

Hanan nodded. As Moab produced the best sheep and wool, any Moab sheep would be valuable, but a ram of top quality, such as the Yidla line, would be even more so.

The farmer turned to another man standing nearby. "I accuse Rapa of luring my ram away from the flock and then concealing it from me."

"What evidence is there for this?" another elder inquired.

"Rapa has coveted this ram for some time. He offered to purchase it on several occasions and was very put out when I refused to sell." Kalkol looked at the elders. "Some of you may remember last month when he made an offer here in the gate for my ram in exchange for one of his fields. Three days ago one of Rapa's shepherds was seen lurking about my flock, and the ram disappeared soon after."

He turned back to Rapa. "My shepherd has searched, tracking the sheep as far as he could, but there is no evidence that anything attacked the sheep. We have not been troubled by lions or bears lately. There is a wolf that sometimes tries for one of the flock, but the shepherd swears he has seen nothing of this predator for several days. The ram's trail headed into the area where Rapa keeps his flocks. I demand that his flocks be searched for my ram," he ended, turning stiffly away from his neighbor.

Hanan looked at the other farmer, who shifted about indignantly, glaring at Kalkol. "Rapa, what do you have to say?"

"I deny this false accusation! Yes, I have tried to purchase the ram, but I didn't steal it! His shepherd made up this story because he's afraid to admit he sleeps on the job. Kalkol is known as a hard master, and undoubtedly his shepherd wanted to avoid a beating."

Several of the elders nodded. Boaz kept silent, his eyes on a tassel hanging from Hanan's robe, but he agreed. Kalkol was a very hard man, and any servant of his would hate to admit a fault of this kind.

"I demand that Kalkol look to his own pasture to find the ram, or what is left of it by now. His shepherd can scarcely be trusted to be truthful about how diligently he searched."

"How do you know my shepherd sleeps?" Kalkol asked.

"Because my own shepherd has seen him doing it," Rapa retorted.

"So your shepherd was skulking about the area," Kalkol sneered. "Likely while he was there, he made off with my ram!"

Hanan put up his hands for silence, and both neighbors quieted.

"Where are these farmsteads?" Boaz asked Shahar, the man next to him.

"Southwest of town about four miles."

Boaz frowned. If he remembered correctly, some extremely rough country lay between Bethlehem and Timnah. The region must have a thousand places where a sheep could stray or disappear.

But to be that careless with a Yidla ram? The bloodline was becoming widely known for its abundant wool and good disposition. Kalkol and Rapa continued to argue with each other.

As Boaz eased back against the wall behind him, he remembered something. He had just been talking with Ladel about getting a Yidla ram himself, but his brother-in-law had wanted to wait. Some shepherds had reported a strange sickness that appeared only in flocks that included imported Moabite animals. The sheep would fall down, kicking and sometimes foaming at the mouth. Their owners slaughtered them as quickly as possible to prevent the strange disease from spreading.

On impulse Boaz leaned toward Shahar. "Can we talk to the shepherd personally?"

The other man glanced at him. "We could. What would we ask?"

"A few details."

With a shrug Shahar turned to Hanan. "Perhaps the situation would be clearer if we could speak to the shepherd," he suggested.

"Where is your shepherd, Kalkol?" Hanan asked.

"He is in the west market. I can easily send for him."

"Do so."

Boaz motioned to a small boy, watching with wide eyes. "Do you know Patah, the servant of Geber Tobeh?"

"Yes, Adon Boaz."

Being called "adon" startled him a moment. Then he shrugged. It was only a lad, and no one else had heard him. "Would you find him and ask him to meet me at the south gate?"

"Yes, adon."

The lad scurried off, and Boaz settled in to wait. In spite of Kalkol's words, it took longer than expected to find the shepherd. Several people drifted away, finding more interesting things to do than wait. Patah appeared at his side.

"Yes, geber?"

"Do I remember correctly that you are acquainted with the area between here and Timnah?"

"Yes."

"Do you know those two men?" He pointed at the two disputants.

"Yes, and where they live."

"Good. Kalkol charges that Rapa has stolen his Yidla ram. Rapa claims the ram wandered away. Kalkol's shepherd should be here soon to act as witness. I want you to listen to what he has to say."

Patah settled down in the shadows by the wall, his stillness making him hard to notice.

When Kalkol's shepherd finally arrived, Boaz frowned. The man looked familiar, but he couldn't think where he had seen him.

"Just where did the ram disappear, and how far did you follow his trail?" Shahar questioned.

"From our second pasture, in the valley two hills east of the farmstead. From there the ram wandered south, down through the oak groves. It crossed another stream, and I followed it for almost another mile."

When he sensed Patah stir, Boaz tilted his head but didn't look around. "Ask if the ram went straight south," Tobeh's servant whispered.

"Did the ram go straight south?" Boaz interrupted the questioning. "It didn't wander about much?"

"No, geber. It went almost in a straight line. That's why I knew it was led. A sheep alone would never do that."

The onlookers murmured agreement with the observation.

"He's lying," Patah said. "You can't go straight south from that pasture. An extremely steep gully leads down from the hills close to that side. My grandfather noted it well, for it is large enough to be trapped against, or to trap an enemy against. Not even a silly sheep would go there unless driven. And no shepherd would try to take an animal across. It's too steep."

"Thank you, Patah," Boaz said. "I suspected there was a lie somewhere. Now if I could just remember where I've seen that shepherd before."

"Last time I saw him he was on the road to Jebus," Patah said before rising and slipping quickly away.

Jebus! He'd been there on business three days ago and noticed the shepherd with a sick-looking ram. Someone joked that he was probably taking it to Shiloh— Of course, he suddenly realized. If the ram had shown signs of the mysterious sickness, Kalkol would have wanted to get rid of it, but would have hated to take the loss himself. Boaz knew that some of the priests at Shiloh would accept any animal as long as it was still standing. Everyone recognized the bad blood between the two farmsteaders, and stealing a valuable ram would be something easily done in the rough country. Kalkol might have sent the ram as a sacrifice, then claimed it had been stolen in an attempt to recover its price from Rapa.

"Shahar, ask how many Yidla rams Kalkol has," Boaz murmured.

The elder cleared his throat. "Kalkol, how many rams of the Yidla bloodline do you own?"

"Only the one," the farmsteader replied in disgust. "That's why I demand redress for this wrong. I cannot afford to lose such a valuable animal."

"Why then did your shepherd take a Yidla ram to Shiloh for sacrifice?" Boaz eyed the man from where he sat in the shadows. "I saw him take it through the north gate of Jebus myself."

Sudden silence settled over the people listening to the dispute. Kalkol turned red, then white. He turned on the shepherd. "You thieving wretch! How dare you steal my ram?"

The man's mouth dropped open. "Steal? You ordered me to take it to Shiloh as fast as I could so it wouldn't die on the way of the kicking sickness. You even told me which priest to have inspect it and—"

"Silence!" his employer roared. "Now you add false witness to your theft. I shall demand full retribution for this."

"I think not," Adon Hanan said. "Your face betrays you, Kalkol. I think we can give judgment on this case immediately. You shall pay Rapa the price of the ram because you tried to gain it from him falsely." He glanced around at the other elders. "Are we agreed?"

"We are agreed, and we are witnesses to this," the others replied.

Boaz did not stay to hear Kalkol's protests. It was almost time to go to Shiloh for Yom Kippur, and he wished to choose the animals he would take for sacrifice. However, when he arrived home, he found Eliram waiting for him.

"Shalom, Geber Eliram. How are the figs at Tekoa?"

"I found it, Geber Boaz. I found the secret," the man announced triumphantly.

"Have you? Come in, then, and tell me about it." He led the way across the courtyard to his office, calling "Gershed?"

"Yes, geber?" The servant emerged from the main house.

"Bring some refreshment for Eliram. We have business to discuss."

"Right away, geber."

Once seated and suitably supplied with food, Eliram looked at Boaz eagerly. "It is simple, so simple. You know the other trees we planted had not produced any figs as sweet as the first tree."

"Yes."

"This year three of them did!"

"But why now?"

"They were big enough to," the farmer said, a huge smile on his face. "Their roots were down far enough. I studied the land carefully, and I believe there is an underground stream running beneath the field. When the trees get large enough, they produce the sweet figs because they have a constant supply of water while the fruit matures."

"Good work, Eliram. Now, how many more trees can you plant, and how long before the figs will be ready to market?"

"It will need several years, I'm afraid. I am not certain of the path of the stream, and it may take trial and error to find it. But I shall work as quickly as I can. Once the trees are planted, it should be four to five years before they produce the sweet figs."

"Good. Let us work toward that, then. And in the meantime, sell the produce from the good trees to only a select few. We don't want to draw unnecessary attention."

"As you wish, geber. Also, there is something else I would like to ask. My family and I like the land there near Tekoa. I have heard that you sometimes allow the tenants to work toward a purchase."

"Yes, I do. Is this something you would like to arrange?"

"Yes, geber, very much."

"I'm sorry I kept you waiting so long, Ladel," Boaz apologized much later.

His brother-in-law shrugged. "I used the time to bring some animals for you to inspect for the sacrifice. They're in the courtyard."

Boaz followed his overseer outside. Every animal was without blemish, healthy and glossy-coated. "These will do nicely. Can you stay for the evening meal? We should discuss the work arrangements I want you to handle while I'm at Shiloh."

"Tashima is visiting her mother today, so I'll be glad to stay."

Later, as they sat in the upstairs room of the large house, a silence fell. "Why do you worship Yahweh?" Ladel asked.

Boaz turned in surprise. "Why wouldn't I?"

"Most people in Bethlehem don't seem to. I saw what happened to the Levite who came to the market last week. If you hadn't stepped in, the people would have stoned him. Tobeh ranted for an hour about your 'betrayal.' What was wrong about that poor man?"

"The fact that he was a Levite," Boaz sighed. "Some years ago Besai's oldest sister was concubine to a Levite and died as a result. Levites have not been welcome since."

"Why would that produce such anger years later?"

"She died in Gibeah of Benjamin."

Ladel jerked his head around. *"That* concubine?"

"Yes. That's one reason men like Tobeh can gain such influence here. Many people turned against the Levites and rejected the God of the Levites—at least in their hearts."

His friend snorted. "But certainly not with their lips! Bilgai, Tobeh, and Raham go to Shiloh three times a year and sacrifice at Bethlehem's altar every new moon, to say nothing of the shrines in their houses. They pray to Yahweh in the streets and call on Him in the market as they turn a bargain so sharp they should leave a trail of blood to their door!" Ladel leaped up from his stool, too indignant to stay seated. "I grit my teeth listening to them boast about all the favor they have garnered with Yahweh. And I would no more trust them than I would an adder."

He stopped in front of Boaz, looking at him accusingly. "On the other hand, you sacrifice at the altar only on major feasts and only attend Shiloh at Yom Kippur to pay the required tenth of your increase. You never mention Yahweh, and spend Shabbat out in the hills with the Habiru. But," he raised his hand, "if I was in need, I would come to you like everyone else, knowing I would find hesed."

"It is not hesed!" Boaz exclaimed, annoyed. "I do only what any decent man with my means would do, and no more. What Yahweh has blessed me with I'm bound to—"

"Blessed you?" his friend interrupted. "Your God took your son, Boaz—and my sister. I watched when Yatom lay ill and you accused Yahweh. I wanted to shake Him from the heavens and make Him answer you. I know why you have that scar on your forearm. What stopped you from killing yourself?"

"I'm not certain what you're asking, Ladel," Boaz said, rubbing the scar, his stomach in knots as he remembered that night.

His brother-in-law sighed. "You changed the night Yatom died.

Tashima said the first thing you did when you got back here from the forest house was to put Rahab's teraphim into a storage room."

"There's nothing in that," Boaz shrugged. "I've never used them."

"Half the town never uses them, but they don't insult the household gods by putting them into storage!"

Boaz flushed. "I have Yahweh. I don't need teraphim."

"And you're certain enough of that to banish the teraphim from your house? What did Yahweh say to convince you?"

"He didn't say anything. I finally remembered some things my abbi taught me, and it helped me understand."

"Understand? You lost your family name that night!" He threw up his hands in exasperation. "When Raham's wife died in childbirth, he could hardly wait for a decent mourning period before getting an heir from another wife. You haven't looked at a woman since Mena died. Zakkur says Yahweh turned against you and your name will be forgotten in Israel."

Boaz shrugged. "Zakkur can think what he wishes. I haven't looked at another woman because I still love Mena. Maybe I always will."

"What did Yahweh tell you?" Ladel persisted.

Sighing, Boaz rubbed his face. How could he explain? To worship Yahweh was more than reciting prayers, or refusing to eat at certain times, or giving offerings at the altar or the shrine. When he was up in the hills with Pashur, the solitude and beauty drew an awe from him impossible to describe.

How could he explain that sparring with Pashur, when the blood ran strong in his veins and his muscles responded exactly to his will and the clang of swords rang in his ears, that these things felt like prayer, a celebration of life? Would it make sense to say that settling the details of a business deal was worship, reminding him of Yahweh's work of supplying the needs of His creation? How could he express the wonderment of knowing that Yahweh accepted him, accepted his life and the work of his hands each year at the tabernacle? That Yahweh knew his name?

"I don't know how to describe it," he finally said. "I realized that Yahweh can't be bought or influenced, that He chose Israel to bless all the nations with his Promised Seed, because that's what He decided to do. And somehow that Seed will redeem Mena and Yatom and my little daughter from the grave, like a goel redeeming land for a kinsman," he added slowly.

His brother-in-law cocked his head to one side. "I see! If you honor Him this much, Yahweh will be obligated to give back your family."

"If Yahweh created the world, Ladel, He created Mena and Yatom also. How can I obligate Him to give me something He made? If He made the world, sacrifices don't enrich or sustain Him, and so can't buy His favor. They simply shield us from Yahweh's justice until Abraham's Seed makes an end to the evil in the world. Yahweh cares for us because He said He would. That's what I remembered that night."

Boaz looked him in the eye. "If Yahweh cares, it doesn't matter if I die without an heir, for He will remember. And as long as Yahweh remembers, not even death can obliterate my name. In the face of such hesed, how can I refuse to serve Him?"

"You couldn't," Ladel said thoughtfully after a long pause.

Fall
Heshvan, eighth month
(1115 B.C.)

Boaz walked alertly down the narrow twisting street from the Tekoa market to the inn, if one could call it that. Arranging to have Eliram earn the farmstead with the fig trees had taken longer than he planned, and it was dark now. Knowing that his expensive robes were an invitation to robbery, he kept a sharp watch. As he entered the open space in the center of the village he paused. The compound belonging to Domla, the little settlement's most wealthy citizen, was directly across from him, forming the south wall of the enclosed square used to shelter the villagers' animals each night. Tekoa was too small for defensive walls, and any scavenger from the forest, human or otherwise, could roam the town at will.

He stood beside a small house made of stone, its courtyard walls extending to meet the walls of the building that passed for an inn on his left. The latter had been abandoned, and the current resident had patched the courtyard gate back together before spending his days at the market inviting strangers to sleep on his floor and eat ill-prepared food for payment.

The uneasy feeling wouldn't go away, and Boaz began to watch the darkening alleys leading into the square, some of them already blocked for the night.

With his attention distracted by the arguing voices raised from behind Domla's walls, he almost missed the feel of a hand on his purse. Automatically, his left hand swept down to clamp on the thief's wrist, and he threw his weight backward to pin him against the wall.

His shoulder bruised itself against the rock, and his fingers overlapped around the wrist his hand crushed. He immediately loosened his hold, wondering what a child was doing here. The argument faded away as a door slammed, and Boaz dragged his captive into the fast-fading light in the center of the square.

"You're a quiet one, I'll give you that," he said, studying the thin youth.

The lad pressed his lips together, staring back defiantly.

"And very hungry if I'm not mistaken."

His captive remained silent, but he swallowed.

Turning the boy's face so that it caught the last light, Boaz studied him further. He looked healthy enough and on the edge of manhood. His eyes were bright, intelligent, and wary, the slight body tensed.

"You've a good deal of sense for one so young," Boaz said with a laugh. "I could snap your wrist so you won't struggle, but if I drop my guard, you'll be gone. And you haven't been on your own for long, either. You're not ragged yet, but you were quick enough to try for my silver."

"You have no need of the little I'd take!"

Boaz chuckled again. "Well said, but I worked to earn it, and you didn't. What did you plan to do with it?"

"I'm going to join the Habiru," the boy said proudly.

"And which band of mercenary robbers were you hoping to attach yourself to?" Boaz asked, his amusement increasing.

"The Habiru aren't robbers. They're soldiers—warriors, as I want to be."

"Some are that, yes, but many are not. How do you propose to tell the difference?"

"What would you know about it? You're just a rich merchant concerned with his silver."

"Very concerned about it. And I may know more about the Habiru than you imagine." Boaz smiled. "All right, lad. I'm going to give you a choice. I should call the watch and haul you before the town elders"—the boy stiffened in his grasp—"but that would take my time and leave your belly empty, both of which seem a waste. So I'm going to let go of you. You can run if you wish, and I'll go on to the inn, where I have supper waiting. Or you can come with me and I'll feed you supper, and we can talk a bit more about you." He let go of the boy's arm.

The lad jerked backward, retreating several steps.

When Boaz walked away, the boy trailed behind him as if drawn by invisible cords. Boaz smiled again. Hunger could be a very powerful motivator.

He provided the promised supper, which was barely tolerable as a meal, but the lad ate hungrily. Boaz ate lightly, as he normally did at night, an unusual habit he had from the years when he'd been too exhausted at night to eat a large meal as people normally did.

"Now, lad, I'm going to check on my animal in the stable. You can sleep in the inn with me, in the stable with my animal, or in the street."

"Aren't you afraid I'll steal your donkey?"

"Thieves and robbers steal. Warriors fight."

The boy flushed.

Out in the courtyard Boaz ducked his head to enter the lean-to that passed for a stable, checking that someone had watered and fed his donkey. Most of the fodder was moldy, and the donkey had pawed it all over, looking for bits fit to eat. Boaz grimaced in annoyance. He'd have to stop on the way back tomorrow and let the animal graze. The other donkey in the place looked familiar, and he paused, checking it over. So the man already asleep on the inn floor was Pashur. Why would the Habiru pay to stay here when he was so close to home? Maybe for the same reason as himself. He was too tired to go anywhere.

"Have you decided where you'll sleep?" Boaz asked before heading to the inn.

"Here." The lad raised his chin defiantly.

Ignoring the implied challenge, Boaz said, "You willing to tell me your name yet?"

"It's Gaddi."

"Shalom, Gaddi." He headed back to the inn, glad he had his heavy cloak to wrap himself in. The bedding in the place left much to be desired.

The innkeeper shook him awake just at dawn. "Geber Boaz, Geber Boaz! Please wake up."

He blinked in the dim room. "What is it?" he demanded, struggling to sit up.

"Geber, a thief has been caught trying to take your animal from the stable. You must come see about it."

"A thief?" Boaz stood, disappointed that Gaddi would steal from him and wondering who had stopped the lad. In the courtyard the early sun shone directly into his eyes when he walked out the door.

Next to the lean-to stable the boy waited defiantly, watched closely by Pashur.

"I thought the donkey was yours, Boaz," Pashur said, hearing his steps but not taking his eyes from Gaddi. "I found the boy here untying it."

Boaz looked at the lad.

"I was taking it to water it," he said sullenly.

"You were stealing, and from my inn," the innkeeper hissed. "Geber, shall I call the watch?"

Thoughtfully Boaz examined the donkey standing patiently with its rope in Pashur's hand. He rubbed his hand over the donkey's back and down one leg. The animal had been carefully groomed, probably within the last hour.

"Missed that, did you?" he asked the other man, indicating the donkey's shining coat.

His friend gave a half smile and rubbed the back of his head. "That's why I didn't summon the watch, but had the innkeeper call you. I didn't think a thief would curry the animal before taking it, but I'd never seen this lad before, nor heard that you had taken one on."

"Cautious as ever. What do you make of him?"

Pashur looked the lad over and then cocked his head. "Fierce as a mother bear, but young enough still to have heroes."

"He wishes to become a Habiru."

"Does he now?"

"Shall I call the watch, geber?" the innkeeper asked again.

"No," Boaz said. "The mistake is mine, good innkeeper. I had engaged the lad late yesterday to tend the animal. My friend wished to make certain that all was well when he saw a strange person handling my donkey. It is but a misunderstanding."

The tension in Gaddi's posture eased slightly, and he looked at Boaz with round dark eyes.

"Are you certain, geber? I've seen this one about before, and he looked ready for trouble."

"I am certain, innkeeper. The lad took supper with me last night. I trust you do not doubt my word?" he added testily.

"Not in the least, geber," the innkeeper hastened to assure, wringing his hands and bowing slightly. "But you can understand my concern. If it got to be known that stealing occurred at my inn—"

"But it hasn't. What more needs to be said?"

"Why, nothing, nothing at all." Looking flustered, the man moved off, his dirty cloak trailing over the unswept stones of the courtyard.

Pashur handed the lead rope to Gaddi and ducked under the lean-to to see to his own donkey.

The lad stared at Boaz, who noted with approval that Gaddi had neatly tied his dark hair back and tried to wash his face. "Well, hasn't that poor animal waited long enough for a drink?"

"Y-Yes, geber," he stammered, and, still wide-eyed, led the donkey away.

Pashur emerged from the lean-to, his gray-blue eyes amused and the sun glinting on his carefully bound black hair. "I warned you he was young enough to have heroes, and you've just become his biggest one."

"I hope not for long. Bring him in for breakfast, otherwise he will starve himself thinking he's not invited. Not that that would be ill-advised," he added ruefully, remembering the half-baked bread, gravelly lentils, and nearly raw squash he'd been served the previous night.

"I'll see to him," the wool buyer said, disappearing.

Boaz went back inside to prepare himself fully for the day. When the innkeeper announced breakfast, Pashur and Gaddi were already waiting. Once they had eaten and settled accounts with the innkeeper, they started back to Bethlehem.

Once out of sight of the village, Pashur turned his donkey off the road and followed a valley east to its end. Angling sharply around a patch of thornbushes, he led them to a shaded clearing with good grazing. The sun already promised a hot day, and Boaz sat on the ground as the donkey buried his nose in the half-dried grass. Pashur gave his animal a slap and glanced at the boy. "You wish to be a Habiru?"

Cautiously, Gaddi nodded, straightening his thin shoulders. "I want to be a warrior and fight in battles."

"They're not as much fun as you might think. Usually people just get hurt."

The boy's chin jutted out. "I wouldn't get hurt. Being a Habiru would be a wonderful thing. No one would push me around."

Boaz raised his eyebrows at Pashur.

"No one—until you met a better Habiru," the warrior said.

"I'd be the best."

Pashur chuckled. "I'll take him. Patah will like someone closer to his own age to spar with."

"Take me where?" Gaddi asked, his quick eyes darting from one face to the other.

"You wanted to be a Habiru," Boaz said. "Pashur can teach you to be the best Habiru in the country. Do you want to go with him?"

Gaddi looked at the other man in amazement. "You're nothing but a traveling wool buyer!"

"He's also the brother of the new dahveed of the local Habiru," Boaz said. "And he's got more tricks than a baby goat."

Pashur grinned. "Speak for yourself."

"You're from Mattan's band, and you'd really teach me?" Gaddi asked, regarding Pashur with newfound respect.

"Looks like you have an apprentice, Pashur," Boaz said with a grin. "Feed him every now and then."

"I'll consider it," his friend replied, putting his arm across Gaddi's shoulders and steering him onto a track that led into the hills. His donkey twitched its ears, yanked a mouthful of grass from the roots, and followed after them. Boaz watched them go, then settled down to give his animal a chance for a decent meal. He couldn't stay too long, however—he had much to do.

While his inheritance prospered under Ladel's skillful management, Boaz turned most of his attention to his pursuits outside of Bethlehem.

He went to Jebus twice a week to handle business there, using a room rented from Ahinadab, the Ammonite pottery merchant who had become a good friend. Through him Boaz joined the network of merchants and caravanners that covered the land from Egypt to Ur. Rather than bargain over the value of every piece of gold and silver they might carry, the merchant networks used a system of sealed pouches of predetermined value that circulated as a single monetary unit. With Tahat transporting goods from Beersheba to Damascus, Boaz lost no time taking advantage of the system. One day a week he went from Jebus to Jericho, where he could pick up the news from the caravanners and better learn which markets needed his goods.

In Bethlehem he maintained a modest appearance and home, spending his time in his own fields, checking with farmsteads in which he had an interest, or working with Ladel and enjoying his brother-in-law's children.

Mindful that Tobeh kept watch on his business dealings, Boaz made certain that most of the produce from his father's fields went either to his private granaries or the communal ones, leaving him with only a small amount to market in Jebus. Most farmers sold there, since the city, being more fortress than settlement, depended on Bethlehem for the majority of its grain.

The proceeds from harvests in which he had an interest, now more than twice what his father's fields produced, he channeled directly to his scribe in Jericho and had it handled from there. Wealth did not accumulate quickly, for Boaz often found himself helping the small farmsteaders, shopkeepers, or day laborers who ran afoul of Tobeh or other misfortunes. However, since his own needs were few, his treasury did increase. He sent discreet tithes to Shiloh at odd times, and Rahab's teraphim gathered dust in the back corner of a storeroom, for Boaz never took them out again.

Tobeh increased his wealth much more quickly, careful never to cross the line that would label him greedy, but retaining his love of display. He cultivated a selected list of elders and townspeople who contributed to the power his growing fortunes afforded. The day after Tobeh celebrated his thirtieth birthday, old Eprah called him to the gate to help with a judgment. Boaz was not surprised, for his rival had married Eprah's granddaughter, Deborah, and already had two sons.

After his summons to the gate Tobeh refused to answer anyone who called him "geber"—he was "adon" now. He acquired control of more and more land around Bethlehem through business contracts with the landowners or by buying the debts of the smaller farmers, who muttered in the markets that Tobeh acted more like a king every day.

Then the drought began.

The Time of Cultivating

Boaz is growing well, don't you think? Yes, life has been difficult for him, but without the rains, would there ever be a harvest? Dark days lie ahead for Bethlehem, for the drought will be long and hard, and there will be little to eat. But even in the hard times Yahweh works His will. For during those hard times Boaz set down his roots, reaching far for the nourishment needed to live, and finding it better than he knew. He will not realize it until later, but those times were the birthing of his triumph, although they little seemed it at the time.

So while the years pass over Boaz's head in Bethlehem, let us journey across Jordan to the land of his nightmares. Yes, again and again Yahweh brings our salvation out of the stuff of our fears. It is well to remember that, for He is a God who works in His own ways, and strange to us they may be. But Yahweh is the great God who moves where He wills and chooses those He wants regardless of our opinion. And foolish indeed we look when we try to tell Him how He may work and whom He may choose! For Yahweh wanted a special child again, and He found what He wanted in Moab. That's right, Moab, among the people despised and hated by Israel. He placed His hand on Heshbon, across the Jericho fords, and drew to Himself a young girl.

Yahweh had carefully preserved this child, although she had no idea He even existed. Now, however, it was time to cultivate in Moab. Time to encourage the growth so carefully begun 11 years ago. But before things can grow, they must burst out of their old confines, and that can be painful. It is always worth it, however, as Ruth found out, for now it is that she enters our story.

Winter
Shevat, eleventh month, Ruth's eleventh year
(1112 B.C.)

As I hurried past, wrapped snugly in my dark gray cloak against the possibility of more rain, I glanced in the alley. I had only a couple hours before Immi realized that I'd slipped out, and I didn't want Orpah to get into trouble for letting me out on my own. At the leather seller's stall at the corner of the north market I turned down the narrow street, pressing against the wall to let a loaded donkey by and keeping my head down to hide my face from its driver. The midwife should be at the third door.

Lifting my hand to knock, I hesitated, suddenly uncertain. How would I make her tell me what I wanted to know? I had but lately outgrown childhood and was not yet a woman. Through the fabric of my robe I tightly gripped the signet ring on its cord. I had to know. Immi had sent Orpah and me out to the fields one time too many when soldiers came to town, and I had to find out why she always did that. I already knew Immi would never tell me. She would just get that look of quiet fear in her eyes and hug me tight.

Orpah said it had to do with my birth and the signet ring I always kept around my neck on its cord of pale brown hair. She told me I had had it even as a newborn. One night I overheard my parents discussing it. Immi wanted to hide it, but Abbi said it wouldn't matter, since I had the joined fingers as well. The skin between the middle and ring fingers of my left hand came up just a little higher on them than the others. It made using those fingers awkward sometimes. Abbi added that I should keep the ring with me because if anything happened, there might not be time to retrieve it.

I had puzzled over that whispered conversation for weeks. Now, while Immi was busy talking with her cousin on her yearly visit, I had slipped away to find the midwife who had birthed me.

But as I faced the door I couldn't bring myself to knock. Did I really want to know what was so bad about me that Immi was frightened and Abbi talked about things I couldn't understand? A gust of wind drifted down the street, chilling my feet. I shivered, knowing I should go home before anyone missed me and forget about it all.

Only I couldn't forget. I'd already tried that, but my dreams insisted on creating all sorts of terrible things tied to that ring. If I could find out the truth, I could banish the frightful guesses. Unless, of course, the truth was even worse.

The wind whipped about me again, and I looked up at the sky. The clouds were breaking apart, their heavy gray undersides drifting away, taking the fluffy white tops with them. Rays of sun peeked out overhead. It looked as though Baal was done thundering for the day, and Kemosh was dismissing him. I looked back at the door. I had to know. I couldn't stand the uncertainty any longer.

No one was about, the quiet of the noontime rest filling the streets. I should know better than to disturb anyone at this hour, but she was a midwife, used to being summoned at any time. Raising a shaking hand, I knocked feebly on the door, jumping back to wait in the street. No one answered, and I knocked louder.

"Just a moment," someone yawned, footsteps shuffling toward the door. It opened, and a woman looked down at me sleepily. "Yes?"

"Please, I'd like to see the midwife," I managed to say.

"And what would you want with her?"

"I want to talk to her, please."

"Well, she can't be disturbed at this hour! Run along, little girl. Don't go about bothering your elders."

She started to shut the door and, in desperation, I darted through it, nearly making the woman stumble backward. She turned to me angrily.

"I want to talk to her now, please. It's important," I said firmly, projecting my voice as Immi had taught me to do when I sang.

The woman stared at me.

"What is it, Karmet?" someone called from a back room.

"It's a saucy young snip that demands to see you, Hamir."

"Well, let her see me, then," the amused voice replied.

"That way, girl." Karmet pointed, shaking her head.

I walked into the next room. Two oil lamps provided light, and a woman looked up from her place on the floor. "Are you the midwife?" I asked.

"Yes, I am. What did you want to see me for?"

Taking a deep breath to still my heart, I pulled out the signet. "What can you tell me about this?"

She leaned forward to see better, then sat back suddenly, staring at me. "May Kemosh preserve us! Where did you get that?"

"I don't know. That's what I want to find out."

Hamir remained silent for several seconds, looking away and biting her lip, the lamplight flickering across her face.

I waited, half afraid she would tell me, but more afraid that she too would refuse. "Please," I added softly. "I have to know."

The woman rose and held out her hand for mine. "Come. Let me take you home."

My shoulders slumping, I looked down and gave her my hand, disappointment welling inside. "Can't you tell me anything?" I blurted out, pausing in the street and staring up at her.

She shook her head, although her eyes were kind, and started on again.

I bit my lip to keep from crying. Now I would never know what had happened, and the dreams and guesses would go on and on. Distracted by my thoughts, I followed the midwife through several streets before I realized she wasn't headed for my parents' house. Half afraid, I stopped again, looking around.

My guide looked down at me, a faint smile on her face. "Karmet is an invaluable help to me, but she has a loose tongue. No one must hear when I answer your questions." Then she took my hand again, and I followed her mechanically, my heart pounding. I had expected to be elated to find out what had happened at my birth, but dread filled me instead. Would I hear something very bad? Some horrible mystery or disgrace? Did I really want to know?

We walked through the south gate, past the local gardens and most of the vineyards. The sun shone from the rapidly clearing sky. The light-green shoots of new grain contrasted with the darker green of the evergreens, oaks, and terebinths on the hills. As we started down the slope we passed a woman grinding the next day's flour beside the wooden door into the cave that was her home. Such caves riddled these hills, and most of the townspeople lived in them. Only wealthy families like ours had houses.

Just then I looked up and suddenly stiffened. Instead of being in his office at the palace for the noon rest, my father stood not far away as a witness to the transfer of a nut grove of chestnuts and almonds. The new owner was just stepping onto the land, laying his claim. I opened my mouth to say something when the midwife turned away, following a little valley lined with fields to the west. The grass felt crisp under my feet, and I looked around at old olive trees from someone's orchard. They were dormant, waiting for warmer weather.

"Do you like the fields?" Hamir asked.

I nodded. "And the forest. It's cool there, and so quiet. I can hear things better."

The midwife nodded. "What do you hear?"

"Songs, words, sometimes just the wind."

"Let's go into the trees, then, for you will need to hear as best you can. It's an appropriate place to tell you what you ask, for in the fields and forests the gods talk to human beings. Did you know that?"

I shook my head.

"The towns belong to humanity, to be built and made into whatever pleases us. The forests and wild places are home to gods and demons and beyond human control. They are dangerous, as all places of great power are. The cultivated fields are a sort of blending of the two, where gods and humans can meet and speak on middle ground. Roads are like fields: a halfway point. Be careful if you leave either fields or roads, for you may find destiny or death when you walk with the gods."

Looking through the open spaces under the trees, I shivered in the cool green light and stopped in my tracks.

Hamir glanced around. "We have come far enough. Sit down, girl. May Kemosh guard us while we stay."

Somewhat reassured by her blessing, I sat down, bunching my cloak under me to protect me from the chilly ground.

"Your mother is Shimrith, wife of Ithmah the scribe?"

Surprised that she knew, I nodded.

The midwife sighed. "I've never forgotten you. I always thought the truth should be known, but Elsa forbade it. She was the midwife and I was her apprentice then, but I made certain Shimrith knew enough to figure things out, which she did quickly enough. We never told Elsa, and she went to her grave thinking no one knew."

Hands pressed together so hard my arms ached, I waited.

Hamir pushed back her light-brown hair, and her bracelets tinkled. "What a storm we had that night! Lightning made it bright like day, and Baal's thundering shook the ground. Ithmah arrived at our door about midnight, soaked to the skin. Elsa didn't fancy going out into that wind; but babies wait for no one, so we went, prepared for trouble. It was too soon for Shimrith to be birthing, but she was in labor. Two hours later the storm had passed over, and we knew that the babe was probably dead, or soon would be. Elsa sent me to get more herbs to ease Shimrith's pain, and on my way back I found a woman huddled in a doorway, big with child and crying in desperation.

"She was a beautiful one, with hair as soft as thistledown, a robe so fine it seemed made of spiderwebs, and a face that would turn heads. She had started her labor there in the street, amid all that noise and rain. I couldn't leave her, and she hung on to me all the way back to the house. We barely made it before the poor woman was in hard travail.

"While I tended Shimrith in the other room Elsa saw to the newcomer, who was very weak, although she was obviously well cared for and the labor was going easily for a first child. After checking Shimrith twice, Elsa took me aside, telling me to take the child when it came without letting her see it. That's when I suspected what she planned to do."

The midwife stopped, her eyes distant as she looked into the past, one hand idly turning one of her bracelets around and around her wrist. "Not long after, Shimrith's little boy was born. I couldn't resist her eyes, and I let both Ithmah and Shimrith hold him briefly. They knew the babe wouldn't live, and it died only minutes later.

"Elsa fought so hard to keep the other woman alive, but she just slipped away. There wasn't much bleeding, but the poor woman looked so pale, I'd have sworn she had no blood at all in her body. Afterward, we found the sword wound. It had bled fiercely more than once. It's a miracle of Kemosh that she even had the strength to birth a child at the end."

When Hamir paused again, I looked up at her. "That woman was my mother?"

"Yes. And a fine woman she was, too. All during labor she kept murmuring about keeping the baby safe, and made Elsa promise that if there was no one to care for you, you wouldn't be left out to die, but would be sold, so at least you'd live and be cared for. She loved you, although she never got to see you."

Shaken by what I'd heard, I stared straight ahead. Who had wanted my mother dead? If she was rich and favored by the gods, as her clothes had indicated, why hadn't someone protected her? Or had Kemosh turned against her for some reason?

Hamir brushed her hair back again, looking at me from her place beside me on the grass. "While I was folding up your mother's clothes, I found the ring."

My hand went to it automatically, clutching it through my robe.

"I guessed it was royal, and not just from a local king's house. It was carved from ivory, and set with tiny rubies all around. Only an overlord would use a royal dove over a man, flanked by Baal's bull and Kemosh as the sun, on a signet."

My hand shook. She had described it perfectly. I'd never realized how valuable it was. Ivory and rubies? I looked up at her.

"Now you know," she said softly. "Guard it well. I kept it hidden from Elsa, knowing she would take it, for I had a feeling that ring shouldn't be ours. It would bring trouble on all but those who rightly owned it. So I plaited a cord from your mother's hair, put that ring on it, and tucked it into your wrappings.

"Then Elsa took you to Shimrith, exclaiming how Kemosh had blessed, and her child had survived after all. Shimrith never said a word. She just took you right to her breast, and a noisy work you made of your first meal!" The midwife smiled at the memory.

I swallowed at the lump in my throat, thinking how Ithmah and Shimrith had accepted me like that, even though they knew I wasn't their body and blood. Tears stung my eyes as Hamir continued.

"I wasn't surprised when Shimrith returned two days later. By then, word had reached us of Kemosh-dan, Moab's overlord, slaughtering Prince Mesha's line. Shimrith was no fool. She'd seen the clothes that woman wore and had found the signet.

"I took her out to the graves and stopped by the one where we'd laid both the woman and the infant.

"'She wanted her babe to live with all her heart,' I said. 'She prayed that it would be safe.'"

"'It will,' Shimrith replied, 'There's love enough. I hope she's not lonely in her death.'

"'No,' I said, 'she has a tiny son tucked in her arms, who took but a few breaths before going to her breast.'"

"'Then we both have what we need to comfort each other,' she said before walking away."

I sat very still. "She goes back to that grave often," I said softly. "She always takes me. Said we had family there."

"And so you both do," Hamir replied.

"Why didn't she tell me?"

"Because she's a mother and you're a child, and mothers want their children to be safe."

"Safe?"

"Prince Mesha was your father, girl, and King Eglon of Moab was your grandfather. What do you think Kemosh-dan would give to know that?"

I jerked my head up, staring at the midwife, beginning to realize the implications of what she had told me. "How can you be sure?"

"That signet. It's a royal seal from Eglon's reign, though Kemosh knows how Mesha got hold of it." She reached down and took my left hand in hers, touching the skin between my middle and ring fingers. "You have the joined fingers. That comes with the royal line, too. You're Eglon's blood, no doubt."

"But I don't want to be," I gasped, snatching my hand back, frightened by the possibilities yawning before me.

"And well you shouldn't!" she said tartly. "Especially now, with the overlord set on killing his own kin. Right now your blood is nothing but trouble, and so is that ring. But later, well, who knows? The ring's yours more than anyone's, so you keep it hidden. Someday it will be important, and it needs to be in the right hands when that time comes."

Hamir pulled me close to her side. "Don't you blame Shimrith for keeping her secrets. You weren't old enough till now to understand the story and what it means to you, both the good and the bad. But you can't go chattering on about who you are. You belong to Ithmah and Shimrith, Orpah is your sister, and they will keep you safe. They love you, you know."

I nodded, but looked down. Yes, I knew, but my whole world had suddenly shifted, and I was now uncertain about everything.

Rising to her feet, she held out her hand again. "Come, it's time we got back. Never stay too long in god places—we are human and must keep to our own."

Summer
Ab, fifth month, fourth day, Ruth's eleventh year
(1111 B.C.)

It really bothers you, doesn't it?" Orpah asked, glancing up from the robe she was mending.

Reluctantly, I nodded, putting down the old harp I used for practice. Immi was teaching me to play it.

"I think it's exciting."

"It's not exciting to know the king wants you dead," I replied.

After my visit to the midwife, I had confided in Orpah. She hadn't seemed very surprised, and told me that she had wondered about things for a long time.

"Is that why you always watch out for me?" I had asked.

"Immi wants me to. She never told me why, just that we must be very careful and keep you away from soldiers. It was a game at first, but then I started to wonder about it."

Leaving Orpah to her mending, I climbed restlessly down the inside ladder to the ground level storage rooms. To one side were the stalls for the three goats our family kept for milk. The goats were out to pasture with the animals of several other families, watched over by a neighbor boy.

Avoiding the covering on the floor over the cistern, I wandered outside, trailing my fingers on the plaster over the stone that formed the lower walls of the house. The second story was mud brick, also plastered over, and above that was the roof, where Immi had her loom. The noon rest was nearly over, and I knew I should be spinning or practicing my fingering on the harp instead of roaming about as if I had nothing to do.

Immi emerged from a storeroom across the courtyard, shaking the chaff used to pad the storage jars from her robe. "What is it, Ruth?" she asked, seeing me there.

"Nothing. I'm just restless."

"Then why don't you and Orpah go visit your grandparents? Your father would like news of the olive crop. You could take your harp and practice," she went on. "And check on that wild apricot tree your sister found. The fruit should be ripe soon."

I knew Orpah would rather stay here, but I felt trapped inside the house today, and I was never allowed out alone.

Immi smiled. "You can't stay too long since you need to go with me to the temple later, so Orpah won't miss much."

"I'll ask her," I said, wondering how Shimrith knew what I'd been thinking.

Orpah already waited at the door, and I got the old harp. She was worse than Immi. Although she couldn't have heard our conversation, she still knew that I needed to get away. Shaking my head, I followed her down the street to the south gate.

We hurried along the main road and turned off into the valley where our grandparents lived. Their house perched on the side of the hill where the trees met the fields. They had a large two-story house, like ours in town, with a courtyard in front and back surrounded by a wall. A large vineyard stretched halfway up the hill, and beyond that were the olive trees.

I walked in the dried grass beside the dusty path and felt myself relaxing. Somehow, out in the fields or forests my troubles didn't seem so big. Grandmother greeted us at the door and invited us inside.

"Your grandfather is at the olive grove," she said when Orpah explained that Ithmah wanted news of the harvest.

"I'll go find him," I volunteered, wanting to get out of the house. "Orpah can stay here with you while she spins."

Grandmother smiled, picking up her hand spindle. "We can both spin."

Leaving them twirling the spindles and winding yarn, I headed through the back courtyard for the hill behind the house.

Some farmers cleared the forest before planting olive trees, but Grandfather and Abbi chose to plant them between the oaks and pines. It was quicker, and the trees seemed to thrive just as well. But then, olive trees would survive just about anything.

"How is my little singer?" Grandfather greeted me when I found him filling his basket.

"I have to practice," I replied, showing him the harp. "I go to the temple later with Immi. I'll be on the hill above Yidla's flock. And Abbi wanted to know how the olive harvest is this year."

Grandfather nodded. "We'll have plenty of oil and much to sell. Run along now, and remember not to wander off the hill."

"I know, Grandfather."

Resentment against his caution rising inside, I slipped away. I wouldn't dare wander off on my own, since I'd lose the privilege of coming here by myself if I did. As it was, the only reason Immi let me visit my grandparents was that Yidla watched out for me, and she knew how much I needed to be alone sometimes.

As I crested the hill, the trees opened up briefly, and I could see directly north to Heshbon's high place on the top of the next hill. Surrounded by a low wall, the massebot, pairs of large rocks chosen to represent the gods, gleamed in the light. Beyond them and towering over them stood a huge oak tree, its branches shading the place where the qedeshim and qedeshot waited, the male and female prostitutes available to celebrate fertility rites.

I hurried past the clearing. Immi kept me away from the high place, saying I wasn't old enough to understand the rites celebrated there. I wasn't certain I wanted to understand them. Overhead, the sky was clear blue, and the sun had lost its midday heat. The breeze rustled, drawing me farther into the forest away from human-places as I followed the sound of the wind through the pines. Pushing through the brambles that guarded the path to my special spot, I tucked the harp carefully by my side and hurried through the trees to the narrow ledge that rounded the crag at the end of the hill.

Abruptly the hill fell away, the bare bones of its rock exposed scores of years before by an earthquake. Under the roots of a huge pine, the rock face bellied out to provide a narrow foot trail to an indentation in the hill itself. Over the years shrubs had sprung up in the cracks of the face, shielding the niche from casual eyes. Its coolness welcomed me as I settled myself on my hard seat.

This was one of the highest hills around, and the end thrust out toward the south, giving me a panoramic view from east to west. To the right, the land gradually rose to the tops of the cliffs before the Jordan rift and the flanks of Mount Nebo. Farther south, they climbed even higher around the east side of the Salt Sea. Directly in front of me, the hills and valleys meandered among each other, the trees still intensely green from the final showers of the rainy season, the valleys varying shades of green and gold, and the fields and orchards dotted with flocks of sheep. To my left, the land gradually fell away toward the desert, with fewer trees and more grazing land as the soil worsened and the rainfall lessened.

I had been coming here since the day I got lost when I was quite small and Yidla found me. He had showed me one of his special places to distract me from my fright, and I had been fascinated by this tiny cave. Now enjoying the cool shade, I gazed down the valley spread out below. Yidla's flock lay in the shade of the shrubs with the shepherd resting beside them. I had to look closely to see him. He wore a short-ened robe, leggings tied with rawhide, and a sling attached to his gir-dle. Even his hair and eyes seemed faded to dusty browns and grays until he blended in with the wild places and rocks.

Wiping my forehead, I settled the old harp in my lap, starting the exercises to make my fingers nimble and quick on the strings. I worked my left hand especially hard, since the extra skin between my fingers made it more difficult to stretch and move those fingers independently. I also avoided the last string, since the old harp wouldn't hold a tuning on it and the sour note made me shudder.

When I finished, I set the harp aside and pulled my knees up to my chin. Yidla must really be asleep. It was the first time he hadn't re-sponded to my playing. I watched the sheep drowsing lazily and squinted at the sunlight dancing on the ripples of the tiny stream from the small spring at the base of the hill. Most of the springs in Moab were closer to the Salt Sea, on the uplands farther south. Heshbon depended on cisterns for water during the dry season, but for some reason there was a small spring here. It gave just enough water for Yidla's flock, every night filling the pool they drank from.

A song formed itself in my mind, its words questioning, asking for help in my trouble. Learning of my parentage had not been the wonderful, exciting thing I had hoped it would be. Now I knew that if the wrong people found me, they would kill me, and I could do nothing about it.

I didn't want anything to do with kings and their rule. Why would anyone still want to kill me?

"Yah, are you here?" I asked aloud. At first, I had been afraid of the strange presence I had felt here, but Yidla had assured me that Yah was a friend. I was very doubtful, since the shepherd lived in a different world than we did. His head wasn't shaped quite right, and he had unfocused gray eyes. He was very gentle and easily distressed by anger, noise, or any kind of roughness. But the sheep adored him, and he knew every animal in his flock better than his dog did.

Shimrith had told me about the "accident" that injured him years ago. His father had claimed the boy fell against the doorstep, but no one believed it. His mother had taken her dying son to her father's house and refused to see her husband or let him near Yidla. Eventually the man left town.

Surprisingly, Yidla had recovered, but his head was never quite right after that, and he couldn't talk very well. He remained isolated from other children and had attached himself to a flock of sheep belonging to Heshbon's local king, Hissil. Before long, Hissil noticed that Yidla's sheep thrived no matter what happened to other flocks.

After the young shepherd solved the problem of the kicking sickness, the king would have sooner killed a son than do anything that upset him. The sickness started in flocks with sheep brought from Mari in the north. At first, only one or two sheep got ill, but then more and more.

In desperation the king gave some of the sick sheep to Yidla, who discovered that the sheep would recover if someone kept them too busy walking to lie down. Left on their own, they would just give up and die from nothing more than the very bad stomachache that caused the kicking and moaning and foaming at the mouth. By watching closely, Yidla found the strange plant that caused the problem. He named it "kickplant," and when he weeded it from his pasture, the problem stopped. Abbi said the seeds for the plant probably came in the wool of the sheep from Mari.

After that, King Hissil gave Yidla the care of his best ewes and rams. In time, Yidla's rams were in great demand, as they were always of top quality and surprisingly gentle and cooperative. Being able to buy one became an honor, since the shepherd would get very upset if he thought one of his sheep was going to a harsh or careless owner. The first few times it happened, he wept and cried in such distress that Hissil soon refused to sell to anyone that the shepherd disliked.

As he was about so many things, Yidla had been right about Yah, so I welcomed the presence to my solitary place and often talked to him. He listened to my harp practice, and when I had trouble with a difficult piece, talking it over with Yah helped me see how to stretch my joined fingers or arrange my hands to play the tune smoothly.

Immi often commented on the quick way I picked up the technique, but I never mentioned my strange friend, for I had promised Yidla that I wouldn't. The shepherd feared that too many people would drive Yah away, and Yah was the one who taught him so much about sheep. I didn't think the spirit would have trouble avoiding people, but rather than face Yidla's distress, I didn't mention him to anyone.

I was glad for his presence now, needing reassurance as I sat hugging my knees. I didn't want to be killed, and if the soldiers came, they might murder Immi and Orpah and Abbi, all because they had helped me.

"Yah, what should I do?" I asked, suddenly starting to cry. I didn't want to be a king's granddaughter—I just wanted to be Ruth, daughter of Ithmah and Shimrith, and go to the temple to sing, and compose songs to play on the harp, and laugh with Orpah about the people we saw in the street from our rooftop, and not have to worry about someone finding out that I was Prince Mesha's daughter and a threat to the throne.

Suddenly I shivered, knowing full well that if Kemosh-dan ever did hear about me, no one would be able to protect me from his soldiers.

"I will," a quiet voice said close to my ear.

Gulping back another sob, I stared around frantically. "W-Who spoke?" I whispered, terrified.

"I am Yah, and I will protect you."

"You're Yah? B-But how can you do anything?"

"I will protect you, my child. Be at peace."

A warm, comforting feeling wrapped itself around me, like that of Shimrith's arms, and the knots in my stomach eased away. Sitting extremely still, I tried to understand just what had happened. Yidla never said that his friend spoke, but then he had never said that he didn't either. Who was Yah, anyway? And how could he protect me?

"The forests are places of great power," I repeated to myself, remembering Hamir's words, and that meant either demons or gods. Suddenly I realized that I sat in a place of very great power, for I was not only in the forest but on a hill and sitting in a rock, all of which were connected to powerful god things.

Yah must be one of the elohim! A hill spirit! I started to shake again. This was his place, not mine. Had I offended him by coming here? I froze, unable to move. But that warm, comforting feeling continued to fill the tiny cave, resting easily on my mind.

"You never know if you will find death or destiny when you walk with the gods," the midwife had warned. Since I was still alive, perhaps I had found destiny.

"I-I thank you," I said, trying to remember how the priests in the temple talked to Kemosh. "You are gracious to your servant—uh, maidservant." I wasn't certain what gracious meant, but I remembered the priests using the word, and it was part of a song Shimrith had taught me.

"Be at peace, my child," Yah's quiet words replied. "Go now to Yidla. He needs you."

Puzzled, I looked down the cliff. Yidla's sheep were scattered more than he normally allowed, grazing peacefully, but he still lay exactly as he had been when I had first arrived. He should have moved by now.

Scrambling to my feet, I hurriedly edged up the narrow ledge to the top of the hill. Then, tucking my harp under my arm, I ran down the path, pushing impatiently through the brambles at the end, finally turning down the shortcut to the bottom of the hill. It was steep, and I had to slow my headlong rush, but I made it to the bottom with only a couple scratches, although my robe had torn in three places.

Calling Yidla's name, I burst out of the brush and into the clearing, startling the sheep into darting off a few paces. My friend lay very still, his face flushed, and he wouldn't open his eyes. The skin on his hand was hot to my touch. I shook him, but he only moaned and tossed his head. Leaving my harp beside him, I ran for help.

Summer
Ab, fifth month, eleventh day
(1111 B.C.)

It was a week before I went back to my god place, as I called it now. No sheep grazed below my perch, for Yidla lay in his mother's cave, too ill to know anything or anyone around him. I had worried so much about him that Immi took me to see him yesterday. He lay motionless, not even knowing I was there. His skin was pale, and he breathed so raggedly that my chest ached from trying to breathe for him.

Last evening, while I was at the temple with Immi learning my part in the grape harvest ceremony, Yidla's mother came to pray. Sobbing and wailing, she had knelt on the porch, cutting her hands and face until the blood ran, crying her plea to Kemosh to heal her son. Incense wafted out of the sanctuary, and as she approached the door, I had followed her, stopping by the first row of pillars.

The smoke from incense half hid the small golden statue of Kemosh visible through the door that led to the holy place where the god lived. A gold chalice set with gems gleamed on the table by a gold plate that had bread on it, and the three-foot-tall incense stand had serpents, which gave and renewed life, molded around its legs.

Yidla's mother had bowed to the floor, choking on her sobs and praying desperately that her son would be healed. I had knelt too, for I must be respectful before the god as I timidly added my own request for my friend's healing. But after a few minutes I had looked around in puzzled confusion. I had been there, and Yidla's mother had been there, but no one else!

By now I well knew the presence of elohim, but the temple had been totally empty. How very, very odd. Since Kemosh was a powerful national god, I had expected a more powerful presence than that of a hill spirit. But I had felt nothing—nothing at all.

Now, here in my god place, I wondered what I would feel. If I couldn't sense Kemosh in his temple, maybe I wouldn't be able to feel Yah either. But no sooner had I settled down on my rocky seat than I knew that Yah was here. How strange!

Taking a deep breath, I spoke out loud. "Yah? I don't mean to offend you by talking to you. I hope you haven't minded all the things I've said before. But this is something different today." I paused, fearful that he would leave and the cave would be as empty as that temple had been last night.

"Yidla got sick, and I'm afraid he's going to die. I know you probably have a lot of other things to do, but you do seem to be interested in him. He says you taught him about sheep and things.

"So if you want him to come back, and his sheep to return, you might have to help him. His mother went to the temple yesterday. She prayed and gave some of her blood to Kemosh, asking him to heal her son. I know Yidla isn't really smart about some things, but you don't seem to mind that. Maybe Kemosh did, or perhaps he was too busy with something else to listen, but I don't think he was in his temple yesterday to hear her pray."

I stopped again, holding my breath. The presence was still there, closer now. "Is there something you could do? I don't know very much about you, but you're an elohim, a god. Can you help? I know Yidla would be happy—he thinks of you as a friend—so if it wouldn't get you in trouble with Kemosh, could you help Yidla get better? Even King Hissil would be grateful, because I heard Abbi say the king was worried about his sheep breeding plans if Yidla dies.

"He might give you a sacrifice or leave some gold if you could help. I'd give you something, but I don't have anything. All I can do is sing and play the harp a little."

I thought for several minutes. What could I do that a god might like? "I know, I could make a song for you," I exclaimed. "Would that be all right? I could teach it to Yidla, and he could sing it whenever you wanted.

"I've got to go now. I promised I wouldn't stay long, since no one's here to watch out for me, and Grandmother needs help in the garden this afternoon. If you want a song, please help Yidla get better. I'll try to make it a good one, but I'm just learning. Thank you, Yah."

I worked all afternoon with Grandmother setting early grapes out to dry as raisins, wondering if anything would happen. Yah was a god, I was certain, but I had no idea how much power he had, or if he was really that interested in people. We worked so late that I slept at Grandmother's.

When I arrived home the next morning, Immi met me at the door with a smile on her face. "Ruth, Yidla's mother came to the temple early this morning. The fever left her son yesterday afternoon just as the noon rest was ending. Would you like to go see him?"

Unable to speak, I nodded. That had been when I had talked to Yah! Was it possible he had been able to help? A thrill went through me, and I hugged the happiness to myself all the way to Yidla's home.

The shepherd and his mother lived in a small cave near the town walls. Outside the steps that went down into the cave his mother was baking bread in the beehive oven. Nearby she had a small loom set up with the swath of cloth half done.

"Ruth wanted to see Yidla again," Immi explained, handing the woman some dates we'd purchased on our way.

"Oh, he's so much better, I brought him outside. He's up on the ledge in the sun. Go see him, Ruth, while I put these away. Yidla loves dates, and we can't always get good ones." She disappeared down the stairs, and I looked longingly after her. I liked the shepherd's home. It reminded me of a warm burrow.

I scrambled up the rocks to the ledge where Yidla lay on a woven mat of reeds. An old cloak stretched on some sticks served as a small awning. The shepherd smiled when he saw me, then looked around.

"Guess," he said in his slightly slurred speech.

"I can't guess, but you are much better today."

Yidla nodded, his face one big smile. "Feel good after Yah come."

"Yah was here?"

"Shhh, not speak," the man admonished. "Immi say Kemosh make better, but Yah come, not Kemosh."

"I'm so glad, Yidla. I went to my god place yesterday and asked Yah to do something if he could. I'm so glad he did!"

His light-gray eyes got huge. "You ask?"

I nodded. "You're my friend, and you said Yah liked you too, so I thought he might help even though he's a god."

Yidla glanced around uneasily. "Not call Yah god. People come."

"Sorry. I forgot. But anyway, you're getting better now, and everything will be all right. Even King Hissil was worried. He complained to my father that he would never find a better shepherd than you, so you've got to get well quick."

Slowly Yidla smiled.

"Ruth!" Immi called.

"I have to go now, Yidla." I left him still smiling.

On the way home Immi stopped at the temple, and I ventured into the sanctuary again. It still felt completely empty.

I didn't get back to my god place for another three days. But I brought my harp with me and worked out a song to teach Yidla, making it short and simple so he could learn it. Since I didn't know if he could sing very well, I tried to make the melody simple too.

"Thank you, Yah, for blessing my days,

"For teaching me sheep, and giving me life.

"Let Yah be praised forever."

The words weren't quite right, but I thought it wouldn't matter, since Yidla would probably shorten them even more when he started singing it.

"I hope you like it," I told Yah when I finished.

The shepherd was back in his pasture in another week. My song turned into a much-shortened chant, since he was completely tone-deaf and could only hum a monotone. But he was delighted with my effort and learned it in a single afternoon. Afterward he assured me many times that Yah liked it as well. I hoped so, since Yidla droned the three lines scores of times each day.

He seemed to feel that he owed me something because I had spoken to Yah for him. For a while he worried about what he could give me, then decided he would teach me all about sheep. I wasn't certain I wanted to learn, but soon found that I didn't have a choice. Every time I came to practice my harp, Yidla insisted on instructing me about each sheep, what they liked, how to care for them, what to keep them away from, what made them sick, what made them well, and a myriad of other things I had no idea his mind could remember.

Altogether, Yidla knew an enormous amount, and he was a very thorough teacher. He quizzed me whenever we met. His delight when

I knew an answer was just as much an incentive to remember as were his tears when I forgot something.

Spring
Abib, first month, third day, Ruth's twelfth year (1110 B.C.)

The sun shone brightly in the market square just inside the south city gate. Everything looked washed and clean from the hard rains yesterday, but no clouds had appeared in the sky yet today, so Kemosh looked down with bright, clear rays. Off to the left, the three-story fortress/palace loomed over the market, its outside wall part of the city walls. Officials came and went through the doorways, and men loitered around in their best garments, waiting their turn.

Abbi emerged from the palace and called a name. The man hurried toward the door, his dress indicating he was from Mari, north on the Euphrates. As a scribe and translator, Abbi kept business records for the palace in both Akkadian and Egyptian, and translated into Aramaic when necessary. Someone's enterprising son wandered among the waiting men, making a few coppers offering wine from his skin bag.

To our right, stalls raggedly lined the square, offering such items as spices, leather, and dyes. Bronze sickles gleamed in the sun as the seller demonstrated their balance to a prospective buyer. Locally made pottery bowls lined the ground next to the field tools, and the seller yelled at his neighbor not to trample on the dishes. I smiled to myself. The bowls were so carelessly made and decorated that the only thing they were good for was to be broken anyway. Criers for merchants who owned shops tried to urge customers away from the stalls to purchase more expensive goods, and the stall owners abused the criers with curses, telling the customers to ignore the lies and buy top quality without the outrageous price.

A Midianite led a late-starting caravan toward the King's Highway. It lumbered through the square to the gate, 10 camels hitched together in a line followed by more than twice that number of donkeys. The

Midianite traders gave thought to no one, and neither did their camels, forcing the crowd to scramble aside while the desert people regally ignored the protests yelled after them. I glanced at the brands on the donkeys. This caravan had come through many times before.

The King's Highway passed through Heshbon. It ran east from Egypt to Edom, then north on the east side of the Salt Sea through Moab and Ammon to Damascus. Heshbon profited from the trade, and Abbi could find most anything he wanted right in our own markets. He'd purchased Immi's rectangular cosmetic palette here, and it was expensive white limestone, decorated with lotus designs just as Egyptian ones were. Heshbon was also the first good stopping place on the route east from Jericho, so we had goods from Canaan and the coast.

My favorite was the expensive pottery that came from an island in the western sea called Cyprus. It wasn't as brightly decorated as some of the other imports, but the clean brown lines on the white background had a simple elegance that fascinated me. Orpah liked the much brighter red pottery decorated in black, especially when it had pictures of animals.

Immi wanted to visit the instrument maker, and I followed her into the alleys behind the square. Someone drove a donkey loaded with sticks past us, and Immi stopped twice to exchange greetings with people. While she talked, I watched the basket weaver, who had set up shop outside his house. His quick, dexterous fingers fascinated me as the line of darkened reeds twined about the basket. At last we turned into a courtyard surrounded by three houses. The woman tending the fire closest to us rose.

"You have come in good time, Shimrith!"

Immi smiled. "I'm eager to see what your good husband has produced."

She laughed and looked at me with twinkling eyes. "The temple singer is here, Zippor," she called to someone in the house.

Zippor emerged from the doorway, and my eyes riveted instantly to the harp in his hands. The wood of the long upright would fit snugly to my chest, and the well-set perpendicular bar at the top held the strings taut as they stretched down to the gracefully curving piece that connected the bar to the bottom of the upright. The careful workmanship of the inlaid wood gleamed in the light, and my fingers ached to touch it, for I knew it would have a very special sound.

When the instrument maker stopped in front of me, I couldn't control myself. I brushed my finger over the smooth curve of the wood. A breeze blew by, and I cocked my head. The 24 strings had sounded faintly to my ear, almost calling my name. The inlay, in a lighter wood than the upright and bar, was a simple direct line that reminded me of my favorite pottery. The harp was a bit big, but I knew that in a couple years it would fit into my hands as if made for them. Unable to speak, I could only stand there and long for that instrument with all my heart.

Zippor held it to me, and I forgot everything as soon as I took it into my hands. Strumming the strings, I corrected the tuning of three of them and then pulled a chord from the harp, cocking my head to test the sound. Mellow and full, it floated on the air, exactly in harmony. I wanted to hear more and struck another chord, humming in tune. The thrill sent a shiver down my spine, and I smiled, plucking a melody to express the joy I felt. I had no words for it—they would come later. Then I repeated the tune twice, altering it slightly each time until I had just the right feeling in it and my fingers worked comfortably. Finally I played it through so I would never forget.

The total silence around me jerked me from my daydream. Everyone in the compound had gathered, standing in perfect silence, their eyes shining. I flushed in embarrassment, then horror. What right did I have to play someone else's instrument, especially one as fine as this? It had to have been made for a master! I looked around wildly for Immi.

Shimrith stood to one side with an older man that I'd seen at the temple. She smiled at me. "The harp is yours, Ruth. We will take it home, and you will never have to let go of it again!"

My heart nearly stopped beating. "Mine?"

She nodded.

"Oh!" I had no other words as I hugged that wonderful harp to my breast.

Zippor came out of his house with a leather case. It was of the finest quality, but simply adorned with spare elegant lines. He showed me how to fit the harp into it and adjust the straps so I could carry it comfortably and not have it getting in the way.

His wife led me to Shimrith, since I couldn't seem to walk on my own. I clutched my harp with one hand and Immi's skirt with the other in a way I hadn't done since I was a child. The man with her chuckled.

"You were right, geberet," he said in a deep resonant voice. "She is something exceptional, and it won't take long for her to outstrip us all. I will teach her, but she will need guidance for only a little while."

"Thank you, Adon Tawy. Shall we go, Ruth?"

As we walked away, I realized that the man must be the master singer and teacher at the Kemosh temple. He was from Egypt and had trained there, then had fallen in love with King Hissil's daughter when the king was at Beth-shean for some trade negotiations and Adon Tawy was on his way to Mari in the north.

I barely had my wits about me when we arrived back at the south market by the gate. Someone brushed roughly by as we crossed the square, and I clutched the harp, turning to see who had bumped me. Sunlight glinting off a patch of color under the man's arm stopped me in surprise. What on earth was Abiaz doing hiding such fine linen fabric under his outer robe? He was nothing more than a ne'er-do-well around town, vexing the local merchants and annoying the administrators of the palace because of the constant complaints about him. Certainly he couldn't have enough money to buy linen that expensive! Glancing back, he noticed me staring at him and hastily covered the folds of cloth before hurrying on his way.

Seconds later two soldiers and an enraged merchant ran into the square, shouting. I looked after Abiaz in time to see the linen passed to a stranger with a donkey. In an instant the man had rolled its rich glowing green into a black cloth and covered it with a dusty old cloak. The man never even stopped. He hurried his animal along and ducked out of the square into an alley.

By now more soldiers had rushed from the palace, and confusion reigned as the merchant screamed for his linen, demanding that everyone be searched. Soldiers shoved their way toward the gate, following the merchant's frantic directions to stop a medium-sized man with dark hair and a brown robe. The description fit nearly everyone in sight.

Immi pulled me to one side. Just at that moment I noticed the donkey with the disguised roll of cloth head up the road to the north gate. I opened my mouth to say something when I remembered the brand on the donkey's flank. It belonged to the Midianite caravan that had departed earlier today. Closing my mouth, I looked away.

With Midianites involved, pursuing the matter could very well lead to bloodshed. The desert caravanners were fierce and quick to take offense, and I had gotten only two glimpses of the cloth and could not identify the man who had received it. In addition, annoying the caravan might make them avoid Heshbon, as might all their kin, and that could mean a great loss in revenue. Besides, Abiaz wasn't all that cunning, and the merchant must have been quite careless to lose the bolt of fabric to him in the first place.

A scuffle started by the gate, and still more soldiers headed toward it.

"Thief, thief!"

"Grab hold of him there."

"Where is it, man?"

A rush of speech in a Canaanite accent followed, almost shrill in protest.

Ithmah hurried toward the gate, and without thinking I pushed closer, dragging Immi with me.

"I tell you, this is the thief," Abiaz said, gripping a middle-aged Canaanite and roughly shoving him toward the center of the square. The soldiers seized the man.

I snorted in disdain. Just like that slippery frog, to blame some innocent, helpless foreigner for his own deeds. The Canaanite stared around in desperation.

"Bring him along," Abbi commanded, leading the way across the square to the palace. I followed while other soldiers dispersed the crowd, knowing that the excitement had probably covered up a dozen or more thefts from the closest merchants and stalls.

Sure enough, the pottery merchant was already yelling that half his bowls had vanished and more had been smashed. I shook my head. Any halfway decent thief would know better than to take the inferior ware that that potter turned out. More than likely a couple of beggars had helped themselves to a much-needed dish.

At the palace Abbi had the guards bring the Canaanite before the magistrate along with several witnesses. Abiaz was not one of them. Soldiers guarded the door, but I could hear the chorus of accusations against the frightened man. As a foreigner, he had no one to speak for him, and no recourse if declared guilty, being completely at the mercy of the magistrate. Neither did he look prosperous enough to purchase leniency.

Shimrith caught up to me. "Let's go, Ruth. Ithmah will be busy with this for some time."

"But he didn't take the cloth, Immi. I saw who did."

She looked at me sharply. "Are you certain?"

"As certain as I can be, and that Canaanite had nothing to do with it. He must have been outside the south gate when the man with the linen left the square, headed north."

"Well, you can't do anything about it now."

"I can if I talk to Abbi."

"Ruth, now is not the time. Besides, don't you want to get home and play your new harp?"

I looked down and realized that I still clutched the harp case to my side. Remembering the soft, seductive sound of the strings under my fingers, I hesitated. I had a thousand songs buried in that harp, and my fingers itched to play them.

The sound of wailing made me look up. Four soldiers escorted a woman and two young men with a cart and two loaded donkeys through the square toward the palace. They were Canaanite, most likely the accused man's family. If he was found guilty, the magistrate would confiscate their goods at the very least, and depending on the value of the linen, all four might even be killed. They were foreigners, after all.

Immi made a sound of disgust. "Let's go home, Ruth. Those are Israelites, from the hills across Jordan. They may even be Benjamites, like those that slaughtered our king. Leave them to the magistrate."

"But Immi—"

"Don't draw attention to yourself, Ruth. It might lead to more—well, more trouble."

It might draw attention to me and whose daughter I was. Again I saw the barely concealed fear in my mother's eyes. Then I glanced toward the palace. The Israelite woman looked so alone and frightened. What if it were Immi standing there in some far place, unable to defend herself?

I had to do something. "Wait, Immi. I have an idea." I darted away before she could stop me. Slipping around the corner, I ducked down a narrow alley that I remembered from my days playing around the palace. An old storeroom had doors to both the outside and an inside passage. From there I could get to Abbi's office.

I felt my way along the hall in the dimness, and soon saw light ahead, then oil lamps. Moving purposefully, I walked through the passageways and climbed the stairs to the private office behind the public room where my father and another scribe recorded the pleas of the terrified Israelite before the magistrate.

Standing half unseen in the doorway, I motioned to Abbi when he glanced in my direction. He raised an eyebrow, and I urgently motioned again. At the moment one of the townsmen was pontificating on his part in the capture, and Ithmah eased away while everyone was listening.

"Ruth, what are you doing here? Where's your mother?" he asked, the small fringe on his robe dancing as he swung his shoulders. He never looked as tall as he really was, since bending over his work all day had left him slightly stooped.

"Immi's outside. We got to the square just as the commotion started. Abbi, the Canaanite is innocent. Abiaz took the linen."

"You're certain?"

I nodded.

"Why didn't you come forward?"

"Because it might not be advisable for the magistrate to know, officially, what happened. The donkey taking the linen out of the square had a brand belonging to the Midianite caravan that left this morning."

"Yes, that could be awkward," Abbi said, stroking his graying brown beard.

"Besides," I added, "it was Abiaz who first caught the Canaanite, and you'll notice he's not here now."

Ithmah sighed in exasperation. "Someday that man will go too far, and we'll have the joy of executing him. Complaints will drop by half the day we do. Stay here. I'll see what I can do."

In a couple minutes Father reappeared, followed by the magistrate. I lowered my gaze in respect.

"What is this you say?" he asked, intently searching my face. "You saw the theft?"

"Not the theft, Nahsi, but the departure of the linen." I told what I had seen, giving descriptions of the men involved as best I could and not mentioning Abiaz's name. My father gave me a slight nod of approval.

"How do we know you really saw this linen?" the magistrate asked.

"It was a vivid green. Ask the merchant what color of cloth was stolen."

"You're a very observant young woman."

"It was very fine linen, after all, Nahsi," I replied.

He burst out laughing. "Trust a woman to notice that! Well, if the linen is the color you say, then this Elimahaz person—or whatever his cursed Israelite name is—must be innocent. But why didn't you come forward publicly?"

"The donkey had the Midianite brand from this morning's caravan," my father replied.

The magistrate stiffened. "I see. You notice more than just cloth, young woman. We are indebted to your discretion."

"Thank you, Nahsi."

"It is a pity you did not recognize the man who took the linen."

When I quickly glanced at my father, he again nodded to me.

"I did recognize him, honored one. It was Abiaz."

"Abiaz! Well now, this is the most interesting information yet," the magistrate purred. "You know, Ithmah, this may be what we've needed to break that ring of thieves that has plagued the wealthier merchants for the past year. If there is a connection to the caravans, that would explain the total disappearance of the stolen goods."

The magistrate turned back to me. "You have done well, young woman."

Before he could ask my name, I slipped out the door, leaving the palace by another side entrance. Someone ducked back from the corner of an alley as I emerged. I was sure it was Abiaz.

Immi was relieved when I walked up to her.

"I talked only to Abbi and the magistrate," I assured her.

"Maybe this won't be a problem after all," she admitted. "Well, from the sounds of things, this will be over soon. Let's wait and go home with Abbi."

Moments later the Israelite woman came out the door, looking around. The boy with the wine skin offered her a drink, which she accepted, then walked over to stand in the shade not far from us.

"Thank you, geberet."

Her words made Immi start, and she glanced at the woman. "Did you speak?"

"I wished to thank you for what your daughter did. I saw her speak to the scribe, and after the magistrate spoke with her, his attitude greatly changed. She saved our lives."

Immi smiled. "I am Shimrith, and my daughter is Ruth. We have not done much."

"It was enough. Your daughter's hesed was a gift from El-Shaddai. I am Naomi, wife of Elimelech." She wore a good-quality brown robe and sash that matched her honey-colored hair and brown eyes.

"You have recently come to Moab?"

"Yes, geberet. Drought has ravaged the hills where we live across the Salt Sea. My husband came here, hoping to start a wineshop. There are many excellent vintners in our land."

"Yes, I have heard my husband speak of them," Shimrith said. "He will be glad to know that someone with such knowledge is here. Where are you staying? Ithmah will want to speak with your Elimelech."

"We have not yet found a place," Naomi answered.

"There is an inn just down this alley and to the right. It is small, but the proprietor will treat you well. Go there. I'm sure Ithmah will contact you soon."

"Thank you, Geberet Shimrith. You are more than kind."

When Elimelech and the two young men emerged from the palace, the soldiers released them in the middle of the square. Naomi smiled her farewell and hurried to join them, waving back to us. I liked her.

Spring
Abib, first month, tenth day
(1110 B.C.)

Shalom. Come in," Naomi greeted us gladly a couple days after they moved into a house. "Almost everything is settled now, and I'm pleased to have company. If we sit up on the roof, we can catch what sun there is." She led us to the stairs outside the house, and we settled on the roof under a thatched awning. Naomi had two woven mats set out, and she took up her spinning while she talked. Immi never went far without her spinning either, and they were soon talking and laughing like old friends. Orpah and I looked over the low parapet into the street below and whispered to each other about what we saw.

"Look, there goes Abiaz," I said. "I wonder what he's doing here?"

"Making trouble as he always does," Orpah replied. "Abbi says he either causes, or knows who causes, most of the problems in this town. Look, there's Sakar!"

"He's just a younger son of King Hissil, Orpah! If you must marry a sar, go for the prince in line for the throne."

She made a face at me. "I don't want to be married to the king. Just one of his family. More fun and no responsibilities."

"Fun until someone decides to take the throne," I reminded her.

With a wave of her hand Orpah dismissed the idea. "Heshbon has been peaceful for a long time because Hissil and his family are perfectly happy to leave the rest of Moab to Kemosh-dan."

"Kemosh-dan rules only the tribal territories north of the Arnon River."

"He doesn't even rule all of that," she reminded me. "The Gadites are firmly entrenched near the Jericho ford, and the Jahaz tribe toward the eastern desert does pretty much as it wants. Anyway, fighting about land seems so senseless. It all belongs to Kemosh, so why argue over it?"

"They argue about who's going to run it for Kemosh," I explained. "Everybody wants to get wealthy."

"Well, if they want to be wealthy, they should go to Egypt. Remember that caravan we saw on its way to Haran? Did you ever see so much gold?"

"The way they flaunted it, it's a wonder it wasn't all stolen," I snorted.

"Abbi said they purposefully showed it to impress us with the greatness of Egypt," Orpah yawned, then turned away from the roof, uninterested now that Sakar had vanished from sight. Joining Immi and Naomi, she took out her own spindle and a hank of wool. I settled myself in the corner, took my harp from the case, and started practicing.

Late spring
Sivan, third month, Ruth's thirteenth year
(1109 B.C.)

Immi, may we visit Naomi today?" Orpah asked one morning.

"Yes, but Ruth must remember to meet me at the temple."

"May we go now?"

"It's a little early," our mother demurred. "Why don't you wait for a while?"

"Naomi won't mind, and I wanted to see how she set up her loom. It's a different pattern than any I've seen, and I didn't have time to really study it yesterday."

Immi gave her a puzzled glance. "You didn't mention a new weave last night."

"I didn't want to discuss it until I knew more."

"All right, you may go now."

I regarded my sister suspiciously as we hurried away. If there was anything Orpah hated, it was weaving. Something else must be on her mind. I almost ran into her when she slowed abruptly, sauntering closer to the house/shop Elimelech had rented.

He and his sons were just opening for business, releasing the shutters and putting up the awning attached to the front of the building.

"Shalom, Orpah, Ruth," the Israelite greeted.

"Shalom, geber," I answered.

Elimelech's face creased with a smile. "Your accent is improving, Ruth."

"Shalom, Orpah," Chilion echoed.

"Shalom," my sister replied, her voice slightly breathless.

I glanced at her, puzzled by her tone.

Chilion had paused in his work and faced my sister. "You're out early."

"Oh, about usual," she said, lowering her lashes.

Usual? My eyes went round. Orpah was always the last one out of bed, and I always had to pry her upright.

"Is your wineshop doing well?"

"Yes, but there are fewer vintners selling than we thought. Some have already exhausted all their stock because of the drought in Judah."

"I hope you have a successful day," Orpah said.

He grinned. "It's already started out that way. Shalom."

Orpah blushed. "Shalom."

Taking my astounded gaze off Orpah, I saw Mahlon giving his brother much the same look. Disgusted, I walked past her. Orpah was getting silly like this with every boy around. Of course, the boys were just as silly about her. She had always been prettier than I, with dark, wavy hair and perfect skin. I couldn't believe the way she fluttered her eyelashes at every young male in sight, drawing attention to her eyes, which were her worst feature. I grinned in private satisfaction, for my eyes, rich light brown with flecks of darker brown, were my best feature, and Orpah coveted my long thick eyelashes.

"Well, you two are here early!" Naomi exclaimed as we entered the living quarters in back of the public room. "I'm glad to have help today. I've got to get that coat for Chilion started, and with you two here I'll have time."

"I have to meet Immi at the temple," I said. "But Orpah can stay. She was interested in the weave you had on the loom."

Orpah cast me an annoyed glance, hastily hidden from Naomi. "Well, of course I'm interested. It's a new weave to me."

"I'd be delighted to show you how it goes," she offered. "It's often used in Bethlehem and is very simple to do once you have the pattern in mind."

"Why don't you go look at it now?" I suggested. "I can finish cleaning up the dishes from breakfast. I remember which jars hold what in the storeroom."

Orpah gave me a mean expression, but she had to follow Naomi into the back courtyard where the loom stood. I didn't think even knowing the coat was for Chilion would make her interested in the least. *Serves her right,* I laughed to myself, returning the uneaten raisins to the storage jar. Beside it were two six-foot pithoi. The huge stationary jars held barley and wheat.

Smaller jars of honey, raisins, figs, and wine leaned against the walls or each other. Sacks of chaff stood by the door, waiting to be spread for padding between the jars, but Naomi still hadn't had time to sort things properly. Setting an oil lamp in the niche in the wall, I swept the room.

Orpah managed to keep Naomi's explanation short, and when I entered the courtyard, the woman already had the beehive-shaped oven hot and was tossing flattened dough against the walls to bake. Orpah ground wheat with a basalt roller, sliding it back and forth in a trough. Some of it Naomi would cook coarsely ground as couscous, but most of it would be pounded into fine flour for tomorrow's bread. A neighbor brought the goat milk Naomi had bargained for, and I put it into the churning bag made of skins cured with pomegranate peel. Tying one end of the skin to an upright on the loom, I shook the bag back and forth until the milk curdled, making leben.

Immi arrived an hour before noon to take me to the temple and my music lessons. Adon Tawy was teaching me to sing and compose. My mother still taught me the harp, since she played better than Tawy did, but he helped me learn the lyre and the different rhythms and techniques on a tambourine.

When I returned in the afternoon, Naomi sat at her loom with Orpah beside her, spinning on her hand spindle. I took a stool by the pile of raw wool near the loom and began carding it, drawing it through combs to separate the fibers for spinning and clean out the burrs, grass, and dirt the sheep had collected.

"Would you tell us another story?" I requested. "A long one. We've got all afternoon."

"Yes, one with a sar, a prince, in it," Orpah agreed, looking up eagerly. By now we both loved Naomi's stories.

"A sar!" Naomi exclaimed. "I'll have to think about that. I'm not certain I know—well, wait. I do know a long story about a sometime sar who became a nahsi as well."

"Was he handsome?"

"Yes, Orpah, very handsome, and it got him into trouble with his master."

"But how could he have a master if he was a sar?"

"Because he wasn't always a sar. He was also a slave."

"I don't want to hear about a slave," Orpah protested. "All they do is work."

Naomi laughed. "This sar didn't stay a slave. El-Shaddai had other things in mind for him, and that's the story."

I settled back happily. El-Shaddai was Naomi's god, and he did the most fascinating things. He reminded me of Yah when Naomi described how he was interested in his people and often communicated with them. I teased the last piece of twig from the wool and picked up another handful to card. "Start now, please," I begged.

She smiled. "Long ago in Canaan lived a very rich sar named Jacob. He had such large flocks of sheep and goats, with donkeys and camels, that he had to pasture some herds far away, or there wouldn't be grass enough. He had two wives and two concubines who gave him 12 sons and one daughter. Now, Jacob loved his favorite wife, Rachel, more than he loved anyone else, and when Rachel died, he turned all his love on her son, Joseph. He gave Joseph a richly embroidered coat, planning to make him sar one day, even though he was younger than all his brothers but one."

The loom clattered, and Orpah wound the yarn from her hand spindle, then twirled it again, pulling out more wool. Naomi went on.

"Jacob's older sons were very angry about this, but dared not cross their father, so they hid their hatred, hoping for some way to get rid of their favored younger brother. But the brothers weren't the only ones who had their eye on Joseph. El-Shaddai had noticed him, and he was very pleased with what he saw, for the boy had a good heart and tried to honor his father and his father's God, even though he was a bit spoiled.

"One day, however, the brothers got the chance they had been waiting for . . ."

Soon we got so caught up in the story that Orpah forgot to spin, and I to card the wool. Even Naomi's hands were still for minutes on end as she told us how Joseph's brothers sold him as a slave to Egypt, and how El-Shaddai put him into the palace as Tate, the highest position next to Pharaoh himself.

Orpah sighed over the romantic way Joseph had won the heart of the woman Pharaoh gave him as wife, but I marveled that El-Shaddai had enough power to raise his follower from a slave to rulership right under the noses of the Egyptian gods. Naomi's god must be very smart to hoodwink the most powerful gods in the world like that. Maybe he was greater than Kemosh. He certainly seemed more interested in his people than Kemosh was.

I considered that on our way to the temple to meet Immi. I wanted to ask the priests about it, but decided not to. It might not do for them to know I had such questions. Maybe I could mention it to Yah. He didn't seem to mind my talking to him about things. Perhaps he was lonely. In any case I could ask and tell him that I wouldn't say anything about it if he didn't want me to. I didn't want to get him into trouble with Kemosh.

While I waited for Immi to finish speaking with Adon Tawy, I slipped into the temple sanctuary. Again I knelt to one side inside the door. Incense clouded the air before the statue of Kemosh, and I saw three gold gerahs left by someone as an offering. Outside, the priest was just finishing a sacrifice. I remained motionless, waiting as I did in my rocky hideaway, but the temple was empty, devoid of any presence. After a while I left, frowning. Was Kemosh ever there?

When we arrived home, Immi called me up to the roof. "Ruth, the temple priest tells me that you have gone into the sanctuary several times."

Wondering if I'd done something wrong, I nodded.

"He's very impressed. It's important for a temple singer to be faithful."

I blushed. How could I tell her that I went there hoping to find Kemosh, but that he was never there?

"Is something wrong, Ruth?" She looked down at me gravely, although by now I had grown almost as tall as she.

"There's something I don't understand," I confessed, twisting a strand of my brown hair in my fingers.

"What is it? Maybe I can help."

"Why is Kemosh's temple always empty?"

She looked puzzled. "What do you mean, empty?"

"Well, when I go to my god place on the hill—"

"God place? Ruth, what are you talking about?"

"That's what I call my special place on the hill near Yidla's flock," I explained, "where I go to practice and everything. Anyway, Yah is always there too. I can feel his presence."

"Who's Yah?" Immi asked, her voice sharp as she gripped my shoulder. "Has someone been watching you or anything?"

"No, Immi, not with Yidla around," I assured her. "Yah's a hill spirit, I think. At the temple, I try to sense Kemosh like I do Yah. I thought I would be able to, since Kemosh is greater than just a hill spirit, but I never feel anything!"

She frowned, her dark brown eyes fastened on me. "Kemosh is very busy," she said absently. "He can't be in his temple all the time. As god of all Moab he has other things to concern him."

Well, if he was rarely in the Heshbon temple, how, I wondered, could he answer people's prayers?

"Does this hill spirit frighten you?"

"No. Yah's nice. He called me his child. I think he's lonely, and Yidla and I keep him company. It's always easier to practice and compose my songs when he's around."

"He spoke to you?" Immi gave me another long look.

I nodded. She didn't say anything more, so I went down to supper.

That night Immi brought several sticks of incense when she checked me for the night. "Take this to your god place, Ruth. Put a little in Yidla's fire whenever you go. Yah may be just a hill spirit, but he is elohim, and if he has shown interest in you, you must be respectful of him. It wouldn't do to offend him."

"I will, Immi."

Early summer
Tammuz, fourth month, Ruth's fourteenth year
(1108 B.C.)

Are you ready, Ruth?" Orpah called, heading for the stairway outside.

"I'm getting my harp," I replied, tucking the beautiful instrument into its case. Orpah took my breath away when I saw her. I was taller than she was now, but she was simply beautiful. Her hair was done in a fancy braid with flowers woven into it, and she wore a bright new green robe Immi had ordered for her. She had hennaed her nails and painted her eyes, and her cloak had a narrow trim of green that brought out the brown in her eyes.

I wore the plain light-gray robes of an apprentice temple singer. When my part in the grape-harvest ceremony was done, I had a new blue sash and matching cloak to put on.

"Oh, what I wouldn't give for your eyes!" Orpah sighed as I entered the room.

"Oh, what I wouldn't give for your luscious figure," I mimicked, still uncertain what to do with my growing height.

She giggled. "You'll be as tall as Abbi soon. But I'll never be able to move in that queenly way you have."

"And I'll never be able to draw men's eyes like you do!"

"Guess we're even. Let's go. Abbi's waiting in the street."

Once at the temple, I hurried through the crowd to join the rest of the singers. I was nervous, for tonight I had a short solo part in the praise anthem to Kemosh. In addition, it was the first night that Adon Tawy would use, for the entire ceremony, music that I had composed. Because I was still so young, he thought that it was better not to say anything about what I had done, and I was more than willing for it to stay that way.

"Here you are," Immi greeted me distractedly. "Alya came down with a sore throat this afternoon and can't sing. Adon Tawy wants you to take her part."

The news stunned me into silence. Alya had several solo parts, and the Egyptian music master had drilled me on them as preparation for next year, or maybe the year after that. But now?

Catching sight of me, he hurried over. "You heard?" he asked anxiously. "Do you think you can remember what to do?"

Rubbing my palms down my robe to dry them, I nodded.

"Just watch me, then. You'll be doing the short solo we planned as well."

"Ruth will do fine," Immi assured him with a brief smile.

As the adon hurried away to remind the back rows of singers where to stand, I sat down to one side, my stomach suddenly in knots. "Yah, be with me," I whispered without thinking, my eyes shut tightly as I struggled to control my fluttering insides.

Immi hurried over. "Are you all right, Ruth? You look pale."

I took a deep breath. "I'm fine now," I replied, clutching at Yah's comfort and feeling some of my tension ease away.

"It's time to line up. Are you certain you can do this?"

Another nod. But as I took Alya's place, my stomach felt tight and sick. I was the youngest apprentice in the temple. The adon had been teaching me for more than two years, but I had only been allowed to join the temple choir two months before. Several other singers could have taken the part. What would they think if I made a mistake?

When Tawy returned, I tried to grab his arm and tell him to find someone else. But he went by too fast for me to catch him. "Yah, what will I do? I've never done anything like this before, and the whole city is out there. Even the king!"

"Sing for me, and don't worry about all the people."

Taking a gulping breath, I followed the singer in front of me outside. "I'll try, Yah," I whispered. That seemed the only way I'd get through this without making any terrible mistakes.

Under Tawy's direction the first part of the ceremony went smoothly. When the first of Alya's solos came, I forgot to step forward out of the choir, and then I was too embarrassed to do it during the other three. By the last one I was dizzy and could hardly control my breathing enough to hold the last note.

My planned solo was at the end of the anthem, and now that Alya's part was over, I relaxed and did my lines perfectly. The choir master gave me a grateful smile. Then the priests prayed to Kemosh, thanking him for the abundant grape harvest just gathered, offering sacrifices and incense, performing the rites that would ensure continued fertility for the vines for another year.

I stood quietly, head bowed, waiting for Kemosh's presence to fill me. Since it was one of the most important ceremonies each year, surely he would be here for it. But again I felt nothing. Only Yah, lingering in the corners of my mind. I puzzled over Kemosh's absence. If he was never here, why did we bother to worship him?

Anticipation spread through the crowd as the ceremony closed. There would be dancing now, and feasting all through the town. My family would go out to the winepress in Grandfather's vineyard for the feast he gave there. Elimelech and Naomi were invited, but I didn't know if they would come. He hadn't been feeling very well lately, and Naomi did not approve of the open fertility practices of the harvest festivals.

I wondered what they did in Judah to keep the land fertile. If the people didn't share their own virility and fertility, becoming one with their god in renewing the land, how could the land continue to produce? Maybe that's what had caused the famine in Judah that Naomi's family had fled from. If the Israelites didn't show their god what he had to do, maybe he'd forgotten. But the El-Shaddai in the stories that Naomi told didn't seem to need reminding about anything. It was all very confusing.

As we arrived at the vineyard the musicians Grandfather had hired started to play. Orpah hurried ahead to join the other girls at the winepress, a large chiseled-out cavity in the rock. The bottom was already covered with grapes waiting to be trampled. Grandfather was putting a large jug under the end of the channel from the press to catch the new wine.

The musicians struck up a dance tune, and my fingers itched to play my harp as the girls crowded into the press, hitching up their robes to trample the grapes. A shout rose as the first wine ran into the jug. Orpah laughed delightedly. The grape festival was a special time for women, and she never missed anything if she could help it. I wanted to rest a bit before joining the dancing, so I saw Mahlon and Chilion arrive. Their robes were plain gray, with darker girdles, making a contrast with some of the colorful robes around them. Watching the young Israelites, I wondered if Naomi knew her sons had come.

Then King Hissil and Sakar arrived. Grandfather greeted them, proud that the ruler had honored him by attending his party. Sakar caught sight of Orpah in the winepress and headed for her as if drawn by cords.

"I heard you singing in the choir at the temple. You sounded scared," Mahlon said right beside me.

Startled, I turned to him. "I was. The singer who was supposed to do those parts got sick this afternoon, and Adon Tawy picked me to replace her."

"Well, you ended well. That last solo was the best."

"That's the one I expected to do," I said. "How's your abbi doing?"

Mahlon frowned. "Not well at all. I doubt he'll be able to get up tomorrow."

"That won't matter," I smiled. "Hissil has been known to take a whole week to celebrate grape harvest."

He nodded. "Abbi is thankful for the time to rest."

I looked down as Mahlon took my hand. It seemed small in his. Usually I could talk and laugh with him, but tonight something was different. I could feel my heart beating, and I couldn't find anything to say.

"I-I didn't know you attended the ceremony," I finally said.

"I went to hear the best singer in Moab," he replied, turning toward me. "Even when you're scared, you outshine anyone else."

I blushed.

Mahlon bent his head. "You're beautiful, Ruth."

"Orpah is beautiful," I corrected.

"Orpah is more exotic, but she can't match your grace and elegance."

His hand tightened on mine, and he stood very close to me. I tipped my chin up to see his face.

"Sometimes I think I'll die without you," he said in a strangled voice. Quickly he kissed me, then rushed away.

I stood there, too stunned to move. Then a little smile curved the corners of my mouth.

Summer
Elul, sixth month, Ruth's fifteenth year
(1107 B.C.)

You look radiant today, Ruth," Adon Tawy said as he entered the room where I waited. "Have you some songs for me?"

"I came to tell you that I'm leaving the temple," I replied.

"Leaving! But you can't—your composing—what will I do?"

"You will have to give me more time to compose instead of demanding songs on short notice," I teased. "I'm getting married."

"Married? Is that all!" he sighed, relieved. "You'll be the death of me, Ruth. How could you frighten your old teacher so rudely? Who is the lucky man?"

I laughed. "Mahlon, son of Elimelech the Israelite. We are to be married at the second new moon from now, so I'll be too busy to do much composing for a while."

"Congratulations. May your home be filled with children. But Ruth, remember your music. You're already a better composer than I, and in a few more years you could be the best in all of Moab."

I averted my gaze, uncertain if the adon was teasing me or not. "I'm just a temple singer who likes to write songs," I protested.

"You are far from being a simple temple singer, Ruth. Your talent is so great you don't even know you have it. Writing songs is not difficult for you, is it?"

"Difficult?" I looked up in amazement. "I just do it. I can't stop doing it."

He sighed in exasperation. "See what I mean? At least you can continue to be a lay singer like your mother. That way you won't forget your music."

I smiled. "Don't worry, adon. I couldn't live without my harp, and if I have that harp in my hands, I can't stop the songs."

The Egyptian smiled back. "I shall hold you to that. Congratulations again."

As I left him, I stopped at the temple for a moment to check if Kemosh was there. He never had been, even during the major festivals, but I wouldn't give up, determined to know the presence of Moab's god. But he wasn't here today either, so I hurried through the narrow streets to Elimelech's wineshop.

Abbi said the shop had not done as well as King Hissil had hoped. Partly, it was the result of the continued drought in Judah, but Abbi had also observed that Elimelech had no business sense. Although Chilion was better at it, his father wanted to do the bargaining himself. My father had wished numerous times that he could put Elimelech's knowledge into Chilion's head and let the Israelite's son try his wings. But the Israelite was very closemouthed about the sources of the wines he sold.

"You are very faithful, Ruth," Elimelech greeted me a bit pompously. "I think you've come here every night for weeks."

"And I'm glad she does," Mahlon said, smiling. "It's the best part of the day."

I blushed as I always did, and we stood talking in front of the shop until Naomi reminded her son that it was time to eat.

The next afternoon he met me at the temple cistern after practice. As we moved out of the way of the other people coming and going I noticed the worry line creasing his forehead. "What is it, Mahlon? Did something happen at the shop today?"

"No, the shop is fine. We had a caravan owner come in. He had heard that we sell specialty wines, and he said he might have a market in Damascus if we were willing to ship that far."

"Then what's the worry line for?" I pressed, edging as close to him as I dared.

He stared down at the ground. "It's nothing, Ruth."

I cocked my head at him, holding his gaze when he looked up.

Mahlon reddened.

"Does it have something to do with me?"

Reluctantly, he nodded. "Are you sure that our marriage is acceptable to your family?" he asked.

My stomach hardened. I didn't like where our conversation was leading, but if there was a problem, I wanted to know. I'd learned years ago that it was better to know exactly what one faced, even if it was frightening.

"My parents are very happy with our betrothal," I told him. *More than you know,* I added silently to myself. Neither Immi nor I ever forgot that my blood was a danger to me. That threat would pass to my children, especially sons. But if I married an Israelite, the political value of my children would be significantly reduced, if not removed altogether. Being half Israelite might protect them if Kemosh-dan or his successor discovered more of Eglon's descendants and started another bloodbath.

"It's Naomi, isn't it?" I asked into the silence.

"Yes," he admitted reluctantly. "It bothers her that you still sing at the temple. She's afraid that I'll—" he stopped.

"She's afraid that you'll start to worship Kemosh instead of El-Shaddai."

A reluctant nod.

"I wouldn't ask you to start," I said, a sudden bitterness welling up inside. "Kemosh is never there." I left him standing alone and ran down the streets to my house in the deepening dusk. Grabbing my harp, I told

Orpah I'd stay the night at Grandfather's and hurried out before anyone could stop me, slipping through the gate just before the soldiers closed it for the night.

Refusing to cry, I rushed down the road, turning down the path in the valley where my grandparents lived. In the twilight I didn't notice Yidla until he spoke.

"Rut'."

I stopped.

"I take you god place. Come."

I almost started crying right there, gratefully following him to the shortcut up the hill. The shepherd led the way until he reached the path through the trees to the niche in the rocks.

"I wait here," he said, sitting down.

Clutching my harp, I almost ran along the familiar path to my god place, tears now flowing freely down my cheeks. Discovering that Naomi didn't want me had wounded my heart as nothing else ever had. I loved her and had looked forward so much to being her daughter-in-law, certain that she would be just as happy as I about wedding her son. The darker shadow of the niche opened before me, and I sat down, putting my harp on the floor, so familiar with the place that darkness was no hindrance. Pulling my knees up to my chest, I sobbed uncontrollably.

Would there ever be a place where I belonged? Shimrith and Ithmah and Orpah loved me, but I wasn't really theirs. I belonged to the woman who had died that night, the one who cradled Shimrith's son in the grave. Then Naomi came, winning my heart with her warmth and fascinating stories. Had she only been pleasant to me out of gratitude for what I had done before the magistrate? Why didn't she want me now? Why wasn't I good enough for her son?

Because I am a Moabite, I thought. My ancestors had lured the Israelite men from their god at Beth-peor, and she feared I would do the same to Mahlon. Ironic bitterness filled me. I went to the temple and participated in the ceremonies only because everyone else did, certainly not because Kemosh was ever there to be worshipped.

Besides, what would be so bad if Mahlon honored the god of the land he lived in? Of course, Elimelech claimed that this land belonged to part of the tribe of Reuben. But King Hissil didn't pay tribute to Israel. He paid Kemosh-dan. And why had Elimelech and Naomi come to Moab in the first place? If their god was so worthy of worship, why was there a famine there? The gods were supposed to keep famine and enemies away—that's why people worshipped them.

I rocked a little on the hard stone, looking out at the night with tear-blurred eyes. Would Naomi be happy if I worshipped El-Shaddai as well as Kemosh? What if I stopped composing and singing at the temple? But playing my harp to accompany the choir, being part of the harmonies and chants, answered some need deep in my soul. I couldn't stop being who I was.

What would I do if giving up my music was the price for marrying Mahlon? I loved him. For the first time, someone ignored Orpah and preferred me. The most wonderful feeling filled me when I saw his love in his eyes. And when I made my music, he reveled in my voice, listening with everything in him, knowing it expressed the deepest part of me.

"Oh, Yah, what am I going to do? Why does my life have to be so complicated? Why can't I just be Ruth, daughter of Ithmah and wife of Mahlon?" I questioned, bursting into tears again.

A bit later I wiped my face on my skirt, rather ashamed of myself. I hadn't cried like this since I was a child. But why couldn't Naomi be happy with me as Mahlon's wife, as she'd been with me as a friend? Or had that simply been gratitude?

Easing back against the cool rock behind me, I sighed. Abbi had warned me the hill people across Jordan were very set in their thinking about gods, but I hadn't thought it would be a problem, since Naomi loved me already. What did it matter what god you worshipped? Because, when it came right down to it, I supposed I worshipped only Yah.

The thought made me laugh a bit shakily. "Did you know that, Yah?" I whispered. "I worship you, not Kemosh. Don't tell him, because even though he's never around, he might get angry if he found out that one of the blood royal family was worshipping a hill spirit instead of him!

"I worship you because I've felt your presence beside me when I needed help. I've heard you speak to me. You've promised to protect me, and you helped Yidla when he was sick. But that won't make any difference to Naomi. To her, you're probably just as bad as Kemosh is. So what am I going to do?"

Automatically I took my harp out of its case and ran my fingers over the strings. Constant practice had made all my fingers strong and quick in spite of the joining on my left hand. I let my hands wander, pulling from the harp an odd, questioning melody that matched my mood. Once again, I didn't truly have the place I thought was mine. Shimrith, Ithmah, and Orpah weren't really my family, and now Naomi didn't want to be.

"I guess you're the only one who wants me, Yah," I sighed. "Although why a god would care, I don't understand. I'm glad you're just a hill spirit and not some great national god who wouldn't have time for people like me and Yidla. Kemosh doesn't know if I worship him or not; I'm an outcast because of my blood family, a danger to those who shelter me, and unacceptable to the mother of the man who wants my hand. So who am I?

"I'll have to be a worshipper of Yah, I guess. Please don't mind that you have just Yidla and me. We're a small tribe, but we'll be faithful."

Yidla! He must still be waiting at the end of the trail, and it was very, very late. Hurriedly, I packed my harp, eased my way past the rocks to the hilltop, and hurried down the trail.

"Yidla, I'm sorry I stayed so long."

The shepherd stood. "Is all right. Yah say you sick here." He touched my chest over my heart. "Say take you god place until you better. I wait."

"Yah told you I was coming and to bring me here?" I asked, scarcely able to breathe.

"Yes. Yah like you. Like songs from you. Like song you give me. 'Thank Yah, Blessing days, Teaching sheep, Giving life, Yah praise forever,'" he chanted proudly.

"How do you know Yah likes my songs?"

"He say," the shepherd shrugged. "Come, you sleep Grandfather's."

I could hardly believe it. But Yidla was too simple to lie. If he said the hill spirit told him something, then the god had. I fell asleep that night still muddled in my feelings, my heart aching. Yet underneath all the turmoil was the quiet, constant warmth of knowing that a god had chosen and accepted me.

The Time of the Latter Rains

Ruth has done well under Yahweh's cultivation, has she not? But she still has much more to do and learn. However, time is passing quickly now, and the plantings are almost mature. Bethlehem is enduring the latter rains, and Yahweh's crop there is fast ripening for harvest, but the crop in Moab needs the rain. Maybe when the Seed of Abraham comes, Yahweh's harvest can be reaped with tears of joy, but until then, let us not despise the tears that water our souls and teach us Yahweh's compassion.

Besides, Ruth is in Moab, and Boaz is in Bethlehem, and for the harvest to be complete, the two must get together. Boaz has roots very deep in Bethlehem now, for he is where he should be. But Ruth? Well, she has grown as much as she can in the soil of Moab, but she has never had the chance to grow as deeply as is her nature to do. Did you notice that? Yahweh did, and it is one of the reasons He chose her.

As rains on our fields loosen the soil, so Yahweh's rain will loosen Ruth until she can be transplanted to her appointed place in Yahweh's fields and produce seed for the reaping.

Early winter
Kislev, ninth month, Ruth's sixteenth year
(1106 B.C.)

Ruth! Ruth!"

The sound of Mahlon's voice pulled me from the courtyard where Naomi and I were weaving one afternoon. I ran to the outside door. He and I had been married for several months now, and I'd never heard him sound frightened.

"What is it?" I asked, pulling the door farther back out of his way as he struggled through it with Elimelech hanging on his side.

"Abbi just collapsed. Chilion ran for a healer."

Elimelech swayed on his feet, his eyes unfocused, his skin pale and clammy. I slipped my shoulder under his and helped my husband half-carry him into the side room.

"Naomi, come quickly!" I shouted, grabbing a sleeping mat and hastily spreading it out. Mahlon eased his father down.

Elimelech clutched his chest, his breathing labored. Sweat gleamed on his face, and he moaned.

My mother-in-law rushed in. "Elimelech, what happened?" she asked frantically, throwing herself down beside him. "Mahlon? Chilion?"

"I'm here, Immi," Mahlon replied. "Chilion went for a healer."

"It hurts so," Elimelech gasped, groping for his wife's hand. "El-Shaddai, don't strike me now; there is so much to do!"

"Why would El-Shaddai strike you?" his wife demanded, gripping his hand. "We have been faithful to Him. Chilion will be here with the healer, and you will be well in no time."

"Waited too long," Elimelech gasped, clutching at his chest again. "Should have told Chilion, but I thought—plenty of time." His body went rigid with pain, and then relaxed, the breath rushing from his chest. His eyes half opened, and his head rolled to the side.

"Elimelech? Elimelech!" Naomi screamed, shaking him.

Mahlon knelt beside her, taking her hands in his. "Immi, Immi, stop it!" he said, tears brimming from his eyes. "It's no use."

"He can't die," she said, staring fixedly at Elimelech's vacant eyes. "He can't leave me here. The healer will come. He'll know what to do!"

I backed from the room, leaving Mahlon holding her while I slipped outside to watch for Chilion and the healer. They arrived in just a couple minutes, but the healer took one look and shook his head. It was too late. Naomi collapsed in Mahlon's arms, her keening a wild and forlorn sound.

"Probably a bad heart," the healer said to me a little later. "From what you describe, I doubt I could have done anything had I been standing beside him when it happened. It takes some people this way, suddenly and without warning. I am very sorry."

"You were kind to come. What fee do we owe?"

The healer waved his hand. "Nothing, for I did nothing. I wish I could have."

"Thank you," I said, ushering him to the door.

A bit later, Ithmah arrived.

"Abbi, how did you know to come?" I exclaimed in surprise, letting him in.

"The healer stopped at the palace on his way home. Elimelech is truly dead?"

"Yes. Mahlon said he collapsed with no warning. We barely got him into the house."

Abbi looked grim. "This will be hard on the family, away from their homeland and all. What about a burial place?"

"I don't know. I'll ask Mahlon." I went to the sleeping room where Naomi and her sons sat with the body.

"Mahlon?"

He got up.

"Do you have a tomb here?"

His frown line deepened. "No. We didn't expect to stay long. It will be hard for Immi to have Abbi buried in a strange land."

Chilion left Naomi's side. "What is it?"

"A tomb," Mahlon replied.

His brother sighed. "We'll have to buy one. Abbi must be buried soon. Where we'll get the silver, I don't know."

"My abbi wishes to speak to you about one," I said.

Chilion came out with us. "Shalom, geber. You know where we can purchase a grave?"

My father nodded. "It's a small cave that could be readied for a burial by tomorrow morning. It will need to be dug out a little and a covering made for the entrance."

"It would be welcome. How much?"

Ithmah hesitated. "Let me look to that. The site itself will be reasonably priced, and the fee for work done should be well within your means."

Chilion nodded gratefully. "Please make the arrangements, and let me know how much we must pay."

I went with Ithmah to the door.

"I'm sorry this has happened, Ruth," he said before he left. "Elimelech was a good man."

"I'm so glad you came, Abbi," I said. He hugged me tightly, then left. If I knew my father, he would make certain the grave was within Chilion's means, no matter how much he had to pay from his own treasury. Even though in many ways Elimelech had been a weak man, Abbi knew that Mahlon made me very happy, and this was a way he could express his gratitude.

In the weeks following Elimelech's burial Naomi became withdrawn and silent. Orpah took to stopping by, and her bright clothes, cheery laugh, and good spirits did much to draw Naomi out. But I was the one my mother-in-law turned to in the night when her sons were sleeping and the pain of missing Elimelech was too much to bear.

My eyes opened the instant I heard footsteps and the creak of the door to the courtyard. In the pitch-dark I felt around for my harp and sandals. Naomi had been more interested than usual in Orpah's gossip from the market today, and I'd hoped that she would sleep better tonight. I snatched up Mahlon's cloak with mine and stepped out into the chill air.

The stars gleamed overhead, their light sharp in the blackness. Naomi sat motionless in front of her loom, her head bare. I draped Mahlon's cloak around her shoulders, noticing how thin they had gotten in the past few weeks. Adjusting my own cloak, I sat close beside her, my shoulder touching hers, and waited.

"He was doing what he thought would help," Naomi whispered.

"We never went to the temple of Kemosh, or the high places, or bowed to your foreign gods. Why did Elimelech die?"

"I don't know, Naomi," I said, putting my arm around her. "But he gave you Chilion and Mahlon. They will provide for us."

She shook her head. "Things had been improving. Another year, and the shop would have provided support for our clan at home. He was so hopeful."

"Chilion will continue," I encouraged her. "He's even better than Elimelech at bargaining and such."

"But he doesn't know where to buy." Her voice quavered. "Elimelech never told anyone where he got his best stock. Why did El-Shaddai turn from us? How have we angered Him that He lets my husband lie among strangers? He should rest with his fathers in Bethlehem."

I hugged her to me, silent before her questions. As Naomi leaned against me and sobbed, I faced the thoughts churning in my own mind.

I kept remembering Yidla's healing. As near as I could tell, Yah had healed the shepherd because he wanted to. Even though I had asked for the favor, I'd had nothing to offer that could sway the decisions of the elohim. And he seemed to like Yidla and me for the same reason: he wanted to. Trying to control him as the gods normally were with incantations or sacrificial bribes seemed an offensive insult to what he had done, so I simply thanked him and did my best to honor him at all times. It made me wonder how El-Shaddai felt about mortals who tried to control him.

Pulling our cloaks around us, I shifted closer to Naomi. Clouds had begun to block out the stars, and the wind felt damp with coming rain. Naomi's sobs subsided to silent tears, and she clung to me tightly. "He was all I ever wanted," she whispered. "He gave me sons and had a high reputation and place in Bethlehem. Now he's gone, and we are far from home and left alone."

Her weeping continued, drawing tears from my own eyes because of her heartbreak. Yet her words puzzled me. Naomi's stories had impressed one thing firmly on my mind. While El-Shaddai accepted sacrifices and praise from humanity, and brought the rains and kept the ground fertile in return, he did it from down here among his people, while all the other gods did it from a distance. The only exception I knew of was Yah, whose presence I felt right now, mourning with us. How could Naomi feel so bereft when her god chose to be close to his people? Was it because Kemosh kept El-Shaddai from reaching her here in Moab?

I picked up my harp. Naomi sat motionless again, hurting too much to even move. Letting my fingers pluck the strings as they would, I played softly, forming a sad melody to echo our sorrow. Gradually a lament shaped itself in my mind, and I named it "Naomi's Song." When I had played it twice, she rested her hand on my knee.

"That harp speaks for my heart."

I didn't reply, but played a restful song, one that I'd composed the first time I visited my birth mother's grave after I had acquired this harp. It was a bit sad, and a bit lonely, as I always felt when I went there.

Naomi sighed when it was done. "Let's go in," she said. I helped her stand, and she paused at the door before we went in. "You are a good daughter to me, Ruth," she said. "I'm glad you're here."

My heart sang as I lay down by Mahlon again. Naomi had accepted me into her family at last!

Early fall
Tishri, seventh month, Ruth's seventeenth year
(1105 B.C.)

You look cheerful today," Orpah said, coming in one morning.

I smiled. "Naomi is almost her old self again. Why are you here? I thought you were busy with Sakar."

Her gray-brown eyes flashed. "Why should I care about him? He can go to Damascus forever for all I care!"

I pricked up my ears. "What did he do to lose your good opinion of him?"

She tossed her head. "I'm not certain he ever had it. Trailing around any girl likely to become a woman as he does."

"King Hissil still hasn't sent for you to be Sakar's wife? How much longer do you plan to wait?"

"I'm not going to marry Sakar," she sniffed. "He chases after anyone. I want someone who'll stay home—like Chilion. Maybe I'll marry him."

Unwisely I laughed. "Oh, Orpah, you'd be miserable with him! He's very staid, spends all his time at the shop, and wouldn't know how to treat you the way you want."

"I would not be miserable," she contradicted. "When I first met Sakar, he was just a nice boy and not at all pompous or uppity. But you should see him now! Just because his father's the king, he parades around like a cock bird showing off to all the hens."

In other words, he's not paying attention to you, I thought to myself.

Orpah dropped by more and more often, and even though I knew she was chasing Chilion to get back at Sakar, I said nothing, since her exuberance helped Naomi throw off her depression. Knowing how my mother-in-law had felt about Mahlon marrying me, I could only imagine what she'd think of his brother marrying Orpah.

But she surprised me. When Chilion announced he was taking Orpah as his wife, Naomi kept any misgivings she might have had to herself. It was Ithmah and Shimrith who needed convincing.

"Will you talk to Abbi?" my sister begged one day. "It's been more than a week since Chilion sent the message asking for me, and Abbi still hasn't answered. I've tried and tried, but he won't let me talk to him about it. If he wants those grandchildren he's always hinting about, he'd best let me get married, so we can get started."

"What makes you think he'd listen to me?" I asked, surprised.

"He always listens to you. Both Immi and Abbi do."

"What could I say?"

"Tell him that I won't marry anyone else but Chilion. You married Mahlon, and they were delighted. Why can't I marry Chilion?"

"Because Ithmah is not certain he can support her," Immi sighed the next afternoon when I ventured to ask that question.

I stared at her in surprise.

"The wineshop is not doing well at all," Immi went on. "Chilion has better business sense, but he doesn't know the vintners the way his father did."

That explained some things, I thought, depressed. I'd known that the shop wasn't doing well, but I hadn't realized that it was that bad.

"What do you think, Ruth? Can Orpah manage with Chilion? I don't want her to be miserable."

"She will be happy with anyone who appreciates her beauty, and Chilion certainly does that," I replied. "I wouldn't have thought she would settle for him, but when I see them together, she seems very content."

Immi laughed shortly. "And she hasn't been content for a long time. I'll speak to your father about it again. Maybe something can be worked out. Orpah's argument about grandchildren may be more persuasive than she knows!"

It must have been, for not long after, Chilion and Orpah were married.

Late summer
Elul, sixth month, Ruth's eighteenth year
(1104 B.C.)

But you can't go out now, Ruth. Kemosh-dan is here! His soldiers are everywhere!"

"You can't leave Chilion as sick as he is, Orpah, and Naomi doesn't know where to go if our usual healer isn't there. With Mahlon gone to Dibon, I'm the only one left."

"Then I'll have to go with you," she said automatically.

"You don't need to escort me anymore, Orpah. I'll be fine. Besides, what could you do if the soldiers did take me?"

"I could scream and weep and throw myself in their way. It might be enough to start a riot so that you could get away."

"And you might get yourself killed. We've got to have medicine for Chilion. There, Naomi is calling. You go see what she wants, and I'll be back in no time."

I escaped, shutting the door firmly behind me. But once in the street, I fumbled under my cloak to be certain that the signet ring was well hidden, then kept my left hand out of sight. I did not want to be out, for with Moab's overlord in town, I felt conspicuous every time

I saw a soldier. But my little hoard of silver gerahs was gone, and Chilion needed more of his medicine. Ironically, the very fact that Kemosh-dan was in town made it a perfect opportunity for what I planned to do.

"Yah, protect me as you promised so long ago," I whispered as I walked quickly through the narrow side streets, keeping my head down and well covered. Tucked in my robe was a song for Adon Tawy at the temple.

The music master was not there. From habit, I stopped in the sanctuary to check for Kemosh's presence. The sacred place was empty, even though Kemosh-dan himself was in town and would worship here. Walking to Tawy's house behind the temple, I wondered if Moab's god ever attended a temple service anywhere in Moab.

Ashamed of my heretical thoughts, I waited in the courtyard while a servant told Adon Tawy I had come.

He hurried in. "Geberet Ruth, I'm glad to see you. Do you have another piece for me?"

"Yes, adon," I said, my palms sweaty. I wanted to wipe them on my cloak, but held them still.

"Good! I hoped you'd bring one this week. Is it for the new moon ceremony?"

Drawing a deep breath, I forced myself to look Tawy in the face. "Yes. I think it's good enough to sell."

The temple musician smiled. "All your songs are good enough to sell."

"How much will you pay for this one?"

He blinked in surprise, then sat down, regarding me carefully. "Why this sudden decision to sell your work? Do you wish to be recognized as the composer?"

"No. I don't care that people think you write the temple music. But I need money."

Tawy's expression relaxed. "Your songs are certainly worth paying for. Will this, uh, be a permanent arrangement?"

I hesitated. The experiences of the past three years argued for such, however much I might prefer to give my songs away. "I believe so."

He smiled wryly. "You have listened to me to my own detriment. If I don't buy your music, people will wonder why the quality has suddenly deteriorated, and with Kemosh-dan here, I dare not let that happen. I don't suppose any of that influenced your thinking?"

"It might have."

His lips twitched. "You are a very shrewd woman, Ruth. Too bad you're married. I have a brother in Egypt who would delight in your business sense. You and he could be wealthy together!"

"But if I went to Egypt, you would have to compose music again, and King Hissil would think Lilith had taken your strength and banish you from Heshbon. Then your brother and I would have to feed you and your family. I'd rather sell my songs and let you feed me."

At that he laughed outright. "Let me hear the song. If it's up to your usual standard, I can offer two silver gerahs."

Astonishment made me dumb. Two days' wages? The most I'd hoped for was 10 coppers, half a day's wage. I stared at him.

"All right, two and 10 coppers," he sighed.

I looked down to hide my expression, hastily revising the prices I had planned on asking.

"Three," I pushed, despite my trembling.

"Done," Tawy agreed.

"I shall expect four silver gerahs for wedding and burial songs, and 15 for complete ceremony music. The small love songs and celebration songs go for one silver gerah each."

"You will bankrupt the temple!" he protested, but his eyes gleamed, and I knew he would have paid more.

"I'm sure King Hissil will show his liking for the temple music as he always has," I remarked. "If I remember correctly, you were thinking of melting some of the silver in the treasury for a lampstand. If you hint that the treasury is low, perhaps Hissil will decide to contribute."

Again he laughed. "Bring whatever you write, Ruth, and I'll gladly pay. Composing was the bane of my life until you came along, and you know that too well!"

With the silver in my hand, I headed straight for the healer's house. Chilion would have his medicine, and more besides. Tucked in my sash were several requests for small songs that would tide us over nicely until Mahlon returned as well as replenish my reserves. I had learned much today. Boldness at the right time paid well.

But never enough. Soon after Chilion recovered, we had to abandon the wineshop. Since Israelites couldn't own land in Moab, we found a moderate-sized cave outside of Heshbon, and Naomi, Orpah, and I settled in while Chilion and Mahlon worked as day laborers in the surrounding fields.

Early fall
Tishri, seventh month, Ruth's twenty-first year (1101 B.C.)

I stood numbly as our neighbor and his son pushed the covering away from the cave entrance. It seemed just yesterday that we'd been here, burying Chilion. It had been a windy day like today, only warmer, and Abbi and Immi had been here for us both. But they had gone to Beth-shean with King Hissil, so Orpah and I stood alone. Low, gray clouds scuttled across the sky, fleeing from the sight of the dead waiting for burial in the ground. Beside me, Orpah held my hand, tears running down her face. I hadn't cried yet. I couldn't.

The sickly odor of decay rushed from the tomb, making the men removing the covering gag. I hardly noticed. They waited to let the air clear, then picked up Mahlon's wrapped body. I carried the few things I could spare to put with him in the tomb, a pitiful reminder of a life now gone. There were no children to continue it. I didn't know if I was glad or not.

Our neighbor's wife supported Naomi as we followed the men into the tomb. The stench was much worse, and the bearers hastily laid Mahlon down on the floor by the narrow ledge where Chilion's body rested. I refused to look at the remains of my brother-in-law. Even Naomi kept her eyes turned away. The men retreated from the tomb, and most of the mourners stayed back from the entrance. I hastily put my offerings with Mahlon, and behind me, Naomi slid to the floor in a faint. The neighbor caught her, and his son helped carry her out.

Bile rose in my throat, and I could do no more than whisper a choked goodbye before following the others. They were already replacing the covering. Orpah bent over Naomi, who wept weakly. With the assistance of others she shuffled slowly down the hillside to the path that led to our underground home. I lingered, looking longingly at the trees covering the hills around me. Who would know if I didn't return immediately? They would think I was still at the tomb.

Automatically I reached for my harp, but I had left it in the cave. With one last look at the tomb, I started back. When our home came into view, the crowd in front seemed more agitated than necessary. I quickened my pace.

"I tell you, it's mine! The debt must be paid!"

That sounded like Abiaz, I thought worriedly. The troublemaker had harassed us much lately. He had hated me since King Hissil had put a stop to the caravanners' thievery among the merchants years ago. After I talked to the magistrate, the authorities had watched Abiaz so closely he had been unable to make much money from his various schemes.

"What do you think you're doing?" Orpah's voice, shrill with outrage, reached my ears. "Leave that! You have no right!"

Pushing through the crowd, I ran toward them. A cart and donkey stood by the door, half filled with our things.

Abiaz appeared, carrying part of our loom, Orpah right behind him, tugging at the wooden frame.

I stood directly in his way, and he stopped so quickly that he overbalanced and nearly fell. It would have been amusing, except that I had just buried my husband and didn't feel like laughing.

"Ruth! I thought you were still at the tomb," he blurted.

"So I see. Why are you stealing our loom?"

"I'm not stealing," he said loudly, casting a worried glance at the glowers of the people around him. "Mahlon owed money. I'm collecting on the debt for the loaner."

"What debt?"

"Goods for the wineshop," he said uneasily.

"The wineshop was sold years ago and the debts paid then."

"Not this one. Mahlon has been paying against it every month. It was from before, when Elimelech started the place."

I hesitated, trying to remember if my husband had ever mentioned anything about such a debt. I had no idea what Elimelech had done to start the shop, but it would have been like him to borrow from the troublemaker.

"Who is the loaner?" I asked.

"It's from the palace," Abiaz replied smugly.

I hesitated again. King Hissil had wanted the shop to succeed and would have lent money to help out. But I rather thought the debt, if it had still existed when the shop was sold, would have been settled at that time. However, Maash, Hissil's heir, was assuming more power, and he was not the forgiving type. He might have revived the old debt and demanded full payment. For that matter, Abiaz might have decided to do that himself, collect what he could, and then share with Maash if he got caught.

In any case I didn't have the time or energy to bring it to the magistrate. "How much are we supposed to owe?"

"That's not something I need to discuss with you, Ruth," he brushed me off. "I'll discuss it with—" He stopped abruptly.

"With my husband?" I finished for him softly. "You might find that a bit hard, Abiaz. Although, if you insist, we can open the tomb again today. I'm a widow now, and speak for myself. Orpah is a widow, and she will speak for herself. So is Naomi."

"I'll speak to your father."

"I'm not in my father's house, Abiaz. I am living in my dead husband's home, and I answer for myself. How much?"

"At least 50 silver gerahs is still unpaid on the loan."

I studied the man. He jiggled his right leg nervously.

"Are you certain, or shall we check the documents on the loan?" I had no idea if there were any, but if the palace had made the loan, a record of it must exist somewhere.

Noticing the quick alarm that flashed in Abiaz's eyes, I hid my smile. He didn't want that done. Likely it would alert Maash to what was happening, and the crown prince would want his cut, *if* such a loan existed.

Anger ran through me, and I studied the contents of the cart. Orpah and I had been cleaning our storeroom four days ago when Mahlon got caught in the sudden cold shower and sickened. We hadn't had time to finish the job, and most of the stuff in the cart was the pots, utensils, and broken tools that we no longer had use for. I had been complaining to Orpah about finding someone to haul it away when

Mahlon had appeared at the door, soaked to the skin and shivering.

Abiaz had obviously loaded anything in sight into the cart from the yard before going into the cave just as we returned.

"Well?" I looked at him.

He smiled. "I do apologize, Ruth. I just remembered the 50 pieces was from another loan. Your loan was much, much smaller."

"Then doubtless you have enough here to cover the payment, if such there be."

Abiaz and I stared at each other. The neighbors and mourners for the funeral shifted uncomfortably. I expected little or no help from them. Abiaz ran with a group of hard men in town, and anyone crossing him openly would be sure to find unpleasant things happening to them or their possessions. But as long as Hissil lived, even they would hesitate at outright robbery of three widows, two of whom were daughters of a palace favorite.

If Abiaz was smart, he'd take the way out that I'd offered him.

"The addition of the loom will finish the payment."

That loom was worth more than everything he had in the cart, and we needed it. "Are you certain of the amount? My father can look it up with little trouble. It seems to me that the cartload and 10 silver gerahs will be sufficient. The loom stays."

One or two of the men stepped forward, faces set and hard. Abiaz dropped the parts of the loom from his arms. "I suppose the loaner will be satisfied with that," he said sourly.

Reaching into my sash, I pulled out a small leather pouch and emptied the 10 gerahs into his palm. It was all we had to live on.

Without a word Abiaz climbed on the cart and started down the road.

"Why did you let him get away with that?" Orpah asked as the crowd dispersed, some people heading for home and others going in to sit with Naomi.

"We needed the stuff carted away, and paying that much before witnesses will prevent him from coming back later to demand more. We'll manage without the silver. It was the loom I was worried about—and my harp."

"That's safe. I hid it under the broken ox yoke in the back passage as soon as I found him rummaging around," Orpah said, glaring down the road at the figure on the disappearing cart. "I couldn't let him have either one. The loom and your singing are all that keep Naomi alive."

Suddenly exhausted, I turned to the doorway, wanting to sleep for the next two years and wake up with all our problems whisked away. I bit my lips to keep them from trembling.

"Why don't you try to rest, Ruth?" Orpah said. "I'll handle everyone here, and you haven't really slept since Mahlon sickened."

"I will," I said gratefully. "Call me if you need me, Orpah."

~ ~ ~

"Ruth?"

"Yes?"

"I hate to bother you, but Naomi won't eat."

I let go of the signet ring around my neck, bumping my harp beside me on the sleeping mat as I shifted position. I didn't want to eat either. My heart ached too much. Orpah's suggestion that I rest had only given opportunity for the dark thoughts to burrow their way in deeper.

"Ruth?"

Pushing the harp aside, I forced myself to move. Naomi needed me. My world was dark and empty now, but hers had completely disintegrated.

Outside, she sat in the gathering dusk, isolated by her sorrow from everything around her. Orpah had a bowl of lentil and barley soup dished out, with unleavened bread beside it.

I took the bowl. "Come, Naomi, you must eat a little," I said gently. She didn't respond, so I scooped up some of the soup with the bread and held it to her lips. Her mouth opened in surprise, and I put the bite in. After a couple more bites, she fed herself. I also ate some in order to encourage her. Then I looked at Orpah.

"Go on," she said. "I'll be fine with the help of the neighbors."

Grabbing my harp, I fled. I needed my god place more than anything, but I was too tired to make the climb, so I sat under the oak trees on the hill above the tomb in the darkness. What little I'd eaten lay heavy and sour in the hard knot that marked my stomach. If Naomi felt the same, she would be cursing me for coaxing her to eat.

"Yah, what will we do?" I whispered. Naomi had not recovered from the blow of Chilion's death before Mahlon joined him. Orpah had her hands full caring for Naomi, which left me to find a way to feed the three of us.

"Help us, Yah," I prayed, utterly weary. "If you saved Yidla when I asked, why not Mahlon? If you were like Kemosh, I'd know you didn't care, but you have called me your child. Could you not interfere because Mahlon belonged to El-Shaddai?"

Responding to the familiar urge to play, I reached for the harp. The feel of the strings as my fingers plucked the notes calmed my thoughts. I didn't understand the ways of the gods, but I could still feel Yah's presence deep in my heart, despite the wounded numbness of grief and puzzlement.

I told the harp of the bruises in my soul, creating a melody of sorrow and loss that at last freed the tears from my burning eyes. The music brought more comfort to me than anything else could have, unless it was Shimrith's arms. I let the last notes fade into the darkness.

"That harp bares the soul. I thought I had finished crying for Chilion," Orpah said, sitting down beside me and wiping her eyes.

"How do you bear it?" I asked.

"Chilion suffered so from the fever that I prayed only for his death those last few days. I had time to get used to the idea of being without him. But Mahlon! Gone in just two days! I can't yet believe it."

"He was never that strong," I admitted. "He covered it well, but some days I almost had to carry him to bed."

"Chilion guessed as much. He used to worry. They were so close. But I thought things were going better after he stopped working in the fields and got the job in the pottery shop."

"They were. Sometimes he would talk to me before falling asleep. He never could do that when he labored in the fields."

As Orpah gazed into the black night a small animal rustled the leaves of the bushes behind us. "What are we going to do?"

I closed my eyes, too drained to think beyond the next moment, let alone come up with answers about tomorrow or the next day. But my sister left the question hanging in the air. "We are going to sleep for another night. Tomorrow I will again convince Naomi to eat something so she will live," I replied, unable to keep some of the bitterness from my voice.

"There's not much left to eat, you know."

Why couldn't she have kept that bit of information to herself? I didn't want reminders of all the problems looming over us.

Rising to her feet, Orpah shook out her robe. "Don't stay out all night." She walked away. Somehow she always knew when I needed to be alone.

I looked at the stars shimmering overhead. My hands strayed to my harp again, and the notes hung on the air. I was as uncertain about the future as my sister was. What were we going to do? Especially with Naomi? My own grief weighed on my mind like a load of potter's clay, but the devastation in her eyes stabbed my heart.

It wasn't right. Naomi was so gentle, so proud of her sons, so destroyed now that both were gone. The harp jangled, the discordant notes harsh in the night. I looked up at the stars, peering through the oak leaves as they trembled in the passing breeze.

"You're not much of a god, are you, El-Shaddai?" I challenged. "Naomi told me many times how powerful you're supposed to be, and about all the wonders you've done. She's recited every story about Israel until I know them by heart. I don't understand how you can deprive someone who dedicated to you both her husband and sons, then leave her to starve. Seems to me the least you could do is provide food!"

Anger choked my throat as I stood. Strangely, the fact that my husband had died didn't matter as much to me as the fact that Naomi had lost her last son. As I unconsciously fingered the signet ring that hung beneath my robe I reminded myself that I expected bad things to happen in my life. Given who I was, I was lucky to still be alive. But that Naomi's god would let all three of her men die left me furious. Orpah would have been horrified at my outburst to a deity, but I was in Moab where Kemosh ruled and Yah protected me, while El-Shaddai was in Israel, miles away across the Jordan River. He couldn't hear me, so I was safe enough.

Racing back to our cave home I welcomed the heat of anger that replaced the empty numbness of my grief. I had loved Mahlon, and now I didn't even have a child to remember him by. What would life be without him?

The smell of lentils cooking with olive oil, garlic, and spices woke me. My mouth watered, and I opened my eyes, wondering who was up so early. Then the memory of Mahlon's death dropped into my mind, and my stomach knotted, warning me that I wouldn't be able to eat very much. Thankful that one of the neighbors had come, I sat up. Maybe that would spark some interest in Naomi.

But Orpah stirred the pot outside over the cooking fire. I raised my hand to shield my eyes from the bright sun.

"That's the first good sleep you've had since Mahlon got sick," she greeted me. "Hurry up; the noon meal is almost ready."

"Noon?" I gasped.

She laughed.

After hastily combing my hair, I went back into the cave to our storage chamber for some dried figs. Stopping in my tracks, I raised the oil lamp to see better. Sacks and jars of food were everywhere, the disorganized confusion making it impossible to determine how much of what was where.

"Orpah! What happened?" I exclaimed, racing to the doorway.

She looked up from the cooking, her face flushed, a small smile on her lips.

"Sakar. He came this morning. Both you and Naomi were still asleep. He left three donkeyloads, even carried them into the storeroom. I was so surprised, I could hardly thank him properly."

Why would Hissil's son Sakar take such an interest in us? I sat down in the doorway. Orpah ladled the lentils into a bowl and glanced at me.

My breath caught. Lovely when she married Chilion, now she was stunning with perfect features, flawless silky skin, and hair that seemed to float around her when it was unbound. She had not had children either, and her figure was youthful and firm. Put her in fine linen and jewels, and she would outshine that Trojan woman who started a war not so long ago with the Greeks. Maybe Sakar's attention wasn't such a mystery after all.

After only a couple mouthfuls, I picked at the food. Naomi still slept, so I didn't have to eat to encourage her. Orpah sat down beside me.

"It's odd that Sakar came after I'd mentioned last night that we needed food."

My stomach lurched, and I froze. Very carefully I set the bowl on the ground and tucked my arms around my stomach, leaning against the doorframe. *Just last night I'd challenged El-Shaddai to feed Naomi, and this morning the most unlikely person in the city showed up with three donkeyloads of food.*

How had El-Shaddai known? Only Yah had heard that challenge.

Early spring
Abib, first month, Ruth's twenty-second year
(1100 B.C.)

Almost six months had passed since Mahlon's death, and it had taken all of that for Naomi to get back on her feet again. Both Orpah and I worried about her. She remained silent and withdrawn, nothing like the welcoming, cheerful woman who had won our hearts before her sons did. She moved in her own gray world, hardly noticing if we spoke to her or not. The look of unending pain in her eyes always unsettled me. Often I made an excuse to get away, leaving my sister to stay with her while I retreated from the world of humans to the regions of the gods, leaving even my familiar god places behind to go east. The dry, rocky savanna emptying into the desert eased the pain in my soul and gave me strength to scrape together enough to keep the three of us alive.

Today I climbed the last few feet to the top of my hill, panting a little, and stepped carefully through the thorny bushes under the pines that masked my trail. Once through the bushes, I hurried along under the trees in the dead calm of near midday, my harp bumping rhythmically on my side.

With the approach of harvest, Adon Tawy had asked for a praise song. I was uncertain how things would go, since it would be the first time I'd tried to compose since Mahlon died. But now that I had my harp in my hands, with the noon sun shining over the quietness and peace of the hills, I knew I'd be able to forget the sorrow and worries on my mind. Besides, I was in my own familiar god place, with Yidla listening below, and the faint smell of the incense burning in his fire drifting up to me.

I ran my hands over the strings, starting a firm rhythm.

"O blessed be the Lord, who has given abundantly to his people,
Who has caused the earth to bring forth harvest for his followers.
Blessed be the god of Moab, of Madaba's people,
For the wine and olive presses are running over,
The threshing floor is buried in wheat, and the sheep have given their wool.
Let us sing to the Lord for all his works,
For all the blessings he has poured out upon his land.
Sing praises to Kemosh, god of Moab.
Give thanks to the lord of Moab."

Below me Yidla clapped his hands in time, head nodding from side to side, always a good indicator of the worth of a song. Smiling, I played the tune again to fix it in my mind. It needed some tightening here and there, perhaps a different twist to the musical phrases in the third and fourth lines. But that was something I could do at home, since Naomi now accepted the music that had brought such comfort to her in her grief. For my part, I understood that the Israelites held a very different view of creation and fertility than that of Moabites, explaining her aversion to the worship of Kemosh, and I did not sing the words to praise songs from the temple when she might hear.

Idly I let my fingers choose which familiar tunes to play as I sang. Tawy's training had disciplined my throat and muscles until I could play my voice almost as I did my harp. Outside of temple celebrations, I rarely let myself go, but sometimes I just had to sing.

Today, remembering the sorrow of my loss, I took funeral songs from my memory, modifying them as I played to reflect my personal grief, the longing I felt for Mahlon, the distress at how Naomi had changed, the melancholy of my life and days. As I sang, the sorrow eased and the quiet peace of this god place seeped into my heart. The slow, heavy rhythm smoothed out as songs of quietness and homes, of peaceful pastures and silent forests worked out of my fingers. I sang quietly, changing the words for myself, letting go of the tension and accepting Yah's peace in my heart.

As I thought of how Naomi had first welcomed me as her friend, I sang of the pleasantness and cheer she carried with her, making her name so fitting for her. I remembered our wonder and joy at the food

Sakar brought, and before I knew it, I was singing of my amazement, plucking the strings sharply at unexpected intervals to lend that same surprise to the music. I ended with my puzzlement and perplexity over what might have been an answer to my challenge of a foreign god who could not have heard me shouting at him.

At last I stopped, my fingers sore and my throat tight from the unexpected exertion. Suddenly I glanced hastily down at Yidla. I had forgotten about him. He stood tall and straight, facing west, his whole body alert.

Having stayed later than I had planned, I took the shorter, steeper way to the base of the hill. Orpah had gone into Heshbon to help at the palace where King Hissil was entertaining an ambassador from Babylon, and the neighbor who promised to check on Naomi was probably more than ready to leave, as it was time to prepare the evening meal.

I went by Yidla's flock. He was so sensitive to the emotions in my singing that I wanted to be certain I hadn't upset him. Hurrying from the cover of the trees, I looked around in bewilderment. Where were the sheep?

"Yidla?" I called.

He appeared from nowhere, his face white and fierce, a look I'd never seen before. Clapping a hand over my mouth and grabbing my arm, he pulled me back into the trees toward the base of the slope.

My heart almost stopped, and I stumbled, nearly falling. Yidla had never before done such a thing! Pulling away, I tried to jerk my arm from his hold. The shepherd missed a step and fell. Yanking my arm from his grasp, I backed up, ready to scream.

Yidla rolled, staring past me and scrambling up on all fours. When I faced him, he half rose, motioning urgently and creeping forward. Warily I backed away.

The shepherd glanced backward again and started toward me, arms spread as I'd seen him herd his sheep. He was trying to get me away from something!

My chest eased, and I took a breath, moving over the rough ground more swiftly. "All right, Yidla, I'm going," I said softly.

Frantically he motioned me to be silent, directing me to a fall of rock concealed by bushes. As I climbed into them, I glimpsed the flock, crowded silently into a shallow, overgrown ravine, invisible from any angle but above. Their absolute stillness and total silence sent a shiver up my spine. Just what was Yidla hiding us from?

After checking behind him one last time, he joined me among the rocks. Moments later two men appeared in the tiny clearing we'd just left, sitting down under an old olive tree that had gone wild. One was a total stranger, the other Abiaz.

Carefully I shifted position so that I could study the newcomer. He was tall, with dark hair, an angular face with heavy eyebrows, and a thin neck that led to a strangely thick body.

"You're certain no one is around?"

Abiaz snorted. "We're alone."

"What about those sheep and that singing?"

"They've obviously moved on. Besides, Yidla is crazy, so even if he heard us, no one would believe him. What brings you from Beth-peor?"

The stranger ignored the question. "What can you tell me about Ithmah the scribe?"

I stifled my gasp. What could this rough-looking stranger want with my abbi?

"Nothing fishy there. He's a stuffy palace scribe appointed to deal with traders and couriers," Abiaz replied, waving his hand at a fly. "Got a wife named Shimrith who's a temple singer, and two daughters named Orpah and Ruth."

"Two? I thought there was only one."

I tensed up. Why would he say that?

"Been two as long as I can remember."

"How long is that?" the stranger probed, obviously unimpressed with Abiaz's certainty.

"Let me put it this way," the latter replied sarcastically. "Orpah was just weaned when Shimrith got pregnant. She birthed early, and they kept the baby secluded until it was stronger. If I remember correctly, she was quite small. Good-looking enough, but can't hold a candle to Orpah. Now, there's a face!"

"I suppose they married?" The unknown man had kept his face away from Abiaz as he questioned him in a bored voice, but I noticed how tightly he clenched and relaxed his hands.

"Wasted themselves on some weak-boned Israelites that couldn't get children by them," Abiaz said in disgust. "Both died. Just recently buried the last one—Mahlon, I think. So now they're widows."

I frowned, angered at the insult to Mahlon even though he was dead, and worried about the man's interest in Orpah and me.

"Is she barren?"

"Who? Orpah? With that figure, I'd not care!" Abiaz laughed crudely.

"No, Ruth."

The townsman shrugged. "Never thought about it. They were married for several years, but then a real man has never tried to cover them. Anyway, you're looking in the wrong place for Eglon's blood."

The stranger sat very still, except for his head, which he slowly turned to face Abiaz. "That's a dangerous thing to say."

"Look, geber, you're the stranger here asking nosy questions. I'm just proving my worth by showing I know why you're asking. You need what I can get, and you can pay me what I want. We both win."

"I don't know what you're talking about," the other man said coldly, standing.

Abiaz snorted. "Everyone knows Eglon's posthumous son, Mesha, plotted all his life to take the throne from his half brother, Kemosh-natan. And everyone knows that Mesha's newest wife fled the palace when Natan's successor got tired of Mesha's plotting and slaughtered the entire family. That sort of nudged him on to wipe out the whole bloodline while he was at it.

"Now that Amarel of Dibon wants the throne, any connection to Eglon's blood would consolidate his position if he manages to get it. But not many of the clan survived, thanks to the efficiency of our dear king's soldiers. Only no one ever found out what happened to Mesha's youngest wife and the child she carried. There are rumors the child will be known by the royal signet ring the young woman stole on her way out the door."

Scornfully the man walked away.

"I'll be available when you come back," Abiaz called after him with a laugh, standing up. He waited until the stranger was out of sight. "And you'll come back," he added. "By then I'll have answers. Imagine thinking Ruth of the blood royal! Interfering daughter of Lilith is what she is. Ruined that sweet deal with the caravans, and foisted off on me a cartload of junk. Then I had to pay Maash all that silver to save my neck. I'd like to—"

He stopped muttering, staring intently at the ground. "Ithmah and Shimrith did keep her very close there at first. Maybe there's something in it after all." Then he slowly wandered off.

My stomach in knots, I leaned against the rock, clutching the signet convulsively. My worst nightmare had just come true. If Abiaz started asking questions, he'd go to the midwife, and I had no illusions about whether or not he'd find out what he wanted to know.

Abbi was old now and not as important as he used to be. Maash was handling more and more of the palace duties, and he had his own favorites. But Hissil could keep Ithmah and Shimrith safe, and with Sakar so taken with Orpah, she was in no danger.

That left only me. I pressed the back of my hand against my mouth. If Abiaz reported what he found to Kemosh-dan, I'd soon be dead. I stared at Yidla, still standing by me and tensely listening into the woods.

Yah, you promised to protect me! my mind screamed. I couldn't stop my trembling. If I ran, where would I go? Without family or clan, I would be lucky to survive more than a few weeks. But if I stayed, I might live only a few weeks anyway—maybe only days.

The distressed sounds coming from Yidla finally penetrated my mind.

"Rut', Rut', no fear! Please, Yah here. Will keep safe!"

I tried to smile. "I'll be all right, Yidla."

"You safe. Yah here. Others gone," he assured me, patting my shoulder.

I struggled to suppress my agitation. "It's all right, Yidla. I'm feeling better now."

"Yah here. Safe." He looked at me anxiously.

"I hope so. I must get back home, Yidla."

"Wait. When others gone far, you go."

I leaned back again against the hard rocks, trying to still my pounding heart. Where could I go? How could I go? As I sat there wondering if I would live much longer, the most irrelevant thought popped out of my mouth. "Yidla, how did you know Yah's name?"

"Pash."

"Who's Pash?"

"Travel man from west. Buy wool. Talk. Say this Yah place. You go now." He reached down to help me stand.

"I will remember how you kept me safe, Yidla."

The shepherd shrugged. "Yah say hide you. Go now."

"Thank you, Yah," I whispered as I hurried toward home, somewhat encouraged that no matter what happened, the hill spirit would know what to do.

"I'm sorry I'm late, Naomi," I called, entering the cave.

"I've been wondering what to do."

Her comment, coming from the darkness and exactly echoing my thoughts, stopped me short.

"About what?" I asked, lighting a lamp and noticing that she seemed more aware than usual.

"I have nothing left. I never wanted to come to Moab."

"Oh?" It was the most she had talked since Chilion had died.

"Elimelech insisted on coming. He said there was always rain in Moab. We could see the clouds across the Salt Sea. He thought a wine export business would help our clan by providing a market for their wines. Now there's nothing left, no one to support me or speak for me. I am as the dead."

Puzzled, I frowned. Naomi said that often, even though she had family and clan in Bethlehem to whom she could turn if necessary. And what about El-Shaddai? He was always rescuing people in just such situations. What made her think he had abandoned her?

Looking at her now, I noticed how white her hair had grown, nearly covering the light brown it used to be. "We can speak for ourselves," I said firmly. We had already paid off debtors and outwitted Abiaz; we could survive somehow with Yah to help.

Naomi didn't seem to hear. "So I've been wondering what to do."

At least it was encouraging to know she had been thinking of something while she sat silently and stared at the walls. Orpah had gotten her to do a little weaving at the loom outside sometimes, but not often.

"Pashur, the wool buyer, came today."

My scalp prickled. Pashur? Pash? "Do you know him?"

She nodded, only her head moving, as if the rest of her were truly held by death. "He's from Judah and comes to buy wool. We knew him in Bethlehem, and he'd buy wines occasionally and gave Elimelech the idea of starting a wine business. He hadn't heard that my sons died." Tears fell from her eyes. She ignored them.

I put my arms around her shoulders, so thin and frail and still. "I'm sorry I was gone, Naomi. I could have told him had I been here."

"It was good to see him. He's from home and brought news."

"What did he say?"

"The rains came to Judah. There was a good harvest last year, and another on the way this year. I am going back to Bethlehem. I will die there, not here." Her voice carried no expression, as if what she spoke of had no interest to her whatsoever.

"You want to leave?" I asked, surprised. "But your home is here. Elimelech and your sons are buried here!" I searched her face. How could she think of abandoning her dead like that?

Naomi shook her head. "This has never been my home. I lived here because it was where Elimelech came, and where Chilion stayed. I can decide now, and I'm going home to Bethlehem." Her voice was suddenly firm with decision.

"What about Orpah and me?"

"You will return to your mother's house and remarry. Yahweh has brought the rains back, given us bread, and nothing can stop me from going home."

My heart stopped. "Who is Yahweh?" I asked in a shaking voice, backing away from her.

"El-Shaddai's name is Yahweh. But Abbi always called him El-Shaddai, so I do too. I will leave day after tomorrow," she finished, getting up and unfolding her sleeping mat.

I scarcely heard her. Pashur had to be the man who bought wool and told Yidla which god lived at the hill. Yahweh. The shepherd shortened everything.

I sank down in a daze. It was all the same god. *And I had taunted Him with His neglect of His people!* I curled up on the floor. Why wasn't I already dead? To show such disrespect to a god! How much more of a fool could I be?

"Yah, be with me!" I whispered frantically, then stopped in horror. Yah was Yahweh! How could I ask Him for protection from Himself?

My world came apart again. Without the hope of Yah's protection, I would soon be dead. Fear and shame flooded through me. I had been so angry at El-Shaddai. He would surely strike me down or send demons to drive me insane, punishing me for my blasphemy.

"Yah say hide you." "Yah like you. Like your songs." Yidla's words forced themselves into my terrified thoughts.

"I will protect you, My child."

But that was before I mocked Him. Before I presumed to tell Him what He should do and how He should act. Before He answered and sent us food. My breath caught. He sent us food. Why would He answer me when I had been angry and had turned on Him, blaming and mocking Him?

"I will protect you, My child."

What sort of a God was this? Finally daring to move, I stood. I had to get out of the cave. From force of habit I took my harp as I started down the familiar path to the tomb. I walked in a daze, expecting Yahweh to strike me dead any moment.

Who was this God? I continued past my husband's grave into the forest crowning the hill, needing a god place. If Yahweh wished to slay me, He would find me easily enough. I had nowhere else to go.

Clutching my harp, I crouched against the wide, stubby trunk of a terebinth, the thick branches like a huge spreading mound over me. I don't know how much time passed before I gradually realized He wasn't going to kill me immediately.

"I will protect you, My child."

The words kept running through my head. Could He possibly still accept me? After what I had said and thought?

"Yah say hide you. Yah like you. Like your songs."

"You told Yidla to hide me," I whispered. "Why?"

As the silence and peace of the night settled around me, I relaxed, tears streaming down my face. "How can You care about me? I'm not even an Israelite. I'm a Moabite, an enemy, and worshipper of Kemosh." But I wasn't. I hadn't worshipped my people's god since I had declared myself a follower of Yah.

"You chose Abraham," I said, remembering the stories Naomi had told and retold. "He didn't choose you. You must have chosen me, even though I didn't know who You were. And You chose Yidla, too. You choose the strangest people."

I groaned, putting my head in my hands. "Forgive my tongue, Yahweh. I'm so used to speaking all my mind to You. Please do not be angry with Your handmaid."

Yah's presence filled the forest around me, full of comfort for my fears, peace for my troubled heart, and laughter. Laughter?

My eyes opened wide. A God who laughed? Sarah had laughed, and Yahweh laughed back, and Isaac was born. This was very confusing. What kind of a God laughs? What kind of a God wrestles physically with His worshippers, puts slaves on thrones, turns rods into snakes, shakes city walls to pieces, and talks to Moabite shepherds? What sort of God turns laughter into babies, transforms hatred into salvation, and stubbornness into deliverance?

The sort of God who would answer my anger with food and protect a small child who did not know His name. A God who taught an injured boy about sheep, and who liked songs about Himself although they named another god. Who listened to my chatter, answered my fears, and accepted me no matter what I said or did.

Hugging my harp, I sobbed uncontrollably. And this God chose me! I was a follower of Yah, and I would be so the rest of my life. If He wanted me, He could have me—all of me, the good and the bad, the anger and pain and grief. I didn't need to worry about other gods. If Yah was great enough to put Joseph on a throne in Egypt, if He could go into the land of other gods and live in a small cave to be near a simple shepherd and a frightened girl, if He could seek followers from Ur, if He cared enough to point out which maiden a servant should choose for his master's wife, I had nothing to worry about. Least of all Kemosh, who had never graced his temple with his presence. If Yahweh was present in Ur, Haran, Canaan, Egypt, and Moab, He had to be the most powerful God in all the world.

"Yahweh, I am Yours," I said. "I am honored to be chosen by You. And I will follow You for all my life. No matter how short it is. Oh, Yah, what shall I do?"

"Go with Naomi." I couldn't tell if the words had been spoken aloud or not. But the simple solution to my problem took my breath away. With her, I would have a place, and a connection to a new land, however tenuous. Besides, I couldn't stay in Moab. Abiaz would see to that.

"I'm going with you."

"Orpah, don't be unreasonable," I pleaded. "You don't have to."

"I'm going with you."

"Immi and Abbi will be heartbroken if you leave. You have a future here. Sakar would have married you yesterday if you would let him."

Our low voices barely carried out of the storage room; she had that stubborn look on her face I knew well from my childhood. "I'm going with you."

I sighed. "Orpah, I'm not a child anymore. You don't have to watch me like a hen with one chick. I'm a hen just like you. And I'm leaving Moab. That way I'll be out of reach of Kemosh-dan and his soldiers. I'll be safe. Will you please stay here?"

Refusing to answer, she sat there on the storage jar with her hands clenched, the oil lamp in the niche above us casting a wavering light in the darkness.

"Don't leave Sakar! You've loved him all your life."

"I loved Chilion. And I love Naomi. I'm going."

"Chilion is dead. There are no children. All you've ever wanted was to settle down with a husband and have children. You can do it now, without worrying about me. Orpah, see reason!"

"No."

"Think of Sakar. You can't leave him a second time." Frustrated, I went into the main room of the cave. There was no need for her to go. I would be fine. Naomi would be fine. Orpah could stay and live the life she longed for with the prince she'd always wanted.

In the corner Naomi breathed evenly in the darkness. She would be up early, eager to start. Today she had moved with purpose and energy, though without the cheerful conversation that had once made her so pleasant to be around. The bitter sorrow that haunted her brown eyes cut my heart. How would I cope with that when I could no longer roam my beloved god places to get away from it?

Perhaps I would find a god place in Judah. But it would be different there. As a Moabite and foreigner, I would have to be very circumspect. Here I was known and protected by my family.

I thought for a moment. I wanted to pay Abiaz back somehow for forcing me to leave my home. But there was no way I could. Maybe later. Maybe never.

"Remember him, Yah," I muttered. "Remember what he has done."

The next morning Naomi was up before either Orpah or I. She had dressed and combed her hair and sat at the door staring down the road as she waited for us. Orpah cooked some breakfast, and I checked the small bundles we would take. Most of the things in the cave would remain behind as settlement for the last of our debts.

After eating and tidying up for the last time, we walked out. People filled the courtyard. Immi and Abbi were there, the neighbors, and Sakar, standing with a stony face to one side. Orpah went to him, and he touched her cheek.

"I'll wait," he said between clenched teeth.

Her hands shaking, Orpah averted his face. Then with a nod she went back to Naomi, who patiently answered everyone's good wishes and looked longingly down the road.

Slinging my harp case over my shoulder, I picked up the bundle of food. The several coppers and couple silver gerahs tucked in my sash would have to last the week it would take us to walk to Bethlehem.

Shimrith looked at me with tear-filled eyes. "I will miss you, Ruth."

"And I you, Immi. But I must go."

She nodded, her eyes telling me that she had feared this very moment all her life.

"Take something to the grave we visit, will you?"

"Of course, Ruth. I will not let her be lonely. Will you come back to her?"

The catch in her voice made me look away quickly. My voice shook. "I dare not, Immi. Tell her I didn't want to go, that I don't mean to abandon her."

"I will."

"And tell Yidla that Yah will go with me."

"I wish for your father's sake that Orpah would stay, but I haven't been able to convince her to."

"Nor I. But with Sakar here, she may change her mind yet. I hope she does. There is no need for her to go."

Immi bit her lip. "I impressed on her too much her duty to stay with you. I had no idea she would hold to it this long."

I hugged her. "I think she's wavering. I want her to stay. I would not rob you of your only child."

She looked at me sternly. "I have two wonderful daughters, Ruth, who have given me much joy. Do not exclude yourself again."

"Thank you, Immi," I said, fighting back the tears.

"Now go, and don't forget your music. You must keep singing and composing. I'll break the news to Adon Tawy. He'll be devastated."

"He will have to hire another composer at decent prices, you mean," I corrected, smiling through my tears.

She smiled back. "Something like that."

Glancing around, I saw that Naomi had started down the road. Pulling myself away, I gave Abbi a hard hug, whispered "I love you," and went after her.

Midmorning we stopped in the shade of a tree by the road. I added my cloak to the bundle I carried. The sun grew warm quickly now that spring was here. Up the valley, someone's barley field was beginning to turn gold, the breeze rippling through the grain as it passed. Orpah looked back, biting her lips. Her steps had lagged more and more, and indecision crossed her face. I rejoiced. She should return home.

Naomi hadn't looked back once. That vague, empty sadness sat on her face, and when she turned to us, she spoke distantly, as if we were strangers.

"Neither of you needs to come any farther with me. I know the way, and I know where I can stay at night. It's time for you both to return home to Shimrith."

At the mention of Immi's name, tears leaked from Orpah's eyes and her lips trembled.

"We'll go with you," I said softly.

"No, go back," Naomi insisted, gazing down the road. "El-Shaddai should show you as much hesed as you've shown to your dead and to me."

Then she faced us directly for the first time today, and I saw the total aloneness in her eyes. I couldn't understand why she didn't take comfort from El-Shaddai. He would surely care for her.

"Go back," Naomi repeated gently, putting her arms around Orpah and kissing her forehead. "Shimrith needs you, and Yahweh will give you happiness and children with another husband."

Clinging to Naomi, Orpah broke into sobs. "I want to go with you," she cried. "I can't leave you alone. I'm all you have left of Chilion."

Naomi turned to me, her eyes brimming with memories. She touched my harp. "You too, Ruth. You made Mahlon so happy. Now you must do that for another. Go." She kissed me as well, with all the tenderness of a mother.

I found myself crying as hard as Orpah was, but I shook my head. "I'll not go."

"You must return," she insisted. "I can't do anything for you. I'm dead and useless, beyond childbearing, with no more sons to be your husbands. Even if I could lie with a man tonight and get sons of him, it would take too long for them to grow to manhood. Why should either of you remain unmarried that long?

"If you return to Shimrith, you'll have a better life. Mine will only be bitter now that Yahweh has turned His hand against me. Go back."

Orpah cried harder than I'd ever heard her. She looked at Naomi, then me, indecision plain on her face.

"Go, Orpah," I urged softly. "Sakar is waiting, and it's time for you to live the life you've longed for. I must go on without you. Naomi and I will take care of each other, and you don't have to worry about either of us."

"Naomi, are you certain?" Orpah slowly asked.

"Yes," she replied firmly. "I have nothing for you. Your life is here in Moab, not with one already dead in Israel."

Suddenly she threw her arms around our mother-in-law, hugging her for a long time, crying as if her heart would break.

At last Naomi loosened her arms and pushed her away. "Go, Orpah. You've been a good daughter to me, and Yahweh will reward you with many sons."

Turning, my sister wrapped her arms around me, her face white. "What about you?"

"It's time to let me go, Orpah. Think of Immi. She'll be overjoyed to see you, and you can give Abbi the grandchildren he wants so badly."

I was shaking by now. I had never known a time when she hadn't been there. To see her walk away now felt as if she were tearing the roots from my soul. I gritted my teeth to keep from calling her back.

"Join her," Naomi urged as Orpah glanced back one more time. "Shall I take both Shimrith's daughters from her? You belong there, bearing children to another man. Besides, Adon Tawy will be lost without you and your songs. You have a place in Moab with your people and gods. There is nothing in Israel for you."

Her last words stung. Nothing in Israel? The God who had chosen me, protected me, and accepted all my foolishness, anger, and pain was of Israel. Yah had shown me hesed. He was the only one who could protect my life, and He had done it. The least I could do was take care of Naomi, His follower. Even if that meant never marrying again.

"I won't leave, Naomi, so stop telling me to go back," I said, looking her in the eye. "I'll go wherever you go and stay wherever you stay. I'll take your people as my people and your God as mine, also. Wherever you die, Naomi, I'll stay until I die and am buried beside you."

The intensity of my feelings startled her. She clearly hadn't expected me to react this way.

"And may Yahweh curse me with being cut in half like a sacrifice to this covenant if even death separates us," I added.

Naomi stared at me with wide eyes, the breeze from the west ruffling the robe on her statuelike form. That I would actually abandon, forever, the land holding my ancestors, let alone take the name of Yahweh as my covenantal God, astounded her. "Ruth—"

"I will not leave, Naomi."

She opened her mouth, then shut it, looking at me helplessly, a frown appearing between her eyes. Her lips tightened, and she looked away. Finally, she started toward the Jordan in silence.

Harp bumping against my side in time with my pounding heart, I followed. The expression on her face as she had turned away had revealed her feelings, and my heart sank. I would have to prove myself to her again. She didn't want me with her in Israel.

Can I blame her? I thought, smiling grimly to myself. I was a seductive Moabite, a tempter of Israelite men, bringing death and destruction. I was an enemy. What would people think if she returned with someone like me in her shadow? They would probably assume that her sons had died as punishment for marrying Moabite blood.

Her back rigid, Naomi walked without looking back. For all I knew, the same thoughts had been running through her mind. Maybe I would never convince her I was good enough in Israel. Well, whatever happened, Yah had chosen me, and that would have to suffice. Besides, I dared not stay.

~ ~ ~

About noon we came to a small inn by the road. Stopping, we both took long drinks from the well. Without a word Naomi went to a bench beneath a shade tree. I followed her. The inn was small but neat, the stones by the door and around the well carefully swept. The aroma of fresh bread filled the air, and my mouth watered.

Naomi sat stiffly, as if next to a stranger that she didn't want to know. In uncomfortable silence I watched the shadows crawl across the stones, wondering again why Naomi continued to struggle with such bitter grief.

I mourned Mahlon, but Naomi seemed certain that all that remained for her was the grave. As a widow without sons, she might be on the fringes of society, which classified women in relation to a man, but then as a widow, she also had complete freedom to conduct business, own land, and make a place for herself. It would take work, but she didn't even seem willing to try.

Another figure approached us on the road, the man obviously used to traveling with a donkey following along behind him. He wore a plain brown kilt and shirt. We watched him stop at the well, water his animal, and drink. After wiping his mouth on the back of his hand, he adjusted the short sword at his girdle before approaching us and nodding his head at Naomi.

"Shalom, Geberet Naomi. Who is your companion?"

"This is Ruth."

The man waited, but she refused to look at either of us or say anything more.

Puzzled, he turned to me. "I'm Pashur, a buyer of wool. I understand that Naomi wishes to return to Bethlehem."

"I'm going with her, geber," I replied, liking the steady way his grayish eyes studied the two of us. His movements reminded me of King Hissil's sword instructor, and I suspected the man would be skilled with the weapon he carried.

Pashur turned to Naomi again, waiting for comment, but she let the uncomfortable silence stretch. "Have you eaten?" he finally asked.

I didn't think she heard him—she had that blank look in her eyes. "No, we have not," I answered for us both.

"I'll get something then," the merchant said. He returned shortly with some bread, goat cheese, and dried figs. Naomi paid no attention until I placed some of the food in her hands and urged her to eat.

After we finished, he checked the pack on his donkey, and I joined him. There were some things I needed to know. "Geber Pashur, how was Yidla?"

"He's fine," the man replied without thinking, then jerked his head up. "How do you know Yidla?"

"We've been friends since my childhood," I answered, satisfied that I had guessed correctly. "He taught me many things, among them to worship Yah."

"Would you be the Rut' Yidla has talked about for so many years?"

"Probably." My harp strap slipped from my shoulder, and I pulled it up again, settling the instrument more securely with my left hand.

For an instant his eyes sharpened, taking me in, his glance lingering on the slight bump made by the signet ring under my robe. Then he turned and looked at Naomi, who was still staring into space.

"Why would a Moabite worship Yahweh?"

"Why would Yidla?"

Pashur rubbed his black hair and stared at me.

"Do you object to traveling with a Moabite back to your land?" I asked directly, knowing it was better to face things up front than let them sour in the background.

"That depends," he said, turning back to the donkey and tightening the pack saddle. "How long has Naomi been like this?"

"Since Mahlon died six months ago," I answered, adjusting the harp strap again.

"I didn't realize she was grieving this deeply. It will be a welcome help to have someone along who can care for her. I'm just puzzled over why you would do so."

"Would you expect a daughter of hers to leave her?"

"Of course not!" he said indignantly.

"Then why ask me? Because I'm a Moabite?"

At least he had the grace to blush.

"You must not think much of my people."

Stung, he glanced up, leading the donkey from the patch of grass beside the inn toward the bench where Naomi waited. "I would expect it of you with your own family and people."

I jerked my chin up. "She became family. I loved her before I loved her son."

Pashur rubbed the back of his head again, studying me anew. "Have you any idea what you're in for?"

"If your assumptions about me just now are any indication, I think so."

"Yahweh be with you, Ruth. You'll need Him. I'll take you and Naomi into Judah." He took the bundles I carried and tied them onto the donkey, making sure to keep the load balanced. Then resting his hand on the animal's neck, he gazed down the road. "Yahweh works in strange ways, Ruth, nor is He limited to means that are acceptable to us. I'm traveled enough to understand that, but others won't. Especially the hill people in Judah. Naomi obviously requires someone to take care of her, and she will never go to her clan for help, so she's going to need you. Let's hope that makes enough difference."

After a final look around, he announced, "I'm ready, geberet," and Naomi left the bench and started down the road without noticing either of us.

What am I getting myself into? I wondered. *What did Pashur mean about Naomi not going to her clan for help?* I watched her straight, unyielding back in front of me, and sighed. I would just have to win her acceptance again. The first time all she had needed was the assurance that I wouldn't woo her son away from El-Shaddai. What would it be now?

"Yah, go with me," I whispered as I followed the wool buyer and my mother-in-law down the road.

~ ~ ~

We paused at the Jordan ford at noon the next day, the river still high from the winter rains and the snowmelt from Mount Hermon. The tops of brushy Euphrates poplars protruded above the muddy water. Pashur told me it was an odd tree, with different-shaped leaves as it aged. Soggy debris drifting down with the flood floated against the bank, momentarily free of the current. On Jordan's other side the road continued to wind through the blindingly white valley to Jericho, where palm trees clustered thickly in the distance. Farther south, the land rose again to the escarpments around the Salt Sea.

As we waited for the ferry, I stared at the water. This was truly the point of no return for me. Once I crossed Jordan I would be in territory controlled by the tribe of Benjamin, the people who had assassinated my grandfather. Over there I would be the foreigner, invading the land of Kemosh's rival and trusting completely in the hesed of a God who had no reason to keep faith with me. How could I be such a fool?

Pashur eyed me. "Second thoughts?"

"Yes, but I dare not go back." I answered so softly I wasn't certain he heard.

Most of the trees left by the ford were young elms. We avoided the better shade of the plane tree, not wanting to chance the irritation to the skin and eyes caused by the tiny hairs that covered the leaves. Naomi sat on a stump, looking at nothing, lost again in her world of grief.

Our guide shook his head. "I can hardly believe she's the same person."

"I know." I bit my lips, unable to continue. The donkey yanked a mouthful of grass from the ground and blew through its nostrils.

"Pashur, you've been very kind to me, and I would presume on your kindness a little," I said, setting my harp beside me. "Why won't Naomi go to her clan for help?"

The wool buyer rubbed the back of his head, a habit of his, I decided, and twisted his mouth wryly. "It's an ugly story. But maybe it is something I should open your ear about."

I stiffened, the phrase tightening my stomach. What could be vitally important about the answer to my question?

"Naomi comes from a respected clan in Bethlehem," he continued. "Her mother, Madana, had a much older half sister and brother named Abigail and Besai. Madana's mother was never well after her birth, so Abigail took care of her.

"One day a Levite named Ushna arrived in Bethlehem, looking for a place to settle. He saw Abigail and took her for a concubine. From all appearances, she was willing at first, and her father and brother were favorable to the match. Having a Levite in the family had its advantages. But you might not understand that."

"Naomi has told me much of Israel," I replied, pushing my hair back over my shoulders. "I'm aware of the Levites' place in the worship of Yahweh. I can imagine that such a connection would bring advantages."

Pashur nodded. "Ushna never found anything in Bethlehem that really satisfied him, so he went back to Ephraim, taking Abigail with him. No one knows what happened in the hill country, but she arrived back home alone one day, and whenever anyone mentioned Ushna, her lips tightened and her eyes flashed. Then about four months later he appeared with two loaded donkeys and a servant. A man named Micah in the north had hired him to be a priest, and he wanted Abigail to go with him.

"Besai and her father were delighted. Ushna stayed about three days longer than he wanted to while Abigail's brother and father tried to convince her to go with him."

He paused, looking at Naomi, but she seemed completely oblivious to our conversation. Still, he lowered his voice. "Eventually Ushna decided to leave without her, but Abigail's father coaxed him to delay while Besai did everything he could to persuade her to go. She finally consented. Even though it was late in the afternoon, Ushna refused to stay in Bethlehem any longer. They left for Jebus.

"For some reason, the Levite didn't take accommodations there, but continued on to Gibeah in Benjamin another four or five miles north. He went to the marketplace as any stranger would, but the Gibeanites weren't feeling hospitable that day, and no one invited him to stay the night. It was almost dark when a fellow Ephraimite offered to take them in, knowing it was dangerous to sleep outside of house walls."

Pashur spat on the ground, then swallowed. He cast a side-glance at me. "Gibeah was a rough town, and not all that safe even within house walls. Some of the townsmen had noticed Ushna's arrival and decided they could have some sport with him. I don't know if they planned on acting like Sodomites, or if they got drunk first, but they went to the house and demanded that the Levite be sent out to them, if you take my meaning."

I nodded. I knew such things were done by some.

"The householder offered the men his daughter and Abigail instead. But they wanted that Levite. To make a sordid story short, Ushna shoved Abigail out the door. When he went out in the morning, she was dead on the doorstep."*

Turning away, I clenched my teeth, stomach churning. "I think

* See Judges 19.

I've heard the rest of this," I said. "Naomi's aunt was the woman cut in pieces and sent to all the tribes. That started the war with Benjamin. As I recall, it almost completely wiped out that tribe."

Pashur grimaced. "Naomi's mother, Madana, never forgave her father and half brother for practically forcing Abigail to go back to Ushna. She passed on her dislike to her daughter, and for good reason. Besai would do nearly anything for gain, and his son, Tobeh, is the same. Tobeh's a big man around Bethlehem now. You, especially, should stay clear of him. He's not to be trusted."

Although I fully understood why I needed to know this, it still shook me. But I steadied my mind with the thought that Yah already knew the circumstances and would take care of them for us as He had for Jacob when he met his twin brother that first time coming back from Haran.

"I'm glad you told me, Pashur. It will be difficult to get along without clan help, but difficult sounds preferable to what could be our lot in Tobeh's household."

"Infinitely preferable."

The Time of Ripening

What a decision to make, to leave behind everything that makes you who you are! Truly, Yahweh selected well when He chose this woman. She did more than even our ancestor Abraham did, for Abraham had the promise that Yahweh would be with him and give him the land to which he traveled. Ruth had none of that. She had only the faith that a strange and wonderful God had chosen and loved her. Do you wonder that He gave her so many years of happiness? Can you not see the ripening kernels of grain waiting to burst out as soon as the rains cease?

Yahweh is working swiftly now, for harvesttime is all but here. While those in Bethlehem reap their fields, Yahweh will be working for the final ripening of His harvest, and He must complete the job of transplanting his precious crop from Moab. It will take a little time, but there is just enough left, for Yahweh's timing is always perfect.

Spring
Iyar, second month, first day, Ruth's twenty-second year
(1100 B.C.)

Pashur had left us. I walked slightly behind Naomi, since she seemed to prefer me there rather than beside her. She hadn't said a word all day.

We had only one more mile to Bethlehem, and farmsteads lined the road most of the way. Naomi looked around in surprise as we walked. Things must have changed a lot in 10 years. We crested a hill, and across the tiny plain, Bethlehem crowned the opposite rise. To me, It looked large. Probably 150 people dwelled inside its walls, with another 100 living in caves and adjacent farmsteads.

Naomi slowed. I followed silently, carrying the one bundle of things we had left. We'd eaten all the food days ago, and I'd spent all but one silver gerah since then. If it hadn't been for the wool merchant, I don't know how we would have managed.

Adjusting the harp strap on my back, I studied my new home. The walls were mostly continuous, but I saw some places where gaps still existed. Many of those were being built up, even though it looked as if the town had escaped attack for years. People stared as we passed by. Most of them looked well, but I could see the lingering effects of hunger on the very young and very old.

Picking our way across the streamlet still running through the valley, we followed the road between the walled vineyards on the slope leading up to the town. Gardens crowded the walls on each side of the gate. Not much was going on today. Three or four town elders sat in the shade on the stone benches at the gate, discussing something among themselves and watching the people come and go.

I noticed one man in particular, dressed in a brightly colored robe. He had a long thin nose with a scowl under it and stared at Naomi intently. When his gaze focused on me, his gray eyes widened with desire as a flush suffused his face. I drew my harp closer to my side. Something about him said that he'd take anything he could, and his expression told me he wouldn't be particular about whether or not I wanted to give it. I tensed inside, feeling cold and frightened.

Turning away, I edged closer to Naomi. In the square the lazy noise of late afternoon bargaining swirled around us. For the first time, my mother-in-law hesitated. Had she finally realized we had no place to spend the night? Elimelech's family would have long ago put their old rooms to use, and if what Pashur had told me was true, she would not go to her own clan.

The scent of dates drifted by, and Naomi glanced toward its source. Both of us were hungry, and the dates smelled very good. I fingered my last gerah. I had enough to get us some bread and dates for supper, with a bit left over for the next day or two. By then I'd need to find some way to get food.

Taking Naomi's arm, I led her to the date stall. "How much for a bunch?" I asked.

"Five coppers," the man replied, studying us.

"Five? For these dates? They've been in the sun all day. One copper should be enough for two bunches."

"One! These are the sweetest dates in the whole valley! The sun only makes them sweeter. Four coppers."

"But I don't need four bunches. I want only one—this one." Another hour in the sun would dry them out too much. "I can take this off your hands before it completely shrivels up. If someone bought then, what would people say of your fruit?"

At the sound of my Moabite accent, the man at the gate turned away in contempt. I sighed in relief. A woman about Naomi's age emerged from behind the stall, watching me narrowly. Her yellow robe and brown sash showed little wear, so her family was probably well off.

"They will say the same of my fruit as always," the vender said. "It's the best around. Now, I can give you this bunch for only two coppers." He picked up another one.

"No one would pay even half a copper for such fruit," I jeered. "Come, one copper for this bunch is a very fair price."

"If I sold all my fruit at that price, I'd starve," he said indignantly.

"But you've already sold all of your best fruit and are left with seconds, so anything you sell now is pure profit. One bunch for hungry travelers, and we shall call on Yahweh to bless your fields for your act of kindness."

A faint smile appeared on the woman's face, and she turned her gray-green eyes on the merchant, who hesitated.

Picking up the dates I wanted, I reached for my gerah. "A bargain?"

Reluctantly the man nodded, and the woman's eyes danced, especially when I handed the silver piece over and the merchant had to produce change. The sour look on his face told me he would have tried harder for a higher price had he known I had any silver.

As I took my coppers, I saw the woman studying Naomi with a puzzled frown. My mother-in-law had her face turned to the side, apparently looking at something else. I touched her arm again. "Naomi?"

"It is!" the woman gasped. "After all these years! Madiya, Madiya, come quickly; it's Naomi!" she shouted, gesturing to a woman about my age with a pretty, animated face in the next stall.

"Naomi!" Madiya shrieked, running from the stall. "Tashima, are you certain?"

Laughing, the two women converged on Naomi, pushing me aside, their cries of shock and delight drawing a crowd. Word spread rapidly, and soon other women ran toward us.

"Who is it?"

"Naomi!"

"Can it be true? After so long?"

"Where?"

"There, see, with Tashima. Naomi, how are you? What has happened?"

Some of the men at the gate looked in our direction and drifted closer to swell the rapidly growing crowd. In spite of the chattering, I stayed at Naomi's side. She hadn't said a word, just looked from face to face, accepting the hugs of welcome, tears streaming from her eyes.

"Quiet, now!" the one called Tashima finally ordered. "She can't get a word in edgewise. What a surprise this is to see you, Naomi!"

The women subsided, some shushing children who were asking impatiently what the fuss was about.

"It will be so good to have you back again," Tashima added. "Our grandchildren can play together, and with the drought over, things will be pleasant again!" The crowd laughed at the wordplay with Naomi's name.

"I'm not Naomi," my mother-in-law said in a low voice, drawing amazed looks from the women around. "El-Shaddai has made my life very bitter, and I am Marah now." A buzz of whispers and comments rippled through the crowd as the smiles of welcome faded.

"What has El-Shaddai done against you?" Tashima asked, looking from Naomi to me and back again. "Why should we call you 'bitter'?"

I felt the rich man's eyes on me again and shivered. He pushed his way closer, listening intently for my mother-in-law's answer.

"Elimelech, Chilion, and Mahlon lie in a Moabite grave," she said, her voice trembling. "El-Shaddai condemned me without trial, falsely stripped me of everything, and brought me back with nothing of value. He has made bitterness my lot, and that is how I shall be known."

Naomi's words brought my attention back to her. I'd been right. If she thought of me at all, it was as a useless weight tied to her.

"All dead!" Madiya gasped, her eyes round. "We'd heard of Elimelech's death, but your sons? Oh, Naomi, how terrible! When did this happen?" The women crowded around again, this time to offer comfort.

My mother-in-law couldn't answer.

"Chilion died more than seven months ago, and Mahlon not long after," I said.

Tashima and Madiya looked surprised that I would speak. They had probably assumed I was Naomi's bondwoman. But I paid little attention to them, keeping my eye on the rich man. His mouth turned up in a nasty-looking smile, and his eyes wandered over me again before he shoved his way out of the crowd and strode off.

Naomi's back had gone rigid when I spoke. She was probably afraid I would say I was Mahlon's widow. While I knew the truth would come out sooner or later, it didn't have to be right this minute.

The buzz of conversation swelled as she still remained silent, unable to control her weeping. Tashima took her into her arms, and the other women murmured condolences, many crying in sympathy. The men drew away with much to discuss, for with the males of Elimelech's line dead, something must be done about the family land.

I suspected that the man I had seen had already thought of this, and I'd bet anything he was Naomi's kinsman, Tobeh, whom Pashur had warned me about. He hadn't offered help, or even let Naomi see him. No wonder she wanted nothing to do with him.

As Naomi continued to weep in her arms, Tashima told the other women, "Don't bother her now. Madiya, send everyone home. We can all talk to Naomi later. She's exhausted and needs rest. Go on home."

Gratefully I watched the crowd disperse in excited groups. Tashima shooed the last ones away and drew Naomi into the shelter of the house behind the stall. I followed, sitting beside my mother-in-law.

"Tashima, is there somewhere we could go?" I asked. "I'd like to get Naomi to eat something if I can."

Giving me another startled look, the woman rose. "Come to my house. We can discuss things there." Her hair was streaked with gray, and she had a quick wit and ready tongue as she replied to several comments on our way to a large compound in the middle of town. A two-story house like my parents' stood on one corner. A large common courtyard separated it from another smaller house and some rooms opposite.

After she led us across the courtyard, we sat by the door of the smaller house. Setting my harp and bundle on the ground, I turned to Naomi. "It's time to eat now," I said a bit loudly, trying my best to get her attention.

She didn't respond.

"They're good dates, Naomi. Eat them."

Tashima frowned, looking into her old friend's vacant brown eyes.

"Eat the food, Naomi," I encouraged. "They're your favorite and very good."

At last Naomi put the fruit into her mouth. Tashima watched as I pitted more for her and gave her the last of the bread I'd purchased yesterday. Our host brought some wine, which we drank.

"Thank you," I said. "My name is Ruth. Do you know a place where Naomi and I can stay?"

"But surely you are going to her family?" the woman asked, looking surprised.

"Naomi doesn't want to," I explained. "I understand Geber Tobeh is not an attractive situation."

Her eyes narrowed. "You're right about that. I can see several objections to becoming part of his household, especially if Naomi truly has no one."

I told her in more detail how Chilion and Mahlon had died.

"So you were married to Mahlon?" she asked, studying me.

"Yes." I pressed my lips together and took a deep breath. "He was a good man."

"From the clan of Ephrath, he would be," she remarked, then stood. "Now for a place to stay. Most of the suitable caves nearby are already taken, but if you don't mind tiny, I think I know of a place. It's too late today to do any inquiring. Stay with us tonight, and in the morning we can check into the house. It's just a single room in the corner of the wall, but the roof is good, and it's not far from the market."

"Thank you, Tashima. Yahweh will grant you hesed for this."

Iyar, second month, second day (1100 B.C.)

The next morning I followed her to the living quarters she had mentioned. It was indeed small, and had probably been a storeroom at one time, but new construction had isolated it and enclosed it in a pocket approached by a narrow opening between another house and the city wall. A small cleared space in front would serve for a courtyard and cooking fire, the roof was in good repair as Tashima had said, and we should be able to find some way to separate the small space into storage and living quarters.

It was extremely dirty, however. As I went inside, some sparrows fluttered past my head in dismay, scolding loudly. From the looks of the floor, bats as well as sparrows had roosted here. There were no windows. I thought of Ithmah's house in Heshbon with its two stories, windows, and shaded roof, and sighed.

Well, I was destitute now and would have to accept what I could find. "This will do, Tashima."

"I know it's not much," the woman said doubtfully, "but it's the only thing I can think of right now. There are a lot of empty rooms in family households because of the long drought, but I doubt anyone would offer any of them."

I shrugged. "I can't blame them. Two indigent widows couldn't pay much rent, and we can hardly expect another clan to support us, especially since I'm a foreigner."

Tashima gave me another look from her sharp eyes. "A lot of people here will treat strangers courteously, unless Adon Tobeh says otherwise, and then most will simply leave you alone."

"The adon's influence is that strong?" I asked, staring at the wall, wondering if staying out of his clutches might be harder than I thought.

"I'm afraid so. Only one man in town is willing to ignore Tobeh's displeasure, but until he returns, no one else will dare. Tobeh has a reputation for repaying those who don't agree with him."

"I'll keep that in mind," I murmured.

"You're wise."

"Here you are," Madiya exclaimed, peering down the narrow opening to the space. "Shalom. I've been looking all over. I wanted to help Naomi move in. When will your things be here?"

I held up the bundle I carried. "They are here."

"But surely you have more?" the woman exclaimed as she hurried toward us, her gray robe and sash nearly as worn as my brown one.

I shook my head. "We lost everything."

"Do you have more silver?"

"No, I used the last gerah to buy the dates last night. All I have left are the coppers I received in change."

"Quickly, Madiya, start collecting necessities," Tashima directed. "If we hurry, we can get most of what they'll need before Tobeh has a chance to interfere should he want to. That room is completely empty. See if you can find storage jars or a couple of pithoi and something for Naomi to sit on. I'll worry about dishes and cooking utensils."

"We'll need a loom," I added.

Tashima looked at me, amazed.

"Weaving is the only thing that Naomi responds to right now."

Madiya looked up, her bright eyes curious, black hair bouncing. "What do you mean?"

Tashima gave her a grim look. "After you collect things, come to my house and see for yourself. Naomi just sits and stares. Hasn't said a word since yesterday. She acts just as old Helas did when we were little."

"Oh," Madiya said, her faced strained. "He died."

"Naomi considers herself dead already," I put in.

"I wondered about that yesterday when she accused Yahweh of injustice," Tashima said with a sigh. "They always worshipped faithfully and brought offerings and sacrifices, so Naomi would expect blessings. And they were always prosperous when many others weren't."

"Until the drought?" I questioned.

"Yes. Off with you, Madiya. Ruth, come back to my house and get a broom and some rags to clean with. You'll have to carry water since this place has no cistern. Then you can clean while Madiya and I scrounge for you."

I followed them down the alley and into the market. "You're very kind, Tashima. I didn't expect so much."

"You're with Naomi, and she's a favorite around here—or she was. Many's the time she helped us out in any number of ways. It's our turn now."

"Here's a broom and some rags," she continued when we reached her house. "You can find your way back?"

"Yes. I'll go as soon as I check on Naomi."

With a nod, Tashima hurried off.

Naomi sat by the cooking fire in the courtyard, staring into space. She hadn't combed her hair this morning, and I noticed her faded green robe was nearly worn through in places. We'd need clothes soon.

"Naomi, I found a place for us to stay," I said. "It's pretty small, but it will keep the rain off, and we'll manage. Tashima and Madiya are helping me get it ready. When I come back, I'll take you to it."

My mother-in-law nodded absently.

Her lack of interest disturbed me. What could I do to help her regain the will to live? What did she need? I must find out soon.

By noon Madiya came puffing into our little courtyard with a mended stool, an old cloak, and two more pottery dishes. "It's a good thing we started when we did," she commented, surveying the pile of miscellaneous castoffs in front of her. "Tobeh has the word out, and two people who promised me things refused to give them when I went to pick them up. I think this is all you'll get."

"It's not much," I replied, struggling with my dismay at what little I had to start housekeeping with. I had four lids for pithoi, but no pithoi; two broken brooms out of which I could make one good one; three cracked cups; five bowls, no two alike; one water jug with a crack in one shoulder; a very dull bronze knife; a large krater bowl with an edge broken off; and a three-legged stool with only two legs, in addition to the stool, cloak, and pottery dishes Madiya held.

Yah, what am I to do? I cried inwardly. *Please, send us all that we need. Especially the loom. Naomi will die without one.*

"It's not enough," Madiya said. "You can't possibly live with just this. Where will you put food?"

That was a moot question, since we had none at the moment.

"Madiya, are you back there?" someone called softly.

"Yes. Who is it?"

"It's Gershed. I'm to dump these two storage jars. Do you know a junk pile I can put them on?"

The man was a stout, cheerful Phoenician with thin brown hair and a hooked nose.

Madiya stared at him. "But we need those!" she sputtered. "You said—"

"Perhaps you better not hold him to that promise," I said, eyeing the man. "We wouldn't want trouble with Adon Tobeh. But if you're looking for the nearest trash heap, we've got one right here. Bring them on back."

He disappeared, then struggled down the narrow entrance with the first of the jars. His eyes widened at the sight of our pathetic pile, but he kept a straight face.

"Definitely a trash pile. Couple more trips, and I'll be done."

Madiya could hardly control her laughter as Gershed solemnly placed the large jars on the ground. As he left, he looked at her.

"You know, I saw Banael wandering toward the gate with a bundle. He said something about his wife not wanting it any longer. He should be almost to the gate now."

The woman ran down our alley.

I finished sweeping out the room and had started sweeping the walls to remove the cobwebs and dust when I heard Tashima call my name.

"It's indecent, Ruth," she said in frustration, "but Tobeh has let it be known that he doesn't like Moabites. He said they deserved no better than the trash heap. Now he's had one of his servants following me, making sure no one would give me the time of day whenever I asked people for whatever they could spare. If I'd known he would do this, I would have started collecting things yesterday."

"This the new trash heap?" someone asked from the entrance to the alley.

"Yes," I replied. "Just leave whatever you have."

With a wink, the man did, Tashima sputtering as he departed.

"How dare he say that!" she fumed. "When I get my way with Tobeh, I'll tell him who's the trash heap in this town! And you shouldn't let him trample on you this way," she went on.

"I don't mind being part of a trash heap," I said with a smile, my heart suddenly light with anticipation. The bundle contained two robes, one for Naomi and one for me. Obviously, Yah could supply what we needed from the town's garbage if He wished.

And He did. All day long various householders, wives, servants, and messengers found their way down our little narrow entrance while taking out their trash. Before long, Tashima and Madiya had to help me sort through the items.

As evening approached, the contributions slowed down. I glanced at the piles of items spread around our little courtyard. We had more than enough to begin housekeeping. By now we had four pithoi, all that would fit into our small room, three empty storage jars, and three more full ones, two with olive oil and one with wine. The servant who delivered them solemnly assured us that his geber had declared them spoiled and unfit to use. Tashima and I had been able to put together a curtain to separate off the storage area. The curtain was quite colorful and somewhat varied in length, but it did the job.

A carpenter had come, sorted through our "trash" to find the materials to repair three stools and a small table, then, declaring he was too tired to carry them off, left them with me. The various bundles contained enough food to last us for a little while.

"Well, I must say, this has been quite a day," Tashima sighed, stretching her back. "I never knew so many people to decide to clean house on the same day before. What's the matter, Ruth? You keep looking at the alley. Expecting something?"

Embarrassed, I glanced away. How could I explain that I expected a loom? Yah had seen to it that we had everything but the one thing absolutely necessary to Naomi, and I couldn't imagine He'd forget that.

"Madiya? You still there?" Gershed called.

"We're here," she answered.

"Here, help me get this off the street before anyone sees."

"What is it?" Tashima asked.

"It's a loom," I said without thinking. "Put it here. The sun will warm Naomi in the mornings, but it will be shaded in the hot afternoons."

"No one is going to throw out a loom!" she gasped.

"Tashima, it's a loom!" Madiya squealed.

"Shush!" Gershed commanded. "Help me get this off the cart."

We all carried the pieces of it into the courtyard, and he set them up again before he left. As he worked, Tashima kept looking at the loom with the strangest expression on her face, while he carefully avoided her eyes. I wondered why.

"Gershed, carry our wishes for Yahweh's blessings to your mistress," I said. "She is kinder than we deserve."

"She has no need of this any longer," he said with a sad smile.

Tashima insisted on going back with him, much to his dismay, puzzling me further. She said she'd bring Naomi when she returned.

While Madiya sorted through the last of the items, I prepared supper. We borrowed coals from a neighbor and burned the wood from a stack the local woodcutter left because it was "too short" for his customers.

Naomi looked no farther than the loom when she arrived, clinging to Tashima. Quickly inspecting it, she then sat down in front of it.

"I'll speak to Geber Hasi, the cloth-merchant," Tashima said to me. "I know he needs some help, and it will give Naomi something to do. You said she's been like this for how long?"

"Ever since Mahlon died."

"And for all the help Tobeh is being, she may as well be dead, too," Tashima said in disgust. "He's probably sitting at home now wondering how to get his hands on Elimelech's land when he should be making sure Naomi has the necessities to live."

"But he doesn't have to, so long as she doesn't go to his house."

"No, but that doesn't remove his moral responsibility. Naomi is his own cousin!"

"Maybe he would have helped if I hadn't come," I sighed.

"That had nothing to do with it. It just gave him a convenient excuse," she snorted. "If you hadn't arrived, he would have just found another, or forced Naomi to turn her rights to the land over to him."

"Rights?"

The woman nodded. "As Elimelech's widow, Naomi has usufruct rights to the land as long as she lives. She has the right to gain her living from it. Either she can sell that right, or the land, or ask for it to be redeemed in lieu of sale."

"Redeemed?" I'd heard of land redemption before, but didn't understand anything about it.

"If a landowner becomes too poor, he can sell the use of his land, or the land itself, to another for a certain length of time. At the end of that time, if he cannot buy the land back, he can go to a close relative and ask them to be a goel, a redeemer. The goel then is responsible for purchasing back the land so that the man and his family will not lose their inheritance."

"What happened to Elimelech's land when he went to Moab?"

"It's been a long time now, but I think he sold the rights to it to a couple people. One man got the fields and another the vineyard and olive grove. The term was for five years, I think. The elders would remember."

"But Elimelech was gone 10 years. What happened then?"

"The same men are still using the land. Not that Tobeh didn't try to get his hands on it, but he didn't have quite enough influence then. Now that Chilion and Mahlon are dead, however, you may be sure he's got a plan to obtain the property."

She stopped, her eyes flashing. "You know, I'll bet that's why he didn't want anyone to help you two! If Naomi is forced back to his household to stay alive, he'll automatically get control of her rights. Then he wouldn't have to buy them."

I stirred the stew over the fire, trying to decide the best way to use Naomi's land rights. "When could we sell or ask for redemption?" I asked.

"You'll have to wait until after harvest for Naomi to put forward her claim. It might be best to sell them for part of the harvest next year. But you'll have to find someone who will be willing to brave Tobeh's displeasure as well as stay out of Tobeh's control until the harvest comes in. That's a long time, and Tobeh's been known to do almost anything." Naomi's old friend spread out a cloth on the ground and set out my "new" bowls and some bread and cheese.

"Sounds as though Tobeh has a stranglehold on the town." I checked the stew again. It was nearly done.

"In some ways he does," the woman replied. "He either owns, controls, or has influence over half the land in the area. I've heard stories about how he does things, but no one's willing to take him to the gate and accuse him openly. Several of the elders favor him because of his wealth, and Boaz is the only one in town who cares nothing about him and is also wealthy enough to ignore him."

"What's his name again?" I asked, thinking of what Ithmah always said. "The enemy of my enemy is my friend." I needed all the friends I could find if I was to support Naomi and myself through an entire year and fight for land rights with the wealthiest man in town.

"Adon Boaz. He's gone now; otherwise, Tobeh wouldn't have gotten half as far against you as he has. If things get really desperate, go to him. He's helped many people in the past, especially those that Tobeh gets his claws into."

"I'm a Moabite," I said doubtfully, ladling out the stew into the bowls Tashima held for me.

"But Naomi is not. He'll help," she assured me. "He's the only reason Tobeh hasn't gained control of everything. Well, I'd better go get food ready for my own family."

"Yahweh reward you, Tashima. You've been so helpful."

She smiled. "Naomi and I grew up together. I couldn't let her sleep in the streets. Shalom."

"Shalom." I watched her leave. *Well, Yah, I think I made a friend today, or maybe two. Even though we arrived with nothing, You've already begun to fill us. We have what we need for our house, and I know You'll provide more food when this is gone.*

I went over to Naomi, who was still sitting by the loom.

"Tomorrow we'll get something for you to weave," I promised, taking her hand and helping her to the mat by the fire so we could eat. Afterward, I sat outside and played my harp to help her sleep.

Iyar, second month, second day, Boaz's forty-third year (1100 B.C.)

Taking a seat in the shade of the gate at Tekoa, Boaz prepared to be patient. The gate was hardly more than a standing stone on each side of the pathway with seats for a couple people. It looked a bit odd because of the absence of any town walls. Today was the second one he'd spent waiting for Domla the merchant, who should arrive at any moment according to the servants. His tall frame drawing glances even in repose, Boaz stirred restlessly. More than one woman's glance lingered on his thick chestnut-brown hair.

Lost in thought even while alert for the appearance of Tekoa's principal inhabitant, he didn't notice the attention he attracted. Under his gray cloak, his linen robe reached to his ankles, woven of dark blue with discreet red stripes for contrast, the required tassel on each corner. A red girdle of fine wool had a short fringe, the one obvious mark of his status. Other than that, he let the quality of the cloth speak for itself.

Normally he would have enjoyed watching the people entering and departing the little settlement, but the memory of last night's nightmare wouldn't leave his mind. During the past few years his habitual nightmare had become vague and shadowy, generally coming in fragments, waking him with his body bathed in sweat and a knot in his stomach. But last night it had been vivid and disturbing, and he couldn't shake it off.

Leaning his head against the rock behind him, he clenched his fists to stop the trembling in his arms. That faint, mocking laugh echoed in his imagination, taunting him. A frown appeared between his eyebrows. In all the years he'd had this dream, he'd never realized before how familiar that laughter was.

"Ah, Boaz! Shalom. What brings you here so close to harvest?"

He glanced up. "Shalom, Ahinadab! I should be asking you that question. Surely you have not come to little Tekoa for elegant pottery for your shop."

The Jebus merchant chuckled as Boaz rose. "Hardly, although I wish I could. The last shipment had two items arrive in pieces at the Jebus gates, and that lice-infested caravanner tried to charge me for them."

"Naturally you didn't pay," Boaz said, amused.

"Naturally. And by the time I was done with that scraggly-bearded maggot, he was only too happy to depart."

Knowing the range of scorching epithets at the Ammonite's disposal, Boaz could well imagine this was strict truth. "So what does bring you here, Ahinadab? Surely you have not followed that unfortunate caravanner to these gates?"

Ahinadab snorted. "And waste more of my valuable time on that braying toad? I have dispensed with him entirely, and when I return, I must find a new man to transport my orders from the Joppa port."

"I may be able to help you with that. Contact Tahat of Jericho. He should be in the Jebus area. Tell him I recommended him to you."

"I'll do that. Your recommendations are always good ones. But I am here to find figs. I bought some from a new vendor in the market last month, and those were the sweetest figs my wife ever tasted. She insists it must be something in the soil where they were grown that makes them that way, and she must have more."

"And how is Anamot?" Boaz asked, walking with his friend into the marketplace.

"Crying for sweet figs," the merchant answered resignedly, brushing away an impertinent lad selling trinkets. "Nothing would do but for me to leave the shop in the care of my worthless assistant and traipse the country inquiring after a common fig seller, as if I had nothing better to do than cater to my wife's desires. I shall probably return home figless to find my shop a rubble, my assistant and any proceeds gone, and my wife so incensed at my failure that she will turn me into the streets like a common beggar."

Boaz couldn't keep the little smile off his face and tried to hide it by stroking his beard. The Ammonite merchant's gloom always amused him, since it concealed an extremely shrewd mind and an undying passion for the maligned wife.

One look at Boaz, and Ahinadab fought to suppress a twisted smile of his own. Hastily he looked away.

"Which means that you have tasted something very unusual indeed," Boaz laughed, "and sense an opportunity to take yet more silver from your hapless customers. Just how sweet were these figs?"

"When I find the seller of them, I'll let you buy one from me and try it yourself," he retorted.

Again Boaz smiled to himself as they walked on, for he knew well enough who marketed those figs. It was the first year Eliram had begun to sell them, and the word was spreading rapidly. He'd let Eliram attend to that. The man had shown himself as good a businessman as he was a fig grower. Before long he would pay off his debt, and he and Boaz would begin a formal partnership.

Ahinadab's voice brought his mind back to the present. "But what is your business here? This close to harvest, I expected you to be in Bethlehem."

"I expected to be in Bethlehem," Boaz sighed. "But Geber Domla still owes me for the wine he bought three seasons ago, and I'm determined to get payment. So I sit here like the stones, hoping to trap him."

The merchant thought a moment. "Is Domla a rotund little man with a beaked nose and close-set eyes?"

"Seen him, have you?"

"He's hiding out down the valley. The way he danced around so nervously talking to someone drew my attention as I rode by. I doubt you'll find him coming by this way."

Boaz slapped his thigh in disgust. He should have known that withered old stick of an overseer would find some way to keep his geber out of town.

Ahinadab grinned. "What will you do now?"

"Leave. What else can I do?"

"He'll likely come scuttling into town before the day is out as soon as he thinks you're gone."

"I'm counting on it."

"I thought so. Shalom, Boaz."

"Shalom."

Boaz returned to his seat in disgust. He'd have to play the farce out, sitting here all day, then leaving tomorrow in full view of everyone. After spending the day out in the hills somewhere, he'd slip back into town and beard Domla in his own house about suppertime.

Well, it would be the last time he'd deal with the man. Yet he couldn't resent the sale of the wine, for it had put money into the purses of several struggling families who had entrusted their shares of the vintage to him, and Domla had agreed to a good price. When the Tekoan had failed to bring payment on time, Boaz had quietly paid the others out of his own treasury, knowing he could afford to wait on the defaulter, while the others couldn't.

Settling back and stretching his long legs, Boaz returned to his thoughts and his scrutiny of the people entering the gates. He smiled slightly, remembering Ahinadab's complaints against Anamot. The smile turned a bit sad. The Ammonite's devotion to his wife reminded him painfully of Mena.

From long habit Boaz suppressed the pain that crossed his face. By now he'd gotten very good at hiding it. Suddenly he wanted to be away from the village with its activity, the noise of market hawkers, and the smells of cooking food that floated on the breeze. He longed for the clean, fresh scent of the dark pines, the rustle of the oak leaves, the green of pasturelands below, and the coolness of the deep shade over his head.

With a sigh, he waited out the warm afternoon on the hard seat. Close to sunset, he left for what passed as an inn here. The service and food hadn't improved since his last stay, but he'd have to endure another night.

He ran his hand through his hair, streaked now with gray. As he walked past the entrance to an alley, the corner of his eye caught the movement of someone starting forward, then pulling back. A smile tugged at his lips. Wealthy he might be, and clothed in better garments than most, but he was nonetheless someone an average thief would hesitate to attack.

Ears attentive to any footsteps behind him, he shifted his hold on his staff slightly. Someone else might not be so intelligent as the man who had pulled back into that alley. It was close to dark in the narrow street that led to the inn. He should have departed the market square earlier. And he should also have taken a different route. As he'd traveled this way the two previous nights he'd noticed at least one man watching him.

Something stirred ahead and to the right, and the hair on his neck rose. Although he continued without a break in stride, he'd marked the corner where the movement had been. At least one man there. The tiny street was nearly dark. His imagination might be playing tricks on him, but he didn't think so.

Probably two, he corrected himself. Maybe another behind him. He carefully eased toward the right side of the street. Doing so would give him room to react to whatever might come from the left. Drawing his robes closer, he tightened the girdle.

Was that a darker shadow by the house wall on the left? Maybe. Every sense alert, he kept going, eyes scanning the deserted street. They came from both sides, the one on the left of the narrow street emerging from the shadows first and rushing toward him as the second burst from the corner Boaz had marked.

At the last second he jerked backward, thrusting his staff between the legs of the attacker on the right, his hand gripping the man's arm and shoving him forcefully into his accomplice. The man grunted with the impact, and Boaz pushed past, driving the end of his staff into someone's side, eliciting a gasp of pain. Ahead, a narrow space between two houses offered a sanctuary, and Boaz threw himself into the darkness, pulling his cloak tightly around him lest its lighter color betray his presence.

Flat against the wall, he listened to the confused grunts and thuds from the street.

"Get him! Get him! He's got my neck!"

"I've got him. Get the purse, will you? He's like—"

"Fool! Let me go!"

"What—"

Boaz shifted so he could see better.

The would-be thieves stared up and down the narrow street, now darker than ever. "Where did he go?"

"Idiot! Why didn't you grab him?"

"I did! You shoved him into me just as we had planned."

"That was me, dolt. We'd have had him and his purse if you could be brighter than an ox now and then."

"Me? Why would you come hurtling into my arms? Oh, ho! Missed him, did you? And trying to lay the blame on me! Just wait until I tell this story. You, of all people, missing that large a target. It's worth it to lose his purse for this!"

"Missing the target? He wasn't human. Haven't you figured that out? If he was human, why didn't he shout for the watch? Eh? Or call for help? He just vanished, and there's no way he could have gotten out of the street. I don't know what it was, but that was not a merchant."

His companion snorted. "And if anyone believes that, there are fish with feathers swimming in my wine cup! You just messed up, that's all."

Amused, Boaz watched the two disappear, then made his way to the central square where the inn was. Several animals were already there, and the smaller alleys had been blocked off. He glanced at the corner where he'd caught the young boy stealing his purse years ago. What had been the name? Gaddi. He wondered how the lad was doing and if he had fulfilled his wish to become a Habiru.

Thinking of them brought Pashur to mind, and Boaz knew what he could do the next day while he waited for Domla to return home.

Iyar, second month, third day (1100 B.C.)

Early the next morning Boaz rode his donkey out the gate and down the road. Once out of sight of the town, he turned off into the hills, working his way steadily deeper into the surrounding forest. There he paused in a familiar clearing, one of the places where the Habiru often trained.

Pashur stepped out from the trees, dressed in a soldier's short kilt and with guards on his arms and head. "Took you long enough."

"I didn't know if you were around, and I have all day," Boaz replied, dismounting.

"Good. Just enough time for me to remind you of all the things you've forgotten."

"Maybe," Boaz said, taking off his cloak and laying it carefully out of the way. He stripped to his loincloth, donning the kilt and guards that Pashur tossed him.

"Spears first," Boaz said, adjusting the guards. "It's been awhile."

Nodding amiably, Pashur reached for the long spears leaning against a tree. He tossed one to Boaz, who whirled it in his hands once, shoved the head into the ground, and snapped the shaft in two.

"Now, you demon, give me a good one!"

Laughing, Pashur tossed him a second one, which Boaz looked

over carefully. The shaft was smooth with use, but the head was still firmly attached. Tall as he was, the spear reached over his head. Facing his friend, they began the familiar drills.

It felt good. As he warmed up, his movements became smooth and sure, the muscles in his arms and legs responding to the exercise like those of a younger man. Although Boaz knew he was middle-aged, the training and hard work of his youth had given him immense strength, which he still retained.

"Ready?" Pashur asked.

Boaz nodded. Abandoning the drills, they sparred, and the Habiru soon bested him.

"You always could beat me with a spear," Boaz gasped, rubbing his right arm where his friend had struck, making him lose hold of the weapon.

"Only because you can't bring your strength to bear easily," Pashur admitted. "Amos, bring the water skin, would you?"

When Boaz looked around in surprise, a young man grinned at him, handing him the water. The sparring partners drank deeply. Then they took up swords next, each slipping a shield on his left arm.

"Drills?" Pashur asked.

"Not for me. I feel loose enough."

Nodding, the wool merchant raised his shield and began to circle. Boaz followed him, advancing and striking first. His friend blocked with the heavy bronze center of the hardened-leather shield, the clang of the blow ringing in the small clearing.

As they continued, a light sweat formed on Boaz's face, and his breathing deepened. The grass was trampled around them, and the sun broke through the clouds overhead. What would the townspeople think now, Boaz wondered, blocking a blow with the sword, then lunging forward immediately, only to meet his friend's shield.

If word got out that he still trained with the Habiru and had such close contacts with them, Tobeh would undoubtedly assume it was for nefarious purposes and hint of it to whoever would listen. And that would mean more challenges to his honor and less time to attend to his business, he thought with irritation. Maybe it was time to go on the offensive with Tobeh and—

Pashur suddenly feinted before striking, throwing off Boaz's timing, very nearly landing a solid blow that would have ended the bout. Recovering swiftly, Boaz frowned, his annoyance causing him to pick up the pace of the sparring. The Habiru warrior pushed a little harder, quickening the tempo of his own blows. Suddenly Boaz felt the flat of the sword on his leg. His irritation rose higher. If it had been a real battle, he'd have been down and seriously injured. How had he dropped his guard that much? The glint in his friend's eye didn't help.

Stepping back, Pashur stopped the exercise for another drink. "You haven't forgotten much," he admitted, rubbing his arm.

"But it takes awhile for it to come back," Boaz replied. "If I were in a real battle, I couldn't afford that kind of time."

"I don't know. The danger of a fight often brings things back quicker than you expect. Ready?"

Boaz raised his shield, and they started again. Determined to win, he took the same tack he had on other occasions, subtly driving Pashur into a corner and then wearing him down.

This time, once unable to break out from the corner, Pashur laughed. "Somehow I can never best you on this one. I yield." He tossed the sword to the ground and loosened the shield on his arm. "Amos, bring the water again," he called. The youth approached with the skin, looking at Boaz with undisguised awe.

After drinking, Boaz eased himself to the ground, groaning. "I'm going to be very sore in the morning, I'm afraid."

"You're not the only one," Pashur replied, stretching his arms.

"While I remember, how's Gaddi doing?"

Pashur frowned. "He left us about two months ago. He's been dissatisfied for some time. Although he did well in the training and was the most promising young man with a sword I've ever seen, the routine of practice, chores, farmwork, and more practice grated on his nerves. I think he expected more excitement in a warrior's life."

Boaz shook his head. "I sure hope he doesn't get himself into any trouble. I liked him in spite of the way he tried to take my purse!"

"Too many find themselves too deep in robbery and killing to stop, but I hope he comes around."

"What's the news?" Boaz asked, leaning back and using the arm guards to pillow his head. He closed his eyes.

"Naomi returned to Bethlehem. She came back with a Moabite daughter-in-law and nothing else."

Boaz opened one eye. "But Elimelech was well-to-do."

"They lost everything, including Chilion and Mahlon."

Both eyes now open, he half raised himself from the ground. "I knew Elimelech had died, but not her sons! Who's supporting her?"

"Boaz, think a moment. Who's the closest male relative on her side?"

"Tobeh!" He sat up fully, facing his friend. "She'd die before going to him for help. You said she's alone?"

"No. Mahlon's widow, Ruth, is with her. Good-looking, with uncommonly beautiful eyes. I've never seen any like them before—light brown with darker flecks. She's devoted to Naomi, and right now Naomi's so sunk in grief she hardly knows what's going on around her. Ruth takes care of her as if she were a child and gets no thanks for it. I don't think Naomi is very happy to have her."

"She wouldn't be, since Ruth isn't an Israelite. How do you know all this?"

"During my last trip to Heshbon I heard of Mahlon's death," Pashur explained. "I went to see Naomi, and she wanted to return to Judah, so I offered to bring her. We agreed to meet at an inn. When I arrived at the rendezvous, Ruth was with her. The Moabite did everything for her except chew her food, and Naomi never said a word."

"Is Ruth also alone?"

Pashur rubbed the back of his head. "No. Her father is a scribe for King Hissil, and the family is well-off. Last report we got, Ruth's sister, Orpah, was betrothed to Sakar, one of Hissil's younger sons. Maybe Ruth intends to stay with Naomi until she can live on her own and then go back to Moab. I don't know. Something else interesting is that Ruth worships Yahweh."

Boaz looked up in astonishment. "What about Kemosh?"

"She was a temple singer."

"Did she also serve as qedeshah in the high places?"

Pashur shook his head. "I asked about that, and she said her mother kept her away from the high places. Then she added that she didn't worship Kemosh anyway, just Yahweh."

"It's hard to comprehend Elimelech allowing his sons to marry women of Moab, even ones that worship Yahweh," Boaz said softly and a bit bitterly. "He was always so—righteous. And what Naomi must have thought!"

Pashur cocked his head. "Surprised us, too. From what we gathered, Naomi wasn't too happy with the situation, and I have my doubts about whether she's accepted Ruth even yet. Elimelech probably had his eye on the good connection with the palace she brought."

"That doesn't say much for Elimelech."

The Habiru shrugged. "He always was a weak man. In any case Naomi is not pleased to have Ruth with her now. She's facing enough problems without having a Moabite temple singer for a daughter-in-law, even one who worships Yahweh.

"It would be a big help if you gave them your protection though. If you accept the situation, Tobeh won't be able to turn the entire town against them, and Naomi may have a chance to stay out of that man's clutches."

Boaz did not reply for some time. "You say Ruth cares well for Naomi?"

"Like a true daughter."

"And worships only Yahweh?"

"As near as I can tell."

"Her behavior?"

"During our journey together she conducted herself better than many of the women in Bethlehem."

"She will have to continue that in order to remain here." Boaz's voice was sharp. "I'm trusting you on this, Pashur. I can't afford to lessen my influence in the gate. Tobeh has been generous in all the right places and has gained much support. And Elimelech's land is a prize he can't resist." He leaned back again, thinking intently, speaking mostly to himself.

"My clan has first claim to redeem the *land itself* if Naomi sells, but Tobeh has first claim to redeem the *usufruct rights,* since they are Naomi's. I'm the only one in the Ephrath clan right now who could redeem that large an inheritance, which means Tobeh will have the chance to purchase it outright. If she tries to sell the rights, he can claim his duty as goel to get control of them. Either way he'll get that land," he ended in disgust.

"But you just said you could redeem it," his friend broke in.

"Naomi won't deal with me, Pashur. Have you forgotten?" He sat up slightly.

"But that was years and years ago!"

Boaz shrugged. "I'm just as much a Canaanite now as I was then. She won't consider me trustworthy."

"That's ridiculous, Boaz! After all you've done for the people in Bethlehem?"

"She's been gone 10 years, and her father taught her well. Naomi won't trust me."

The Habiru pounded the ground with his fist in frustration, and Boaz lay back again. After a short pause, Pashur said, "My nephew Patah brought word that Tobeh has begun to gather supporters. He's been giving very select feasts in his home and spending freely. His generosity has about convinced half the town that having him in charge would be a good thing."

Boaz snorted. "He'll get Bethlehem destroyed like Shechem was when Gideon's son Abimelech tried to be king. Yahweh is Israel's king, as that woman in Thebez reminded Abimelech when she dropped the grinding stone on his head."*

"That doesn't matter to Tobeh. He's got Bilgai, Zakkur, Raham, Eprah, and Yattir solidly behind him. They've already discussed details of administration when Bethlehem has a king."

"If he'd keep his mind on his business instead of trying to become king, he'd be twice as wealthy and better off than most kings. He's always been an excellent businessman. What's he thinking?" Boaz shook his head in dismay.

"When it comes to his family honor and position in Bethlehem, Tobeh hasn't been rational since his father died," the Habiru reminded him. "He's a menace to the peace of this land, and we have enough threats coming from outside, what with the Philistines pushing farther and farther into the hill country."

"Maybe it *is* time I gave Tobeh something to occupy his mind," Boaz said with a sigh, gazing up at the sky.

Pashur chuckled and brushed at a fly. "Halve his profits! That'll keep him busy."

---

* See Judges 9.

"All right."

"I'm joking, Boaz." The Habiru shifted to face him.

"I'm not. I'll cut his profits off entirely if he continues to push his idea of becoming a king."

The Habiru stared at him for an uncomfortably long time. "I'm beginning to understand the reputation you have everywhere but here. Does Tobeh have any idea of what you can do?"

"If he took the time to think about it he would. I believe Zakkur has mentioned me to him several times, but Tobeh doesn't appear to have listened."

"You mean he's ignoring something Zakkur said to him?" Pashur asked in amazement, sitting up.

"He thinks Zakkur is chasing phantoms," Boaz said innocently.

"Tobeh won't believe you're wealthy, because you don't flaunt it. Is that it?"

His brown eyes twinkling, Boaz grinned.

Pashur laughed until he lay gasping on the ground. "How long have you had him in a corner?"

"You and Tahat did that for me a couple years before the drought ended."

"But you used up all you had then," the warrior exclaimed, "and all we did was transport grain. How could you have cornered him then?"

"By the end of the drought most landowners were unwilling to ship grain because of the risk of attack. Thanks to the training you gave Tahat's guards, he was able to stay in business, and now he's the only caravanner that serves Bethlehem."

"So Tahat transports anything Tobeh sells or buys?"

Boaz nodded. "Tobeh never should have forced that man off his land. It made him angry enough to break away instead of trying to repay his debt."

"Maybe he's not as oblivious as we think," Pashur suddenly commented, straightening up. "Tobeh met with a Habiru late one night, and Patah overheard them mention taking care of Tahat once and for all. The Habiru was from a southern band. They're trouble and can be vicious when paid to be. I sent a warning to Tahat to be extra careful."

"Good. Tobeh can be vicious too, and he was especially hard during the drought. If he suddenly finds himself in difficulties, he'll receive little help."

"Whereas you emptied your treasury," Pashur said. "And I heard the story of your trip to Shiloh, too."

Boaz flushed, getting up and reaching for the water skin. "There's nothing to that."

"Whether there is or not is immaterial. People believe there is. How many families did you keep alive during that drought as well as sending food to us more than once?"

"I just did what I could. No more nor less than anyone else in my position."

The wool merchant snorted. "Tobeh and those like him did nothing but gain power, and the Elimelechs in town ran away."

Finishing his drink, Boaz passed the skin to Pashur. "Elimelech took a gamble. He wanted to provide an outlet for the vintners in our area to sell for better prices. Had that shop in Heshbon been a success, a lot of families would be better off."

"Maybe, but most people think he deserted during a time of great need. Your trip to Shiloh about wrapped things up for a lot of them." The Habiru climbed to his feet, stretching.

"How do you know about it?" Boaz asked, uncomfortable.

"Did you really think you could keep it a secret?" his friend chuckled. "People sat up and took notice when you left town with two oxen, a ram, and a goat in the middle of famine. When you returned with only one ox hitched to the cart, and word leaked that you'd been to Shiloh, people looked to the sky. The early rains came, right on time, and people drew their own conclusions. They credit you with breaking the drought."

Flushing angrily, Boaz swung around, his fists clenched. "Nothing of the kind. All I did was—"

"—go to Shiloh, offer sacrifices, and pray for rain. And the rains came. Results like that are hard to argue with."

"But others had been praying just as hard, Pashur."

"But the rain didn't come until you went to Shiloh."

Irritated, Boaz picked up the sword he had used and tossed it beside his friend's. "Yahweh determines the times, not human beings."

"Yes, but Yahweh listens to the likes of Abraham."

"I'm not like Abraham."

"You'd have a hard time convincing people around here of that. Obviously you've been blessed greatly, a sure sign of Yahweh's favor." He collected the arm guards and water skin.

"I lost my wife and two children, Pashur. What good is my wealth?" Boaz said quietly.

"You certainly made good use of it during the drought. People remember things like that, my friend." As Amos picked up the pile of equipment, Pashur tossed Boaz his robe. "Now, it's almost time for you to beard Domla. Want some help?"

"I can still collect my own debts, Pashur," Boaz said drily, stripping off the soldier's kilt and dressing again. "If you really want to help, tell me how to get back into Tekoa without anyone knowing."

Pashur had been right about this alley, Boaz thought later, looking around in disgust. It stank with garbage, waste, and slime. Holding his robes carefully, he made his way down it, pausing at the end to glance into the street. Stepping out, he adjusted his clothes, turned left, and hoped the stench hadn't settled onto him permanently. He should be just two corners over from Domla's house.

A bit later as he brushed the last of the slime from his sandals in a shaded puddle left from the last rain, he listened to the sounds from Domla's house before setting aside a barrier to the central square and entering, urging some goats out of his way. It appeared the merchant had guests. Knocking with his staff on the compound gate, Boaz turned slightly to hide his face in the deepening shadows.

When the old overseer opened the door, he stepped inside.

"Geber, uh, adon," the overseer changed the title when he saw Boaz's robes, "please, whom shall I announce?"

"Just show me the way; I'll announce myself."

The man paled when he recognized his visitor in the light of the oil lamps. "If you please, adon, this is not a good time," he began.

Boaz sighed. "Not for me, either, but some things cannot wait on a convenient time. Will you show me the way, or shall I wander about on my own?"

Swallowing his outrage, the overseer led the way through the courtyard.

As he passed a doorway, Boaz glimpsed Domla in a room. Leaving the overseer to continue by himself, he slipped into the doorway, moving silently.

"I wasn't certain I would be here," Domla was saying. "Boaz hung around for two days, and I had to stay out of town."

"I'm surprised you have trouble with him," Tobeh's familiar voice answered. "I find him very easy to handle."

"You don't owe him money," the wine merchant snapped.

"I'm so glad you remember that, Domla," Boaz said cheerfully, privately thinking it was definitely time to go on the offensive with Tobeh. "And since you have so much spread out on your table this minute, we can settle the debt immediately."

Domla jerked his head up, and the other man in the room turned around swiftly.

"Shalom, Tobeh," Boaz greeted. "Such a surprise to see you here. How is business for you this year?"

"Where did *you* come from?" Domla gasped.

"Bethlehem. Lived there all my life. I believe you owed me 10 gold gerahs. I see you have it all counted out. Please put it in this pouch." Boaz tossed a small leather bag on the table and turned to Tobeh. "I thought that southern field you have looked a bit sparse this year. Bad seed from last fall?"

Staring with contempt at the flustered Domla, who still hadn't moved, Tobeh bared his teeth in a semblance of a smile. "That and poor workers. It's so hard to get good help these days."

"I hadn't noticed. Now, Domla!" Boaz added, staring straight at the debtor.

Mopping his forehead with a shaking hand, the Tekoan fumbled 10 gold gerahs into the pouch and slid it across the desk.

Boaz seized it and tucked it into his girdle. "Nice to get this little matter cleared up. I'll leave you to your business. Shalom, Domla. Oh, Tobeh, try fertilizing your fields, your yield might improve." Hiding his smile at the flash of rage in the man's eyes, Boaz slid out the door. In the courtyard he found the overseer frantically searching for him.

"Here you are, adon. I've been looking all over for you."

"Unnecessary exercise, I assure you." Boaz strode toward the gate.

"But adon, you wanted to see Geber Domla."

"I have." As he shut the gate in the face of the gaping overseer, he heard, faintly, Tobeh's contemptuous laughter from the house. It was the same laughter as that in his nightmare. Stopping in midstride, Boaz swallowed the gall that rose in his throat. Rage flashed over him, filling him with something more, sharpening his senses until he could stand the town no longer.

Swiftly retracing his steps, he turned into the filthy alley, uncaring of his clothes, and fled the settlement, using the low ground to make his way to the trees where his donkey patiently waited.

He paused a moment, his hearing catching the slightest sound, his eyes already adjusted to the denser darkness of the forest. His rage made his fingers tremble as he untied the donkey, but instead of mounting, he led it behind him, moving unerringly for the nearest trail. Needing to work off his anger, it wouldn't be the first time he'd run on the silent night ways of the Habiru.

Iyar, second month, fourth day, Ruth's twenty-second year (1100 B.C.)

Shalom, Ruth. How is Naomi today?" Madiya asked as I paused in the market, wondering what food I could bargain for with the few coppers I had left.

I shook my head. "The same."

The woman sighed. "The weaving hasn't helped?"

"It doesn't seem to matter. She spends all her time at the loom—I have a hard time making her stop to eat—but she hardly notices anything else."

"It's so sad," Madiya replied, blinking the tears from her eyes. "Even though I was young, I remember what she was like before. To see her so silent and bitter almost breaks my heart. She was such fun."

I nodded in agreement. "I wish I knew what she needs to pull her out of her grief. If she doesn't stop thinking of herself as dead, she'll soon be dead."

"Did Tashima have any other suggestions?"

"I haven't seen her to ask. I think she's been binding sheaves in the barley fields."

"Most of us are," Madiya said with another sigh. "It's such hot work—Ruth! Why didn't I think of this before? Don't you go out to glean?"

"Glean? But Elimelech's fields are in use. I couldn't take grain from there. Someone else owns the harvest."

The woman laughed. "Ruth, you can glean in any field you want to! It's part of our law. Yahweh commanded that the edges and corners of a field may not be harvested by the owner. And after the grain is cut and bound, the owner must leave the gleanings for widows, orphans, and others in need. It's the same with the grape and olive harvests. After the owner picks the vine or tree once, he must leave the rest for the gleaners."

"Would I be able to glean enough to keep us?" I asked, feeling encouraged for the first time since leaving Moab.

"Well, that can depend on whose field you go to. Tobeh's stingy. If he owns the field, he won't let anyone but his own workers glean, and he harvests everything. And if he holds an interest in someone else's field, he can make himself obnoxious about gleaning. The trick is to be in those fields when he's not there. Most landowners don't mind."

I scanned the market as we walked toward the gate. "I can work in any field I wish?"

Madiya nodded. "Of course, you have to be careful about the people you work with. Last year some troublemakers bothered the women a lot, and after Ladel's daughter nearly got raped, the elders drove them from the town. I doubt they'll be back this year, but you never know. They were probably Habiru, hiring out during the busy season."

"You have trouble with Habiru?" I asked in alarm. I had wanted to go out into the hills to find a god place, but if there were Habiru around, I would be foolish to do so.

"That depends," Madiya said. "There's one band that sort of stays here. They're peaceable and decent and have kept away the more vicious bands. When they hire on, they work hard. Well, I've got to go. Give my love to Naomi. Shalom."

"Shalom. I will." I felt in the pouch again. Ten coppers, and we had barely enough food for another day. I might be able to save my coppers by gleaning tomorrow. If I worked both barley and wheat harvests, and later the grapes and olives, we'd have a small store of food. By then I might be able to earn something playing at weddings and feasts. With what Naomi made weaving, we shouldn't starve until we could find someone to redeem Elimelech's land, and if I could figure out what Naomi needed to be happy, life could be good again.

Naomi rested during the heat of the day. She didn't ask for food, and I didn't prepare any. I'd make supper tonight. We had enough flour for two more meals if I ate only one, and we had raisins. I could save my share to take with me tomorrow, though I might spend a copper on bread at the market if I had to.

When my mother-in-law eventually emerged from the house, I greeted her. "Shalom, Naomi. Did you have a good rest?"

With a shrug she walked to the loom.

"Will you be all right here? I want to go into the countryside for a little bit."

"Go, daughter," Naomi replied, sitting down. Picking up the shuttle, she started to work.

Well, now that I had said I was leaving, I'd have to, I thought wryly. Had I expected that she'd ask me to stay? Constantly pushing for some kind of acknowledgment wouldn't make her see me any differently or cause her to take an interest in life again.

Slipping the harp into its case, I strapped it on my back, going carefully down the narrow access alley so I wouldn't scrape the instrument on the walls. I told myself that I could go look over the fields near the town and decide where to glean tomorrow, but I really needed to get away from Naomi's unremitting sorrow.

Outside the west gate, I turned right, twisting down the narrow paths between vineyards and gardens on the north side of town. Numerous fields spread out on the small plain, most of them thick with grain. A small path turned off to the right, and on impulse I turned with it and followed it past the fields and up the opposite hill into the forest.

In spite of the danger of Habiru, I desperately needed a god place where I could rest and talk to Yah. So much had happened and changed. We needed so many things, and Naomi was so different. I yearned to feel His comforting presence. The path wound deeper into the hills. A few rivulets still ran down the slopes. Most would dry up in a few more weeks. The final showers of the rainy season were about over, and there would be no more for four months. Then once again the cool winds from the Great Sea would bring rain to the land, and crops would be planted for another year.

The path branched, and I climbed higher into the forest, the coolness of the evergreens closing around me. Cresting the hill, I nearly tripped over a sheep on its side in the path, kicking erratically, foam rimming its mouth. I halted, startled by the elder standing near it.

"No need to fear, young woman," the man said with a smile.

I looked down, noticing the budding horns, along with the wide chest and boxy lines hidden by the thick wool that went with Yidla's stock. The yearling ram kicked more.

"If we can get him on his feet, he'll be better," I said automatically, thrusting my harp onto my back. "Walk him for a couple hours and he'll be fine."

"Fine?" the elder asked in surprise. "He looks close to death."

"He ate some kickplant and just needs to work it out of his system."

Giving me a strange look, the elder approached, and we tried to get the ram up. Three times we almost made it, only to have the sheep groan and roll back to his side again.

"We need some more help," I panted. "Otherwise he'll just give up and die. A ram like this is too valuable to lose."

"Valuable? It's just a ram my grandson received as wages for three years of service, but it sickened on the way home."

"His master must be blind, or extremely generous. That's a Yidla ram."

"Yidla ram!" someone exclaimed, and I whirled around as a Habiru warrior stepped out from the trees.

Clutching my harp, I backed away. *Yah, please protect me,* I prayed silently, glancing around in alarm.

"Don't be afraid, young woman," the elder said again. "This is my son, Mattan. I am Meshullam."

The ram bleated and kicked again, flinging foam from its mouth.

"Will it really be all right?" a third voice asked, and a youth stepped around a dense laurel bush on the other side of the path. "I'm Patah, and that sheep was my wage."

My heart pounding, I stayed very still, wondering how many more there were. I never should have come out here alone.

"Walk it, you said?" Meshullam inquired.

Hesitantly, I nodded, swallowing my fear. "About two hours. He should be fine if he doesn't get into any more kickplant."

With Patah and Mattan assisting, the ram made it up this time.

Hoping they'd forget about me and I could get back to Bethlehem, I edged farther away. *Yah, keep me safe!* I prayed again.

"How do you know this?" Mattan asked, watching his son urge the sheep down the trail.

"Everyone in Moab knows about kickplant," I replied, then could have bitten my tongue! First I come out to the forest alone, then I admit to being a Moabite, if my accent hadn't told them already. *Yah, please get me out of this,* I pleaded.

"Would that by chance be a harp?" Meshullam asked unexpectedly.

I nodded, clutching the case tighter, wondering if they would take it.

His dark gray eyes lit up with amusement. "Ah, you must be Ruth, Mahlon's widow from Heshbon. Pashur warned us we'd likely find you in the unlikeliest places."

"You know Pashur?" I asked cautiously, taking a deep breath.

"He's another of my sons," Meshullam smiled. "Mattan, my oldest, is now dahveed of our band. We are Habiru."

"Madiya of Bethlehem mentioned a band who had helped the town more than once."

The older man laughed. "And having said that, you challenge me to prove it true! Pashur said you had a quick mind. What are you doing out here alone?"

"Looking for a god place," I replied, not liking the amused glance that took me in.

"What's that?" Mattan asked, turning his attention from watching Patah struggle with the ram back to his father and me.

"It's a place where the gods are," his father explained, staring at me. "If I may ask, how do you know the ram's ancestry? Covered with as much wool as he is, I can't tell anything at all."

"I grew up around Yidla," I said, loosening my hold on the harp and concluding that I might have found destiny again instead of death. "Your grandson has a real prize. Breed him to your ewes, and you'll improve the quality of your wool and the hardiness of the flock. If you don't have ewes, you can breed the ram at a price."

Meshullam laughed. "Perhaps Geber Tobeh outsmarted himself this time. He undoubtedly thought the sheep would soon die when he gave it to Patah."

I cocked my head, my trained ear picking up the dislike for Tobeh in the man's tones. "Would that just happen to be Adon Tobeh, son of Besai?"

Mattan made a sound of disgust. "He's not adon to us!"

I relaxed a little more, swiftly calculating the advantages of friendship with someone who was not afraid of Tobeh.

Meshullam's dark gray eyes laughed at me again. "We make questionable allies," he said. "Friendship with us will automatically lose for you the regard of a number of people in town."

I couldn't stop the blush. How had he known what I was thinking? Then he smiled and shrugged. "I'd get the better side of the bargain," I replied.

Mattan's mouth nearly dropped open, and for an instant blank astonishment showed on Meshullam's face. But instead of commenting, the old warrior turned to his son.

"Who would know for certain about this yearling?"

"Geber Ladel. I'll take the ram to him. Provided it's still alive."

Then Messhullam turned to me. "What did you call the plant the ram ate?"

"Kickplant." I described it to them and then told Mattan where he could find some on the road to Bethlehem. "The seeds get caught in the wool," I added. "Make certain none grows where you pasture your flock, and you should have no problems."

With a nod Mattan headed down the path to help Patah with the ram. His father turned to me.

"It's fortunate we met, Ruth. But I think we've interrupted your search for a god place long enough. Come into the hills anytime you wish. You'll be safe. And you might find a good god place down that way." He pointed to a path that started by a large tree locally called a cedar, but that was really a kind of juniper. "Bethlehem is that way," he added, pointing.

"Shalom, Meshullam. I'm pleased to have met you."

"Shalom, Ruth. The pleasure is all ours, especially if this does turn out to be a Yidla ram!"

When the men had gone, I sank down on the path, shaking all over at what could have happened, but hadn't. "Thank You, Yah. Help me not to be so foolish again!" I exclaimed. For a few seconds I debated returning to town at once, but after I'd calmed down a little more, I remembered Meshullam's promise that I would be safe in the hills and decided to trust him. I didn't know how much longer I could survive in Bethlehem without some place to talk to Yah.

Following the path he had pointed out, I discovered a small hill with a stand of huge common oak that seemed strangely still. Ivy and myrtle grew here, some moss-covered boulders formed a protective hollow, and through the trees I could see down a valley. Squinting, I made out smoke against the sky, so Bethlehem was probably not more than a mile or two away.

As quietness settled over me, I took the harp out of its case. Tuning the strings, I began to play Yidla's song. Before I was half finished, tears streamed down my cheeks. I longed for home. For Shimrith, Orpah, Ithmah, Yidla, and even Abiaz! Closing my eyes, I remembered the hills and valleys by Heshbon dotted with sheep and grain fields. I thought of the warm sun, cold rain, and harsh hamsin wind that could ruin a crop in one night if it came at the wrong time. When I opened my eyes, I expected to see the great sweep of land that spread out before me from my god place above Yidla's pasture.

The sight of the pines, valley, and hill close to me jarred my mind painfully, and I stifled my sobs. Had I made a mistake in coming here? What would we do if I could not earn anything with my music? Especially, what would I do if Naomi died? I was without ties to the land, a seed blown far by the wild hamsin. Could I grow here? What if the soil was hard, or the rains unfriendly? I had abandoned my home and family, tearing myself from the mother who lay sleeping with Shimrith's son in her arms.

"Yah, don't let Naomi die!" I pleaded incoherently. I had told her I would stay with her, had vowed I would lie beside her in her grave, but how could I know the future? If the Habiru I had met today had belonged to any other band, I could be lying dead in the forest or enslaved for the rest of my life.

I curled up around my harp, crying for all that had been left behind. Finally my tears subsided, and I rested against the moss of the boulder, gazing at the valley in front of me. My mind quieted, and I felt the sense of Yah's presence creeping over me.

"Thank You," I said aloud. "I needed the reminder that You are never far away. Today You opened the way for me to come out here in safety. You have already given much to us, and I feel that there is still more to come. For surely You would not have given me four pithoi without knowing that they will be filled up. Why would I have a grinding stone unless You will give me grain to make flour from? Three days ago we had nothing but a bundle and one silver gerah. Now we have a household with all the necessities—sleeping mats, clothes, and a loom for Naomi to work at. Surely I can trust You for food."

Taking up my harp again, I played a restful afternoon song that soon drowsed into a quiet lullaby. Liking it, I went through it again, working it over until I was satisfied with the melody line and rhythms. Then I played it twice to commit it to memory.

"This is a good place," I whispered. "You have even given me a new song. I will play it for Naomi tonight so that she will not waken and weep with grief for her family.

"Yah, You know what I plan to do tomorrow. Please guide me to a field where the owner will let me glean. Give me a place here in this land. Show me what Naomi needs to heal her heart and live again. Do not let her wander any longer in the shadow of the dead."

Although I wished that I could stay longer, I stood, knowing that I must be back in town well before dusk. Already I had seen speculative looks from some of the men in the market. It would have been much easier if I belonged to a particular family or clan, but living under Tobeh's protection would probably be worse than staying alone. The memory of the way he'd stared at me made me shiver.

"The enemy of my enemy is my friend," I repeated, walking out of the trees and into the little valley. I must strengthen the ties to what friends I had, and as soon as possible discover who Boaz was, the one man in town who cared nothing for Tobeh. In only eight weeks, when the grains were harvested, Elimelech's fields would be free, and Naomi could claim her rights. But as a destitute foreign widow fighting with a rich townsman for that land, I had no illusions about my chances of winning.

Iyar, second month, fifth day (1100 B.C.)

Early the next morning I drew water from the common cistern before anyone else came. I filled the water gourd that hung by the loom for Naomi to drink and then prepared breakfast with the last of our food. I didn't eat much and had only a few of the raisins to take with me for a lunch. I hoped I would find a good place to glean—otherwise it would be a very long, hungry day.

"Shalom, Naomi," I said when she came out of the house.

"Shalom." She sat down and ate a little.

"Naomi, finish your food," I reminded her. "Will you weave again today?"

She nodded, eating a couple more bites.

"Geber Hasi will be astonished at how much you've done," I said, surveying the work on the loom. It was a simple black, gray, and white-striped weave with undyed wool, and Naomi had worked steadily since Madiya brought the yarn two days ago.

"If you'll be all right here alone, I'd like to go out and glean during the harvest. Do you think that would be a good idea?" I waited for her reaction to my words.

My mother-in-law set her bowl aside and sat at the loom.

"Maybe I could bring home enough grain to give us food for several days," I tried again. "There are so many fields near Bethlehem. Surely I can find someone who will let me glean."

"Go, daughter," Naomi said without turning around.

Sighing, I picked up the few raisins I had wrapped in a cloth and tucked it into my sash. What could I possibly do to awake her to life again, or make her see me as more than just a burden?

Carrying my basket, I stopped uncertainly at the end of our tiny alley. Harvesters and laborers hurried through the gate to the fields. Which field should I try? I had no idea what Tobeh owned, and I didn't want to end up in one of his. Madiya would know, or Tashima. I waited a while, but didn't see either of them, and I dared not linger longer. People might get the wrong idea, especially the men.

"Yah, help me find a good field to glean in," I whispered, taking the street to the south gate of Bethlehem. Trying to look as if I knew where I was going, I walked out of town, ignoring the curious glances of some and replying to an occasional "Shalom." Beyond the gardens and vineyards close to the town began groves of fruit trees and an olive grove set in tiny terraces on a small hill. Fields of grain stretched down the valley, and larger terraces climbed the hillsides, glowing golden in the early-morning sun.

Day laborers left the road and threaded their way to various fields. Undecided about how to proceed, I slowed. Then up ahead I glimpsed a familiar cart with Gershed prodding the donkeys. Well, whoever had given us that loom was a good and generous householder. I'd follow his servant.

He kept a steady pace, and soon most of the workers had already disappeared into the fields. I wondered if I had made a good choice. What if Gershed wasn't going to a field? The road wound around the arm of a hill, hiding Bethlehem from sight. Hurrying, I closed the gap between the servant and me. On my left, several more fields lay thick with grain. Gershed turned up the path between them, and I sighed with relief. He stopped to talk to a man standing to one side.

He must be the owner, or overseer. I paused, looking the situation over. Behind me, a laughing group of men carrying sickles turned up a path to the first field. The overseer greeted them and assigned them places.

"Ruth, you did decide to glean," Madiya said, her voice surprising me. "I'm glad to see you here. I stopped at the house to see if you wanted to walk with me, but you'd already gone, and Naomi couldn't tell me where. Didn't you tell her?"

"I didn't know where I'd be, and she wasn't interested. Is that the owner or an overseer?"

"Geber Ladel is the overseer. Just ask him if you can glean. You can follow along behind me if you want to. I'll be binding sheaves." As she went over to speak to the man named Ladel to get her assigned working place, I wondered if he was the man the Habiru intended to show the ram to. If so, my connection to Messhullam might be an advantage.

While I debated, Madiya began binding sheaves with practiced ease behind a large man cutting grain with a well-made bronze sickle instead of the more common flint ones. She had probably assumed that I had worked in the fields before. However, Immi had kept me home during harvest, ostensibly to keep my hands from stiffening, but surely with other motives as well. Thinking back, I realized that Shimrith had sheltered me from a good many things.

But my family wasn't here now. Uneasy, I curled my left hand into a fist and hid it in my robe. Madiya's description of the attack on a girl last season ran through my mind, and my stomach tightened. I couldn't afford even the slightest hint of scandal. Every eye in town would be watching during the coming days to see if I would confirm the common belief about a Moabite.

Realizing that I had clenched both my hands, I forced myself to loosen them. We needed food. All I had to do was go to the field and pick up grain. That couldn't be too hard, could it? I glanced at Geber Ladel. What if he wanted to know who I was? Would he send me away when he found out I was the widow from Moab that Adon Tobeh didn't like? But Midiya seemed to assume I'd be gleaning behind her, so this couldn't be one of Tobeh's fields. In any case, I didn't have time to stand around debating with myself.

Trying to still my pounding heart, I approached the geber.

"Shalom. May I help you?" he asked.

"Shalom, geber. Madiya said that you are the overseer. I would like to glean if I may."

"Are you a relative of Madiya's?"

The question I dreaded. Better not mention Moab. "I'm new in Bethlehem, and Madiya has been very kind to me. My name is Ruth, and I live with Naomi."

"Ah, the Moabite daughter-in-law." He looked at me intently.

I held my breath, meeting his gaze.

"Yes, you may glean. Follow after Madiya."

"May Yahweh return your kindness," I said in relief, nearly dropping the basket I carried.

The man gave me an odd look.

Madiya smiled a quick welcome when I walked over. No one talked, since everyone wanted to get as much done as possible before the day grew hotter. She was quick with her work, gathering the handfuls of stalks dropped by the reapers after they scythed them and piled them up into a bundle that she tied with more stalks of grain, then standing the sheaf upright.

I looked carefully over the ground she had covered, alert for any stalk that she had missed or that had fallen from the bundles. Any that I found, I put into my basket. Madiya was a good worker and only occasionally left more than a few stacks ungathered.

As the morning wore on, I noticed other gleaners entering the field. Some stayed, working steadily behind the binders, while others soon left, looking for a place where more grain had gotten dropped. The fields followed the contours of the hills and had odd corners and nooks where barley had also grown. When we passed one along a wall, Madiya reminded me that I could gather any grain there that the reapers had left.

As the sun climbed higher my stomach started to growl. I'd had nothing last night and very little this morning. Knowing I had the entire day ahead of me, I resisted the temptation to eat. I'd be hungrier later. Some of the other gleaners had small water juglets or cruses with them. Madiya had one fastened to her sash. I'd have to remember to bring one tomorrow.

"How about a drink?" Madiya offered, pausing in her work.

"I'd like that," I said gratefully. "By the way, whose field is this?"

"One of Boaz's. Didn't you know?"

I shook my head. "No, I chose this one because I followed Gershed here from town. I thought anyone who would give us a loom had to be wealthy and generous."

She giggled. "Boaz is certainly both. He saved my family during the drought. That's why I'm working in his fields. We're trying to pay him back. Because we don't have much silver, Boaz agreed to have us work the debt off. We'll serve two more years during harvest. Ladel says we'll be paid off then, but Abbi says that's ridiculous. Ladel won't budge, though, so there's nothing Abbi can do."

"We'd better get started again," I said, noticing the overseer watching me. Madiya turned back to her work.

The gleaner next to me left, and I searched the ground after that binder as well. She was a bit more careless, and I had half my basket full by midmorning, about enough grain to make bread for one meal. I bit my lips. At this rate I would collect only enough to keep us from hunger during harvest, with nothing to store for later. Well, I'd just have to trust Yah for that. He was certainly providing what we needed now, after all.

With my back aching from the constant stooping, and my stomach cramping with hunger, I decided I would rest. While we had worked, Gershed had put up a shelter to one side of the field. It looked inviting.

"Madiya, is it all right if I sit in the shade for rest?" I asked in a low voice.

She turned to me. "Oh, yes, Ruth. That's what the shelter is for. You're not used to this, are you?"

"Not really."

With a grin she went back to binding sheaves. I carried my basket to the edge of the field and glanced at Geber Ladel. He smiled and nodded to the shelter, so I sat down to rest.

"Shalom, Boaz," Adon Hanan called.

Reining in the donkey he was riding, Boaz turned to the elder. "Shalom. How is your harvest this year?"

"We have a good crop again, thanks to you."

Boaz flushed. "I did nothing."

Hanan chuckled. "You prayed."

"Everyone prayed."

"But Yahweh listened to you."

"Hanan, please!" he said in exasperation.

The elder chuckled again. "Why do you think people call you 'adon' now? Elimelech's widow is back in town, and she apparently has no plans to go to Tobeh's household." He changed the subject.

"Can you blame her?"

"No. And that's why I wanted to see you today. Tobeh wishes to control Elimelech's land. Naomi set up house in a hovel by the wall, and Tobeh has made it clear he doesn't approve of the daughter-in-law from Moab who lives with her. If he can starve them into coming to his house, he'll get that land."

Boaz stirred uneasily on the donkey, staring down at his hands. "From what I've heard, Naomi's daughter-in-law is devoted to her."

"She has conducted herself very well so far, but that won't matter to Tobeh. He wants that land. We've joked for years that he is determined to own everything in this town. Maybe we were speaking the literal truth and just didn't know it. Some whisper that he wants to be king."

"Israel doesn't have kings," Boaz said testily. "Yahweh leads us."

Hanan cocked his head. "Don't ignore the facts, Boaz. The tribes are tearing themselves to pieces or being torn to pieces. People want secure lives, to know that they'll eat the rewards of their labor in the fields and vineyards. They see the peoples around us do that more often than we do. And the most obvious difference is that the other nations have kings.

"Bethlehem has been fortunate for many years, thanks in a large part to Meshullam and his Habiru. Our only hardship lately has been the drought, and very few actually have died as a result of that, thanks in most part to you."

"You did your share too," Boaz interjected, nodding a greeting to a townsman walking by.

"Other places are not so lucky," Hanan continued seriously. "My last trip to Shiloh was a revelation. The whispers are growing louder. People are discussing the possibility of a king."

"They're foolish, then. Yahweh is better than any king—if we follow His instructions and remember His words."

"Others feel that way, and when they say so, the answer given is that we need a war leader, a dahveed, over all 12 tribes to protect the land."

Boaz shifted again on the donkey and stared out the gate. "It's getting that bad?"

"Yes. It will be a while before anything comes of it, but the tribes will demand a king someday, and it won't be far off."

"Of whom will they demand it? Yahweh Himself?"

"Probably of the high priest at Shiloh."

"They won't get much help there!"

"I don't know, Boaz." Hanan stood and rested his hand on the donkey's neck. "The Philistines are getting more and more threatening. We don't have too much trouble up here in the hills, but it's getting harder and harder to buy anything metal. How many bronze sickles have you seen this year? The day may come when all we have left are slings and arrows."

Boaz smiled. "A well-placed sling stone is worth more than a spear or a javelin. We won't be helpless."

"No, but do you really want to fight them or pay tribute?"

"Of course not. But installing a dahveed won't solve the problem."

Hanan lowered his voice. "No, but it provides an opportunity, which brings me back to Tobeh and his ambitions. He has effectively hidden his goals behind his wealth, avoiding a reputation for greed by giving feasts for a select group, especially in the past six months. He has the ear of many of the elders now. And he's hinted that such feasts will be common for everyone if Bethlehem had a king."

Not liking the situation as the elder sketched it for him, Boaz frowned. Tobeh must feel it was time to make another move.

"Only you stand in his way," Hanan said urgently. "Your influence became enormous when the drought broke. You've always excluded Tobeh from the Ephrath clan; and if you let that man gain control of Elimelech's land, it will destroy a lot of your power, and then no one will be able to stand in his way."

Hanan looked up at him. "I'm old, Boaz. I wish to live out the rest of my days sitting in the sun, not here at the gate with all the problems of Bethlehem troubling me. If I leave now, Tobeh has a good chance of taking my place, and that would be a disaster for the town. I want you in my seat, Boaz. You have the balance and discipline to listen and judge justly even those you dislike. Don't let Tobeh gain more power."

Boaz stared at the ground. He knew he had to respond to Tobeh's challenges—and not just for his own personal honor, but for the good of the town, as Hanan said. "You're not the only one who has spoken to me of this," Boaz sighed. "But Tobeh is goel of usufruct rights to Elimelech's land. I can't change that. Nor can I alter Naomi's attitude toward me."

"I know," the elder admitted, stepping back. "If only there was some way you could make that scheming parasite refuse to be goel!"

"That would take a miracle of Yahweh!" Boaz said with a wry grin. "But I *can* make it more difficult. Shalom, Hanan." He prodded his donkey into motion.

On his way to his fields Boaz checked the gardens and vineyards. He had a very good grape harvest coming on, and the olives were abundant also. All in all, he'd have an excellent year if the hamsin stayed away.

As the donkey jogged along Boaz decided that he should speak to Ladel about Hanan's concerns. However, that must wait until after the day's work. Right now he had fields to inspect.

Rounding a bend, he halted at one of his fields and studied it. It looked much different now than it had during the year of the drought, when the grain had been bedraggled and thin, like the hair on an old beggar's head. This year the crops were like fur on the earth, heavy and full. From the appearance of things, not even Jebus would be able to buy up the excess. Satisfied, he rode up the path where Ladel waited. Several of the workers saw him approaching.

"May Yahweh be with you," Boaz called to them.

"And Yahweh bless you," they responded.

"Is all well?"

His brother-in-law smiled. "It's the first week of harvest; of course all is well. Wait until the end of wheat harvest, and then I will have a list of complaints that stretches from here to Bethlehem."

"By then it will be time for Feast of Weeks, and you can send everyone to Shiloh to complain there."

Ladel chuckled.

"Have the day laborers been worthwhile so far?"

The overseer nodded. "We have several hires from town, and I've scattered the Habiru among them. I wish I could get all my workers from those warriors. They *work,* and I don't have to supply them with sickles either. They bring their own, which are usually better than any we've got."

Boaz grinned. "Just don't ask where they get them."

"I wouldn't dream of it. But I do wish there were more."

"What's Madiya doing here? I thought her family had worked off what they called their debt."

"I tried, Boaz, but her father absolutely insisted that he supply labor for two more harvests. I can't get him to stop, and I don't want to send her away without an escort. I've seen a couple of the same troublemakers from last year again."

"Well, let it ride. It won't hurt anything and will please her father." Glancing around, Boaz noticed a strange woman sitting in the shelter.

Even as she sat there quietly, something about her posture caught his eye and quickened his interest. "Who's the good-looking woman* in the shelter? I don't recall her. What family does she belong to?"

Ladel flicked a brief glance at the shelter, then turned back to Boaz. "That's Ruth, the Moabite who came back with Naomi." He shifted his weight to the other leg and eyed his brother-in-law. "I gave her permission to glean when she asked. Although she's worked steadily, I doubt she's done much of this kind of labor. Still, she held out longer than I thought and sat down only a couple minutes ago. She's acquainted with Madiya, so I told her to glean after her friend. It's worked well."

Boaz turned his attention back to the field so it wouldn't be obvious he was studying the newcomer. Moabite women were known for their beauty and allure, and he began to understand why. Something about her stirred feelings in him that he hadn't had in a long time. He wondered what she'd look like walking toward him, then hastily pushed the thought from his mind.

"Have any of the men bothered her, she being a Moabite and alone?"

The overseer also faced in the direction of the field. "One of the day laborers tried, but the Habiru next to him put a stop to it. I don't know what he said, but the laborer hasn't so much as glanced at her since. She's kept strictly to herself and her work."

"What do they say about her in town? Has your wife heard anything?" Boaz asked, sliding off the donkey.

Ladel gave him a slightly puzzled look, then shouted a reminder to one of the field hands to be sure to leave the corners for gleaning before answering. "I can always tell who worked last for Tobeh!" he said in disgust. "According to Tashima, Ruth has been a surprise. Many thought she was a servant, but word soon got out that she was a daughter-in-law. Have you seen Naomi yet?"

Boaz shook his head.

"She hardly speaks and spends most of her time at the loom or staring at nothing. Which reminds me," he added, shifting uncomfortably.

---

* The Hebrew word Boaz used has the connotation of a woman eligible for marriage.

"The only thing that remotely interests Naomi is weaving. When Tashima told me she and Madiya were collecting necessities for Naomi—and Tobeh interfered with that as much as he could—I sent over Mena's loom. Tashima was appalled. I hope you don't mind," he finished sheepishly.

For a moment Boaz was too stunned to move. Then anger flashed through him. His wife's loom? How dared he! Mena had loved weaving and had been working on an intricate robe for him when she died. He didn't want that loom touched! It was—it was—to his surprise, he couldn't remember where the loom had been anymore. The thought quenched his anger like a splash of frigid water. Forcing open his clenched hands, he rubbed his donkey's neck.

Beside him, his brother-in-law stood stiffly. "Forgive me, Boaz. I can get it back if you wish. I should have asked."

Knowing that hanging on to Mena's loom wouldn't bring her back, he smiled wryly. "No, you were right to send it. Mena wouldn't want it to go unused, and if it helps Naomi, so much the better."

"I'm glad you feel that way," Ladel said, unable to hide his relief. "I thought Naomi was kin to you in some way."

"Elimelech was." The donkey thrust its head down and pulled off a mouthful of grass to chew, Boaz still rubbing its neck ridge. "Ruth seems to be a decent woman?"

Ladel nodded. "According to Tashima, she stayed with Naomi instead of returning to her family after Mahlon died. I'd guess the family is well-to-do, but she hasn't shirked today, and she's most grateful for the help they've had since they arrived in town.

"My wife says Naomi would have died without Ruth's care. The woman's constantly on the lookout for anything that will rouse Naomi's interest in life again, but nothing has helped so far except the weaving. It's upset Tashima a lot."

Boaz squinted at the sun. He had much to do today. "Has Gershed met her?"

"Yes. He said Ruth has been very circumspect. Apparently a few of the men tried to catch her eye in the market, but she'll have none of it. One or two were very put out. They expected more from a Moabite."

"What's your opinion?" Boaz asked, looking at his brother-in-law.

"She's a decent woman, intelligent, well-spoken, and determined."

"Be sure the men leave her alone, then. Call her over." With both Pashur and Ladel giving such glowing reports, he was curious about her.

The overseer motioned to Ruth, who had returned to work.

A shout from the field distracted Boaz's attention, but it was just an unexpected snake close to the terrace wall. The men soon disposed of it.

"Ruth, Adon Boaz would like to speak to you," Ladel said.

Boaz turned back to see the Moabite.

~ ~ ~

Automatically I hid my left hand in the folds of my robe and touched the slight bulge where the signet ring hung on its cord. I looked into Adon Boaz's face before I wondered if I should keep my eyes down instead. He stiffened, staring at me as if he'd never seen a woman before. I couldn't look away either, held captive by the shadowed sorrow I saw in those deep brown eyes. His rich, dark chestnut hair was lightly streaked with gray, and I twisted my hands in my robe to keep from touching it. I didn't know what to do. I'd never seen such an expression on a man's face before, at least not when he was looking at me.

Sakar had looked at Orpah like that just before we left, when he thought he'd never see her again. But not even Mahlon had stared at me with such intensity. It made me blush.

The overseer coughed gently, and Adon Boaz blinked. I hastily looked down, half afraid of what had just happened.

"I'd like to speak to you, daughter," he said.

Amazed at being named far above my social situation, I jerked my head up to stare at him again, the blush draining from my face. What could this mean? Quickly I looked down again, for although his face was composed, there was nothing calm about the burning fire in the back of his eyes. That look had frightened and repulsed me when Adon Tobeh had it, but seeing it in Adon Boaz's eyes brought a completely different feeling. Something in me responded, and it took a moment for me to concentrate on what he was saying.

"Stay in this field. Don't glean anywhere else. The binders will follow the reapers, and you should marry yourself to—uh, stay close to them. The binders. So you can glean."

I froze a moment, trying to sort out what he'd just said—or hadn't said—and what it meant. Cautiously, I risked another glance up. His face was fiery red as he avoided my gaze, clearly flustered at his slip of the tongue. But had it been a slip of the tongue? Did he see me as an easy woman because I was from Moab?

"I've ordered the men not to bother you," he continued, getting redder if possible, and looking everywhere except at me. "They'll leave you alone and not harass you while you're working."

Feeling extremely confused, I shot a quick glance at Ladel. Was Adon Boaz really—babbling? I'd seen men fall for Orpah in an instant and sometimes say the most absurd things. Had that just happened here? Should I say something? I looked at the overseer again. He watched the workers in the field with a perfectly solemn face, which aroused my suspicions.

Adon Boaz glanced around also, seemingly a bit desperate for more to say. "And if you get thirsty—when you get thirsty—you go and drink from the water jars in the cart that my young men filled, that Gershed filled. The water is there for my workers, if they get thirsty."

He was really babbling, and his eyes kept meeting mine as if he couldn't stop staring at me. Geber Ladel bit his lip to stifle a smile. Not certain what might be so amusing to him, I turned my gaze to the ground and kept it there, more and more uneasy.

As a widow and a foreigner, I was as far down the social ladder as it was possible to get. I'd do best to keep to that place, in spite of what Adon Boaz had called me. At the same time, I must determine exactly what had happened here, but I wouldn't find out anything if he didn't stop repeating himself every other word. This was the one man who didn't care about Adon Tobeh, and my life and Naomi's might depend on his goodwill.

Sinking to my knees, I touched my forehead to the ground, being as courteous as I possibly could, since I must be very direct with my words. "Why are you so concerned about me when I am just a foreigner?" I said, glancing up at him.

Adon Boaz looked down at me, his gaze riveted to mine, making me very aware that I was a woman, and he was not. He moved his hand as if to touch me. I held my breath, but he stroked his beard instead. The sharp disappointment that flashed through me appalled me! What I was thinking could lead to nothing but trouble. Unfortunately, I suddenly realized that I didn't care, and I had to sternly remind myself that my life wasn't the only one in the balance.

It was Geber Ladel's hand that helped me stand, although I would certainly have preferred to stay kneeling. I felt safer with the ground digging into my knees to remind me of what was most important at the moment.

Adon Boaz had himself under control when he answered this time. "I've heard all that you've done for your mother-in-law since the death of Mahlon, your husband. I know you left behind your family and the land that holds your dead to come and live among strangers for the sake of Naomi. This is—unusual."

I didn't reply, thinking wryly of what my real family would do if they found me.

"Yahweh of Israel will surely give you many sons now that you have chosen Him to cover you—uh, trusted Him to take care of you." The redness crept up his face again.

Geber Ladel bit his lip once more and stared very hard at the reapers in the field.

Surely no one could deliberately be this clumsy with words, I decided. At the implication of the thought, a wave of heat rushed over me again. I forced myself to think. Here in a field I was again in the halfway places of the world. Was this destiny coming to me? We desperately needed this man, but I dared not presume on comments that might be misinterpreted. Yet neither could I afford to turn away any chance to gain his favor.

The silence had stretched, and I must answer. Again I humbly bowed. "I hope I will always please you, adon. Your kindness"—I emphasized the word slightly—"has given me the comfort of a lover, and your words are as gentle as if I belonged to you. I know I do not, but you have given me a pleasurable welcome."

Geber Ladel's brown eyes opened very wide, and he coughed. "Madiya has moved quite a ways since I called you here, Ruth. Perhaps you should return to work."

I glanced at the field, forcing myself to resist the invisible current that seemed to be drawing me closer to the adon. "Yes, geber." I felt Boaz's eyes on me all the way back to work.

~ ~ ~

"You going to check the other fields?" Ladel asked without looking at his friend.

"What? Oh, yes. Yes, I guess I should." Still dazed, Boaz mounted the donkey and headed back down the path to the road. He had four or five more stops to make before noon, and he had to be back here by then.

He couldn't forget those clear, light-brown eyes flecked with darker brown and rimmed with long lashes that curled upward toward arched eyebrows. The look in them had been familiar. She had the same confidence as Mena had when he'd first seen her, one born of hardships surmounted and danger survived. At the same time, it was definitely not Mena.

She was taller than his wife had been, with a regal grace in the way she moved that gave him pause. Ladel was right. She was used to wealth. Her clothes were much worn, but had originally been of extremely good quality. Why would she choose poverty with Naomi over wealth with the family? Why would she marry an Israelite in the first place?

And the things he'd said! Boaz flushed again. Every time he got involved with a woman, his mind seemed to run away like an unbridled donkey. He still felt flustered and confused and had just gone right past the field he was supposed to check on!

With a sigh, he reined his donkey around.

Must he always make a fool of himself over women? He'd all but proposed! To take a Moabite as his wife in a community such as Bethlehem would forever damage his reputation. With Tobeh scheming to rule the town, he dare not let something like that happen. Like it or not, what opposition there was to the man now revolved around him. He'd have to be very careful.

At the same time, he now had the perfect opportunity to be certain that Ruth and Naomi had enough to eat for a while, which would protect them from Tobeh, though he'd have to walk a fine line. Still, it was possible, provided he kept himself under control and didn't lose his head again. Although he was embarrassingly aware that his desire had been plain to her, he couldn't forget the flash of response he'd noticed before she looked down and—

"Adon Boaz, did you want something?"

With a start, he looked around. His donkey had stopped beside the overseer of the field, and he hadn't even noticed.

Pay attention to business, he admonished himself. *Forget about her. Forget all about her.* But the thought of having that strange, exotic Moabite in his house set his heart to pounding.

"Adon?"

"Sorry, I'm quite preoccupied today," Boaz mumbled. "How is the yield this year? Any trouble with the laborers?"

~ ~ ~

When Boaz returned about noon, Ladel looked surprised. "Something wrong?"

"Oh, no. I just thought I'd eat the noon meal here."

"Well, if eating is on your mind, you'd best stop watching your new gleaner so intently. The workers are noticing."

Flushing, Boaz averted his face. "Has anyone bothered her? Any of the Habiru?"

"No, they haven't, and unless I miss my guess, they let the other workers know they wouldn't stand for it. I get the feeling they know and respect her. Makes me wonder just who she is."

"Now who's watching her?" Boaz said testily.

Ladel raised his eyebrows. "That way, is it? Laid claim already?"

"I have not laid claim to anything!" he retorted, turning on his brother-in-law.

"Boaz, this is me, remember? I was there when you first saw Mena. You haven't been this incoherent since I pushed you into asking for her hand. But you had best be careful."

Sliding off the donkey, Boaz turned it loose to graze. "She's still in mourning for Mahlon, and I'm old enough to be her father, so there shouldn't be much chance for me to make a fool of myself," he said. "But I can make certain that she and Naomi don't starve, and I might be able to put a decent young man in her path if she's interested. Other than that, I'm outside her circle."

"I wonder," Ladel said, studying the Moabite.

Boaz joined the workers on the blanket on the ground in the shade of the shelter. Many reapers had brought something to eat, but

Boaz also supplied food for them. Ruth sat a little apart, holding a cloth with a very few raisins in it. He watched carefully to see if she had anything else but didn't see anymore food.

Worry creased his forehead. Were things that bad already? Didn't they even have enough that Ruth could bring a decent lunch to the field? He watched her finish the raisins and then take a couple heads of grain from her basket, rub off the hulls, and chew on that.

Something had to be done, and now might be a good time to challenge Tobeh over treating the two widows as if they didn't belong to his clan. His face hardened at the thought. Then he took a deep breath. He was betting everything on Pashur's and Ladel's assessment of Ruth. If she was indecent in any way, his support of her and Naomi would turn into the worst mistake of his life, irreparably damaging his influence.

He turned to his brother-in-law. "Bring Ruth here," he said quietly. "I don't think she has much to eat."

The overseer went to her, telling her to sit closer to Boaz.

"Here," Boaz said, picking up some bread and holding it out to her. "There is plenty. Dip it in the vinegar."

Stunned silence descended as the workers stared in shock. But Boaz noticed only the astonishment in Ruth's eyes as they flickered back and forth between the bread and his face. She understood exactly what he was extending toward her, and she couldn't believe it.

With a smile he held the bread a little closer. His simple gesture invited her to become part of his clan, with all the rights and protection that went with that. And by offering the food with his own hand, he had announced that he was personally concerned with her welfare.

"Thank you, adon." Her quiet words seemed loud in the silence, and she took the bread with a trembling hand, dipped it as instructed, and took a bite.

When one of the townsmen opened his mouth to say something, the large Habiru next to him jabbed a forceful elbow in the man's ribs. The villager gasped and closed his mouth.

Ruth ate the bread, then two more pieces that Boaz passed to her without comment, making absolutely certain no one could misunderstand his position. He also gave her some grain, quick-roasted in the fire to parch it, to be certain she had all she could eat. Noticing that she slipped bits of her meal into the cloth, he guessed she was thinking of

Naomi, so he kept her liberally supplied until she had enough to take back to her mother-in-law. The gratitude that flashed from her eyes in the one glance she gave him embarrassed him.

She rose sooner than anyone else, drank quickly, and went back to the field. There she broke off stalks growing at the edges where the reapers had already gone by and worked the cracks and crannies of the terracing walls.

Boaz frowned. "Ladel, I don't think there's anything to eat in Naomi's house. Let her glean in front of the binders if she wishes." He looked at the reapers. "No one is to bother her. She is not to be molested in any way." The men nodded, still amazed at what he had done.

He turned to the binders. "Madiya, you and any others she gleans around should drop handfuls of grain for her. Make certain you leave a lot."

"Yes, adon," Madiya said with wide eyes.

The large Habiru looked at Boaz intently. "Shall we leave more than usual at the edges and corners?"

"Yes."

Speculation appeared in the men's eyes, and several glanced at Ruth's figure in the field.

Seeing their reaction, Boaz added, "I don't intend for the widow of my kinsman to go hungry."

The townsman beside the large Habiru had a sarcastic smirk on his face. It stayed there as the field hands went back to work.

Ladel looked at him and shrugged. "Nothing will stop that sort of talk completely. You surely made your position plain today," he added.

— — —

That afternoon I couldn't pick up the grain quickly enough. The large Habiru that Madiya worked behind went so fast that she had to scramble to keep up. Twice I had filled my basket and dumped it in the pile by Overseer Ladel before I got suspicious. I took up a position behind another woman, and within a few minutes the field was again littered with grain for me to find. I moved again, with the same result.

No one said a word.

"Yah, what can I do to repay such hesed?" I whispered. I looked toward the overseer, but Adon Boaz had left. Almost crying with joy and relief, I worked as fast as I could, and the pile by Geber Ladel grew bigger and bigger.

As the afternoon shadows lengthened I was so tired I could hardly move, but the thought of the surprise in Naomi's eyes when I returned with so much grain kept me going to the last. Only about half the field had been reaped, and two more fields rose on terraces above it. If this continued, I'd be able to fill at least one pithos with barley.

As the workers left the field, I took my last basketful to my pile.

"Well, you've done very well," Madiya said, giggling.

"More so than I deserve. What happened at the noon meal?"

"Adon Boaz guessed that you and Naomi didn't have any food, so he told us to be certain you had plenty when you went home tonight. I told you he was wealthy and generous!"

"You were right," I agreed. "How am I going to get this home?"

"Let me load it in the cart," Gershed said from beside me. "Did you glean all this today?" he added in surprise.

"Gleaning was very good today," Madiya informed him. "And it will be from now on, so you'd best show up every day to cart it all to the threshing floor. You can beat out the grain there," Madiya added to me. "Then you won't have to carry all the straw. As it is, you'll have enough of a load."

The threshing floor was a wide platform of stone built roughly in the middle of the surrounding grain fields in a place that caught the afternoon wind from the west. Madiya helped me pound the heads of grain with a stick until the kernels of barley fell from the stalks. While we worked, the wind from the sea brought coolness and blew away the chaff as we threw the grain into the air.

"You must have an ephah here!" Madiya exclaimed as we swept up the grain. "How are you going to carry it?"

"I'll have to use my head covering, I guess," I said. "I haven't anything else large enough to put it in. It won't fit in the basket."

"No, but some of it will. Here, line the basket with your head covering, and we'll pour in the barley. You'll have to tie the corners around it, but at least you can use the basket to carry it all. Whew—it's as heavy as my 3-year-old."

"You've been so helpful, Madiya. I'll see you tomorrow."

"I'll stop by, so wait for me."

"I will." I hurried back to Bethlehem, lugging the basket and wondering what Naomi would say. I must have had two weeks' worth of wages in grain to take home. And for Adon Boaz to offer me entrance into his clan still stunned me. I decided I'd better not count on that too much; his gesture might mean less than I thought. I was in a foreign land, after all, so I'd keep that part of the day to myself.

I had to squeeze sideways through the narrow alley to our courtyard. Naomi sat at the loom just staring, but she had obviously done a lot today. The cloth was half done. I almost lost the load when I entered the courtyard. "Naomi," I gasped, "you're going to have to help me. Light the lamp and open one of the pithoi. I can't handle this barley much longer."

Something about my voice made her look around. Her mouth dropped open when she saw the bulging headcloth half supported by the basket. "Where did you get all that?" she gasped.

"Later. Help me get this into the pithos."

Moving more quickly than she had in months, Naomi went into the house and lit our oil lamp, pushing aside the curtain that closed off the storage jars. She pulled the lid off the nearest one and helped me lift the cloth from the basket.

"See if you can just open a corner, then we can pour directly into the jar," I suggested.

"Where did you go?" Naomi asked again, her shaking fingers working at the knot Madiya had tied. "What field?"

"Out beyond the curve south of town. Watch it!"

The knot gave suddenly, and we almost spilled the grain, but Naomi caught the edge of the cloth. Carefully, we carried it over to the jar and poured it in, sneezing from the dust.

"Whose field was it?" Naomi asked again. "You couldn't have just gleaned all this! May Yahweh bless the man that took such interest in you! I will burn some grain tomorrow so that Yahweh will continue to favor you."

For the first time since Chilion died, Naomi actually smiled. It sent a thrill through me. I'd gotten her attention at last. She fussed over me like she used to as I shook out the headcloth and picked out the pieces of chaff that clung to it.

"Oh, here, I brought this, too," I said, remembering the parched grain and bread that I had tucked into my sash. I took it out. "Eat. I'll get the water gourd."

Before Naomi could say anything, I slipped out the door and into the coolness of the night. "Thank You, Yah," I said, brushing away a few tears. "Thank You that Naomi has awakened at last. Help me to keep her out of the shadows of her grief."

Naomi had eaten the bread and had started on the parched grain when I returned. I handed her the water gourd, and she drank, then looked at me.

"Now, tell me, how did you gather all that grain? Whose field did you work in?"

"The field belonged to Adon Boaz."

She blinked. "Boaz! May Yahweh richly repay his generosity!" she exclaimed. Then she looked thoughtful for a moment. "Maybe Yahweh hasn't forgotten to show hesed to me and the dead. You know, Boaz is a relative of ours, a possible goel on Elimelech's side. I hadn't considered him before since—well, maybe that won't matter. He was certainly more than kind today."

I hardly heard what Naomi had said after that third sentence. She had said *"ours,"* not just hers. Maybe she had decided I was not a burden to her after all.

"There's more," I said, breaking into her silence. "Adon Boaz insisted that I continue to glean in his fields. I'll probably come home tomorrow with twice what I have today, and I can glean all during the barley and wheat harvests. That should give us enough to last for a long time."

"Boaz spoke to you?" she asked, surprised. "What did he say? When did you see him?"

"He came to the field about midmorning," I replied. "Geber Ladel had me come to speak with him. Adon Boaz said I was to work in only his fields. I didn't know what to make of it at first; he acted flustered and kept repeating himself. He said I was to 'marry myself' to his reapers," I added, deliberately misquoting him to see what Naomi would say.

She frowned. "What could he be thinking of! You should stay with the binders, the other women. Otherwise, someone could get the wrong idea and try to molest you, especially since you're from Moab. You stay where Boaz can make certain no one bothers you."

"He assured me I would be fine more than once."

Naomi looked up. "You said he repeated himself and acted flustered?"

"Yes."

"Well, that's odd. Boaz isn't usually that way unless—h'mm. Why would he say 'marry'?" she ended, her voice trailing off.

"It seemed to amuse Geber Ladel a lot. At least, the overseer was laughing at something. But it might have been me."

"I don't think it was you," Naomi said, her speculative gaze really paying attention to me for the first time in months.

Iyar, second month, sixth day (1100 B.C.)

I got up the next morning extremely sore from the unaccustomed work of the day before. To my surprise, Naomi already had breakfast ready. It was the first time since we had left for Bethlehem that she had been up before me.

"Shalom," she greeted me with a smile.

"Shalom," I answered and sat down to eat.

While I did, she baked some unleavened bread for me to take for a lunch. She also had a juglet full of water and tied it on my sash herself.

"Remember, stay close to the binders," she urged me, handing me the largest basket we had. "We don't want anything to happen."

I went out to the market to wait for Madiya, meditating on what Naomi had said. Apparently now that I had brought home a significant amount of food I was important to her again. Therefore, one thing she needed was the assurance of another meal. Noticing the stare of a man in the market, I moved to another place. The man looked like a day laborer, probably here to work as a harvester.

He followed, keeping me in sight, and I worried that someone had told him I was a Moabite. Anxiously I scanned the market for Madiya. Fortunately, she arrived before anything more could develop.

"I'm glad you're here," I greeted her. "There was trouble brewing with that man over there."

Madiya looked. "That's Hattush, one of Tobeh's servants. I'm not surprised he'd try to get your eye. Not only is he the type to do it, but Tobeh probably encouraged him to make trouble. He's desperate for Elimelech's land."

That comment got my immediate attention. "Why? From what little I've heard, he has plenty of his own."

"He does, but he hasn't managed it well, and his fields no longer produce much. My abbi says he hasn't fertilized in years and it's a wonder he gets any crop at all. He can't understand what Tobeh's been thinking of."

By now we were beyond the city gates. The gardens and orchards were still green from the final rains of the season. The grapes had begun to swell on the vines.

Halfway to the field, I wondered if Adon Boaz would be there. My heart skipped a beat. After the things he'd said yesterday and the way he had treated me at the noon meal, I wasn't certain what to expect. Maybe yesterday had just been an impulse that he regretted now, or that meant nothing, even though the other field hands seemed to take it seriously.

And what about Adon Tobeh? Everyone assured me that Boaz didn't care about Tobeh, but I still worried. Boaz had been related to Elimelech, not Naomi, and with me a Moabite, I wondered if his hesed would last.

Madiya chattered on, but I barely listened. When we reached the field, Adon Boaz was already there, talking to the overseer. He greeted us and then turned away as Geber Ladel told Madiya to follow Sarnahal, the same reaper as yesterday. Standing close to the adon, I held my breath, wondering if he'd speak to me again. I was so tense that I hardly noticed the other workers headed to the field. And he was nicely taller than I, a pleasant change from Mahlon, who'd been a little shorter. Pleasant. Naomi. *You're here to glean,* I reminded myself and managed to follow Madiya to work without making a fool of myself.

Today was a repeat of yesterday afternoon. I couldn't collect the stalks fast enough. I had brought the biggest basket we had, but it wasn't sufficient. By the noon break I had a larger pile of grain than I'd had the previous day.

Madiya looked at it and giggled. "Might as well put it into

sheaves," she said. "You have enough here for several."

Boaz took the noon meal at our field again, and when I held back from the others, his eyes invited me forward, so I sat close to Madiya. He didn't speak to me, just glanced my way frequently. Madiya made certain I had plenty to eat, and he gave her a nod of approval.

Before the meal was half over a messenger came and spoke to him. After he gave the man some bread, parched grain, and a drink, the two left for Bethlehem, talking seriously about something.

I was surprised at the letdown I felt after he departed, though it did make me smile at my foolishness. An adon such as he would never consider taking a Moabite into his house unless it was as a slave. I should be content with having gained his favor to the extent I had. And if I really wanted to show my gratitude, I should make certain no one had the chance to connect me to him in any other capacity than gleaner and landowner. I should certainly ignore that little tingle that went through me every time I saw him.

With another self-conscious smile at how silly I could be, I tucked some parched grain into my lunch cloth.

"What are you doing?" one of the binders asked.

"I'm saving this for Naomi. She loves parched grain," I explained.

"She does? Here, take this," the woman offered, holding out the last of hers. "Hamioh, give Ruth the last of your parched grain. She's saving for Naomi. I'm Nehebet," she added to me.

The other woman promptly handed over the remnants of her meal as well.

"May Yahweh bless you both," I exclaimed.

Hamioh gave me a strange look, her round face puzzled. Nehebet looked down quickly to hide her own expression.

I looked at Madiya's dancing dark eyes. "Did I say something wrong?" I asked hesitantly.

"No. But Hamioh expected you to use Kemosh's name! You're a Moabite, after all."

The two binders flushed slightly.

"I guess it could sound odd," I acknowledged. "I hadn't thought of it that way."

Both women looked up in amazement, and Madiya laughed. "Naomi taught Ruth to worship Yahweh when she married Mahlon," she explained. "Now Yahweh is the only God she has—just like us."

Pleased smiles crossed the women's faces, and the atmosphere was much more relaxed after that, so I didn't bother to correct Madiya's assertion.

As we went back to work, I asked, "Where did you learn that I worship Yahweh?"

"Sarnahal the Habiru told me," she replied.

I looked at the large man whose arm already rose and fell in the steady rhythm of scything grain. Apparently what one Habiru knew, they all knew. Perhaps I owed Pashur more than I realized for my ready acceptance by the warriors.

While Madiya helped me bind the last of my grain that evening, Ladel came over to me.

"Ruth, Adon Boaz will expect you to glean in his fields on through the wheat harvest. Come with Madiya each day. She knows where all the fields are, and you can work after her as you have been doing."

"Yes, geber," I replied gratefully.

Gershed arrived, and his eyes widened when he saw my stack of sheaves. It took the three of us more than an hour at the threshing floor to beat out all the barley, and the Phoenician had to go into town to get something for us to carry it in. At the house the grain half filled the first pithos.

"What time tomorrow?" I asked Madiya when she finished helping us put the grain in storage.

"Oh, tomorrow is Shabbat," Madiya said. "No one will work until the day after that."

I had forgotten about the rest day, having not paid that much attention to the days of the week since Mahlon had died. But I was very grateful for it now. Two days of the unaccustomed labor had left me stiff and sore. After eating the evening meal, I relaxed on the stool, looking around. Naomi had cleaned, and the small touches that she had previously used to welcome Shabbat were present today. Tears sprang to my eyes.

"How did it go in the fields?" she asked.

Wiping my eyes, I told her all about the little happenings of the day, just as I used to. She eagerly asked after anything I could remember about Boaz. Since he was the foremost thought in my mind, I found it easy to satisfy her curiosity.

The next afternoon Tashima and another woman came to visit. She was astonished at the animated change in Naomi. The other woman was Deborah, a childhood friend who had married Tobeh. She looked extremely tired and carried herself heavily from having borne several children. She eyed me warily before ignoring me. From comments in the conversation I gathered this was the first chance she had had to see Naomi, since Tobeh disliked Moabites so much. I fell asleep listening to them talk.

The days passed swiftly. Adon Boaz always had a kind greeting for me, but other than that, he sent any messages through Geber Ladel. I would have thought him indifferent except for the way his eyes followed me when he was at the field and the look I saw in them when no one else was noticing. That look in his brown eyes always produced an answering desire in me, distracting me from my work and filling me with thoughts I had no business thinking.

But he was constantly on my mind, and I snatched any information about the adon that came my way. I allowed myself to ask only the most general questions, and only when I was certain that nothing could be read into my inquiry. I mulled over each new thing I learned, trying to understand this man who had granted us such hesed. I wished there was some way I could repay him for the help and protection he had given Naomi and me. I knew there had to be something missing from his life, for where else did that shadowed sorrow in his eyes come from?

Iyar, second month, eleventh day (1100 B.C.)

The second week of gleaning I had trouble in the market. Tobeh's servant, Hattush, had stationed himself just outside the entrance to our little alley. When I emerged to go to the field, he stepped up to me and put his hand on my arm.

"It's time you stopped avoiding me," he said in a low voice. "My geber sent me to you. He knows what you are, and so do I. If you want to help your mother-in-law, come to Adon Tobeh's house tonight. If he's pleased, he'll see that you both are taken care of."

When I tried to pull away, his grip only tightened. "Leave me alone," I said.

"Do you think he doesn't know why you glean so much every day? Who is it? Boaz or Ladel?"

"I don't know what you're talking about," I said furiously, although I understood only too well. "Let me go!" I jerked hard against his hold.

"You just settle down. I'm not through talking yet. Just because you glean in Boaz's field doesn't put you above me. I'll expect the same you give to them and my adon, to pay for my silence."

"I'm through listening! Get away from me!" Seeing Madiya approaching, I gave her a desperate look.

"Ruth!" she called, starting to run toward us.

"How dare you, you—" The force that jerked him backward choked the man's words off.

I tore my arm from his grasp and jumped away as Madiya arrived, breathless, beside me.

"I believe the woman said that she wanted to be left alone," Sarnahal commented mildly to the man he held immobile on the ground.

The man twisted in his grip. "She's nothing but a heathen, a Moabite tempter that—*ahh!"* His words ended in a gasp of pain.

"As for her being a heathen, I've heard her use Yahweh's name with more reverence than you probably do, and as for being a tempter, I've yet to see her do more than work to stay alive and worry over her mother-in-law. That being the case, I suggest—strongly—that you keep away from her, because if you don't, I'm liable to get more careless with you than I have already."

The Habiru let go, and the man, giving both of us a glare of pure hatred, scuttled away.

"Who was that?" my rescuer asked.

"Hattush, one of Tobeh's servants," Madiya answered. "Ruth, are you all right?"

Although shaken and upset, I nodded. I couldn't afford to have anything like this happen. The slightest thing could turn people against me, and if we were to have any chance at keeping Elimelech's land under our control, I had to preserve a spotless reputation. More so than ever if Hattush had spoken the truth about Adon Tobeh wanting my favors. He would consider a refusal an insult and would be looking for an excuse to rouse the town against me. I must be very careful of him from now on.

"He waited for you at the alley entrance, didn't he?" Sarnahal asked, watching the man disappear in the market crowd.

Again I nodded.

"Madiya, tell Geber Ladel I'll be a little late today." He started off.

"Wonder what he's up to?" Madiya commented. "Oh well. If you're ready, we'd best be getting on ourselves, Ruth. Or do you want to stay home today?"

"I can't. We need all the food we can get. I'll be all right." But I wasn't all right. I could still feel the man's fingers on my arm and hear his voice telling me to go to Adon Tobeh's house. I had thought his geber hated me. What was I going to do?

"Yahweh, be with me!" I prayed again and again, but I felt as if every eye in the world were watching me, and it was almost noon before my trembling stopped.

Geber Ladel called me over before we left for the threshing floor that evening. "Ruth, are you all right? Tobeh's servant didn't hurt you this morning?"

I wondered how he'd heard about it. "I'll be all right. You are kind to ask," I replied.

"Gershed, be certain she gets back to her house," Ladel directed.

"Count on it," the Phoenician said grimly.

That night I couldn't get to sleep. I kept waiting for someone to jump out of the dark at me and grab me as Hattush had. If anyone did break down our flimsy door and I cried for help, would anyone answer? If the townspeople turned against me and drove me out, how could I survive? How would I protect myself against people like Abiaz? Had he found out who I really was and told Kemosh-dan, or Amarel of Dibon? Amarel would want me to provide an heir, but all those barren years with Mahlon would argue against my usefulness. Kemosh-dan would just have me killed on general principles.

What could I do? When I tried to turn over, I bumped my harp. Feeling it reminded me that I was not entirely alone. Yah had promised to protect me. "I shall have to trust You, Yah," I whispered, "for I surely cannot protect myself." Again shifting on my mat, I tried to make myself sleep.

What if I was barren? Deep in my heart, I had always attributed my childlessness to Mahlon's sickly health, but what if I was wrong? What if I couldn't give Boaz any children? My thoughts froze in mortification. When had I started thinking myself into the adon's bed where I had no right to be? But the thought wouldn't go away, fed by the silent intensity of his look that always made my breath come faster and reminded me that I was a woman.

I tried to find a comfortable position. Whether or not anything could ever come of his desire, I didn't know and should not be speculating on! A half hour later I gave it up, took my harp, and sat in the doorway. After turning it, I strummed it softly, imagining myself in my god place in Moab, looking down at the sheep in Yidla's flock. I played the quiet, contented songs I remembered from then, and gradually peace settled in my heart. When I stopped, I looked for a long time at the stars shining in the sky above me. A movement in the alley caught my eye.

"Who's there?" I gasped, standing.

"One that means you no harm, geberet," a voice answered. "You and Geberet Naomi will be safe. Forgive me for disturbing you, but your music drew me closer."

"May Yahweh grant you hesed," I said and went inside. *Thank You, Yah,* I added to myself.

~ ~ ~

"What do you mean, someone accosted her in the market?" Boaz roared.

"She's fine, Boaz," Ladel soothed. "Madiya got there and so did Sarnahal. He handled it very quietly, with no disturbance. Will you stop pacing?"

"You're sure she wasn't hurt? Did he touch her? Threaten her? Who was it?"

"Gershed says it was Hattush. It's his style."

"If Tobeh is behind this, I'll crush him with my own hands," Boaz hissed between clenched teeth.

"You'll have to take your place in line," Pashur said from the office doorway. "Mattan, Patah, and Sarnahal have already claimed that right, provided Meshullam will let them get ahead of him. Although if they could see you prowling around like a lion, they might think better of getting in your way."

"She could have been harmed, Pashur, to say nothing of what the talk would do to both her and Naomi." Boaz paused in his pacing. "What are you doing here?"

"She won't be harmed. Sarnahal alerted Patah, who got a message to Mattan immediately. As long as there is need, there will be a guard posted day and night by Naomi's house."

"A guard would start even more talk—"

"Would you relax, Boaz? Give us some credit for subtlety. Who's going to notice that a beggar has changed his sleeping place?"

With a sigh Boaz ran his hand over his face. "Sorry, Pashur. This has upset me more than I thought. I haven't felt anything like this since—"

"Since Mena," Ladel finished softly.

Reluctantly Boaz nodded.

"Why don't you ask her to marry you? You took at least a year too long with Mena."

"In case you haven't noticed, I'm old, Ladel. Why would she want me? She could have any young man in the town just for the asking."

"Not yet," Pashur said. "Many people are still making up their mind about her, but if she continues on as she is, and with Naomi's family connections, she'll be very eligible."

Boaz's expression froze. "Yes, she will get the best."

"What makes you think she won't recognize the best when she sees it?" the Habiru asked.

"A young woman deserves a young man," Boaz said with a sigh. "If I were even 10 years younger—but I'm not."

"I don't think that will matter to Ruth," Ladel commented. "Since you're here, Pashur, I'll go to Tashima. She's as upset as Boaz about this."

The wool merchant stood aside to let the overseer out the door and watched him leave the private courtyard.

When he turned back to Boaz, his face was grim. "A word to open your ear, Boaz."

"What is it?"

"This situation is more explosive than you know. Abbi went to his sources for some information. Ruth came with Naomi for more than one reason. Not only is she devoted to her mother-in-law, but some people asked too many questions about her origins. She's Eglon's granddaughter."

As if struck by a blow, Boaz backed a step, then slowly sat down. "I thought Kemosh-dan wiped out the entire bloodline."

"He tried, but it's been rumored for years that a couple people escaped, one being Mesha's youngest wife. Eglon's royal signet ring disappeared the same night, and speculation has it that the woman took it with her.

"I already knew that much, and about the joined fingers in the royal line, when I agreed to bring Naomi back to Bethlehem. When I first met Ruth, she adjusted the strap of the harp case on her shoulder with her left hand, and I noticed the slight oddness in the way she used her fingers. It took me a bit to remember why it seemed important. I also noticed that she carries something on a cord around her neck. She is never without it, and it's the right size to be a signet ring."

Pashur leaned against the wall, staring into the corner. "That was enough for Meshullam to question his sources about. What came back is that the timing is perfect and that Ruth's parents and sister were very protective of her. She was never alone and always kept in the background, even when she sang at the temple. If royal visitors came to Heshbon, the girl would vanish.

"On the heels of that report came an urgent message from Yidla. I just got back from Moab this afternoon and came here as soon as it was dark."

"This wouldn't be Yidla of the Yidla rams, would it?" Boaz interrupted, motioning Pashur to take a stool.

"Yes. I'd gained his confidence, and he trusts his sheep and their wool to me. That's why my business grew so rapidly."

"What's his connection with Ruth?"

"His pasture is close to her foster grandfather's farmstead, and she spent a lot of time with him as she grew up. He's the one who taught her to worship Yahweh."

"How did Yidla learn to worship Yahweh?"

"That's my fault again," Pashur confessed. "When I first met him years ago, I showed him how to clean out a tiny spring in the pasture where he keeps his flock. He was very thankful, then upset because he couldn't ask the god of the place to bless me because he didn't know his name. I said it must be Yahweh. It was a bit embarrassing when he took me seriously, but since then Yidla has worshipped Yah, as he says it."

The Habiru leaned forward on the stool, looking embarrassed again. "I'd never say this to anyone but you, Boaz, but Yahweh loves that shepherd. Yidla claims Yah taught him about sheep. A head injury left him simple, but you wouldn't know it when he works with his animals.

"Anyway, Yidla rescued the midwife, heard her story, and sent for me."

"If I understood Yidla correctly, a couple days before I met Naomi at the inn, Ruth and he overheard a stranger from Beth-peor talking with Abiaz, a Heshbon troublemaker. Amarel of Dibon wants Kemosh-dan's throne and needs someone of the Eglon bloodline to marry. His agent eventually traced Mesha's youngest wife to Heshbon. Abiaz guessed what was in the wind and wanted to be part of it. There was just enough odd about Ruth to attract his attention, and he thought about it for a while, then went to the midwife. From what I saw, she refused to answer his questions for some time."

Boaz winced, noticing Pashur's clenched fists and taut frame.

"Finally, she told him that a richly dressed woman had appeared in

Heshbon the night Shimrith, Ruth's 'mother,' went into labor. The two gave birth in the same house. Shimrith's baby died, as did the woman. The midwife gave the live baby to the live mother."

The Habiru paused again, then stood up restlessly. "After Yidla assured the midwife I was a friend of Ruth's, I heard the part of the story Abiaz didn't get. The midwife found Moab's royal signet ring in the woman's clothes and wrapped it up in the baby's swaddling cloths. Shimrith found it, of course."

For a time Boaz sat in silence. "Well, that explains why she married an Israelite," he mused. "It would provide some protection for any children."

"There's more," Pashur said. "I may not be the only one who knows this. While I was in Moab, Tobeh's agent was asking questions about Ruth. He and Abiaz found each other."

Boaz paled.

The silence stretched. "Can you help her?" Pashur finally asked.

"What more can I do?" Boaz replied, his face drawn. "With the prejudice against Moab in town, I dare not show interest. If I lose any influence in the gate, Tobeh will take over, and that will be the destruction of Bethlehem, to say nothing of Ruth. We have to wait and hope the scales will tip in our favor."

"But Ruth may not have time to wait, especially if Tobeh knows this." Pashur swung himself around. "What about Elimelech's land?" he asked savagely. "Can that tie in at all?"

Boaz shrugged. "All I can do there is make it difficult to redeem. Tobeh is determined to get it, and I have no power to stop him. I suspect getting the land is the last step in his plans to elevate himself."

Pashur sat down again. "That would explain it," he said soberly. "Patah says he's recklessly depleted his treasury with those feasts he's given. This must be his big move, and it must culminate soon, for his wealthy facade won't last long. What does Tahat say about his shipping?"

"That's a bit puzzling," Boaz replied, settling his back against the wall. "Tobeh's not selling. He's apparently waiting, but we can't figure out what for."

"Isn't there anything we can do besides wait?" Pashur fumed, his hands restlessly fingering the dagger in his girdle.

"Not that I can see," Boaz replied with a faint smile at his friend's actions. "We'll have to leave it in Yahweh's hands. What happened to the midwife?"

Suddenly Pashur grinned. "Did you know that Patah is getting married?"

"Already? Is he old enough?" Boaz looked surprised.

"He thinks so. He convinced his beloved to marry now with the assurance there would be a good midwife to attend her."

"I see," Boaz said with a chuckle. "Shalom, Pashur."

"Shalom, Boaz."

The Time of Reaping and Celebration

The harvest is fully ripe and waiting to be reaped. All that remains is to scythe the grain and rejoice with the abundance it produces. But harvest also means sorting the good from the bad. As in all fields, Yahweh has weeds that must be tended to. You've no doubt watched the growth of the particularly large weed in this story. So has Yahweh. He's not blind, you know, and no weed has gotten by His eyes yet. Just because He doesn't deal with them as we wish doesn't mean they escape. But let us not stray from our story. Follow Yahweh as He goes to His field and brings in the harvest He has worked toward for so long!

Spring
Iyar, second month, twenty-third day, Ruth's twenty-second year (1100 B.C.)

Do I look all right?" I asked Madiya as we hurried behind Naomi to Tashima's house in Boaz's compound.

"You look fine," my friend assured me. "This is just a get-together to welcome Naomi. All the women are eager to hear you play."

"I wish Tashima hadn't said so much. What if no one likes my music?"

"How can they not? You play the best songs I've ever heard," Madiya assured me.

Last Shabbat Tashima had come to see Naomi again, and I had been playing my harp when she arrived. Naomi had boasted that I had been the best singer and player in Moab. Tashima loved my praise songs to Yahweh. I didn't tell her that I had originally composed some of them for Kemosh's temple and had simply changed the god's name to Yahweh when I sang them here. When she decided to give Naomi a welcome-home feast, she asked me to sing and play my harp.

Hurrying along, I tugged at my sash. I hadn't been this nervous since the night I had to do Alya's solos in the grape harvest ceremony. When we arrived, Naomi sat beside Deborah, Tobeh's wife. Hamioh and Nehebet, the binders I'd met in Boaz's field, called me over to meet their friends. I found everyone as curious about me as if I were from beyond Egypt instead of just across the Jordan.

"Did you live in a town in Moab?" one woman asked.

"Yes, in Heshbon," I replied. "It's bigger than Bethlehem, and the caves there are grouped closer to the town. Many of the people live in them, like here."

"Was there a high place close by?" Nehebet asked.

The other women gasped at her boldness, and Deborah looked up alertly.

"There was one on the northeast side of town," I admitted. "Immi never let me go there. Then I met Naomi and Mahlon, so I never attended it at all."

Nehebet looked distinctly disappointed. She was married, but the way her eyes followed the men in town made me wonder if she wouldn't have participated in some of the fertility rites of the high places. Not that she'd have to go to Moab to do so. I'd noticed high places here in Judah, and not very far away.

"What are the rites for?" Nehebet pressed.

I glanced around quickly. Some of the women looked uncomfortable, but all of them were curious. Deborah had turned back to Naomi, but her posture told me she still listened.

"The priests say the rites remind Kemosh to replenish the land every year so we will have food," I explained. "But I'm glad I worship Yahweh now."

"Why?" Nehebet asked.

"Because I'd rather not worship a god that needs constant prodding as if he was a lazy ox. Just look at how Yahweh took care of your ancestors in the wilderness. I think He's a better god than Kemosh."

"That's so," Hamioh agreed. "I've heard that the foreign priests have to slash themselves to get their god's attention. I'm glad we don't have to do that."

"Don't you have a song about Yahweh taking care of us?" Madiya put in. "Tashima said you sang one about a goat kid that wandered away."

"I wrote that for some children," I admitted. "It tells the story of a kid who got lost and how Yahweh watched over it until the shepherd found it."

"Sing it for us," Hamioh urged. "I overheard you one evening, and you're good."

I blushed. "You're kind to think so." Getting my harp, I tuned it and started the song. It was a quiet one with a simple melody that alternated between dissonance and harmony as the kid wandered into and out of danger. The happy, spritely rhythm when the shepherd found the kid and it bounced into his arms made everyone laugh and clap at the end. The applause was louder than I expected, for the entire room had quieted and listened, even the children. Only the men's voices in the courtyard continued as they laughed and talked.

"That was wonderful, Ruth," Tashima said. "Sing the one about the fox finding his vixen."

"I don't want to interrupt things," I protested.

"You're not. Sing for us."

I performed that one, and then another, a sad song of two lovers who had to part. When I finished it, Nehebet was humming along.

"You have a good ear," I told her. "Sing one with me."

She looked pleased, and I started a song Mahlon had taught me about picking olives from a tree. I suspected most everyone here knew it, and soon all had joined in. When I began playing Miriam's triumph song about the defeat of the Egyptians, everyone looked surprised, then delighted. We stumbled through it once, laughing at the mistakes everyone made, then tried it again.

"I think we've got it this time," I said. "Once more."

Nehebet had a good voice and took Miriam's solos. I led the chorus and played. I hadn't realized how much I missed singing in a group, and I couldn't seem to get enough of the music. Tashima produced a tambourine for Hamioh, who had a natural sense of rhythm.

> "I will sing to the Lord,
> For He has triumphed gloriously.
> The horse and his rider
> He has thrown into the sea!
> The Lord is my strength and song,
> And He has become my salvation;
> He is my God, and I will praise Him,
> My father's God, and I will exalt Him."

If I had been paying more attention, I would have seen the men gathered at the door, and I wouldn't have jumped so when the male voices, led by Geber Ladel, joined in. Tashima encouraged me to go on, so we continued the piece until the end. When the singing died away, no one spoke for a moment.

"That was wonderful, Ruth," Naomi said. The look she gave me warmed my heart at the same time I became acutely aware that Boaz was watching me. When I glanced back, however, he was walking out the door, so I didn't know if he liked the music or not.

"Yes, the singing was wonderful, but what about the food, Tashima?" Ladel asked.

"I forgot all about it," his wife gasped. "Ruth, your music is irresistible! But we must serve."

I put the harp away, and everyone scrambled to help serve the food while the men good-naturedly starved until it was ready. I stayed busy in the house until everyone went out to sit in the courtyard and eat. Then I remained by Naomi's side. Boaz carried on various conversations on the other side of the court, and only once did I feel his gaze. As I glanced up, his eyes flicked away almost immediately. But in the brief moment we shared a glance, the depth of his feelings set my heart pounding and brought a blush to my face.

"Ruth, are you all right?" Naomi asked.

"I'm a bit hot," I mumbled.

Naomi said no more, but her look strayed to Boaz.

Not long after, Tashima had me play again, and I sang for more than an hour. When we left, she went with us to the gate. "Your music added something special to the evening, Ruth. And Ladel told me this was the first time he'd heard Boaz sing since his first wife died. He took her death so hard, you know. Well, shalom to you both."

"Shalom," we answered.

"How long ago did she die?" I asked Naomi as we started back to our house.

"It was before we went to Moab," she replied. "She died birthing their second child. His son died about a year later, I think, from a bad fall."

"That must have been a hard time," I ventured, wondering why she talked so matter-of-factly about that much tragedy.

She shrugged. "Yahweh knows best, and Mena was half Edomite."

Why would that make any difference?

The beggar sleeping at the entrance to our courtyard roused when we approached. I caught the gleam of metal by his side in the dim light, and something in the way he moved reminded me of the trained warriors I had seen. Silently I thanked Yahweh for the friends I hadn't known I had.

After the feast the stream of visitors to our home increased, and everyone wanted me to play. I always did, including many songs that others could accompany along with me. Even Deborah's attitude toward me softened somewhat. On Shabbat I sometimes sang all afternoon, and before long the whole town had learned many of my praise songs.

The sparkle came back into Naomi's eyes as she reestablished her position as a favorite friend to nearly everyone. With Tashima and Madiya leading the women's attitude toward me, I was accepted as a decent, eligible woman in spite of my origins, and I did nothing to jeopardize that reputation. We hadn't yet gained control of Elimelech's land, and Naomi and I would need all the support at the gate we could muster in order to do so.

Available bachelors started looking my way, and Naomi often discussed this one or that one, asking how I liked them and what I thought. Usually I was too tired from gleaning to consider the subject that much, but I noticed that it became almost the whole of Naomi's conversation with me. I was also aware that Adon Tobeh watched me with hatred now.

Spring
Sivan, third month, seventh day, Boaz's forty-third year (1100 B.C.)

"Adon Boaz, Adon Hanan says you must come to the gate at once," Patah panted, stopping Boaz as he rode out of sight of Bethlehem on the road to Jebus.

"What's wrong?"

"Geber Tobeh is claiming that Bethlehem needs an appointed leader."

Without a word, Boaz reined his donkey about and prodded it into a trot. The young Habiru matched his pace. "He's at the south gate. Adon Hanan says to hurry."

This had to be the opening move in Tobeh's campaign to establish himself as a king. Boaz tightened his lips grimly, urging the donkey on faster. How was he to handle this? Maybe his best course was to remind people what had happened when others tried to gain honor they had no right to. He could also point out that the judges appointed by Yahweh had all refused to become kings. By the time he crossed the west market he had his speech outlined in his mind.

Gershed waved at him frantically as he passed his gate. The servant held out his best cloak. "They're still at the gate, adon. Adon Hanan has been stalling for you, but Tobeh has taken an unexpected tack. He's urging the people to be faithful to Yahweh, saying that the famine was punishment for sin. Hanan is afraid he is targeting Geberet Ruth."

Boaz froze for an instant, his stomach suddenly tight, his planned speech fleeing from his mind. "This is very good to know, Gershed." Putting on the cloak, Boaz strode down the street toward the south gate. If Tobeh had learned of Ruth's ancestry, what could he, Boaz, say to protect her? Having a poor Moabite widow in town was one thing, but having the granddaughter of an oppressor such as Eglon was another. How could he defend Ruth without lessening his influence and thus destroying any chance she had?

"Yahweh, give me words to defeat Tobeh's plans," he whispered. "Ruth is a good woman and cares faithfully for Naomi. She forsook Kemosh and worships only You, entrusting her life to the shelter of Your wings. Wrap Your cloak around her and preserve her from those who would destroy her."

Tobeh's voice reached his ears as he approached the gate. He paused in the shadows to listen.

"Brethren, have you forgotten the punishments rained upon our fathers for their sin at Beth-peor? Dare we to tempt our young men by allowing this Moabite to dwell among us? She will use her wiles to ensnare our sons, drawing them after her into the false beliefs of the Baals."

Boaz clenched his teeth. Hanan had been right. Tobeh was using Ruth as his first challenge, and the extraordinary productivity of Ruth's gleaning played right into his hands. Tobeh would conveniently forget there was no other source of food for Naomi and Ruth, and he would use the Moabite woman to excuse his own blatant neglect of his kinswoman.

Suddenly Boaz sucked in his breath. As a Moabite, Ruth would fit right in with Tobeh's usual diatribes against Canaanite blood. While most people in town had accepted Ruth, there were always those eager to believe the worst, and Tobeh would do his best to connect it with his rival.

"Would you have this foreigner take your sons to the high places to worship there?" Tobeh continued. "Have you forgotten why we all wear a tassel?" He showed one on his robe. "This symbolizes our loyalty to Yahweh and His commandments and our rejection of the beliefs that the world was created by the union of Baal and his consort. We do not believe that the life-giving rain is the seed of Baal, nor that emulating the union of the gods at the high places will magically stimulate divinity to replenish their creation.

"Our God, Yahweh, is above and beyond such things. He created the world by His word—and nothing else. As Moses wrote, 'And God *said* "Let there be light," and there was light.' To worship in these places, to participate in their rites, is a denial of Yahweh as Creator, and tempts us to believe ourselves divine as the idolaters do when they 'join with the gods' in such activities."

A man stepped up to hear better, drawing Boaz's attention to the crowd, larger now than when he'd come. Even as he watched, a few more men drifted up. Boaz smiled. Given the timing of this speech, when many men and elders would be busy with harvest, Tobeh had probably planned for a small crowd packed with his own supporters, thus striking the first blow when his opponents would have no chance to respond.

Boaz scanned the market, looking for Tobeh's friends while the man continued his speech.

"Yahweh's wrath came upon our fathers not only at Beth-peor, but at Sinai when they made the golden calf, for Baal is portrayed as a bull to symbolize strength and virility. To create such an idol and worship it with the fertility rites practiced in the high places was such an affront to Yahweh that He destroyed thousands, both at Sinai and Beth-peor."

To one side, Raham and Yattir the Ammonite gave their whole attention to Tobeh. Boaz located Zakkur standing a little distance in front and to one side where Tobeh could easily see him without shifting his eyes from his audience. Bilgai stood opposite Zakkur, his murmurs to those around him underscoring Tobeh's words. Even old Eprah was here, looking wise. Boaz shifted his position, edging toward Hanan's seat.

"The crowd has grown," he said softly.

Hanan nodded, eyes twinkling. "Meshullam's Habiru asked me to send word if Tobeh made a move. It seems their curiosity spread to almost everyone else as well."

At that moment Zakkur saw Boaz, and his eyes widened in alarm.

"I believe that he did not plan for you to be here," Hanan said, hardly moving his lips.

Boaz barely nodded in reply.

"I have inquired after this Moabite," Tobeh went on. "She was often in the temple to her god, even as a child. How do we know that this harlot is not a qedeshah, a woman of the high places? Would you have Yahweh's wrath descend upon Bethlehem? We must root out from among us anything that would corrupt. We dare not allow anyone, especially a beautiful, enticing Moabite qedeshah, to threaten our sons and daughters."

Zakkur frowned at Tobeh, trying to get his attention, but he was too absorbed in what he was saying to notice.

"Yes, I said daughters," he warned. "Already the leavening of sin spreads among us. More went on at the feast welcoming Naomi than you may know. The Moabite first beguiled the women with her music, and then talked of the religion of her land. And none stopped her. Why? Because she was in the house of Boaz, a respected man, an elder in the gate, someone seemingly blessed of Yahweh."

Tobeh paused, catching sight of Zakkur, who shook his head slightly, trying to warn him, but Tobeh frowned in his turn. Several of the men around Boaz smiled in anticipation.

"But is he blessed? Think back, friends and neighbors. For what reason did Yahweh take his family? Do you think our God punishes in such a manner for nothing? To this day, Boaz remains childless.

"What of his inheritance? His father passed on a rich living. What of it now? Has it been increased? The years have gone, and nothing has multiplied. Surely this is a sign from Yahweh that He has removed His blessing."

Intent silence fell on the crowd, and Tobeh drew himself up to his full height, knowing he had every ear in the square.

"He has Rahab for an ancestor. She supposedly forsook her gods and worshipped only Yahweh after the fall of Jericho, but can we be certain of this? Perhaps worship of her gods has continued in secret, and Yahweh is punishing hidden sins. Perhaps Boaz favors the Moabite because he joins with her in worship of the foreign gods around us. Perhaps his treasury is empty because he denies Yahweh as Creator and thinks to make himself divine in the worship of other gods."

Zakkur's shoulders slumped, a sour expression on his face. He tried one last time to get Tobeh to stop, only to be ignored again. Obviously this was the climax of the speech. Boaz almost laughed in relief. Tobeh could not know Ruth's true ancestry.

Spreading his hands, Tobeh drove his point home. "It is time to know, friends. Why has Boaz favored the Moabite? Is he in agreement with her regarding the gods of Moab?"

"I believe I'm in complete agreement," Boaz announced, striding forward. Heads turned, and the crowd shifted excitedly, astonished at his words. Hanan watched with an expressionless face, and Zakkur eyed him narrowly, suspecting a trick of some kind.

"If I remember correctly, Geberet Ruth characterized Kemosh as an ox, emasculated and lazy, needing constant prodding to do its work. I don't see how I could have said it better myself. Being frequently in the temple as a lay singer, she should know of what she speaks. I doubt a qedeshah would maintain that Kemosh was of any use in such a state."

Laughter burst through the crowd, and Tobeh flushed. "More may have been said," he retorted, covering his surprise at his rival's presence. "Who knows what ideas she may have talked of?"

"Ask your wife. She was listening at the time. Or do you doubt her veracity?"

At the question, Zakkur turned tensely to Tobeh. Boaz caught the look on Eprah's face growing more and more annoyed as Tobeh remained silent. He stifled his own smile as he remembered how Eprah doted on his granddaughter.

Shifting from defense to attack, Boaz said, "I am curious about something, Tobeh. If Yahweh has blessed you as much as you imply, how is it that your kinswoman, Naomi, has received no substance from you? Were the harvests from your fields so bad that you could spare none for your cousin?"

"Naomi does not live in my house," Tobeh replied shortly.

"Nor does she live in mine," Boaz said smoothly. "But I did not see that as an excuse to allow widows to starve at my door. Yahweh commanded that both widows and strangers be allowed to gain a living by such things as gleaning. Even if you feel that such aid taints the purity of your house, surely you cannot condemn others who fill the breach and who keep Yahweh's anger from descending upon all of us in answer to the cry of oppression. Such things are expected in the Ephrath clan."

"I'm sure being of Rahab's blood, you do feel inclined toward alluring qedeshah!" Tobeh sneered, gathering his garments in preparation to leave. "I, on the other hand, am also incl—am *not* inclined!"

Boaz permitted a slight smile to cross his lips, noting the slight flush on his older rival's face. "I pray I will always obey Yahweh's command, regardless of the blood that flows in my veins."

Murmurs of agreement and amusement at Tobeh's slip of the tongue sifted through the crowd.

"I will never risk the wrath of Yahweh by associating with idolaters. To allow a qedeshah among us is an affront to our God, regardless of how tempting I—we may find her!" Zakkur froze at his friend's second slip of the tongue, and Tobeh flushed, causing many in the audience to smile knowingly.

"Oh?" Boaz asked. "With all the evil you accuse her of, you find her tempting?"

"I would not let the hem of my garment touch such a one," Tobeh snarled, trying to undo his mistake. "I will do my duty by my kinswoman should it be asked of me, but I will protect what is mine from corruption." He whirled and walked rapidly from the square.

"Yes, and what he wouldn't give for a chance at that corruption," someone said cynically just within Boaz's hearing. Murmuring and chuckling among themselves, the crowd slowly dispersed.

Hanan rose, leaning heavily on his staff. "You held your own," he said to Boaz. "It's fortunate you were here when he threw out his challenge. Had you not been able to answer immediately, things would have swung heavily in Tobeh's favor."

"Then it's fortunate that you sent for me," Boaz replied, helping the elder across the square.

"Driving that wedge between Tobeh and Eprah was pure genius," Hanan chuckled. "Tobeh's refusal to support his wife is not something Eprah will soon forget, and he's been Tobeh's main support since his marriage."

"Let's hope that I can do enough to block his plans. I hadn't realized how hard Tobeh has become. Life will be unbearable for many if he gains his ends."

"Yes," Hanan agreed. "And any victory of his now, no matter how small, will be seen as a sign from Yahweh."

"That works both ways."

"It may, but do not count on it. Shalom, my friend. I look forward to the day when I can leave this gate with you sitting in my seat."

Boaz waited until he was safely in his office before easing onto a stool and putting his head in his hands. Thank Yahweh Ruth's deportment had been such that the only thing Tobeh could find against her was her position as a temple singer. In spite of the man's admission that she appealed to him, had she been less circumspect, or if Tobeh could have revealed that the town harbored Eglon's granddaughter, things would have gone very differently.

Sivan, third month, twenty-eighth day, Ruth's twenty-second year (1100 B.C.)

I paused on my way to my god place in the little valley, trying to spot my Habiru escort, but as always, I could see nothing. It amazed me how they could be around but not be seen. I owed them so much, and often wondered how I could repay them for the safety they provided when I ventured into the forests alone. Usually I sang some songs I thought a warrior might enjoy before I left.

Tucked up against the rock, I peered through the screen of new oak leaves into the tiny valley to see what would happen today. The doings of the small animals amused me, and once I'd seen an eagle swoop down and catch an unwary coney. But today nothing moved in the lazy heat. My mind drifted, as did my fingers on the strings of the harp.

Last night Naomi had told me a most unusual story about Tamar, the woman married to the oldest son of Judah, son of Jacob. When her husband died, Judah had told his second son to perform a levirate marriage and give Tamar a child to carry on his brother's name. The son refused to do this, and subsequently died. Judah thought Tamar was cursed in some way, and put off giving her his only remaining son.

In response Tamar trapped Judah by playing the part of a prostitute. When Judah heard that she was pregnant, he sentenced her to death. He was quite embarrassed when she produced his own staff and signet to prove that he himself was the father of her child. He acknowledged the rightness of her actions and took her back into his tents, raising the twins that Tamar had conceived through him.*

I puzzled over why Naomi would tell me this story, one so full of trickery and deceit. Why was it on her mind? She rarely sank into her grief now, and sometimes I surprised an intent expression on her face. I sensed that she wanted something very much. But what was it?

I leaned back, glancing at the blue sky above. The old eagle drifted in lazy circles up there, and I wondered what it would be like to see the land laid out as it did. What would be important? What was Bethlehem to the creature? Just a place where it could no longer hunt?

Naomi needed a son to restore her life.

The thought coalesced in my mind from dozens of comments and actions. I let my hands fall to my lap. Her happiness and security depended on a son, and I was the one chance she had. My ability to provide food must have awakened her to other possibilities. No wonder she always wanted to discuss eligible men and had been so interested when Boaz favored me.

Sitting there, watching the eagle soar in smaller and smaller circles, I admitted that I too dreamed of a son. I pressed against my cheek the fingers that had touched Adon Boaz when he handed me some food. Mahlon had never stirred me as deeply as this man did. I had never mentioned to Naomi the intense desire I sensed within the adon or the deep ache it generated within myself. I saved those thoughts for the silence and privacy of the god places.

What would it be like to know that Boaz was my beloved, my dahveed, and I was his? To be able to accept and return the desire I saw in his eyes? I shivered in anticipation and hugged my knees to my chest. Since I'd first seen that look I'd not given thought to another man. The stories I heard about him showed his compassion for and understanding of those in need, explaining his amazing hesed to two destitute widows

---

* Genesis 38.

not of his clan. Mahlon had given me his heart, but he was a boy compared to Boaz, who had been seasoned and deepened by sorrow and trouble, making his regard all the more precious.

I smiled. The adon couldn't hide his feelings from me. His eyes told me of the totality and exclusivity of his need, reminding me of the love between Sakar and Orpah, Shimrith and Ithmah, and my foster grandparents. I wanted that love with a hunger only awakened by the thing itself.

But Adon Boaz had made no advances. Did he hold back because of what the town would think, or because he himself could not accept a Moabite? What would he think if he knew my real ancestry? I didn't know, but that didn't lessen my desire for him to cover me with his garment and father my son.

With a sigh I sternly brought myself back to reality, knowing how foolish my dreams were. The best way for me to repay the adon was to ignore the feelings inside me. He had already done more than we could have expected. His blessing had shielded me from harassment and opened the way for people to accept me for my own sake, not just as Naomi's daughter-in-law or the Moabite from Heshbon. I'd already played for two feasts and a wedding, hoarding the precious gerahs the people gave me against the time when our grain supply would run out.

Madiya had told me that Adon Tobeh was furious over the town's acceptance of me. She laughed at how silly Boaz had made the man's speech seem at the gate two weeks ago. Also, she said that Tobeh wouldn't go out of his house on Shabbat because everywhere he went, he heard people singing songs I had written!

That thought amused me, but I couldn't afford to laugh. Our situation was still precarious, and getting found in any sort of compromising situation could reverse the town's opinion and destroy our chances of controlling Elimelech's land. All the more reason not to let my feelings run away with me. Which brought me right back to where I started. Naomi needed a son through me, and that required a man.

The eagle had gone, and nothing moved in the lazy afternoon heat. I frowned a little, turning over a thought that had occurred to me previously. As delighted as Naomi had been that the adon favored me, why hadn't she ever suggested we go to him for help, asking him to redeem Elimelech's land? He seemed the perfect solution to me.

"Yahweh, I have made my choice," I said. "Naomi wants a son, and I will give her one if I can. Please lead me. I know that You will provide whatever I need, as You did for Joseph.

"I choose Boaz as a father. His goodness runs deep and strong, and I would bind myself to him if I can, for he will be to Naomi and me what we need. But many things stand in the way. Do not let me speak, or try to attract him, unless the circumstances are right."

I bowed my head, feeling the close presence of Yahweh in the stillness of the forest. Taking my harp, I played a new song that I had learned in Bethlehem, a praise psalm to Yahweh. Then I put the harp in its case and started for home.

Sivan, third month, twenty-ninth day, Boaz's forty-third year (1100 B.C.)

Boaz threw down the brush pen, stretching, waiting for the ink to dry on the parchment. In some ways, a stylus and clay tablet were nicer since the record lasted longer, but this new alphabetic script was easier to learn and use. Even though parchment was expensive and papyrus would fall apart at inconvenient times if it wasn't good quality, more and more people used it.

He rubbed the back of his neck and straightened his shoulders. Finally he had the details worked out for his latest business deal with Ahinadab of Jebus. They had concluded it in the Jebus gate two weeks ago, but this was the first time he'd had time to get it recorded. He'd send a copy to the merchant tomorrow.

Stacking the parchment with his other records, he blew out the lamp and strolled across the common courtyard. The small house where Ladel and Tashima stayed during harvest was dark and silent. It was late, and likely everyone had gone to bed. The pounding at the gate startled him. He hurried to answer the summons before anyone else woke.

"Pashur, what's wrong?" Boaz gasped, seeing his friend in the light of the dim torch another Habiru carried.

"I bring bad news, Boaz."

Ushering his friend in, he led the way back across the courtyard and relit the lamp in his office. He sat, and Pashur squatted against the wall.

"What has happened?"

"Tahat is dead. Murdered on the road."

For several moments Boaz couldn't breathe. "On the road? I didn't think he traveled that much anymore."

"He didn't. But he decided to go on this trip to ensure the safety of the goods."

Boaz realized that there must be a lot more to the story, for he didn't like the deep anger in Pashur's eyes, something he'd never seen before.

"Start at the beginning."

"It began when Tahat finally heard from Tobeh."

Boaz felt his own face harden.

"You know that Tahat has been wondering why Tobeh has shipped nothing for so long," Pashur went on. "He has been waiting for a favorable market. Deciding the time was right, he contacted the caravanner to take a large stockpile of wine to the coast. Wine from his vineyards has always brought excellent prices on the Philistine and Phoenician markets."

"A shrewd move that would refill his treasury," Boaz said thoughtfully. "What did Tahat charge for such a valuable load?"

"That's where the trouble started. Tobeh only wanted to hire the animals and four caravanners. He insisted on employing his own guards to keep the price down."

"Surely Tahat refused such an arrangement!" Boaz gasped.

"He tried. But Tobeh absolutely insisted, so Tahat demanded to see the guards. They were all Habiru, with Gaddi among them."

Suddenly feeling sick, Boaz closed his eyes.

"With Gaddi there, Tahat figured everything was fine. He didn't know the young man had left our band. I should have told him," Pashur added brokenly. "I should have told him, but it didn't seem important at the time."

"Go on."

Pashur swallowed a couple times before continuing. "In the rough country around Timnah the guards attacked the caravanners just after they had finished loading the animals in the morning. They expected an easy victory. Tobeh apparently neglected to tell them that all our caravanners can fight. Three of the Habiru died before the first of Tahat's men.

"Tahat and his three remaining men retreated to a more sheltered position. The second one died there."

"What about Gaddi?" Boaz asked, starting to pace the room.

"He and a couple other guards were already on the trail with the animals. He claims he didn't know the caravanners were to be killed, although how he thought anyone could steal and sell the goods without killing everyone, I don't know. But it may be true. His actions seem to bear that out."

Pashur leaned forward, his hands clenched. "Tahat had retreated to an outcropping of rock. Another caravanner was unable to fight, so it was just Tahat and the fourth man, both wounded, facing five Habiru, which was what Gaddi saw when he returned.

"He apparently realized the true situation when he saw Tahat fall."

Sighing, Pashur rubbed his hand over his eyes. "As much as I'd like to execute Gaddi with my own hands, I wish I could have seen that fight, Boaz. The two caravanners survived, although one may die yet of his wounds. The other says he never saw anything like what happened when Gaddi jumped in. Said that young man did things with a sword he didn't believe possible. He killed two and drove off the other three without making a sound. The man swears it was like watching a dream.

"When the fight was over, Gaddi tended their wounds, buried Tahat and those of his men already dead, then brought the survivors to one of our outposts before disappearing. That was yesterday. He showed up in our main encampment this afternoon, told Mattan the story, and yielded himself for justice. Mattan sent me to interview the survivors, who are now in Tahat's house."

Boaz paused with his back to Pashur. "And what did you do with Gaddi?"

"We brought him to you."

"Why to me?" He whirled around.

"Meshullam and Mattan want you to judge this case. All of us love the lad, and he is the best swordsman we have ever trained. But he has betrayed us and a friend who trusted him. We don't know what to do with our anger. Our very existence is threatened. You must decide, and all will abide by your decision."

"Did Gaddi also agree to this?"

"It's not his decision to make," the Habiru said shortly.

"How can I judge? I love the lad too," Boaz protested.

"Please, Nahsi. Do this for us."

The unexpected title bewildered Boaz. "I'm not a governing lord over you!"

"You must be one now," Pashur insisted, standing and bowing his head. "We always knew this day would come. Remember when you asked me why we stayed here, and I told you about Abbi's dream? You asked if he saw the man when we came here, and I said no, *not the man*. He recognized you the instant he looked into your eyes when you were but 7. Why do you think he agreed to let you train with us? He knew someday your word would mean life or death to our band, and he wanted you to understand us. That time is now. What do you think Tobeh will do when he learns that one of us was involved in this slaughter?"

"He arranged it!" Boaz exploded, upset by what Pashur asked and the pleading in his voice.

"How does that make a difference? Will the town believe the Habiru outsiders or the wealthy town elder? But if we can say that you have judged and punished the offender, people will be assured that we hold ourselves within the law, and they will let us live. You know we cannot leave. You must hear us," his friend begged.

Boaz sat down in a daze. Pashur never begged for anything. And certainly not from him! They were equals, laughing at the same jokes, discussing problems with each other, and sparring together on the training field, even though Pashur always beat him when they fought with spears!

"Please, Nahsi."

The entreaty in his friend's voice cut Boaz to the heart. Suddenly he wondered if he had ever really understood how the Habiru lived. For the first time, he glimpsed what landlessness meant. The Habiru stood always outside, excluded from the tripartite covenant that used the earth itself to bind Yahweh to Abraham's descendants. Without land, there was no covenant, no entry into the security of order and society. Consequently, something as small as a lie by a town elder could reduce them to utter dependence on someone's hesed for their lives, regardless of the years of service they had provided. A new sort of anger exploded in Boaz's mind. These people were more faithful to Yahweh's covenant, to say nothing of their own private vow, than most of the townspeople.

Yahweh, if Your hesed is for all, how could You exclude those who have been robbed of their inheritance and yet remain faithful? he raged inwardly, struggling to understand.

"My arrows stand before you, do they not?"

The reply swept through his mind with such force that he gasped. Yahweh's arrows? Suddenly he saw how Yahweh's hesed spilled over the boundaries of covenant, working outside the narrow confines of that promise, to encompass the wanderers in an intimate embrace denied to all others, and it humbled him.

Going to Pashur, he put his hand on the man's shoulder, realizing his friend was trembling. "I will do what you have asked."

The warrior nearly dropped to his knees. "We will never forget your hesed—"

Boaz tightened his grip. "No. It is not hesed!" he said, his voice rough with anger. "Can I do any less for those whom Yahweh honors so greatly?"

Pashur slowly looked up, the amazement on his face mixed with bewilderment. "Honors? We are landless! We have no place among Israel!"

"Your place is higher than mine. I hold my place through the land, but Yahweh holds you directly, with nothing in between. You are His sword and spear and shield, the arrows shot with His own hand, to protect the land of His covenant. And if Yahweh chooses me to be His armor-bearer, to care for the weapons of His body and preserve them for His use, who am I to tell Him no?"

The man's blue-gray eyes widened, and he gulped. "Yahweh's weapons? We are but wanderers—we are nothing!"

"And Yahweh used you as He could nothing else. Your band has been like the fortress walls of Jebus to this place. Do not speak to me of hesed. It is my honor to do what I can in return for the hesed Yahweh has given us through you."

The Habiru stared at him for a long time. "As you love me, do you really believe this?" he asked, his voice hoarse.

"Yes."

Straightening, Pashur stood for a moment in silence. "Then maybe our children do not need to fear for the future. You give me hope, Boaz."

"Not I. Yahweh. Bring Gaddi in."

Still in a daze, Pashur turned to the door. "Yahweh's arrows?" he murmured as he walked out.

As Boaz settled himself again, glad for the moment alone, he was still half afraid of the great responsibility just given him. Pashur was right—Tobeh would take any chance he could to wreak his hatred against the wanderers. Keeping their dahveed's vow gave the Habiru purpose and hope for the future, and they would die to the last man to preserve that chance for their children. Whether or not there would be bloodshed would well depend on his decision here and the town's reaction to it if the situation became known. "Yahweh, give me wisdom," he muttered, closing his eyes, his stomach tightening as he heard approaching footsteps.

Pashur entered, followed by Gaddi and then Mattan, whose hard face and tight grip on his sword revealed his extreme anger. Two more warriors remained outside in the courtyard. Gaddi knelt in the center of the room, hands bound behind him, unable to hide his trembling. He still wore the torn and bloodstained clothes in which he'd fought. The dust and sweat of travel covered him, and debris matted his dark hair.

"You are involved in much evil, Gaddi," Boaz said gently, thinking that in spite of the years that had passed, the man before him still seemed so young.

"Yes, Nahsi," the prisoner whispered.

"When I first knew you, you wished to live as a warrior. Pashur tells me that you became the best swordsman they have ever trained. How did you come to leave?"

"I saw one of the daughters of another band, Nahsi."

"I see," Boaz said, thinking wryly of his own reaction to the Moabite widow. "What did you know about the attack against Tahat?"

"The dahveed said Geber Tobeh had uncovered a plot by the caravan owner to steal his goods. We were to take the goods and sell them for Geber Tobeh ourselves." He blushed as he repeated the story.

Mattan made a sound of disgust. "And someone I trained believed that?"

Gaddi didn't answer, but bent his head still lower.

"And what of the caravanners?"

"They were only to be driven away."

"You little fool," Mattan said between clenched teeth, barely able to control himself, knowing that his women and children stood in danger because of what had happened.

"When did you begin to question the story, Gaddi?" Boaz pressed on.

"As soon as I saw Adon Tahat. I knew he would not risk his livelihood doing such things. But I didn't want to believe anything was wrong. I-I wanted their daughter and I—" His words stumbled to a halt.

Mattan cursed under his breath, and Pashur turned away.

"Go on," Boaz encouraged.

"It was as we drove away the animals that I let myself think that if the story *was* a lie, then Adon Tahat and his men would have to be killed. I made an excuse about having left my cloak behind, and I went back."

"It was fortunate for Tahat's two surviving men that you did, Gaddi. However, your foolishness has brought about some very serious consequences. Did you know that Adon Tahat only agreed to have those Habiru as guards because you were with them?"

Gaddi seemed to shrink within himself. "I feared it was so, Nahsi. I went crazy when I saw that I had caused the adon's death."

Boaz sighed. "How many lives were lost, Gaddi, to say nothing of the animals and goods in the caravan because of what you did?" He thought a moment. "And what of you? Were you hurt?"

The young warrior froze. "What does that matter, Nahsi?"

With a sudden exclamation Mattan took a quick step forward and pulled Gaddi's arm away from his side, making the young man cry out. Under the shirt he found a sword wound, hastily packed with herbs tied on with a rag. Whipping out his knife, he cut the ropes binding the young man and found wounds on Gaddi's chest and leg.

"Why didn't you say something?" he thundered, heedless of rousing the house with his shouting.

Gaddi's face hardened. "Should not my own blood run for my sins?"

Boaz exchanged a look with Pashur and his brother. "Allowing yourself to die will not recompense others for those sins, Gaddi," he pointed out. "Pashur, does Gaddi's story agree with that of the survivors?"

"Yes, Nahsi."

Mulling over what he'd heard, trying to decide which course would best serve the ends of justice, Boaz lapsed into silence. The political aspects of the case he would have to consider later.

"Geberet Hannah, widow of Tahat, is the first to be considered for justice," he finally announced. "What recompense will be needed to support her and her sons?"

"She will accept nothing, Nahsi," Pashur said. "Tahat's men told the story when they arrived at her house. When I came to talk with them, I asked if she had need. She said she and her sons could continue with the business, since her husband had taught her all that was necessary, provided that you and I were willing to continue the partnership." The Habiru bowed slightly. "I took the liberty of assuring her this was so. I also told her that Gaddi had returned and asked what recompense she wanted from him. Geberet Hannah refused any, saying he was a fool but not a murderer. She said she would require justice from those who truly owed it." He paused. "I am very glad I am not Tobeh, Nahsi."

"Then we will leave things to her," Boaz replied. "Mattan, you are next to be considered. Gaddi has endangered you and yours."

The dahveed straightened up. "We have yielded our right to you, Nahsi. You must decide."

Boaz looked down at the kneeling prisoner. "Gaddi, what do you have to say?"

"I have brought shame and danger on those who raised and sheltered me. The blood of three men stains my hands, one of them a friend to my people. You know what I deserve."

Was he determined to die? Boaz wondered. "Yet two men live because of what you did."

"I cannot be both good and bad, Nahsi."

After another pause Boaz replied, "Each of us carries both good and evil in our hearts. Every day you choose which will be revealed in your actions, and some days both will. Shall I take your life and destroy the good which is in you? The law demands death when murder has been committed. You did not deliberately plan to take life."

"But blood still rests on my head."

"Tobeh and those who took his money bear more of the blame than you. I will not sentence you to death, for you do not deserve it."

"I do not deserve to go free, either," the young man replied, raising his eyes to Boaz. "If you will not let me die, then I will be a slave instead."

The look in his eyes gave Boaz pause as he remembered that proud, unyielding gaze from the day he'd caught the boy with his hand on his purse. He had not backed down then, and he would not now.

"Six years is a long time, Gaddi."

"Will Tahat return to his family after six years? It must be for the rest of my life, as I have robbed him of the rest of his."

Pashur raised his eyebrows, and a glimmer of respect sparked in his eyes. Mattan remained rigid, but his face softened.

"Whom would you serve? Tahat's widow will not accept you," Boaz reminded him.

"Tahat was your partner. I will serve you."

"And if I will not accept you?"

"Then I will be free to cleanse the land of blood with my own."

Boaz looked at Pashur, then Mattan. The hardness in their eyes told its own story. As Pashur had said, they dared not shelter the young warrior in any way.

Gaddi swayed slightly, and Boaz saw that the youth was near collapsing. He looked at the two older men. "We will wait for seven days to see how things work out. Then I will pass final sentence. In the meantime Gaddi will remain in my custody. Is this acceptable?"

"Yes, Nahsi," Mattan agreed, bowing slightly. The two Habiru silently left the room.

Early summer
Tammuz, fourth month, third day
(1100 B.C.)

"Shalom, Boaz. I won't keep you long from the wheat fields. How is he?"

Boaz looked up as he left his compound gates, leading a donkey. "Gaddi's fever broke last night, Pashur. He will recover, but it was a near thing, especially since he does not particularly want to live. The shame of what he did will not leave him."

"We should have checked him over," the Habiru warrior said bitterly. "We know you don't make it through a fight like that without getting hurt. Mattan has been savage the past four days, alternating between rage at the lad and worry that he might die."

I'm glad I had good news for you. Is all else well? I haven't been to the fields or the gate since Gaddi sickened."

"Then you're very behind in news. Both of Tahat's men firmly believe Gaddi knew nothing of the true plans of the other guards, and they have talked constantly about how he risked his life against his own kind to save them.

"Our people have a warmer welcome in town than we've had since Tobeh first sat at the gate. Customers are demanding that warriors from our band accompany every shipment, even though we have trained all the caravanners to defend themselves. They are paying extra fees for guard duty."

Boaz chuckled as he headed down the street, the donkey following behind. "Tobeh must be grinding his teeth!"

"He can hardly swallow his gall!" Pashur laughed as he accompanied him. "Patah reported that the Habiru Tobeh hired preferred to keep the proceeds from the sale of the wine for themselves. Their story is that Geber Tobeh did not mean to pay them the balance of their fee. He's lost an enormous amount, and Tahat's widow is doing better business than ever."

The mention of Tahat made Boaz's face harden. "It angers me, knowing Tobeh bought the death of another and may go unpunished."

"He will do anything for power," the warrior observed, stepping around the pile just deposited by another donkey a little way in front of them. "And I can't imagine this financial reverse will stop him for long."

"If what we suspect is true, he can't stop now, no matter what the cost. Does it seem to you, Pashur, that all Tobeh's ambitions are tied to his family honor?"

The wool merchant considered, and the two men slowed. "He *has* been obsessed with it since Besai died, so it would make sense. Maybe the only way to stop him is to destroy his reputation and strip him of so much honor no one will listen to him again."

Boaz stopped, thinking deeply, his hand running down the donkey's neck. "That's the conclusion I came to. But what possible bait would lure him to risk family honor?"

The other man started on his way again. "I have no idea. Maybe the only thing stronger than his obsession is his greed!"

Not until they had crossed the south market and walked out the town gate did Boaz say anything. "But how can I turn that against him?" he asked as they descended the slope.

Pashur shrugged. "I don't know. What I do know is where Tobeh has been getting all the food for his feasts. He's been slaughtering his own mutton!"

"But he invested heavily in Yidla stock. Why on earth would he slaughter them?" Boaz exclaimed, turning to the other man.

"Trying to stop the spread of kicking sickness!" Pashur shook with laughter. "He has ordered more than half his sheep killed, including both his Yidla rams and three fourths of his imported ewes. Patah said his pasture is full of kickplant, which is spreading to his other pastures, since he keeps moving his sheep."

"Hasn't anyone told him to weed out the kickplant and walk his ill sheep?"

"He refuses to listen, claiming no one can trust what the Moabite qedeshah says. And he's spreading it around town that she's a witch, or Lilith herself, and has cursed his flock."

His face white, Boaz halted. "Pashur, how can you laugh about something like that? Do you know what will happen if people believe—"

"Relax, Boaz. He's only made himself a laughingstock. Enough flocks in the area have had trouble with kickplant for everyone to see that what Ruth said was true. The town is rocking with laughter. Eprah is so disgusted he's charging Tobeh an outrageous price every time his Yidla ram covers a ewe for him."

Boaz snorted as the donkey pushed him with its nose, and he started on again. "Tobeh would have done better to go to Yittir for that service. He always could talk him into anything."

"Tobeh stays with Eprah in hopes of family peace. Apparently Deborah was furious when she heard how her husband refused to defend her veracity at the gate. Tobeh's apparently hoping that paying the outrageous fees will encourage Eprah to intercede with Deborah for him."

"He won't find any sympathy there!" Boaz exclaimed.

Pashur shrugged. "He isn't getting it anywhere. At this rate he'll be destitute by next year! Shalom, Boaz. I've got to go."

Mounting his donkey, Boaz pondered what his friend had said all the way to the fields. "Yahweh, I believe that You are taking a hand," he murmured. "All that remains now is to keep Elimelech's land from

Tobeh's grasp. With that, he might hide the extent of his losses, and he is skilled enough to work himself back into a position of power again. Show me how to preserve this land for the widows who are dependent on it, for Naomi does not trust me, and I do not see how I can marry Ruth."

He paused. Marry the Moabite? His mouth went dry, and sweat broke out on his forehead. She would be gleaning today, one of the final days of harvest, and he wanted more than anything to make her his wife. But he couldn't now. Maybe in a year or two. But by then she would surely be married to another. Which was just as well. He was too old. Better just forget all about it. Only he couldn't.

Tammuz, fourth month, sixth day (1100 B.C.)

Pashur and Mattan arrived in the courtyard just after the noon rest.

"What brings you here, friends?" Boaz asked as he went out to meet them.

Pashur bowed slightly. "Nahsi. The dahveed wishes to give you these," he said formally. Dropping to one knee, he presented with both hands a magnificent composite bow.

About to protest, Boaz stopped with his mouth open, staring at the weapon. It was large, the normal crescent shape of a bow flattened and curled back outward at both tips. Without touching it, he knew the bow would send an arrow with destructive force nearly a quarter of a mile. Taking it from Pashur's hands, he examined the weapon.

The bow had been made with two kinds of wood, one chosen for the center to support the handhold, the other for the arms of the bow. Bull sinew stretched over the back, and he noticed the patterning in the wild goat horn on the belly, which faced him as he held the weapon up. Bull tendons reinforced the stress points. He ran his fingers over the handhold itself, the carved ivory inlaid with silver above and below the dyed leather grip. Looking closer, he realized the carvings were symbols from Meshullam's dream. On top was a harp and a sheaf of wheat.

Below the leather was a soldier's kilt and an adon's robe, the carvings so detailed that Boaz could count the 24 strings on the harp and almost see the fringe move on the robe.

Thunderstruck, he stared at Pashur. His face a mask, the Habiru pulled a knife from his girdle, flipped it, and held it out to him, hilt first. The blade flashed like silver in the sun, and Boaz took it slowly. The ivory handle had a carving of a military scene on one side. On the other appeared the same four dream symbols. The silvery blade was a metal he'd never seen. Looking his question at his warrior friend, he tested the edge with his thumb.

"It's a new kind of iron," Pashur said, keeping his voice low. "They make it in the north. It is harder than any bronze or iron and will hold an edge for months, maybe years. Just be sure to keep it oiled and dry." He removed the sheath for it, made from dyed leather studded with ivory, and handed that to him.

Boaz could only stare from one brother to the next. "Mattan, I-I can't—" He stopped. The look on the man's face said that he must. "I don't know what to say," he started again after gathering his wits. "These represent Meshullam's dream, don't they?"

"Yes, Nahsi," the Habiru dahveed replied. "They were made to order two years ago as gifts. The bow, of course, was five or six years in the making, the details added after its purchase."

"You grant me too much honor," Boaz said, bowing his head. "I have done nothing to deserve gifts as valuable as these, which would honor a king."

"You have held our lives precious to you and have shown us that Yahweh, too, shelters us under His hesed. Shall we show any less honor to Yahweh's armor-bearer? We are yours, Nahsi, and we shall serve your house as long as there is need." Mattan knelt beside his brother, and both of them touched their foreheads to the ground, then stood.

"I will try to be worthy of your loyalty," Boaz said, blinking at the tears in his eyes.

"You have already been worthy. We will wait while you put those away," Pashur added, unable to suppress a grin at Boaz's discomfiture. "It is the seventh day since your judgment, and Meshullam is here with four elders waiting outside your gate."

"Why?"

"Because we don't think Gaddi will change his mind."

Boaz took the gifts into the house, knowing he would have to find a secure place to keep them. As he emerged, Gaddi appeared from the room next to Boaz's office where he'd been staying. He carried an awl and a hammer.

"Are you certain, Gaddi?" Boaz asked when the young man joined him. "Much of the trouble we feared has not developed. I will be more than recompensed with six years of labor."

"I require it of myself, Nahsi." He led the way to the gate.

"Was he always this stubborn?" Boaz whispered to Pashur.

"No. He's mellowed some with the years."

"And what reason will he give for enslavement? Surely he isn't foolish enough to tell the entire story of that attack!"

"I doubt he'll mention it. I think old deeds are coming back to haunt you," Pashur said, a twinkle in his eye.

Exasperated, Boaz opened his gate and welcomed the elders.

"What brings us here?" Adon Hanan asked.

"We need witnesses to a contract," Boaz replied.

"Shahar, Qausa, and Yattir are here. Will they do?"

"Yes."

Meshullam stood beside Gaddi, leaning heavily on a staff, his hair now completely white with age. Mattan and Pashur waited on either side.

"Who are these?"

"Witnesses for Gaddi," Boaz explained to Hanan.

The other three elders grouped around, and Adon Hanan looked at Gaddi. "What do you wish, young man?"

"I wish to enter Boaz's service—for life."

The adon looked surprised. "And why do you wish this?"

"Boaz saved me from the streets when I was a lad, sending me to a place where I was sheltered and raised. Now that I am grown, I would repay him with the life he gave me."

Hanan looked curiously at the Habiru warriors. "You were the ones who raised Gaddi?"

Pashur nodded. "Yes, adon, at Boaz's suggestion."

"Well, exactly what Boaz will do with a Habiru slave, I don't know, but I'm sure he'll think of something," the older man said humorously. "If nothing else, he will send you out to help guard his goods in the caravans. That service seems to be in great demand lately."

"I shall be happy to go, adon," the young man replied without flickering an eyelid.

"This is truly voluntary on your part?" Yattir asked, looking at the Habiru closely, his face suspicious.

"Yes."

"What do you have to say, Boaz?" Qausa inquired.

"I have repeatedly told Gaddi that the standard six years of service will satisfy any debt, but he will not listen."

"Then there is no need for that hammer, young man," Yattir said, turning to Gaddi. "As elders we can witness that you are not under obligation for so long."

"I will serve for life," Gaddi said harshly, forcing Yattir to step back.

"Will you serve him personally, or his household?" Hanan asked next.

"Let it be his household."

"Then let it so be done," Hanan declared. "We are witnesses that this day Gaddi of the Habiru enters into lifelong service to the household of Boaz of Bethlehem. Do you have an awl?"

"Yes, adon." Gaddi held out the tools to Boaz.

Going to the wooden gatepost of the compound, Gaddi leaned his head against it. Pashur tugged at the younger man's right earlobe, and as quickly as he could, Boaz drove the awl through it with a blow of the hammer. Gaddi stiffened, clutching the wood beam with rigid fingers, but he didn't move as his blood stained the wood, binding him to the household that the gatepost represented. Mattan came forward, tilting Gaddi's head and pouring wine and then olive oil over the wound.

"By this do you claim Gaddi into your service for the rest of his life?" Hanan asked.

"I do claim him," Boaz answered.

"We are witnesses," the three elders said.

He noticed that Pashur stayed close to Gaddi as the youth returned to his room, supporting him when Gaddi stumbled once or twice. Boaz clenched his teeth. The young warrior hadn't recovered from his battle wounds, yet he had insisted on going through the ritual.

As he left, Pashur smiled. "Looks like you have him back, Boaz. I told you that you were his biggest hero. Feed him every now and then."

"I'll give it serious consideration," Boaz retorted as the three Habiru departed.

Tammuz, fourth month, ninth day, Ruth's twenty-second year (1100 B.C.)

I woke with first light and started to get up when I remembered that wheat harvest was over and I no longer had to glean. Madiya said it would be a couple weeks before grape harvest began. In the meantime everyone was threshing the barley and wheat. I stretched and relaxed on the sleeping mat, thankful I didn't have to face another day of exhausting work. Maybe I could go to my god place and compose another song. I needed one for the feast at Adon Hanan's house next new moon. And I must talk to Naomi about the rights to Elimelech's fields. We would have to plan carefully, but with the people I was meeting through my harp playing, there was a chance we could find someone to buy the rights without letting anyone know until we sealed the bargain at the gate.

"Shalom, Naomi," I said when I got up. I smelled grain burning at the little shrine she had set up between our house and her loom. She burned the grain on a small flat rock set on a cloth, with an oddly shaped taller stone standing by it. The area around it she always kept very clean.

"Shalom, Ruth," she answered me cheerfully. "Breakfast is ready, and so is the second piece of cloth for Geber Hasi. We must take it to him today."

"Already? You have worked hard."

"It was just rough goat's hair for a tent and went quickly."

The day passed, and that afternoon we rested on the doorstep before beginning the evening meal. I had just opened my mouth to ask about the land when she broke the silence herself.

"You should have a husband and a house to take care of, Ruth. Someplace secure, where you won't have to wonder where the next meal will come from."

I said nothing. Behind us, the storeroom overflowed with food. Naomi's weaving and my music brought in an increasing income. And I knew that when our food supply ran out, Yahweh would have something else ready. All I had to do was trust in His hesed, as Abraham and Joseph had done.

Reaching for her hand, I said, "We shouldn't worry, Naomi. Yahweh is providing for us."

She didn't answer, and her reasoning puzzled me. Her stories had taught me about her God's hesed, yet she approached Him as Yidla's mother had Kemosh. Every week since Geber Hasi began paying for her weaving, Naomi purchased two turtle doves and had Adon Shahar, one of the elders, sacrifice them at the altar outside Bethlehem. In addition, she burned grain at the shrine, confident that such things would obligate Yahweh to bless us with food and prevent Him from turning against her again. Ironically, she could not see the caring, listening God that chose people to be His friend, nor did she understand His hesed.

"I have thought much on this," my mother-in-law went on. "I have decided what you must do. And you must do it tonight."

Surprised, I looked at her.

"I bought some scented oil in the market yesterday. Wash yourself and do your hair. I will help you put henna on your nails. We will use the oil, and the perfume I got last week."

"You'll have me decked out like a bride!" I exclaimed with a smile.

She didn't smile. "Exactly. Prepare yourself just as you did for Mahlon on your wedding night. When it's dark, put on your best cloak, the new one, and go down to the threshing floor. Make sure no one sees you. Watch where Boaz goes after he eats at the feast. He usually has a place at one corner in back and will sleep there to guard his grain.

"When he's asleep, go to him, take off your cloak, uncover him, and lie down beside him. When he wakes up, he'll tell you what to do next."

I stared at her. Deck myself out and go to the threshing floor at night? Only prostitutes and qedeshot did that! Naomi was asking me to do the very thing that she despised about the harvest festivals in Moab! The very thing Adon Tobeh had accused me of at the gate!

Amazement held me speechless. Doing something like this risked everything we had done since arriving. And what would Boaz think? Or anyone who might see me with him? He would be in an impossible situation. My thoughts trailed off. Undoubtedly, that was the point, to trap him as Tamar had Judah, and for exactly the same reason. A son.

But why? Could Naomi still think he was unwilling to aid us after all the grain we had stuffed into our pithoi? Or the way he had squashed Tobeh at the gate? Or did she assume that he would be unwilling under normal circumstances to couple with a Moabite? And if he did accept me, why was she certain he'd take me into his house rather than publically denounce me? The elders would take his word at the gate no matter what they might believe in private.

"Will you do this?" she asked.

I glanced at her face. The shadows of grief still clung there. To risk this much, she must be desperate for a son. I hesitated only a moment longer. "I will," I promised, *and more besides,* I added to myself. I'd have to decide quickly how to handle the situation, for there was just enough time to get ready.

Fortunately, my new cloak was dark, hiding me in the deep dusk, and the streets were mostly empty. People were either inside eating, or attending the meal at the threshing floor. I hurried through the gate and down the road, staying downwind as much as possible, for my perfume would attract attention if I wasn't careful.

The feast was well under way, torches lighting the food spread out for all to share. Adon Boaz sat in the same group with Geber Ladel and Geberet Tashima. They laughed at something. I sat down in the shadow of a terrace wall corner, well out of the light.

While I waited I tried to think things through again. I had, by now, realized that Naomi's plan really would put Boaz in an impossible position—because of Tobeh. If anyone saw us together, nothing would convince them that Boaz hadn't brought me there, and Tobeh could champion the defenseless widows against the deceitful conniving of a powerful adon. Or more likely, rouse the town against Canaanite blood. The thought made me sick.

That left Boaz with the choice of marrying me or taking me as a concubine, and Adon Tobeh would still damage his influence severely because of my ancestry. And I thanked Yahweh he didn't know the full truth of that!

Below me, the laughter got louder as the wine took its effect. I noticed that Boaz drank more than normal and wondered why. What was he thinking, that man of my dreams? Did he drink for joy of the harvest, or out of sorrow that he had lost his wife and children, who should have been here to share his harvest? Could he possibly imagine that a woman watched from the hill, one who would bring his world crashing down by her simple presence? Something like despair rose in me. Why did Naomi demand that I bring possible ruin on the man to whom we owed the most?

A son. It all came back to that for her. Marriage or concubinage, either would produce a child—if I wasn't barren. And even that wouldn't totally matter, for if I was sheltered by Boaz, Naomi would also have a male to look to for help. Her need was so great that she ignored the risk she asked me to take, nor could she see the possible outcomes if Boaz lost his influence. But I could.

Geber Ladel and Tashima stood, and Ladel put his wife's cloak around her shoulders. I wondered if anyone would ever do that for me. A third figure joined them, and I was amazed to see Mattan. He bowed slightly to Adon Boaz before leaving with Geber Ladel.

What if, by chance, no one saw me tonight? I could just ask Boaz for help. His hesed was well known. Then what would happen? Would he be willing to marry a Moabite? He would have to live down the disapproval of the town, even though many people liked me personally.

Or would he take me as his concubine? There would be snickers, and some, such as Tobeh, would protest, but it might not be so bad. Unfortunately, he had no right to levirate marriage. That belonged only to brothers-in-law and fathers-in-law, all of whom were dead. No, taking me as a concubine would be his best course, the one with the least possibility of disaster for him.

I sighed. Did I want to be a concubine—a lesser wife with only limited rights?

Down by the threshing floor Boaz now sat alone, finishing a last cup of wine. His face was sober and a little sad. His dark chestnut hair gleamed in the torchlight, and I wished I could bury my hands in it, combing it out. With a slight smile, I realized this was the longest time I'd ever had to just fill my eyes with him. Then he looked straight at me. I froze, my heart pounding. How could he possibly see me? A second later I heard someone walk by on the terrace above, and Boaz dropped his gaze again. He must have seen the person above me.

Suddenly I was shaking. What was I doing up here? Did Naomi really think anything good would come of this? If Boaz rejected me, I could only pray he'd let me slip away and would keep the incident to himself, for public exposure would irrevocably destroy my hard-earned reputation. I'd have to leave Bethlehem, if people didn't stone me first.

Still shivering, I hugged myself tightly. I didn't have to do this. I could go back—and face the shadowed grief in Naomi's eyes every day of my life. This chance to connect herself with a man again meant everything to her. Was I willing to risk everything to give her what she needed?

Someone stopped at Boaz's place, and in a moment they both laughed. A second man joined them, and all three called "shalom" to Adon Hanan as the elder's grandson helped him onto the road back to town.

I wanted to be down there with Boaz, to feel his arms around me and listen to his heart beat under my cheek. I wanted to hear him whisper my name and look at me with the love burning in his eyes. But I wanted him to accept me because he desired it, not because he must.

"I will do this, Yahweh," I decided, "but surely there is a way to give Boaz a choice, as I have had a choice. He loves me, and I think he will accept me. I don't see how he can marry me and preserve the influence he needs to keep Tobeh from taking over the town, so I will be content to be his concubine. He's a good man, Yah, and love for him fills my heart. Show me the way."

The cool west wind blew by, bringing a hint of the Great Sea, where it had been born. Below me, Boaz rose unsteadily. I got up also, staying in the shadows, keeping him in sight as he headed toward the mounds of grain. As Naomi predicted, Boaz settled by several large piles near the edge of the threshing floor at the back. I'd have to circle the entire threshing installation to avoid the road back into town, which was now swarming with returning celebrants. Once there, I could approach him without having to pick my way past any other sleepers guarding their grain.

Taking my time and moving as quietly as I could, I circled the threshing floor, sometimes walking on paths between the harvested fields, other times on the stiff stubble. Twice I heard others in the darkness, soft laughter and low voices. I passed on without stopping.

At last, I hesitated at the edge of the grain piles not far from where he lay. I could still leave and tell Naomi that I had failed. That was the prudent thing to do, the one that wouldn't risk my reputation and perhaps my life. But now that I stood here, so close to the man who had filled my heart with his desire even fuller than he had our pithoi with grain, I seemed rooted to the ground.

Nothing stirred around me. The threshing floor was deserted except for those who slept beside the fruits of harvest. A night bird called, and an owl swooped by. The wind felt chill, the day's heat having faded rapidly. I didn't want to commit myself until I knew how to give Boaz a choice. Then again, maybe this was another crossing of the Jordan, in which I would have to trust Yah and softly go forward without knowing the next step.

"Yahweh, as You led me then, lead me now. I will do as Naomi asked." I closed my eyes. And if Yahweh willed, maybe I could restore Naomi's life with a son.

To have Boaz's son? I could imagine his pride and joy, and I ached to fulfill that need in him, make him complete once more, just as I longed to be completed and filled. For I was as empty as Naomi, needing the love of a man, just as the land required the hand of a man to bring a harvest. I pressed closer to him, wishing he could have claimed levirate marriage instead of just land redemption.

Suddenly a thought startled me. Any male in the clan could be goel for our land. In the absence of any direct-line males to perform the levirate, why couldn't Boaz claim that *as a further duty of the goel,* giving him the right to redeem Naomi and me with a son? He was of the same blood to provide seed. As important as it was to preserve a family before Yahweh, surely that would be acceptable to the town, even with a Moabite, since without it Elimelech's line would perish.

Excitement filled me. I wanted to shake Boaz awake and tell him that Yah had given me the answer, but instead I put my arm across his chest and concentrated on the beat of his heart under my hand. He was my life.

Not long after, Boaz stirred restlessly, tossing his head as though from a nightmare. Boldly, I reached up and stroked his hair. He stilled, and some of the lines eased from his face. His hair was rough from inattention, but surprisingly soft under my fingers. Some short strands edged his face, cut by something, and they curled. The moon rose higher. Pressed against Boaz for warmth, I drifted to sleep.

~ ~ ~

Boaz stirred again. He hated this dream. Why was it returning now? Must he be tortured with it all his days? But he was caught up in the endless walking toward the desert on the other side of Jordan, in the quest for a sleeping place, and in the fear of his shadow that moved and grew on its own.

The wind rose, blowing his hair, tugging at his cloak. He fumbled for it, struggling to keep it on. The scent of perfume reached his nostrils, and a hand brushed his hair, distracting him from the dream. He turned toward the scent, grateful for the interruption, and momentarily slipped out of the nightmare.

Inevitably, the power of it pulled him back into the rushing sound of the whirlwind. Lilith stood beside him with her enticing smile and cruel eyes, bending down to steal his life. Somehow this time, he must resist her! That laughter drifted on the wind, and he knew once again he would yield to her deadly kiss, just as her hand on his chest burned through his skin and the scent she wore befuddled his brain—

He twisted his head. This was wrong. Lilith never wore perfume. But surely he lay on sand. Where was his robe? No wind blew his hair, but Lilith's hand rested on him. Terror struck his mind. She felt real! He forced his eyes open, staring at the stars above him, the moon shining in his face. Had his nightmare become horribly real? Had that fatal kiss burned on his lips so that he could not escape whatever now held him down?

Gasping and shaking in every limb, Boaz very slowly turned his head. *A woman lay beside him.*

"Yahweh, save me!" he screamed in his mind, shoving himself away from the figure, and ramming his back into something behind him that shifted and settled, trickling around him.

Barley. He was trying to force himself backward into a pile of barley. The threshing floor. Not sand. He could still feel the heat of her hand on his chest, and he rubbed at the spot frantically. Then he froze as the woman stirred.

She opened her eyes and sat up as he stared at her. She was beautiful, the moonlight reflecting off her skin, and he almost reached his hand out to touch it.

"Who are you?" he whispered harshly, rigidly controlling himself, fearing he'd hear Lilith's cruel laughter in reply. If he did, he was still in his dream and his mind refused to think of what that would mean.

"I am Ruth, your handmaid."*

Boaz drew in a huge breath, easing the ache in his chest. "Ruth?"

"Yes, adon."

The stars of his dream whirled and vanished, and he smelled the freshness of the west wind. Around him heaps of barley and wheat loomed on the Bethlehem threshing floor, and the sounds of others sleeping reached his ears. He relaxed with a soft groan and put his head in his hands, trying to calm the racing of his blood. *Ruth?*

Jerking his head up, he stared at her. "What are you doing here?" The night air cleared his head more. The threshing floor was empty and dark. Nothing stirred close by. He was sure he had come to bed alone.

Facing Ruth again, he swallowed. Her perfume surrounded him, and once more he swallowed. She rivaled Lilith there in the moonlight, sitting so still and silent. He barely stopped himself from reaching for her. Only the fear that she might not be real stopped him.

"Adon?"

Lilith would never have called him that. *Fool,* he thought. Gingerly Boaz shook the kernels of barley from his arms and slid back to his robe on the pile of chaff. This was Ruth, not Lilith. Her eyes were grave and watchful, not cruel. "What are you doing here?" he asked, keeping his voice very soft.

"I have come to ask you to be a goel."

"To redeem Elimelech's land?"

"I'm not asking you to be goel for the land, but for me. Cover me and redeem me from Tobeh's household."

Boaz closed his eyes and started to tremble. *Redeem* her? Boaz forced himself to think. She had called him goel, and redemption applied to land, not people. She must be confused. That was it. She was from Moab, after all, and had mixed up land redemption and levirate marriage. She hadn't really meant for him to cover her, just make sure Tobeh paid enough for the land to keep them out of his household.

---

*Ruth's word "handmaid" claims for herself membership in the clan and eligibility for marriage.

Besides, there was no one to provide levirate marriage. Naomi would know that.

"You can be goel for us, can't you?"

Her voice was soft. Not daring to look at her, he nodded in reply. Then realizing she might not be able to see the gesture in the darkness, he added, "Yes."

"Then be goel to me. Redeem me like the land. Fulfill your blessing the first day I gleaned and give me a son."

His eyes widened, and he stared at her. The moon cast a glow around her, but left her face in shadows, with only a glimmer from her eyes to tease his thoughts. Her request racing through his mind, Boaz sat back. Redeem her from Tobeh's household as land was redeemed? Bought with a son, a seed for Mahlon? *By a goel?* It had never been done. The idea was outside everything he knew . . .

Then he caught his breath. Yahweh's hesed to the Habiru. That had gone outside the covenant itself, which defined the land, the people, the world! If hesed demanded that Yahweh move beyond the law to provide life for strangers and wanderers, surely hesed could stretch the duties of the goel to preserve a family in Israel. Besides, didn't the promised Seed from Abraham preserve *all* the earth, not just the sons of Israel? And if he claimed the right of levirate marriage as a duty of the goel, he could have Ruth with full support of the town. She'd be in his house for always.

And he wanted her more than anything else—especially now that she had declared that she was willing to be his. Elation seized him. She could be his, with her regal grace, her strong slender body, and those unbelievable eyes. Just then she turned her head slightly, and a slice of moonlight crossed her face.

So many ideas raced through his mind that he hardly knew what to say. Slowly he reached out and tilted her chin up with one finger, turning her face farther into the moonlight. Even that slight contact transmitted her tension and uncertainty—and sent a jolt of joy through him.

"Yahweh has indeed blessed you, Ruth," he finally said, struggling to keep his voice down and his desire under control. "You've given more hesed tonight—choosing me over all the younger men—than you gave Naomi when you came with her to Judah."

A smile crossed her face. "You're better than the younger men, and

I have wanted none other since you called me 'daughter' in the field."

Another surge of joy filled him, and Boaz almost gathered her into his arms. But she remained very still, neither yielding to him nor withdrawing from him.

"Don't worry, Ruth. I'll gladly do what you ask," he reassured her. "Everyone in town recognizes you as an exceptional woman, and I will be envied because you have come to me." He chuckled a little. "You've also shown me how I can, with the elders' blessing, help you. We'll be married as soon as we can, and I'll redeem you." He reached out again and lightly touched her cheek with his fingers. She trembled under his touch, then moved back slightly.

Boaz smiled, sure now that this woman wanted to marry him as much as he wanted her. "As for Elimelech's land, Tobeh will have first right on that. I'll ask about it in the morning. If Tobeh wants it, I'll make certain he pays a good price. If not, I can redeem that also. But either way, you will be mine."

Ruth didn't speak for a minute. "Thank you, adon. This is more than I expected." She pulled her robe about her. The moonlight flashed off something on a cord around her neck.

"What's that?" Boaz asked, leaning closer and gently pulling the robe back. "It looked like a ring."

She went rigid, and her hands closed over it instantly. "It's from my mother," she barely whispered.

"Who was she? I know little about you, Ruth." He took the opportunity to push aside her head covering to let the moonlight dance on the smoothness of her hair. Her perfume filled his head again, and he combed his fingers through a long, soft tress that fell over her shoulder. The rest of her might have been a block of stone.

As the silence stretched out, he felt the fear in her, and sadness dampened his thoughts. Would she trust him with the truth about herself, or was her request tonight born only of desperate need? The flames of attraction were one thing, but the companionship and love born of respect and trust between two people was another. That was the empty ache he still carried from Mena's death. He had no companion with whom to share his life.

Ruth still remained silent, unable to completely hide her trembling. He continued to stroke her hair, allowing his hand to brush her cheek, knowing he could only ask, willing her fear to leave. His chest ached from holding his breath, and his heart sank more with every moment. Would it be like this between them? Brought together by a desire that would fade, leaving nothing behind? Would there always be the sorrow of loneliness eating at his heart?

Then, slowly, as if it hurt to move, she pulled the ring back over her head, the chain running down her unbound hair, pulling its glistening waves over her shoulder. Her hand shaking, she held it out to him.

When he started to take it, her hand tightened convulsively. He covered it lightly with his. "What's the matter?"

Ruth swallowed. "I've never taken it off before," she confessed.

When her fingers loosened, he took the ring, his heart suddenly pounding and his own hand unsteady. He angled it to the moonlight, the feel telling him it was carved ivory, and those had to be rubies set in it. But the chain wasn't gold, as he'd thought. It was human hair, the gold highlights tricking his eyes in the dim light. He studied the signet ring itself, a bull and sun flanking a man with a dove over him. "Baal's bull and Kemosh as the sun protecting the king," he murmured to himself. "It's true, then. You are descended from Moab's kings?" He looked at her.

She tilted her chin proudly. "Yes, adon."

Boaz smiled. Her courage was all that he had suspected. Leaning forward, he replaced the ring, taking his time arranging her hair. When he finished, he cupped his hands around her face instead of taking her into his arms as he ached to do. "You are an incredible woman, Ruth. Kings sired you, and yet you came here to Bethlehem with a destitute widow and choose an old man like me for a husband. Why would you give me such hesed?"

Her body relaxed under his touch, and a tear ran down her cheek, which he wiped away with his thumb. "Hesed?" she said, her voice husky. "You have given the hesed, adon, since the day I first came to glean in your field." She paused. "You weren't surprised at the ring, adon."

"My name is Boaz. No, Pashur suspected something of the kind. The ring simply confirms what the Habiru discovered. We will have to be careful that your identity remains a secret until politics in Moab settle down." As he spoke he slid his hands down her shoulders and arms, bringing her hands up to his lips for a kiss.

"What one Habiru knows they all know." Ruth gave a little sigh, and Boaz laughed softly.

"Yes, that does seem to be the way of things with Habiru!"

"What about politics here in Bethlehem?" Ruth continued, looking him full in the face for the first time. "I'm of Moab, adon, and there will be those who are against this."

He smiled grimly. "Don't worry, Ruth. I've been taunted about foreign blood since I was a child, mostly by Tobeh. I'm descended from Rahab of Jericho."

"You must be proud. She is greatly honored."

His hands tightened around hers. "Some honor her. Others think only of her Canaanite origins."

Ruth freed one of her hands and caressed his head. A little smile flirted with the corners of her mouth. "We Canaanites should cling together, don't you think?"

Chuckling softly, he put her other hand on his chest. "At least as closely as a man clings to his wife. And I want you for my wife, Ruth." He leaned closer, waiting for any pressure from her hands telling him to stop, and when none came, he brushed her lips with his. She was shaking again, but he didn't think it was from fear or the chill.

"The desire of my heart is to be your desire," she whispered, pulling him to her.

Boaz wrapped his arm around her and met her lips with a passion he hadn't experienced in a long, long time.

When Ruth finally pulled away, it took a minute for Boaz to gather his wits.

"I should go, adon," she said a little breathlessly, starting to stand.

Without thought, he reached out, gripping her wrist to stop her. Now that she was finally his, he couldn't bear to let her out of his sight. "Stay with me tonight."

Ruth smiled, and he could feel the pulse pounding in her fingers. Then she pulled back slightly, looking away.

She was going to make some excuse, he could tell. He had to think quickly, speaking before she did. She couldn't leave now.

"You not only asked me to be a goel, and I will," he heard himself say, "but you also asked me to cover you, and I haven't done that yet.

Besides, it's getting chilly, and you shouldn't be walking the road or streets alone at this time of night. Stay until it's dawn."

He waited, afraid she would refuse and Lilith would be his only companion tonight. "Please." When he held out his cloak, she lay down beside him again.

Tammuz, fourth month, tenth day (1100 B.C.)

I woke with the first hint of dawn in the sky. Boaz felt warm and strong beside me, his breathing regular and even, no hint of the restlessness of earlier in the night. But the instant I moved, his arm tightened around me, although his breathing never changed.

Turning my head, I saw him looking at me. "Do you know, with Mena it was her hair that I fell in love with, but with you, it was your eyes. The most beautiful eyes I've ever seen." He traced the line of my brows with his finger. "You should go now. It won't do either of us any good to have people know that you came to the threshing floor."

I knew that to be only too true, but I was strangely reluctant. I longed to stay right here beside the man who had seen past my ancestry and loved me anyway. Never again did I want to live through another few moments like those after Boaz asked to see that signet ring. Only the certainty that Yah could provide for me no matter what happened enabled me to take off that ring and hand it to him. Then to learn that he already knew and didn't care, to find that he had Canaanite blood also, had filled me with a giddy relief that made me foolishly bold. Not that he seemed to mind, I remembered with a little smile. But Naomi would be eagerly waiting to hear what had happened, and reluctantly I sat up. Boaz helped me stand and handed me my sash.

"Here, hold out your cloak," he instructed.

When I did, he scooped barley into it until it was almost more than I could carry. "Take this with you," he said, helping me wrap it up and then lifting it onto my back. "Can you carry that much?"

"Yes. Thank you, adon."

Boaz put his hand on my chin and turned my head. "Call me Boaz, Ruth. This is just an earnest payment. Very soon you will be mistress of everything that I possess, which is quite a lot." Then he kissed me, and I found myself halfway to Bethlehem before I had my wits about me again.

As I hurried through the deserted streets I prayed to Yahweh that no one would see me. Although they might assume I was simply up early bringing grain from the threshing floor, they might also wonder if I had stolen it.

"Naomi, Naomi, open the door," I whispered when I reached our room. I couldn't knock—I dared not let go of the bundle of grain for that.

"What happened?" she asked eagerly, opening the door. "Did Boaz accept you?"

"Let me get this barley put away. He gave me six good measures, and I can hardly carry it. Then I'll tell you everything," I promised.

Naomi's brown eyes got big and round when she saw how much I had. "He gave you all this for me? Surely he will care for us well."

At the delight in her eyes I hadn't the heart to tell her that neither Boaz nor I had even mentioned her. "He said that I shouldn't come back to you without something to eat," I said gently. "He will be a good provider."

"I knew he would. He just needed a bit of prodding," she said, certain her trap had worked. "Now, tell me what happened!"

I told her mostly about what Boaz had said and done, saying little about my own words.

"Now that he has claimed you, he must care for us," Naomi said, the light in her eyes such as I hadn't seen in almost a year. "He will have to keep us well supplied and give us a better place to live! In return, you must be a good concubine to him, daughter."

"I am to be his wife," I corrected her. "He said that we are to marry as soon as possible."

Naomi's eyes widened in amazement. "Are you sure? He's more generous than I dared to think. We must stay home then. Boaz will be busy at the gate. He'll see Tobeh today I'm sure, and decide what is to be done."

I listened as Naomi talked on, torn between her rejoicing and my own sadness that she did not comprehend the willing hesed offered by both Boaz and Yahweh, free for the taking. But her eyes sparkled, and the little jokes and happy comments fell from her lips just as I remembered them, so I let go of my sadness and sighed with contentment. *Yahweh, please grant Your blessing that I may give Naomi a son,* I prayed silently.

Boaz watched Ruth leave the threshing floor, soon losing sight of her in the dim light. When she was safely away he sighed in relief. If news of her visit reached Tobeh, he would lose the upper hand in the negotiations for Naomi's land rights. Shaking the chaff from his robe, he pulled it back on, catching up his cloak. He must talk to Ladel right away.

Prudently he entered Bethlehem at the west gate, having circled around from the threshing floor. Inside his office he lit the lamp and sat down to consider his line of attack. He had to approach this correctly, or Tobeh would slip from his fingers like a wet frog, and Naomi would get less than she deserved for that land. Not that it would matter much, since he planned on marrying Ruth—sucking in his breath, he stared at the flame of the oil lamp. There it was, the perfect way to stop Tobeh! The man would never suspect it, and his own greed would lead to his downfall! Boaz began to laugh.

"I didn't expect you to be here yet," Ladel yawned a couple hours later. "Is everything all right at the threshing floor?"

"As far as I know. With this large crop, every grain pit around town, private or communal, will be overflowing. We'll probably stuff that insatiable maw of Jebus this year, too. I came early because I have some business today at the gate, and I wanted your opinion on how best to handle it."

"I'll help any way I can." His brother-in-law sat down on a stool and leaned back against the wall.

Crossing his arms, Boaz leaned back also. "It's going to be a ticklish situation, Ladel, unless no one knows what preceded it. Let me tell you what happened, so we can plan a response in case someone did see something last night."

An odd expression lurked in the other man's eyes. "I'm listening."

"Not long after you and Tashima left last night, I went to sleep by the grain as usual. I woke up about midnight with Ruth lying beside me."

"Ruth?"

Boaz nodded. "Naomi had to have sent her. I can't imagine she'd come on her own. She was suitably—uh—'dressed' for the occasion."

Ladel straightened so abruptly that he nearly fell off his stool. *"Naomi* sent her to do something like that? And Ruth went along with it?"

Stroking his beard to hide the smile he felt creeping onto his lips, Boaz nodded again. "Naomi's desperate, and she would never come to me directly. She's been aware that I've noticed Ruth and probably guessed what I thought of her, so she set up a very effective snare."

"You don't look unhappy about getting caught."

"I'm not. Ruth added her own particular twist to it. She handed me the perfect opportunity to expose Tobeh, and a 'cloak,' shall we say, to cover a marriage with her."

"This I have to hear," his overseer said, chuckling at the pun. "But why didn't Naomi just come herself?"

Boaz's face tightened. "When I was scarcely more than a man, I asked her father for her hand. I was emphatically rejected because of my Canaanite blood. Naomi had seemed willing to marry, but her father's refusal put a strain between us that has never left. I don't know if she feels guilty for what her father did, or whether she agreed with his attitude and hid that from me, or if she thinks I bear a grudge. In any case, she would never feel free to ask me for something."

"And thus the snare." Ladel nodded in understanding.

"Correct. It would have caught me, too, if Ruth hadn't asked directly for what she wanted."

"Which was?"

"She asked me to act as goel and redeem her from Tobeh's household."

"The goel redeems land," Ladel said automatically.

"Think about it," Boaz suggested, a smile on his face while his brother-in-law turned the idea over in his mind.

"Since there's no one else, she put levirate marriage under the duties of the goel!" Ladel finally exclaimed. "And the town elder dare not object to raising up seed to Elimelech and Mahlon! Who is this woman?" The overseer shook his head in wonder.

"A gift from Yahweh, and I mean to treat her as such," Boaz said, leaning forward across the low table. "I could have a son again, Ladel."

"Yahweh will surely bless you with one. But how do you plan to handle Tobeh's objections? And be assured—he'll make them!"

"Here's what I thought I would do," Boaz said, outlining his plan.

When he finished, his brother-in-law shook his head again in wonder. "If that works, it'll ruin him, Boaz! He'll be despised for the rest of his life. But you're betting an awful lot on his greed."

"I know, but as Pashur said, that may be the only thing stronger than his thirst for power. And I don't think he'd dream the elders would accept the plan. He hates Canaanite blood too much."

"He probably can't conceive that anyone will go against him, either," Ladel added, his face expressing his distaste. "The man's despised people for too long. Yet he'll need all the support he can get, now that he's in financial difficulties."

"Oh?"

"Don't play innocent with me, Boaz. How you engineered that, I don't know, but the rumors say that Tobeh's scraping the bottom of his pithoi."

"I haven't engineered anything. Tobeh sowed his own seeds, like everyone else." He pulled some written records toward him. "It's time to start work, Ladel."

"Work?" the overseer snorted. "I wouldn't miss this for the world! Someone else can oversee the threshing today. I'm sticking close to the gate."

~ ~ ~

"You're here early, Boaz," Adon Hanan said. "Usually I am the first to the south gate in the morning."

"I needed a good seat," he replied with a smile, helping Hanan to the bench along the wall. "I've some urgent business to attend to. If you'll judge a case with nine more elders, I would be grateful."

"You want the full 10 elders?"

"I think it would be best," Boaz replied, seating the elderly man on the cushion Hanan's grandson placed for him.

"We'll have to wait a bit then."

"I thought to send for them. This must be settled now."

Hanan gave him an odd look, but leaned back, adjusting the cushion slightly. "My grandson can call them. Whom do you wish to come?"

"Bilgai, Shahar, Zakkur, Gaali, Negbi, Raham, Qausa, Eprah, and Yattir. After you have notified them, please tell Adon Tobeh he is wanted at the gate." Boaz emphasized the word "after" slightly.

The grandson nodded and set out.

"What is this about?" Hanan asked curiously as Boaz sat down.

"Elimelech's land."

"Be careful," Hanan warned. "Half those elders are backing Tobeh."

"Yes, I'm counting on that," Boaz said with a smile.

Moments later he saw Patah hurrying toward the gate and called to him. The Habiru youth came immediately. "Yes, Nahsi?"

Hanan's eyebrows rose, and Boaz reddened a little. "Tell your dahveed that I need him at the gate."

Patah's face showed nothing after a brief moment of astonishment. "As you wish, Nahsi." Then he trotted back the way he had come, breaking into a run as he started down the slope.

"Nahsi? I must keep better track of you, Boaz. I didn't know one could command the Habiru," Hanan said, his voice amused, but his eyes questioning.

"It's nothing," Boaz replied. "I was able to be of some little assistance in a private matter for them. They are more grateful than I deserve."

Hanan sat back, but a thoughtful frown appeared between his eyes, and he glanced at the fleeing figure of Patah uneasily.

The streets became more crowded as the sun rose higher, but no one headed toward the threshing floor. Word had spread that Boaz had requested Tobeh to appear at the gate, and no one wanted to miss anything.

Bilgai appeared as he left his compound gate. Boaz nodded when he approached, and the elder sat opposite him, keeping his face neutral. Looking around, Boaz noticed Pashur's lean figure lounging against the wall in the shadows. He smiled, picking out more than six Habiru in the market or just outside the gate, all strategically placed, and all hardly noticeable. Mattan had interpreted his message correctly.

The dahveed himself entered openly, nodding to Boaz and Hanan without speaking, and going directly to the leather seller's stall, engaging in a lengthy bargaining session there.

Just then Tobeh arrived.

"Ah, Adon Tobeh," Boaz said, rising and stepping into the man's path. "A word to open your ear. There is business between us."

"I can think of nothing vitally important," the man protested. "Is this really necessary?"

"It will only take a moment. I'm sure we can find enough elders for witnesses in a short time."

Shahar and Gaali arrived together, sitting with Hanan, and greeting Tobeh and Bilgai. Zakkur came next, then Yattir and Raham. Negbi and Qausa hurried up, joining Hanan and bringing word that Eprah was on his way. The old elder arrived last, helped by his son and grumbling about being summoned so early.

"My apologies," Boaz said, standing courteously, "but the matter is important."

"Just what does this involve?" Tobeh demanded, irritated.

"You all know that Naomi has returned from Moab where Elimelech and her two sons died," Boaz began.

Tobeh's gray eyes lit up, and he almost rubbed his hands together. The elders with him stirred and glanced at each other, Yattir smiled briefly, and Zakkur looked at him sternly.

"The harvest is over," Boaz continued, "so Naomi can exercise her rights for use of the land. She has decided to sell them, since there are no males left in Elimelech's line.

"Her kinsmen must decide if they will redeem those rights. Tobeh, since you are the closest male in Naomi's clan, the right to redeem falls to you first. I come after you as Elimelech's next of kin."

The crowd pressed close, absolutely silent, not wishing to miss a single word. The disposal of Elimelech's land was important to everyone, but even more significant today was the power struggle between Boaz and Tobeh. The Habiru, who would be neutral, mingled with the crowd, listening intently.

"What are you doing, Boaz?" Hanan hissed quietly. "You are handing us to him on a silver platter!"

"I have no choice," Boaz replied in an undertone. "Just pray he takes the offer."

His gaze never leaving his rival's face, Tobeh stood, apparently deep in thought, and stepped closer to Boaz.

"I was too much for you, was I?" he said contemptuously and for

Boaz's ears alone. "You couldn't find a way to prevent me from taking over Ephrath land, could you?"

"State your decision, Tobeh. Will you redeem Naomi's rights, or shall I?" Boaz kept his own voice just as low as Tobeh's; his face was like a mask.

"I'll do it, Boaz, as you well know. Because with that land as part of my own line's inheritance, I'll have what I need to make it *all* mine!"

"Think carefully, Tobeh. Grasping for more honor than is yours can be dangerous for everyone." Somehow he managed to keep his voice level and calm.

His eyes glittering, Tobeh smirked. "I have thought, Boaz. I have thought for years. Naomi is beyond childbearing, and when she dies, there will be no one of the bloodline to ask for redemption. That land is mine. You never could best me."

Boaz pressed his lips together, holding his rage in check.

Turning to the crowd, Tobeh cleared his throat, putting on his best concerned expression. "I will redeem the rights," he declared loudly. "It is not good for one of my clan and family to sell rights to land when I am able to redeem them for her. I will pay a good price and manage the land as well, just as I stated here not long ago."

Bilgai and Zakkur nodded in approval as the crowd murmured among themselves.

Hanan frowned, unable to stop an anxious glance at Boaz.

Boaz kept his expression under tight control. He could hardly believe how much Tobeh was playing into his hands. "You are certain of the decision? The land is very valuable and will require quite a price."

"I am certain," Tobeh assured him with a triumphant smile. Boaz managed to look faintly disappointed. "I have taken some losses lately, but this is important enough that I will come up with the redemption price anyway. It grieves me too deeply to let an inheritance go when the widow has need of it."

People murmured in agreement throughout the crowd, some nodding, others looking puzzled or worried. "Boaz, he is winning more friends every moment!" Hanan whispered.

"Let it be as you wish, adon," Boaz said heavily, ignoring the older man and looking down.

Tobeh swelled visibly at the title, then exchanged a triumphant glance with Zakkur. When the beginnings of an uneasy growl rose from the crowd, Boaz looked up. "There is one thing more," he said quietly. Something about his tone stilled the crowd instantly, and Tobeh turned back to him. "On the day that you acquire the land rights from Naomi, Elimelech's widow, I shall take Mahlon's widow, Ruth, to my house to raise up seed to the family of the dead."*

Suddenly Tobeh turned to stone, his unbelieving eyes on Boaz. "You—you will what?"

"As goel for Elimelech's clan, I shall take the duty to raise up sons to the dead, and I will take Ruth as my wife," he repeated.

Envy and desire sprang into Tobeh's eyes, quickly transforming into speechless rage. "But—but you can't—that will—" he sputtered at last. "I'd have to give the land back to her heirs! You can't do that! She's a Moabite!"

"To redeem the land is your right, Tobeh. But to raise up seed to a family in my clan is *my* right."

The man stared at Boaz, a flush spreading over his face at the thought of Boaz married to Ruth. "Levirate marriage applies only to the immediate males in the clan, and they are all dead. You are outside your rights!" he charged, envious anger plain in his voice.

The crowd seemed to hold its breath, and all eyes turned to Adon Hanan.

"As goel for his clan, if Boaz wishes to offer himself in levirate marriage to raise up sons to Elimelech and Mahlon, I don't see why he may not," the chief elder observed, stroking his beard and struggling to control his expression. "The duty to preserve a name before Yahweh is of first importance, correct?" he asked, looking at the other elders seated around.

"Correct," Eprah agreed, watching his grandson-in-law in disgust.

"Don't you agree, Zakkur?" Shahar asked, pinning Tobeh's best friend with his stare.

"Well, I-I would suppose that such a thing should—should un-

---

*I have followed the original Hebrew from the oldest manuscripts on this point. Much later manuscripts list an alternate translation that most English translators have followed. However, the original Hebrew makes much more logical sense. There was no way Boaz could force the other kinsman to marry Ruth, yet it is obvious he is trapping his opponent with marriage to her.

doubtedly be of—of—"

"Of first importance, correct?" Shahar pressed.

Zakkur looked at the faces of the townspeople gathered around, and sweat formed on his forehead. "Of first importance," he ended faintly.

"You cowardly toad!" Tobeh growled just barely above a whisper.

Shifting nervously in his seat, Zakkur refused to look at his friend.

"Bilgai? Gaali?" Hanan continued.

"We have always held it of first importance," Gaali stated. "Yahweh Himself made provision for this by mandating levirate marriage."

Under Hanan's hard stare, all 10 elders assented.

"We are agreed, then, that Boaz may exercise the right of levirate marriage as goel, since no other males remain alive in the line. Since this is so, what is your will regarding Naomi's land right, Tobeh?" Hanan asked.

Saying nothing, the man glared his fury as his victory crumbled around him.

Just then Boaz glanced up and caught the understanding gleam in Pashur's eyes as the Habiru warrior shook with silent laughter.

"You cannot possibly mean to lie with her," Tobeh raged. "She's of Moab! A tempter cursed by Yahweh. How can you possibly lower yourself to her?"

"Blame it on my Canaanite blood, Tobeh."

His rival turned white. "You—you polluted piece of—" he choked, his hand fumbling at his girdle as he looked around wildly. Then he froze as Pashur pushed himself off the wall, his face devoid of any amusement now, and three other Habiru in the crowd edged closer to him.

"The elders are waiting to hear your decision," Boaz said with what courtesy he could muster. "Will you stand by your decision to redeem the land rights?"

Still unable to speak, Tobeh trembled with fury and humiliation, and the longer he hesitated, the more the crowd turned against him.

Boaz waited. No matter which choice Tobeh made, he was finished. If he redeemed the rights, he would be nothing more than a steward to the Moabite he desired and hated. But if he refused, he would be despised by the townspeople, especially after the pious speech he had made about the importance of supporting a widow in his clan. Backed into a corner and beaten to his knees, all that remained was for him to acknowledge his defeat.

"I will not redeem the land rights under those circumstances," he snarled at last. "I have a first duty to protect the inheritance of my own seed. Take my right to redeem for yourself. And may the land be cursed for you!" he added under his breath.

Boaz held out his hand, and Tobeh bent down, removing his sandal. "Buy the land yourself," he said, handing it to him.

"I will," Boaz replied, handing it back. He faced the crowd. "Let these elders and everyone here be witnesses that I have redeemed all the land, the orchards and vineyards which belonged to Elimelech, Mahlon, and Chilion from Naomi, widow of Elimelech. Also witness that I have taken to myself Ruth as a wife, so that the name of Elimelech and Mahlon will not vanish from the inheritance in Israel or from being spoken in the gates of this town. You are witnesses."

"We are witnesses," the elders answered, echoed by the crowd. As soon as the words faded, the babble of excited voices filled the market as the townspeople discussed the transaction.

Tobeh hurried away, pushing his way through a crowd that yesterday would have opened in deference to let him pass.

"Brilliant, brilliant, Boaz!" Hanan congratulated him. "At first I thought you had handed him his dream on a platter."

"So did he," Boaz said, still tense from the encounter. "He just couldn't conceive that I would marry Ruth."

"He's about the only man in town who couldn't," the elder laughed. He rose, Boaz helping him stand.

"Leaving already?" the younger man asked, puzzled.

"Yes. I don't think I'm needed here any longer. Sit down, Boaz."

And before Boaz could reply, Shahar and Qausa gently forced him into the most honored seat at the gate.

"Shalom, Boaz," Hanan said, walking stiffly away, his grandson at his side.

"Adon Boaz has Hanan's seat!" someone shouted, and the crowd surged forward to look, laughing and then cheering and shouting as they crowded around.

"Congratulations, Boaz! Hanan has waited long to do this! When will the wedding be?"

"May your house be filled with children, Boaz, as Rachel's and Leah's were!"

"She's a good woman, Boaz. May your name never grow less in

Bethlehem. May it always be spoken in the gate, and with you in this seat, I'm sure it will!"

"The wedding will be soon," Boaz answered amid the happy confusion. "Your good wishes are so kind and more than I deserve. May Yahweh bless you all. Do excuse me. I must be going now. The threshing will not wait and—"

"That should settle Tobeh, Boaz. Marvelous planning!"

"Thank you, Shahar. Please, everyone, I do need to get back to—"

"Congratulations! May your house be as fruitful as Tamar and Judah's son Perez!"

Boaz flushed. "It will be as Yahweh wills. I really must go." At last he eased himself from the crowd of excited well-wishers.

"I'll escort you home, if you want the company," Pashur said from beside him.

"Your company is always welcome."

"You did it," his friend commented, eyes twinkling. "He never knew what hit him until it was too late. He still doesn't know just how overwhelming your strength is, does he?"

"No, because it wasn't my strength. I wonder if he'll ever figure out that he engineered his own defeat."

"Oh?"

"Yahweh simply took all the decisions Tobeh made in the past and brought them to harvest today."

The wool merchant laughed delightedly. "I'll say he did! It does my heart good to see this happen. Patah will be unable to contain himself for days. He has endured many things working in that man's household. Today is a great time of rejoicing for him."

"Let him be careful how he rejoices," Boaz warned. "Tobeh will hate me for the rest of his life. There is no need for that hatred to spread."

"Wise words, as always. I shall warn him, or maybe replace him. He has earned a rest. Here's your house, and I'm overdue at the threshing floor. May Yahweh give you rest, Boaz."

"Shalom, Pashur."

~ ~ ~

Unable to do anything else but wait, I went to my sleeping mat and took out my harp, letting my fingers run through a few chords to loosen them up. Naomi sat in the doorway, mending. Tension made me unable to play any one song for long, and I finally gave it up. My fingers wandered the strings in a questioning tune that reflected my own thoughts. What would Boaz do? Would he really marry me knowing my ancestry? Was I deluding myself about what I saw in his eyes? How would the townspeople react? Would they support his decision, or shun him?

The shadows in the courtyard moved slower than they ever had before. At last we caught the muted sounds of excited voices from the market, then unexpected laughter mingling with shouts and cheers.

"They have finished," Naomi said, looking up. "People sound excited, but not upset. That is good. It went well." She came into the house, leaving the door barely ajar.

Heart pounding, I set my harp aside and waited. Surely he would arrive soon. But time dragged on, and no one came. I didn't know what to think. Perhaps he had changed his mind, or maybe something had happened at the gate that would prevent our marriage. Perhaps Tobeh had too many supporters and had turned the town against Boaz. I pressed my hands together to stop my arms from trembling. Memory made me pause. I hadn't done that with my hands since the day I learned who my real mother was. How much had changed for me that afternoon! How much might change now.

The knock at the door startled us both.

"Who is there?" Naomi asked.

"Shalom, Geberet Naomi. It's Boaz. I would like to speak to Ruth, your daughter-in-law."

The formality of his request sounded distant. I swallowed. Had he brought bad news?

Naomi opened the door, one hand clenched. Was she as uncertain about the outcome at the gate as I, or was something else bothering her?

"May I come in, geberet?"

When I saw her back stiffen, I realized that she didn't want him in the house. Puzzled, I stood. Did she think our room too humble for him? Maybe she didn't think it would be proper.

"I can come out," I said, stepping to the door. Naomi moved aside, the relief on her face quickly hidden. Why? If she wanted me to marry him, why wouldn't she allow him in the house?

I left the door open, and Naomi hovered near it.

"I came to say that everything is settled," Boaz told me. "Tobeh will not redeem the land, so I have agreed to. I also announced that I will take you as my wife so that Elimelech's and Mahlon's name will not disappear from among the people."

Through the crack, I saw Naomi's face ease into a smile, and her eyes sparkled as she turned away. Instantly I caught my lip between my teeth, a sudden sinking in my heart. Was this just levirate marriage, a duty that he had agreed to perform?

"Is that the only reason?" I asked directly. I wanted to know for certain what my position would be. If this was only a duty, I might expect to have a second wife or a concubine also in the house, or even find myself shunted aside in the near future.

"That is the reason I gave at the gate, but it is the least of them," Boaz said, running his finger down the line of my chin. "I love you, Ruth, and I wish you always by my side. I want to wake in the morning knowing that you are with me, and I want to know every day that you are in my house, waiting for me to come home. I have done nothing to deserve you, but Yahweh has given you to me anyway. You are my hesed, and I will not forget it."

A warm glow started in my stomach and spread all through me, even though the words were said awkwardly. He ran his hand through my hair, his gaze telling me he would gladly take me into his arms but for Naomi standing there watching.

"I still cannot believe it," my lover continued. "Waking last night to find you beside me was such a shock. I had longed for you, but when you were there, I didn't know what to do. Why should I find such hesed?"

"Maybe because you give such hesed. We have a storeroom overflowing because of you."

He flushed. "I couldn't let you starve."

"Tobeh would have, and others would have ignored our need."

Boaz bent toward my lips, and a polite cough from Naomi startled us both.

"I must go. The threshing does not wait," Boaz said, straightening hastily.

"When shall we be married?" I asked, catching his hand.

"I will wait until the next full moon, no longer. I can have rooms for Naomi ready by then."

"Can't she stay in the house? It's large enough."

"Naomi will be more comfortable in her own place."

"Why?" I pressed as we slowly walked across the tiny courtyard, knowing that I needed to understand his reasons.

"Naomi learned to despise Canaanite blood from her father," he said softly. "She will not be comfortable in the same house with me."

I looked down, many things I had wondered about spinning through my head. "That explains much," I said slowly. "I have wondered sometimes what she thought about me. Yet I know she cares for me."

"She is a good woman in her own way. Let us respect that, and maybe she will come to respect our way. I have to go, my hesed. Have Naomi take you to the market in Jebus for wedding clothes and whatever else you need. She knows just what to do."

"I will, Boaz. But if I do that, I will not be able to glean," I protested, leaning against his chest.

Boaz chuckled. "You don't need to glean. There is much more than enough in my storerooms."

As I looked into his face, he stroked my hair, tucking it back under the head covering. "Then would you pick another person who is as needy as Naomi and I, and let them glean all that I would have found?"

"I'll speak to Ladel about it today," he assured me, his eyes promising even more. "Shalom, Hesed."

"Shalom, Boaz."

He gave me a tender lingering kiss and went out to the market square.

Summer
Ab, fifth month, fifteenth day
(1100 B.C.)

Once again he walked the wasteland across Jordan, and once again he sought a place to sleep in fear of the shadow that haunted him. "Not now," Boaz cried. "It's my wedding night!" But the dream would not be denied and took his mind to itself. But when Lilith turned her gaze on him, he felt only revulsion. He was enmeshed in the sweet scent of perfume, and a cool hand stroked his hair.

Lilith started toward him, then stopped, unable to continue. "Call me! Call me," she urged. But Boaz refused, turning his mind to the soft singing that surrounded him, replacing the derisive laughter that usually haunted his dream.

Lilith's spell was broken! Relief washed through him. The singing strengthened, accompanied by the skillful music of a harp, mellow and full such as he'd never heard. He turned his head, opening his eyes. The blankets of the sleeping mat were still warm, and Ruth sat on a stool, fingers pulling the most beautiful sounds from the harp in her hands. Again, her voice, soft and happy, added to the music, the words telling of a woman who waited for her love in the darkness of a summer night.

"Hesed," Boaz whispered to himself. "Yahweh, let me always treasure Your gift."

— — —

"Ruth?" His soft voice startled me.

"Yes?" I answered, the light of the single lamp providing just enough illumination to reveal the man waiting for me on the bedroll.

"You are really here!"

Where else would I be? I wondered. Perhaps the restlessness and muttering in his sleep had been a nightmare. "And I will never leave," I reassured him. "Is it a dream that troubles you?"

Boaz reached up and stroked my face as I laid aside the harp. "A dream of waiting for you, Hesed."

"I'm here now," I told him, and I smiled as his hands drew me to him while the faint sounds of the feast still going on swirled outside our room.

"Come to me, Hesed," he murmured, and I responded willingly. His arms held me fiercely, and we were husband and wife.

Spring
Iyar, second month, twenty-first day, Ruth's twenty-third year (1099 B.C.)

Naomi, it's time," Tashima called, running from my room.

It was more than past time, as far as I was concerned. The past two weeks had been extremely hard. The child I carried made me clumsy, and my back ached constantly. Now I felt the muscles tighten, and I struggled onto my side.

Madiya burst into the room. "Oh, Ruth, it's time!" she exclaimed.

"I think I know that, Madiya," I said testily. If one more person said it was time, I was going to scream.

"Is it time?" Ladel's voice asked from outside the room.

"Yes," Tashima answered. "Go tell Boaz."

"Why not just blow the rams' horns and send messengers through the whole town?" I muttered. My muscles tightened again, and Madiya rubbed my back.

"Relax, Ruth, and let the child come," she said.

Let the child come? Did she think I was holding it back? It was more than time for someone else to carry this child!

"It will soon be done, Ruth," Madiya assured me. "When the time arrives, it goes swiftly. Just relax. Let the child come."

I gritted my teeth.

"Oh, do be quiet, Madiya," Naomi said by my head. "Ruth is not you. She wants this child more than any of us. You enjoyed yours so much that you didn't want it to end. Ruth is ready for this."

A rush of gratitude ran through me, blocking out the pain momentarily. Naomi and I had grown much closer this past month. After our marriage, I saw the wisdom of Boaz's granting Naomi rooms of her own. Gradually I realized that she seemed afraid that he would say or do something that might upset her, though he never did.

At last I had asked her about it. "Is it because your father refused his offer for your hand?"

Naomi had looked at me in surprise. "You know of that?"

"Yes. Boaz talked of it more than once."

She was silent for a moment. "What did he say?"

"He said that you made Elimelech an excellent wife, and that Yahweh had guided when you married, for he could not have made you as happy as Elimelech did."

"That's all?"

"Yes. Did you expect more?"

"No, no, I guess not," she had replied, averting her face. But after that, things between them relaxed, and they talked together often as my pregnancy progressed.

I was very relieved, for I found myself hard enough to handle without worrying about tension between Boaz and Naomi. I don't know how he endured me the final month I carried his child. I was restless and fretful, constantly wandering around the house, wondering if everything was ready, and unable to sleep because I needed to check on the linens in the room set aside for the birth. More often than not, I snapped at anyone who so much as asked a simple question.

No one else seemed to think anything of this, but I had never felt this way in my life, and I didn't like it.

I hung on to Madiya's hand with one of mine, and Naomi's with the other. The midwife arrived, looking with approval at the preparations made.

"You're coming along just fine. This should be an easy birth, even though it is a first. The babe is positioned well, and it won't be long."

"Where's Boaz?" I asked. I wanted to see him.

"He's pacing the roof with Ladel," Tashima answered.

"I want to see him." I turned restlessly on the bed.

"Not now, Ruth. You have a child to bring into the world."

"It's his child. I want to see him."

"Ruth, he'll be fine. Just concentrate on the baby."

"Tashima, if you don't get him, I'll go see him myself," I threatened, starting to sit up.

"Ruth, lie down," Naomi commanded. "Boaz will be here just as soon as the baby is born, but not a minute sooner."

I subsided, sulking. It wasn't fair. He was up there on the roof in the sunshine, and I was here in this hot, stuffy room with a body that wasn't mine anymore. But then I didn't have time to think, as my muscles tightened again and again, leaving me exhausted and gasping for breath.

"How much longer?"

"It's time for the birthing stool," the midwife replied. "It would help if you could think about something else. You want this so badly that you have tensed up, and it's making it hard for the child."

"Think of something else? Like what?"

"Tell Naomi about your god place up on the hill in Heshbon," she suggested as the women helped me sit up.

"A god place in Heshbon? What was it like? On a hill, you said?" Naomi asked, taking my hand.

Of all the impossible things to ask! "Yes, it was on a hill," I snapped, trying to settle myself as my muscles tightened again.

"At the top? What could you see?"

"I could see the entire country," I retorted. "A full view from east to west and south across the Arnon."

"Could you see the fords of Jericho?"

"Almost, on a clear day. It was wonderful, the sky so wide."

The midwife nodded to Naomi, and I groaned as my muscles contracted.

"Did you sit under a tree?" Naomi asked, patting my hand to get my attention.

"No. There was a niche in the rock—from an earthquake. I sat there. It was cool, even in the summer. Yidla kept his flock"—I gasped—"at the bottom of the hill."

"Yidla? The one who bred the rams?"

"Yes. For King Hissil. He taught me a lot. I used to help him."

The pain eased, and I loosened my grip on Naomi and Madiya.

"Feel better?" Madiya asked.

"Yes, doesn't hurt so much."

"Good. You're doing fine."

"Naomi, pass the word to Pashur about my child. Have him tell Shimrith."

"Shimrith will know," the midwife promised.

And then it was time. All else fled from my mind but bringing Boaz's child into the world, and he came, deliberately and without hurry, despite my impatience and eagerness. Then he was there, a fine healthy boy, protesting the cold and light until he was washed and wrapped snugly, and I held him in my arms.

"It's a boy, a boy," Naomi repeated again and again. The delight on her face doubled the joy in my heart. Tears streamed from her eyes, and she could hardly see to help the midwife.

"There now," Tashima said, giving Naomi a hug. "See how Yahweh has blessed you again? You are Marah no longer, but Naomi, with a fine, strong son who will restore your life and keep you in your old age."

I looked at the bundle in my arms. His face was puckered and red, but he was perfect. "Thank you," I said to the midwife. "Thank you so much."

"Having birthed you, could I miss birthing your son?" she asked, laughing.

For the first time, I really looked at her. "Hamir? Hamir, what are you doing here? You were in Heshbon. Did Shimrith—how is this possible?"

She laughed at my confusion. "I, too, have come to live in Judah. Adon Boaz passed the word to Pashur months ago that he wanted me to attend the birth. When word got out that the adon had specifically asked for me, my business improved immediately. I'm very busy now."

"Someday you will have to tell me all about it," I said, sensing that there was much more to the story, and wondering about the scars I could see on her arms.

"I will. Right now, you enjoy your son!"

Naomi came in to take the baby out so the friends gathering from across the town could see him. Their happy voices drifted into the room where I rested.

"Yahweh has blessed you again, Naomi."

"Here's your little goel to restore your life, Naomi. He'll grow strong and be with you in your old age!"

"You'll live to hear his name in the gate yet, Naomi! Let me see him. A big strong one he is."

"See, Yahweh did not bring you back with nothing," Tashima encouraged. "You had Ruth, and she's been better for you than seven sons!"

"Yes, yes, she has," Naomi's voice replied happily.

Content, I lay back. All the light had come back into Naomi's eyes as she proudly displayed the desire of her heart.

Later, after most of the excitement had died down, Boaz stood in the doorway, gazing at us both, joy beaming from his face.

"Come and meet Obed," I invited.

He knelt down by the sleeping mat and bent over the baby, who was eating greedily for the second time. "Well, little man, you look quite content," he said. "Named already. Who decided on Obed?"

"Do you like it?" I asked anxiously. "The women named him, and Naomi agreed to it."

My husband smiled. "Obed he shall be. And how are you?"

"Tired," I admitted. "But I feel wonderful just the same."

"You look wonderful. Are you too tired? Shall I go?"

"No. Stay."

He stretched his long length beside me on the floor, leaning on his elbow. "Yahweh has been good to me. I didn't think I would know the joy of a son again, but here he is. I love you, my hesed."

His hand stroked my face, and I closed my eyes, feeling sleep pull at my mind. And stealing over me came the sense of Yah's presence, filling the room with gentle, joyful laughter.

"Thank You, Yah," I smiled.

And so Yahweh's harvest is complete, and with the coming of the new seed, bringing the whole story full cycle from planting to reaping to seed for planting again. How much Zadok missed by insisting that only the end of the tale be told!

Well, our story has been long in the telling. And yet, like all stories, its ending is but the beginning of another, and another, and another, for Obed grew and had a son named Jesse, and Jesse grew and had sons of his own.

And now it is getting late. It has been pleasant here with the lamplight gleaming off the polished wood of the harp on the table. Yes, the wood is solid still, and the harp produces a sound like no other, mellow and full, for Zippor wrought better than he knew in its making. It is still the best of its kind, and although battered and scarred from much use and hard travel, it is still beautiful. Yes, this beside it is the royal signet ring of Moab, bearing the impress of the house of Eglon. How did I come to have Ruth's harp and her royal signet? Well, those are the things of another story.

Tamar,
Daughter of Dahveed, king of Israel
Third month, twenty-first day, second regnal year of Solomon
(968 B.C.)

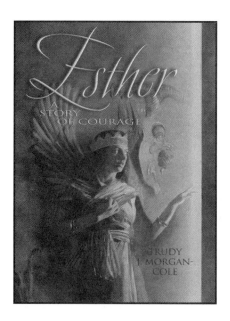

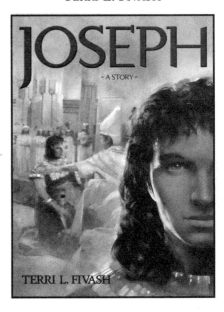